ANOTHER WAY TO FALL

Amanda Brooke is a single mum in her forties who lives in Liverpool with her teenage daughter Jessica. It was only when her young son was diagnosed with cancer that Amanda began to develop her writing, recording her family's journey in a journal and through poetry. When Nathan died in 2006 at just three years old, Amanda was determined that his legacy would be one of inspiration not devastation. *Another Way to Fall* is Amanda's second novel and is drawn from her own experience of having to re-imagine the future after loss.

Also by Amanda Brooke

Yesterday's Sun

AMANDA BROOKE

Another Way to Fall

HARPER

This novel is entirely a work of fiction.
The names, characters and incidents portrayed in it are
the work of the author's imagination. Any resemblance to
actual persons, living or dead, events or localities is
entirely coincidental.

Harper
An imprint of HarperCollins*Publishers*
77–85 Fulham Palace Road,
Hammersmith, London W6 8JB

www.harpercollins.co.uk

A Paperback Original 2013
1

A catalogue record for this book
is available from the British Library

ISBN: 9780007445929

Set in Sabon LT Std by Palimpsest Book Production Limited,
Falkirk, Stirlingshire

Printed and bound in Great Britain by
Clays Ltd, St Ives plc

MIX
Paper from
responsible sources
FSC® C007454

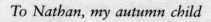

To Nathan, my autumn child

Acknowledgements

This book was inspired by my son, Nathan Valentine, and I would like to take this opportunity to thank those who cared for him during his two-year fight against leukaemia. My immense gratitude goes to the staff at the Oncology Unit at Alder Hey Children's Hospital; it's a credit to you all that not all my memories of the hospital are bad ones. I would especially like to thank Nathan's consultant, Russell Keenan, his bone marrow nurse, Helen Webster, and the nurse he fell in love with, Pat Wood. I haven't been able to return to the hospital since Nathan's death but I think of you all often.

By the same token, I also wish to thank: Jane Bullock at Cancer Research UK; Eddie Hinks at CHICS; Tracey Cunningham at Click Sargent; Vikki George at Postpals; Madeleine Fletcher at the Imagine Appeal; Eleanor Moritz and the team at BBC North West; John Lippitt at the Alder Centre; and all the truly amazing volunteers at the Child Death Helpline.

Writing this book wasn't easy and I am indebted to Natalya Jagger for all of her assistance in my research. I have been truly inspired by Natalya's dedication and commitment to BT Buddies, a small charity that aims to help those suffering from high-grade brain tumours. Thank you, Natalya.

As always, I want to thank my family and friends, especially my mum, Mary Hayes, and my late father, Gordon Valentine, both of whom have been 'invisible' in my life at times (Mum, if you haven't read the book yet then don't worry, being invisible is a good thing!). I also want to thank my sister, Lynn Jones, and my brothers, Chris Valentine, Jonathan Hayes and Mick Jones, whose support I would be lost without.

Thank you to all of my friends for their continuing support and encouragement. You have asked me often enough if I've written any real-life characters into my books and as always the answer is, no . . . or at least not quite . . . but one or two references might sound familiar. On that note, I would like to give special mention to 'the team' who make office life far more entertaining than it should be. You are: Paula Pocock, Lynette Lockyer, Ronnie Farrell, Colette Gill, John Lally, Jenna McCool, Lee Jones, Jane Nolan, Abi Looker and honorary member, Nicola Hodge.

This novel has gone through many iterations and it is the book it is because of the invaluable advice and guidance from my agent Luigi Bonomi of LBA Literary Agency and my editor Sarah Ritherdon of HarperCollins.

Thank you both as always for your continuing kindness, generosity and support.

And finally, a big thank you to my daughter, Jess, who deserves an acknowledgement all to herself. She's the one who puts up with my glares if she comes within ten feet of me when I'm writing. I hope I make it up to you the rest of the time and, if I don't, then I will . . . we still have a lifetime to go.

1

I was sitting patiently to one side of Mr Spelling's vast desk, which took up most of the floor space. The doctor paid me no attention, too intent on the images that flashed in quick succession across his computer screen. As I waited, I became vaguely aware that my fingers had developed a life of their own, tugging at the seams of my jeans then playing with the cord hanging from my padded jacket. I slipped my wayward hands between my crossed legs in an attempt to bring their fidgeting under control, but a moment later the soft whisper of denim across denim drew my attention. My right foot had broken ranks and had started tapping rhythmically in midair.

The sun streamed through the window and it stung my eyes as the rays of light bounced off the butter-cream walls. It was late November and bitterly cold outside but you would never have guessed in the snug little office. I made a point of averting my gaze from the window and the world beyond, choosing instead to concentrate on a collection of health and safety notices pinned to the walls explaining how to wash your hands, how to find the fire exit, how to wipe your nose. I knew every crease and tear of each poster by heart. Likewise, I was familiar with the gilt on the picture frames that protected Mr Spelling's prized certificates, the ones that assured his patients that he was more than qualified to peer into the deepest crevices of their brains and read their fortunes.

My foot froze in midair as the doctor shifted in his seat. I waited for him to look up but he remained focused on his work. With my attention briefly diverted, my hands had broken free and I found myself twisting a dark curl from my ponytail around my fingers. My foot resumed its tapping.

Shifting restlessly, I started to regret wearing so many layers. I could feel my skin tingling with sweat beneath and was about to take off my jacket when Mr Spelling raised his head and this time he did meet my gaze. He had kept me waiting all of sixty seconds but it had felt like a lifetime. In my defence, my waiting had begun long before I entered his office. My life had been held in limbo for almost five years.

When Mr Spelling smiled, I had absolutely no idea if it was drawn from hope or sympathy. His deep green eyes had hidden depths that gave no clue to the news he was about to impart.

'So go on then. Tell me,' I demanded, my tone light

but insistent, my patience exhausted. I held my breath, pursing my lips tightly to stop them trembling.

'It's over,' he said.

That simple statement had numerous connotations but for me the message was clear enough for me to catch my breath. 'All clear?' My question came out as a tremulous whisper.

'Complete remission,' he confirmed.

At last I allowed myself to look out of the window, beyond the treetops that were being stripped of all remains of life by autumn gales and towards the clear blue sky. Freedom, I thought as I allowed a smile to ease away the pain and fear that had cast an ominous shadow over my life. It had been a long time coming but I was only twenty-nine. I had my whole life ahead of me and an awful lot of catching up to do.

'Emma, it's time,' Meg whispered.

Emma felt her body stiffen, her fingers left hovering motionlessly over the keyboard as the connection with her words was broken. The smile on her face faltered as she looked up and caught a glimpse of Mr Spelling and his entourage in deep discussion further down the ward. The thudding of her heart sounded like a drum roll preparing for the fall of the executioner's axe.

It had taken her a huge amount of concentration to block out her surroundings as she began to write, drawing herself into a world over which she had complete control and one she was loath to set aside. At least she was feeling well enough to write, she told herself as she tucked a rogue curl back behind her ear, sweeping her fingers towards the dressing at the back of her scalp as if to remind herself that the nightmare was far from over. Reluctantly, she pulled down the lid of her laptop and pushed it to one side.

Emma's marked improvement was not a result of the operation itself, which had been purely exploratory. It was the new regime of drugs she had been taking that made her thoughts feel clearer and the headaches that had plagued her for weeks had all but disappeared. Her vision wasn't perfect but then it never would be; damage to her peripheral vision was an old war wound. She had been diagnosed with a brain tumour four years earlier and had been in remission for three of those. She was now awaiting the results of a biopsy that was likely to confirm that her future was in doubt once again.

Emma looked towards her mum and she had no doubt that the fear she could see etched on her face was a mirror image of her own. There were other similarities between mother and daughter. They had the same dark auburn hair that fell in soft curls, the same round hazel eyes, high cheek bones and tall willowy frames. Meg had often been mistaken for Emma's sister and there were those who would be genuinely surprised to know that she was already the wrong side of fifty, but not today. Today, her age was showing.

Meg was sitting upright in an easy chair next to the bed; her hands gripped the neatly folded newspaper, which she had been reading moments earlier. She looked tired in her creased blue cotton dress, which matched with the cold blue walls of the hospital ward. As Emma reached out a comforting hand towards her, it didn't escape her notice that the skin tone of her own arm, semi-transparent and tinged blue, also matched the decor.

Meg quickly discarded her newspaper and gripped Emma's outstretched hand. 'Ready?' Meg asked as they both looked towards the huddle of doctors heading their way.

Emma bit down hard on the inside of her lip to hold back the scream building inside her. She wanted to say, 'No! I'm not ready, I'll never be ready. Please, oh, God, please send them away!' Her unspoken words burned like acid at the back of her throat as she nodded in silent submission, never taking her eyes off Mr Spelling as he approached the foot of her bed. Emma had an assortment of consultants involved in her care and it was the neurosurgeon who would have assessed the pathology results of her biopsy. But it was her neuro-oncologist whom she relied upon and listened to most and she had asked for him to deliver the news. Mr Spelling was in his late fifties. He had a full head of thick, brown hair but it was peppered with far more grey than when they had first met. Back then Mr Spelling had been confident and the treatment offered had been intensive – major surgery followed by months of chemotherapy – but remission had been her reward.

Lately, however, each time she had met Mr Spelling,

he had looked just a little less confident, less eager to give Emma one of his winning smiles. He felt Emma's gaze on him now and, when he looked up, he smiled at her but the smile didn't quite reach his eyes, their hidden depths a little closer to the surface than Emma would have liked.

'Writing anything interesting?' he asked her, nodding towards the discarded laptop.

Emma tried to return his smile but the corners of her mouth were being pulled down by invisible weights. She could feel herself not just sinking back into the bed but shrinking in size too, like a small, defenceless child gripping her future like a comfort blanket that was about to be torn from her grasp. 'Just idiotic ramblings,' she answered with a dismissive shrug.

In the days when she had counted on endless tomorrows, Emma had nurtured great ambitions and writing a book had been amongst them. Her first battle with cancer had derailed her dreams for the future and she had spent the last three years prevaricating rather than picking up where she had left off. The blind spot that her cancer had left in her peripheral vision unnerved her and she hadn't been able to shake the feeling that there was something still there inside her head, lurking out of sight. She had been hoping for the best but all the time preparing for the worst, questioning every twinge, every headache, panicking each time she had a lapse of memory. She had told herself it was paranoia but the phrase *I told you so* was echoing across her thoughts now and with it, a sense of regret. There had been so much she could have achieved in the intervening years but she had waited too long. Panic bubbled inside her as she felt time slipping through her fingers.

As Mr Spelling put down her medical charts and walked to the side of the bed, there was an ominous silence, filled only by the continued pounding of Emma's heart. His entourage followed in his wake and when they had fully encircled Emma, her nurse, Peter, pulled the curtain around the bed to provide a degree of privacy. She felt trapped and glanced anxiously from one face to the next, searching out a pair of eyes that might hold a hint of hope. There was none.

'Right, then,' Mr Spelling said, taking Emma's free hand as Meg squeezed the other even tighter. Imperceptibly, the gathering of registrars and nurses leaned in a little closer, eagerly awaiting judgement to be passed.

'Tell me,' Emma commanded.

'We've ruled out necrosis,' Mr Spelling told her, knowing that Emma would immediately understand what this meant. The mass that had shown up on recent scans was not scarring around the site of the previous tumour and that left only one other explanation. Any further attempt to soften the news was futile and Mr Spelling left no pause before delivering the final blow. 'There's a tumour in your temporal lobe, Emma. A grade-three Glioblastoma Multiforme.' He let the words sink in. The brain tumour wasn't only back, it was more aggressive than it had been before. 'We need to plan some radical treatment, a programme of radiotherapy and chemo.'

'No operation this time?' Emma asked, doing well to hide the tremor from her voice. 'Even if the NHS can't afford to sharpen its knives any more, I would have thought the surgeons here could do a decent enough job with a butter knife from the hospital canteen. Or is that what they used last time?' Emma's false bravado was betrayed only by the gentle trembling of her knees beneath the blue cotton blankets.

'If my colleagues' knives were as sharp as your wit, I'm sure we wouldn't be facing this problem right now,' Mr Spelling argued gently. 'I'm afraid we can't operate on the tumour without seriously compromising your brain function. We could remove some of the growth but each time we operate there are more risks and the results are less effective. We'll reassess as we go along but I think for now at least, radiotherapy and chemo offer the best option.'

'And will it get me back into remission?' Her mum's grip on her hand was practically cutting off Emma's circulation now.

Mr Spelling broke eye contact briefly, looking down at his feet to take a breath before facing her again. The look he gave her wasn't in the least bit enigmatic. He couldn't hide his feelings, not when his eyes were brimming with sympathy. Emma sensed that he was about to sugar coat his answer so she jumped in before he had a chance to reply. 'What's the five-year survival rate?'

'It's difficult to say,' Mr Spelling began but then checked himself, knowing Emma wouldn't accept anything but a straight answer. 'A small percentage. A very small percentage.'

'I'm dying, then,' Emma said matter-of-factly. 'This time, I'm dying.'

'No,' gasped Meg, 'no, you're not. We'll go somewhere else if we have to. We'll find a clinical trial somewhere.'

Mr Spelling raised an eyebrow as he looked at Meg but then turned his attention back to Emma. 'There are a number of overseas clinics that have had some success treating cases similar to yours and we'll do our best to investigate all the options, but I don't want to raise your hopes. The clinics may not accept you and even if they do, there are no guarantees. Right now we have to be realistic and plan the treatment that we can offer you here but you have to understand that this is palliative treatment, not curative, not in the long term.'

'So I am dying,' repeated Emma.

Mr Spelling's silence told her more than her mother's knee-jerk reassurances had. Fear tore through her body as she felt her future being wrenched from her grasp, taking with it all her hopes, dreams and foolish whims. Everything was gone.

Emma had heard enough and tried to close her ears to the conversation that continued around her, which was now just noise. Her hand went limp in Mr Spelling's grip and he placed it gently on the bed. She shouldn't have wasted so much time, she told herself as cold terror was replaced by a slow-burning fury. She had been waiting for that magical five-year marker before resuming her life and what a life it was going to be, one where all her dreams were there for the taking. She had faced death head on and she deserved a better future. Perhaps in another lifetime, she thought as she turned her gaze towards her laptop, which looked back at her, its half-open lid smiling benevolently, letting her know her escape route was still open.

'How long?' she asked, her voice barely audible as she forced herself to rejoin the conversation.

'Did you say something, Emma?' Peter asked, interrupting Meg in mid-sentence.

Emma silently thanked her nurse as she returned her attention to Mr Spelling. 'If I haven't got five years, exactly how long do I have? I started writing a book this morning. Will I have time to finish it?' she asked, not taking her eyes off the doctor for even a moment. Her question smacked of desperation but she needed to know that at least this ambition could be realized. She wasn't about to accept defeat, not yet.

'Emma, you can't be thinking of writing now,' interjected Meg.

Emma ignored her. 'I need maybe a year. Can you give me that?' she asked with a tone that dared the doctor to deny her dying wish.

'You know I can't give you a firm answer but twelve to eighteen months would be a reasonable expectation. It really depends on how the tumour develops and how you respond to treatment, but if it was down to sheer determination on your part then my guess is you'll finish your book, and I'll do my damnedest to help.'

'Thank you,' replied Emma, reaching up to squeeze Mr Spelling's arm gently in gratitude. Her mother slowly released her fierce grip on Emma's other hand and Emma surreptitiously flexed her fingers. She didn't want Meg to know that she had caused her hand to ache, she would be feeling bad enough already. 'So when do I start treatment?'

'I'm working on the schedule now but I'd say within the month.'

'But it's Christmas in a month's time,' Emma told him. 'How about we relook at those schedules and make it the first week in January?'

Mr Spelling glanced towards Meg for support but she remained uncharacteristically silent on the subject and simply shrugged her shoulders. 'It gives us more time to consider other options,' she offered.

Mr Spelling sighed. 'OK, January it is,' he conceded.

'Which gives me six more weeks of freedom, so my next question is, when can I get out of here?'

'We'll play that one by ear but if you're going to be your usual determined self,' he said, emphasizing the word *determined*, 'then I'd say you could go home early next week.'

'Monday,' Emma said, nodding her head as if Mr Spelling had already agreed the date.

Mr Spelling suppressed a gentle laugh. 'Yes, Monday should be fine,' he said.

The white-gowned bodies disappeared as quickly and silently as they had arrived, ghostly spectres that had completed their dark deed for the day. The screen curtain was pushed back against the wall, officially releasing Emma from her visitation, but she felt more trapped than ever.

Meg cleared her throat, swallowing a torrent of unshed tears that she wouldn't allow Emma to see. 'Want to talk about it?'

Emma shook her head slightly. 'Not yet.'

'You should get some rest then.'

Emma knew she was right but the steroids she was taking made her edgy and restless and the temptation to pick up her laptop was becoming hard to resist. It felt safer filling her mind with words than allowing time to reflect on what else might be lurking in there. 'I will when I'm ready.'

Meg remained frozen to the spot where she had been sitting throughout Mr Spelling's visit. 'You're not on your own, Emma,' she said, taking a deep breath that lifted her head and pulled back her shoulders. Emma was reminded of a lioness raising her eyes to the horizon, sniffing out the dangers that threatened one of her cubs.

'I know,' she said although right now she would have been quite happy to have some time on her own. As that thought registered, Emma realized that she hadn't thought about Alex once.

She had been dating him for almost a year, her longest relationship to date and her only relationship in the last five years. Whilst her friends from university had been busy settling down and starting families, Emma's future had followed a different path, one that felt like walking a tightrope where each step was a leap of faith. There had seemed little point in searching for someone to share her life with when she didn't know how long, or how brief that life might be. It had been a complete surprise when her close working relationship with Alex at Bannister's Kitchens and Bathrooms turned into something far more intimate, although, she noted, not so intimate that he was there by her side today.

At first, his claim to have a phobia of hospitals had seemed a tad convenient but when she had seen the look of abject terror on his face on the one occasion he had visited her, she had been tempted to believe him and hadn't pushed him since. 'I should ring Alex,' she said.

'And I need to let Louise know what's happening,' Meg said, standing up and taking a tentative step away from the bed.

'I'll be fine, Mum,' Emma replied. Louise was four years younger than Emma and was still considered the baby of the family but she hoped her sister would provide a better shoulder for her mum to cry on than she could. 'But tell her she doesn't have to come in. Friday nights at the bistro are too busy and she can't afford to pay for extra cover.'

13

'Now isn't the time to worry about the bistro,' Meg told her forcefully as she picked up her purse. 'Louise is going to have to learn to stand on her own two feet.'

'Yes, and she will,' agreed Emma, as if prophesying her own doom. 'But I'm still here and she's still my little sister. I want to help her while I can.' Meg nodded and her forced smile squeezed out the first tear, which they both dutifully ignored. 'I meant what I said, Emma. You're not on your own and I'm going to do my damnedest to get you through this. If Mr Spelling can't help you beat this thing then I'll find someone who can.'

'You can't fight this for me, Mum,' Emma told her.

Meg looked down, playing with a seam on her purse rather than meeting Emma's gaze. She looked more vulnerable than Emma had ever seen her. 'I know I can't. I wish I could but I know I can't.'

'I need to be realistic and I don't want to hold on to false hopes. Do the research if you must but in the meantime, let me deal with this my way. I want to make the most of the time I have left,' Emma began but the words caught in her throat as she realized what she had said. 'I mean the time I have before I start treatment, the treatment Mr Spelling is offering me.'

Meg smiled through her pain. 'All right, but I am insisting on one thing. I want you to move back home with me.'

Heat rose in Emma's chest, a toxic mix of panic and anger. She felt like she was being pulled back in time to

14

when she had first been diagnosed. Back then she had been forced to give up a promising marketing career in London and return home to Liverpool and her mother's care. She had stayed with her for nearly two years before summoning up the courage to move out. The thought of giving up her independence once again was too much to bear.

'But your apartment isn't big enough for all of us,' Emma told her, playing for time as the dust settled on the latest bombshell to hit her that morning.

At the moment, Louise was staying in Meg's spare room, having rented out her own flat above the bistro when her business started to flounder six months ago. 'Don't worry, I'm not under any illusions that you and your sister could share a room,' said Meg. 'But right now your needs come first and I've already run the idea past Louise. She's going to move out.'

'So much for positive thinking,' accused Emma as she realized her mum had been planning for the worst despite insisting that everything would be alright.

Meg chose to ignore the comment. 'You can't manage on your own, Emma. There's your medication to keep track of, not to mention the possibility you could have more seizures, and then there's just the simple fact that someone needs to keep an eye on you, look out for any changes which you might not notice yourself. At the very least, you need help building up your strength so you're strong enough to deal with, well, whatever awaits us.'

'Me, whatever awaits me,' corrected Emma. 'I'm

twenty-nine years old, Mum, and I've grown up a lot in the last few years. I've had to. I can look after myself and, besides, I don't live alone.'

Emma shared a house with Ally and Gina. She had known Ally from school and it had been her oldest and dearest friend who had been instrumental in securing her a job at Bannister's as well as aiding her escape from her mum's clutches. She would do all she could to help Emma stay in the house if it was what she wanted but Emma already knew that placing that kind of responsibility on someone's shoulders was too much to ask of anyone, anyone that was except the one person who would always give her love and support unconditionally.

'And I have Alex,' Emma added but as the words slipped off her tongue in a last desperate attempt to make her case, she knew the argument had already been lost. The idea that Alex would be there for her wasn't particularly credible when he was already conspicuous by his absence. 'I'll have to speak to the girls first. They'll have to find another lodger.' Meg shifted uneasily and Emma's eyes widened in shock. 'You've already spoken to them too?' she gasped.

'They said not to worry. You come first. We all want what's best for you.'

'I think you had better go and phone Louise,' Emma said.

In her wisdom, Meg nodded but said no more. She had won the argument but the tone in Emma's voice suggested that the decision could still be overturned.

As Emma watched her mum disappear down the ward, she desperately felt for her phone. Pulling it from her pyjama pocket, she imagined Alex anxiously waiting for her call.

Emma's phone had been switched to silent mode all morning. No telltale vibration had announced a missed call or text message but the empty call list still left her disappointed. With a heavy heart, Emma tapped briefly on the keypad and waited for the call to be answered.

'Emma?' Alex shouted over pounding music and inane chatter.

'Where are you?' Emma asked, as loudly as she dared. The ward was deathly silent other than the occasional groan from a fellow patient or the clatter of a hospital trolley.

'We're having lunch at the pub,' he explained. 'The latest sales figures are looking really good and Mr Bannister insisted. I couldn't refuse.' There was a pause as Alex waited for Emma's response. Her silence prompted him to ask what she had expected to be the first thing on his mind. 'But enough about me, I've been thinking about you all morning. How did it go? What's the news?'

Emma became acutely aware of how life beyond the confines of the hospital walls had been carrying on regardless – another blow to her bruised emotions. Her earth-shattering news hadn't even caused a ripple. She felt a brief swell of anger as she imagined their celebrations, celebrations that she should be party to. She deserved a pat on the back as much as anyone but her anger was swiftly quashed by a more powerful wave of despair. There were worse things in life. 'My tumour's back,' she said stoically.

The background noise continued unaffected.

'Alex? Are you still there?'

'I'm sorry, Em. I really am,' he said. 'I feel so bad that I wasn't there for you. I wanted to be with you, honestly I did.'

'It's alright,' Emma said, surprising herself that she should be the one comforting him so quickly but that was so often the way. She hated her illness, not simply for what it was doing to her but the hurt it inflicted on those around her. 'I'll speak to you over the weekend when you're less busy but I should be out on Monday anyway.'

'I'll come over to see you then, I promise.'

'There's just one thing,' Emma told him. 'I'm going to have to move back in with Mum for a while.'

'Maybe that's for the best. You'll need a lot of looking after.'

Emma was tempted to tell him that she wanted him to look after her. She wanted him to be the one to wrap her in his arms and tell her she was going to be alright but she took the easy option. She said nothing.

'We'll get you through this,' he added. 'We'll all help.'

'I know,' she said, but she didn't know at all. It was an automated response to an automated offer and perhaps they both knew it.

'I'd better go,' Alex said to fill the pause, 'but we'll speak soon. Love you, Em.'

Emma kept the phone to her ear until her link to everyday life was severed and silence returned. She felt drained as she closed her eyes and she didn't resist when she began to slip towards slumber, freeing her mind to take her on a journey of its own.

In her dreams she was still sitting in Mr Spelling's sun-filled office, looking out of the window towards a group of forlorn trees. A handful of bedraggled leaves, silhouetted against the crisp blue sky. Her focus centred on a single leaf that had survived the autumn gales, holding on staunchly to its branch as it prepared to brave the winter frost. Without warning, a vicious gust of wind spun it into the air, where it twirled out of control, leaving sparks of orange and gold as it fluttered in the sunshine. Its descent was inevitable and it came to rest on a pile of leaves whose skeletal remains were being crunched underfoot by passersby who were blissfully unaware of the devastation around them. Emma tried to look away but the vision followed her as she twisted and turned to escape its grasp.

'Emma, are you OK?' Meg asked as she gently brushed away strands of Emma's damp hair from her sweaty brow.

Emma opened her eyes but struggled to emerge from her dream. She felt disorientated and for a moment she was transported back twenty years. She half expected her mum to tell her that she had the flu and wouldn't be going to school that day.

'I'll get you some water,' Meg said when Emma didn't respond other than to open her mouth to expose dry lips.

As Meg busied herself pouring water from a jug, Emma's eyes settled on the window opposite. The afternoon was growing old but there was still enough light left in the day to reveal a thin scattering of autumn leaves clinging to the denuded treetops. Autumn had been her favourite time of year as a child and she had loved stomping through the deep layers of crisp autumn leaves as she collected conkers with her dad. It was only following her diagnosis that she realized there was nothing beautiful about nature's death throes and she had firmly switched her allegiance to spring, preferring the life that erupted from the depths of winter with a shock of apple blossom.

She had greeted each spring with a sense of victory but now more than ever, she wondered how many more victory dances she had left. As that thought settled on her mind, she gave up holding back the crushing weight of fear that had been growing for days if not weeks.

'I'm scared, Mum,' she said, the confession slipping out as easily as the first tear that slid down her cheek. 'I don't think I can go through it all again.'

'I'm scared too,' replied Meg, turning to face Emma, her tears a mirror image of her daughter's.

'Why me? Why is this happening to me?' Emma demanded, neither expecting nor wanting an answer. 'It was bad enough first time around but now, now it's just so damned unfair.'

'I know,' Meg said, stepping towards Emma and wrapping her in her arms.

'I thought I'd paid my dues.' Emma's voice was muffled as she buried her head within her mother's embrace. 'I was almost at the five-year mark, I was almost there. That was meant to be the start of the rest of my life. I was going to look for a better job, maybe even move back to London.'

'I know,' repeated Meg, her voice raw with emotion. 'And to think, a month ago I wasn't happy about the idea of you moving back there. I should be careful what I wish for.'

'There's so much more I wanted to do,' Emma whispered as she let her mind dip into the pot of dreams she had once kept sacred. 'I wanted to do everything, see everything, travel the world.'

Meg pulled back a little and chanced a look at Emma. She was clearly about to hand out another dose of blind faith but one look from Emma told her not to make promises that could not be kept. 'We'll see,' Meg said.

There was another desperate hug as Emma and her mum clung to each other. Their bodies shook, muscles contorting and throats constricting as they tried to control their sobs. Emma heard the curtain being pulled around her bed and assumed it was Peter giving them some much-needed privacy. That simple act of kindness only intensified her pain and desperation. Somewhere between muffled gasps for air, she thought she heard her mum whisper, 'Please don't break my heart.' Emma felt the crack in her own heart cut a little deeper. Time ticked by, precious seconds that she knew she shouldn't waste. Slowly the sobs subsided until Emma was ready to face the world again. She sat up straight and unceremoniously sniffed back the tears until her mum handed her a tissue with an unspoken reproach.

'I suppose I can expect this from now on,' Emma said. 'Being mothered.'

'Mothered but not smothered,' Meg assured her. 'I know I had no right to interfere and make plans without speaking to you first. You're not the frightened young woman you were four years ago. You're old enough and certainly experienced enough not to have me telling you what to do. I promise I'll give you more space.'

'Easier said than done in your apartment,' answered Emma as she thought back to the time she had already spent there. Her memories of the place were not pleasant. Meg lived in a modern two-bedroom apartment that overlooked the river Mersey, not far from the city centre. She had bought it after her divorce seven years earlier. At the time, Emma had her own life in London and Louise was away at university – it had been sufficient for her needs, or so she had thought.

She gave her mum her best impression of a rueful smile but it was forced. 'So how did Louise take the news?'

'She's going to do whatever it takes to help,' Meg answered.

'She's OK about moving out? She has somewhere to go?'

'It's all arranged. Ally and Gina will help over the weekend to move your things into the apartment ready for Monday.'

Emma let her body slump back against her pillows in resignation and as she did so, the corner of her laptop pressed against her thigh, vying for her attention. She was no longer in control of her own destiny and she was desperate to find a way back.

I ran down the corridor as if the hounds of hell were at my heels, driven by an all consuming desire to get out of the hospital. As I pushed my way through the exit doors, it felt as if I was crossing a finish line. I'd done it. At last I could stop running.

I came to an abrupt halt as soon as I hit fresh air. The sun had disappeared and the sky was leaden but it couldn't dim my mood. I looked down at the dog-eared appointment card still clutched in my hand. Its list of dates marked my passage through the hospital corridors over the years and the final entry was today and then, well, nothing. No more appointments, not one. The bitter November wind slapped against my face and my jacket flapped around me but I stood tall. I took a deep, cleansing breath and my chest felt lighter. The fear I had carried around with me for so long had finally lifted. I could face anything now, I told myself as I tore the appointment card to shreds.

I was tempted by the idea of launching the torn pieces of card into the air to shower myself in winner's confetti but I wasn't quite ready to throw caution to the wind. It was going to take a while to get used to my new sense of freedom. I tried to recall my life before cancer had come crashing into it. I had been confident and carefree once . . . hadn't I?

I had left home with a handful of dreams and headed for university. From there, I had moved to London where, unlike many of my peers, I had landed on my feet. I was taken on by a big PR and marketing company that had offices all over the world and amazing career prospects, and it wasn't long before I started to climb the ladder of success. I loved a challenge and I knew straight away I was well suited to the work. That was when the first symptoms had started to appear. The blinding headaches and blurred vision had made working difficult and then the diagnosis of a brain tumour had made it impossible. I was forced to turn my back on my dream job and return home. I later heard that the young woman who had taken my place was now based in New York and taking on all kinds of amazing assignments.

The tumour in my brain had been removed but the surgeon's knife had taken away much more than simply my cancer. My ambitions, my desire to be a wife and a mother one day, these were things that required an undisputable belief in the future and I had lost that. So I had buried the dreams that I feared would always be denied me and spent the last few years treading water, taking

24

a job as an office manager with a small family business that made fittings for kitchens and bathrooms. The business was expanding, and a new position came up as Marketing Director. I had already shown that I had the experience and the capability, but it was Alex who got the job, not me. Alex, whose father just happened to be a close friend of Mr Bannister, the owner of the company. He had the confidence and the contacts. The lost job opportunity was only a minor addition on a long list of life's injustices so I had swallowed my disappointment and trudged onwards.

But all my troubles were behind me now and I was ready to take back what was mine. I took another deep breath of cold, November air and held it as I waited for inspiration to strike. A frown began to crease my brow as I let go of the breath in a long low hiss. What exactly did I want from my second chance at life? Other than savouring every minute, I hadn't really thought it through.

I suppose I had imagined that the rest would be easy. I was free! If I could beat cancer, surely I was entitled to pick and choose what else my life would hold. I'd had my fair share of misery and pain, now I wanted to get to the good bit. I half expected to be met at the hospital gates by a kindly shopkeeper who would magically transport me to his store of dreams. He would stand with his hands deep in his pockets, watching me intently as I scanned shelf upon shelf of boxes in an assortment of colours and sizes, each one containing *something different but equally exciting. He would wait patiently for me to make my choices from a vast array of delicious adventures. It was all mine for the taking.*

But sadly, there was no kindly shopkeeper to greet me so I stood transfixed, not knowing what to do. The next step I took was an important one and I didn't want to get it wrong. I lifted my right foot up nervously, holding it in midair, still unsure where it would lead.

2

It was Monday morning and Emma was alone, or at least as alone as she could be in a crowded ward. So confident was she of being discharged that she was already fully dressed and ready for her escape. She sat patiently on the edge of the bed, her legs crossed and her wayward foot tapping to the beat of the rain hammering against the window. Despite the miserable weather, the thought of being set free was no less enticing. She had already instructed her mum to stay at home, knowing that she would be busy enough preparing for Emma's arrival. It was Louise who would be on call to pick her up as soon as Emma was ready, so now all she had to do was convince Mr Spelling that she was fit enough to be released. Leaving hospital and moving in with her mum may not be a complete escape from her nightmare but it was the nearest she was going to get to a semblance of normality.

Emma closed her eyes as she pondered the next phase

of her life but her thoughts immediately took her to places she didn't want to go. She didn't have her mum's unerring belief that there was a miracle cure out there somewhere and she wasn't sure she should go chasing rainbows simply because her mum believed in them. Emma suspected that any experimental treatment would need to be unimaginably intensive to give her any chance of survival, involving what Mr Spelling would describe as 'heroic measures'. She was already war weary and the question that haunted her was, did she want to let other people decide how much more treatment she should endure or did she want to take a more painful decision?

'Penny for your thoughts?' Mr Spelling asked.

When Emma opened her eyes, her doctor was standing next to her and for once he had arrived without his entourage. 'You know the inside of my head better than I do,' she countered. 'I'm surprised you need to ask.'

'I'm good, but I'm not that good.'

'So why are you so happy?' Emma asked suspiciously as Mr Spelling grinned at her.

'Because,' he said, still smiling, 'all the arrangements are now in place to escort you off the premises.'

'What? You don't want me to perform any more tricks for you?' demanded Emma. 'Wouldn't you like me to walk in a straight line even? I've been practising,' she said as she made a move to slip off the bed, but Mr Spelling lifted a hand to halt her.

'No more tests today. You're free to leave.'

'And then you'll breathe a huge sigh of relief.'

'For now, at least,' he replied with a note of regret.

Emma wrinkled her nose at him. 'You don't like accepting defeat, do you?'

Mr Spelling shifted uneasily. 'We haven't given up yet. We'll start radiotherapy in January and take it from there. I've told you before and I'll say it again: I will do my best for you, Emma, whatever that may be.'

'Do you think it's a waste of time trying to find a clinical trial?' Emma felt nervous asking the question, not sure if she really wanted to know but at least without her mum by her side she stood a chance of getting an uninterrupted and open answer.

'There's a programme in America that looks promising but . . .' Mr Spelling's words trailed off but Emma waited for him. 'There's hope. There's always hope.'

'Is there? I can't help thinking that it might be better to simply accept my fate. If you told me right now that there was nothing more you could do for me, no more treatment, then I swear, I think I'd actually feel relief. It's hard clinging onto hope, knowing how bad the effects of the treatment are going to be and as you've been keen to point out, with no guarantees.'

Emma's emotions were in complete flux and she couldn't completely blame the cocktail of drugs she was taking for the mood swings. At times, she was ready to take on the world, whilst at others, she keenly felt its weight on her shoulders and could barely lift her head to the horizon. And then there were the darkest moments when all she wanted to do was curl up into a ball and literally die. To make matters worse, she could switch from one mood to another without warning, but at least Mr Spelling's calming presence gave her the confidence to dip a toe in each of her emotions and test the water.

'It's ultimately your choice, Emma. Whatever treatment we can offer you, there will always be choices.'

'Quality versus quantity, by any chance?' asked Emma.

'Yes, I'm afraid in my business, it often comes down to that.'

'It's not only me I have to consider though,' she said with a sigh of resignation. 'I have to do what's best for other people.'

The doctor gave Emma a stern look. 'You have to do what's best for you, Emma. What helps the people you love in the end is knowing that you got to do what you wanted.'

'In that case, I want to see Paris in springtime, stand on the edge of the Grand Canyon and stroll through the Valley of the Kings,' Emma quipped. Mr Spelling didn't respond other than to raise an eyebrow and she held up her hands in surrender. This was not the time for smart remarks and Emma's heart quickened as the words to her next question formed in her mind. 'Are you really telling me I can call it a day now?' Her tone remained light but, in Emma's mind, a serious temptation was taking hold.

'You have choices,' repeated Mr Spelling sagely.

Emma was briefly lifted at the thought of bringing

her treatment to an abrupt and total end, but then she let her body sag. 'Then my choice is to make my family happy. My mum's not ready to give up yet, so neither am I. I don't want to be responsible for breaking her heart, not if I can help it.'

'Then I'll support your decision one hundred per cent,' replied Mr Spelling with an unreadable poker face.

'I suppose my next challenge is to build up my strength so I'm ready to take whatever you can throw at me. If memory serves, you don't do things by half measures.'

'And neither do you. It will be a tough fight, I won't deny that,' he agreed. 'So is there anything else you need to know while we've got the chance?' He had also recognized that the conversation would be quite different if Meg had been there.

'No, I think I've taken up enough of your time,' she told him, fearful that if the debate continued about her treatment plan she might just change her mind, but Mr Spelling didn't seem ready to leave. The smile had slipped and he had a look of sadness on his face that Emma was finding all too familiar. She felt obliged to ease his pain. 'Can you keep a secret?' she asked.

'Trust me, I'm a doctor,' Mr Spelling said, his eyes brightening with interest.

'In the story I'm writing, I survive this thing.'

'Would this be the book you want to finish?'

Emma nodded. Her book was another reason she had to fight, for time at least. She'd had many visitors over the weekend, her closest friends and family with the notable exception of Alex, and all of them had heard that she had started to write. Every single person had tried to find out more about what exactly she was writing but so far Emma had remained tight-lipped. She wasn't prepared to share her flight of fancy, unsure if she was ready for their judgement, but Mr Spelling was different. She could trust him with her life.

'Yes, and my biggest problem will be how to fill that life I have in front of me.'

'So tell me, do I play my part in your story or have you discovered that doctor with the sharper knives?'

'You give me the all clear,' she assured him.

'Good. I like a happy ending.'

'Ending?' Emma laughed. 'Oh, no, that's just the beginning. Cancer is not the sum of my life, I am,' she said firmly. 'My story begins with me getting the all clear, an alternative to what happened last week really. Another life.'

'Your life as you would want it to be,' observed Mr Spelling.

Emma smiled, liking the description. 'Yes, but I've already hit a hurdle. I haven't got a clue what I would want if I could have anything!'

'Springtime in Paris? Walking through the Valley of the Kings?' Mr Spelling reminded her.

'They're certainly pretty snapshots from an interesting and varied life but I still need to add more depth to my story and the truth is, I don't have any great ambitions, not any more.' Emma sensed she was talking herself out of writing her book. Her tumour was about to take away the last of her dreams.

'Any more?' So you had ambitions once? You hold such power at your fingertips, Emma,' he said, taking hold of her hand and looking at it. When he looked up at her again there was a shadow of regret in his eyes. 'Just think, you have far more control over your destiny than any doctor. Your hopes and dreams are still there waiting to be handed to you on a plate.'

'Or off a shopkeeper's shelf.'

Mr Spelling shrugged his shoulders. 'You say tomato, I say tom-A-to,' he said.

'In New York, I think they say tom-A-to,' Emma said with a surge of enthusiasm. 'Mr Spelling, I do believe you've just given me the inspiration I needed.'

I was still dangling my right foot in midair as I pondered my next step but then I looked up and was met with an encouraging smile from the kindly shopkeeper. I forgot all about my feet.

'So, what would you like first?' he asked, tipping his head towards the shelves of boxes that were lined up behind him where the hospital car park should have been.

My heart quickened as I realized that everything I could possibly want was within easy reach. 'I . . . I don't know where to begin,' I said.

'Don't worry, I have a reputation for being able to size up my customers and I sense that what you want most

is a purpose in life, something with a bit of a challenge. How about we make a start with your dream job?'

'I had that once.'

'Then you shall have it again,' he replied, sweeping a brightly coloured box off a nearby shelf. It shone with promise. 'But if you don't mind, I've made some improvements.'

I didn't need to ask what he meant. The colour of the box reminded me of a juicy green apple or, more precisely, the Big Apple, and I couldn't wait to begin peeling away its skin to take a closer look.

With my career sorted, the shopkeeper naturally wanted to know what romantic aspirations I had. He looked me up and down, fingers curled around his chin. 'Is Alex good enough for you?' he asked sceptically.

I wrinkled my nose as he pointed to a shelf full of various other options, an enticing row of boxes in eye-catching gift wrap. 'Not if you ask my friends and I have to admit that I had been contemplating moving to London and was expecting to have to make the break but . . . well, I still think there's some potential there,' I told him. I wasn't ready to start my life from scratch and I didn't have to. I could work with what I had and even make a few of my own modifications.

'I'll leave that one in your hands then but your decision isn't binding. I can do a good deal when you're ready for a trade-in.'

'Don't you mean if?' I asked but my words were drowned out by the beeping of a car horn.

I was standing in front of the hospital, my foot still dangling in midair and if the noise of the horn hadn't already startled me, then the face of the person behind the wheel would have been enough to knock me off my feet. My arms flailed and as I stumbled, the torn pieces of card I had been holding in my hand were snatched away by a gust of wind. As the winner's confetti fluttered around me, I stepped forward to claim my prize, not even registering that first step that I had been debating, or the next.

'I thought you couldn't bear the sight of hospitals?' I said. The sun had broken through what had seemed impenetrable cloud cover. I shaded my eyes with my hand and Alex beamed a winning smile at me, his olive skin pulling taught across his square jaw. He had the decency to look just a little shamefaced. As he absent-mindedly smoothed his hair, hair that was slicked back so neatly that it needed no taming, I noted the delicate sprinkling of grey at his temples and knew Alex was proud of this first sign of aging. He was only thirty-two but he was embracing the more mature look, he thought it made him appear more distinguished. 'I couldn't keep away, I've been thinking of you all morning. So tell me, how did it go?'

It was my turn to smile. 'Complete remission,' I said and the tremor in my voice travelled down my spine in a delicious shiver.

'Then that makes your next decision rather easy,' he said with a meaningful look.

'And what decision would that be?' I asked.

Alex leaned over and opened the door for me. He waited until I was safely secured in the passenger seat before he answered. 'I would love to tell you but Ally took the call and she's insisting that she should be the one to tell you,' he said, picking his phone up from the well between the seats. He thumbed a few buttons briefly and then passed it to me before the call was connected.

I gave him a quizzical look as I took the phone but Alex's face was unreadable.

'Ally, do you have some news for me?' I asked when the call was answered.

'Oh, no. Tell me your news first,' Ally demanded into my ear.

'I've been given the all clear,' I said. I had already made frantic calls to my mum and Louise but it didn't matter how many times I said it out loud, it still hadn't quite sunk in. 'All clear, Ally. At last, I have something in my life to celebrate.'

'More than you think.' Ally's voice broke and there was a pause. I could hear a nose being blown. 'I'm so relieved that you can finally get on with the rest of your life.' There was another pause as Ally took a deep breath. 'And what a life it could be. Someone called Kate rang from your old firm, when you worked in London. She wouldn't give me all the details but she told me enough. She, or rather they, Alsop and Clover, want you back. She wants you to call her urgently. I'll text the number to your own phone, OK? Emma, the job will be based in New York!'

My eyes widened in shock. I was speechless.

'Emma?'

'New York? Seriously?'

Ally laughed. 'I'm so happy for you, Emma. Enjoy the moment. It's been a long time coming.'

I was still stunned when the call ended and I handed the phone back to Alex. 'Why me?'

He laughed. 'One of the biggest PR and marketing firms in the world is offering you the job of a lifetime and you make it sound like it's a bad thing.'

'Oh, my God, Alex, I don't think I can take this much good news in one day.'

I could feel a scream building inside me as I took one last look at the hospital before Alex drove away. The pavement flickered white as the wind continued to play with the discarded remnants of my appointment card. I had left my mark on the hospital but then it had left its mark on me too and, in fairness, it was I who had taken far more of a beating. But I wasn't interested in keeping score; we were even as far as I was concerned and I was ready to put it all behind me.

It was only once we had driven through the hospital gates that I regained my power of speech. 'And are you OK with me moving to New York?' I asked, surprised at how selflessly Alex was basking in my glory.

'I want what's best for you and only you,' he told me

earnestly. 'It doesn't matter where you are, I'll always support you. You can count on me.'

'Are you ready, Em?' The voice was familiar but held a note of trepidation that would be out of place anywhere except perhaps an oncology ward.

Louise's face had the same shadow of fear across it as her own but that was where the similarity ended. Louise was a complete contrast to her sister, taking after their dad's side of the family. Emma coveted her blue eyes and the blonde hair falling poker-straight halfway down her back, not to mention her body, which was the picture of health. What she didn't envy was the weight of responsibility that would be placed on her little sister's shoulders. Louise wouldn't only have to stand on her own feet as her mum had said, she would need to be strong enough to keep the family together if the worst happened. One of Emma's legacies would have to be preparing Louise for the task. Judging by her red and swollen eyes, Emma suspected that she was asking too much of Louise, but there really was no choice.

'I have to wait for my prescription but other than that, I'm ready to go,' Emma replied. Even the sudden surge of enthusiasm to write couldn't delay her further. She eagerly closed down her laptop before slipping it into an oversize holdall, which was already crammed full of all the detritus of her latest hospital stay.

'Shall I take that?'

'I can manage,' Emma said. She wouldn't play the

part of helpless patient any longer than necessary but as she stood up, her determination faltered. The dizzy spell was more of a ripple than a wave so she did her best to hide it, taking longer than needed to pack up the last of her things.

'Did you bring my jacket?' Emma asked, thinking about the rain that was still coming down hard.

'Oh, no. Sorry, Em, I didn't think. Here, take mine.'

Louise had already begun to take off her coat but Emma stopped her in her tracks with a warning glare. She was still the older sister, which gave her an air of authority that she would cling onto until the bitter end. Louise raised an eyebrow in defiance but then shrugged her coat back on and as she did so, her eyes were drawn to something or someone behind Emma. She began to suppress a smile.

When Emma turned around, Peter was standing behind her. He had collected Emma's medication, a cocktail of anti-seizure drugs, steroids and painkillers that would hopefully keep the tumour and its symptoms at bay in the weeks running up to her treatment. They were piled up high on the seat of a wheelchair. 'That thing had better not be for me,' she growled.

Peter was about to answer but Louise cut him short. 'Don't even try. You won't get her to use it.'

Peter and Emma locked eyes. 'OK, I give in,' he said, having stood his ground for only a fraction of a second.

'I tell you what,' offered Emma. 'We can use the wheel-chair to carry all of my stuff to the car. In the meantime, you can have a quick break and collect it from the entrance in, say, ten minutes.'

'If there was an element of compromise in there, then I think I missed it,' he told her but, keen to take advantage of an impromptu break, didn't argue.

With a few brief goodbyes to staff and patients alike, Emma and Louise meandered through the hospital towards the main exit. 'You are alright about moving out of Mum's, aren't you?' Emma asked. They had already had the same discussion over the weekend but Emma suspected that her sister had barely taken anything in, the news that the cancer was back was still sinking in.

'Of course I am and I have a long list of friends offering to put me up. I'll be fine, honest,' Louise told her.

'If I'd known this was going to happen, I would never have convinced you to rent out the apartment above the bistro.'

'And if I had known this was going to happen, I wouldn't have depended on you so much to get me back on my feet after Joe and I split up.'

The breakup of Louise's relationship had been a double whammy because Joe was also her business partner. He had been the head chef whilst Louise provided the front-of-house service and the bistro had been going from strength to strength. Joe had walked out on her just over a year ago and it had been Emma who had convinced her to go it alone.

This had all happened around the time that Emma

had been overlooked for the marketing job at Bannister's and she had been keen to concentrate her efforts on the bistro, where she knew she would be appreciated. It also allowed her bruised ego time to heal. Louise had bought Joe out with a substantial investment from her mum and she had eventually found a new head chef. Emma's involvement had begun to dwindle when she started going out with Alex but she was still called upon to firefight now and again. The cash-flow problems that had resulted in Louise renting out her flat only served to prove that she wasn't quite ready to go it alone.

'What I wouldn't give for a crystal ball right now,' mused Emma as the main exit doors came into view. 'But don't think for a minute I'm going to spend all my time at Mum's with my feet up.'

Louise took her eyes from the wheelchair she was trying to manoeuvre and checked Emma's expression. 'You're not thinking of going back to work are you?'

Emma looked sheepish, as if she was still considering the possibility. 'I need more in my life than hospital appointments. I need a purpose, I always will,' she said with a smile as she realized that her kindly shopkeeper would say the same thing.

'But . . .' began Louise as she narrowly averted ramming the wheelchair into the back of an old man who had been walking down the corridor at a more sedate pace.

'Don't worry, even I think it would be a bit too much

to go back to Bannister's but there's nothing to stop me interfering in your business.'

'Yes, there is,' Louise corrected.

Emma knew her mum would do her utmost to prevent her from exerting herself. 'We'll see,' she said as they hit fresh air.

They came to a halt beneath a wide canopy, which gave some protection from the elements. The rain was thundering against the roof above their heads but it was music to Emma's ears. The damp taste of freedom on her tongue felt fresh and revitalizing. She was about to ask Louise where she had parked when a car beeped its horn, making Emma jump in fright, as much by an alarming sense of déjà vu as by the sound itself.

When Emma's heart stopped pounding, a strange silence descended. It wasn't complete – she could still hear the wind whistling around her – but it was the absence of one particular noise that drew her attention. The rain had stopped abruptly and as Emma looked up, the sunshine breaking through the cloud was blinding. She squeezed her eyes shut but as she did so, she caught a glimpse of what could be snowflakes falling around her. She blinked against the sunlight to take a better look. It wasn't snowflakes in front of her eyes but tiny pieces of white card. Emma knew that if she gathered them up and glued them back together, she would find herself in the possession of a dog-eared appointment card. A shiver shot down her spine and she grabbed at her jacket to wrap it tightly around her but she couldn't make purchase with the material and she began to panic.

'Emma, are you alright?' Louise asked, putting her hand on one of Emma's flailing arms.

Emma blinked and the noise of the rain crashed into her world. 'My coat,' she said, still trying to close it around her.

'You're not wearing a coat, Em.'

Emma felt the panic rise in her chest and then slowly ebb away. She could remember the sound of the horn beeping, the silence broken by the sudden roar of rain above her head but nothing in between. She slowly recognized the familiar signs of a partial seizure. The position of her tumour meant that she could expect unsettling effects such as déjà-vu episodes and even hallucinations. Her medication was intended to reduce swelling and control the symptoms but it would appear that her drug regime was still far from perfect.

'Do we need to get you back inside?' Louise asked.

'Not a chance,' Emma said as she looked towards the car that had stopped in front of the entrance. It was the van that Louise used for the bistro and there was a man in the driving seat. Ben was the bistro's new head chef and he had been the one bright light in her sister's darkest hour. Despite the sight of such a familiar and welcoming face, Emma still had to swallow the bitter taste of disappointment. She was surprised with herself for even entertaining the idea that it might have been Alex.

With no recollection of her hallucination, she was even more surprised when she scanned the ground around her, in search of the remnants of an appointment card that existed only in her imagination.

Meg had been working hard. With the help of Ally and Gina, she had already transferred all of Emma's belongings from the house she'd shared with them to the apartment. The whole process had been exhausting and Meg looked nervous as she opened the door to her daughter.

'Let me help you with those,' she said, wrestling a large carrier bag crammed with medical supplies from Emma's grasp. Emma felt the first tug of frustration pull at her mood but she put on a brave smile.

'Did everything go alright? Did you see Mr Spelling? Is there any news?' continued Meg.

The questions came out like bullets and Emma expertly deflected each one. 'Yes, yes and no,' she said.

'What about when we were outside the hospital?' Louise interrupted.

'Why? What happened?'

Emma gave Louise a warning look before answering. 'Nothing. Louise forgot my coat, that's all. Now, are we going to stand here all day? Poor Ben's arms will be two inches longer if he stands holding my bag any longer.'

'Sorry, of course you can, come in. Welcome home, sweetheart,' Meg said, her words choked with emotion.

They all squeezed into the entrance hall. Doors to the left and right led off to the two bedrooms and the bathroom and the door immediately in front of them gave access to the open-plan living area. Emma suspected that the apartment wasn't quite as claustrophobic as it seemed in her current state of mind but the place brought back painful memories she had hoped to have put behind her. Meg opened the door to what was to be Emma's bedroom and Ben put her holdall onto the double bed, the floor space having already been taken up with a mass of bags and boxes.

'I haven't put your things away yet,' Meg explained. 'I thought you might want to decide where everything should go.'

'Or decide what needs to be kept and what doesn't,' Emma said, swallowing another bitter pill of disappointment. She had been living in a large Victorian terrace for the last few years and space had never been an issue.

Emma turned away and headed for the living area, which had a compact kitchen with a small dining area to the left and the living room to the right. The soft lime-green walls gave the room a modern twist and the creams and purples of the soft furnishings added light and shade but the colours were lost on Emma. Her world had turned as dark as her mood and she ignored the balloons and WELCOME banners, her eyes drawn instead to the wide patio window that led onto a balcony and the panoramic view over the River Mersey. In the distance, she could just make out the silhouettes of brooding hills, the most distant of which marked the Welsh border. Their peaks were smeared by dark, heavy clouds as they scraped against the sky.

'Am I interrupting?'

It was perhaps the one voice that could draw Emma back into the apartment. 'Alex! You came!' she cried.

'I said I would,' he said reproachfully as he proferred a bouquet of blood-red roses, which were crushed as Emma rushed into his arms. As she buried her head in his shoulder, she breathed him in. She could smell after-shave and soap overlaid with an unmistakeable musti-ness. Bannister's offices adjoined the workshop and Emma was surprised by the sudden rush of longing for the place.

Meg and Louise busied themselves in the kitchen whilst Ben stepped into the shadows. There was an air of judge-ment in their collective silence.

'We'd better head back to the bistro,' Louise said at last, her tone brusque to match the speed at which she headed back towards the door that she had walked through only moments earlier.

'You're the boss,' added Ben, but he was still looking at Emma. 'If there's anything you need, Emma, you know where I am.'

'Thanks, Ben,' Emma said, lifting her head over Alex's shoulder.

'Any cravings for my Moroccan chicken or chilli beef, you only have to pick up the phone. Day or night.'

Emma held his gaze. She was used to offers of help being thrown at her, platitudes that would never be followed through, but Ben's offer was direct, definitive and she didn't doubt for a minute that he would be there if she needed him.

'Come on,' Louise told him, pulling at his sleeve. 'Before she gets any ideas about us starting up a takeaway business.'

'I'll see you out,' Meg offered.

'And remember to shut the door after you this time,' mumbled Louise as they disappeared.

'Actually, I can't stay long either,' Alex said as he unravelled himself from Emma's arms and dropped the crushed bouquet onto a nearby table. 'I just wanted to let you know that I've really been missing you.'

'I've missed you too,' Emma replied, hoping it wasn't the cold reception from her family that had made him eager to leave.

'You look so well,' Alex said. There was a note of disbelief in his voice. He already knew the painful detail of Mr Spelling's prognosis and Emma wondered what he had expected to see. Alex hadn't known her when she had first been diagnosed with cancer, he hadn't seen her brought to her knees by the rigours of her treatment and, more importantly, he had never seen her as a cancer victim. But that was what he saw now.

Emma fought against the urge to raise her hand self-consciously to the dressing that still covered the back of her head. She had pulled her hair loosely across the wound in a ponytail and that, with the help of carefully applied makeup to cover the dark circles under her eyes, had meant to complete her disguise. 'I'm not dead yet,' she said, surprising herself by her directness.

If she had wanted to shock Alex, then the way he

surreptitiously inched away from her embrace confirmed that she had succeeded.

'Sorry,' she added quickly.

'You're a fighter and you're going to beat this. You have to.'

'I'm not sure my doctor would agree with you there.'

'Will you come back to work?'

'No, not at the moment,' Emma said, although she desperately wanted to say yes. She wasn't ready to quit on every aspect of her life and as she had said, she wasn't dead yet. But Emma also had to accept there were limitations and the seizure she had suffered earlier that day served as a timely reminder of that fact. She could push herself but not too hard, not until she was sure that her medication levels had reduced or completely eliminated some of the symptoms. She wasn't ready to consider that she might never return to work but returning in the near future was an unrealistic target.

'We could really do with your help right now,' persisted Alex. 'Mr Bannister has brought Jennifer in to help but she's on a steep learning curve.'

'Jennifer's covering my job?'

Jennifer was Mr Bannister's wayward daughter and although she was about the same age as Emma, she had never worked as far as Emma was aware and she had certainly never shown an interest in Daddy's business before.

'Needs must,' Alex said. 'She's trying really hard but it's not an easy job stepping into your shoes. I think she would really appreciate it if you dropped by some time, when you're up to it.'

'Maybe I will call into the office,' Emma told him but she had no intention of helping Jennifer step into her shoes. She had thought that they were still hers and she would be telling Mr Bannister just that.

Alex smiled and kissed the top of her head, his lips making a satisfied smacking sound. 'I knew I could count on you. We make a good team, you and me.'

'Yes, we do,' agreed Emma as she tried to match his smile. 'Give me a few days and then I'll come in. I promise.'

'And if there's anything you need, you know where I am,' Alex said as he peeled himself from Emma's arms.

There was only a brief kiss on the lips and then Alex was gone. Within moments, Emma felt the walls closing in around her so she busied herself in the kitchen. She was filling the kettle when Meg reappeared. She had been in Emma's bedroom on the pretext of sorting out boxes, keeping a safe distance and, by all appearances, giving Emma some privacy.

'How about a nice cup of coffee?' Emma asked.

'There's decaf in the cupboard, or if you fancy something else then I've got pomegranate juice or there's green tea. I tried to get that smoothie drink you used to have but they're going to have to order it in for me.' Meg had clearly resurrected her knowledge of cancer-fighting nutrients. Foods high in antioxidants or containing phytochemicals would be high on the list of essential groceries from now on.

'I'm OK with normal coffee for now,' Emma told her with a mixture of irritation and sadness as another door in her past life reopened. 'You don't have to nursemaid me.'

'I know,' Meg agreed and the familiar crackle of emotion accompanied her words. 'I'm sorry.'

Emma's heart bloomed with a new emotion. She had been so intent on controlling her own emotions from the moment she had stepped over the threshold that she only now appreciated how difficult this was for her mum too. The sense of loss and fear Emma had been battling with was nothing compared to what she felt now. Guilt.

'I'm sorry too,' Emma told her and, for the second time that day, she let herself be wrapped in someone's arms. It was even more difficult to extract herself from her mum's fierce embrace.

Tears were sniffed away and eyes averted as Emma continued making drinks and Meg started unpacking the bags of medication from the hospital.

'Do you think it's a good idea going back to the office so soon?' Meg asked.

The pause lasted only a heartbeat. Emma extinguished the anger that flared before it was allowed to catch. Now was not the time for arguments and accusations of eavesdropping. 'I only said I'd call in. I know I'm not ready to go back yet.'

'Good,' Meg said as she continued with her task. In no time at all, row upon row of medicine bottles were lined up in tight formation on the kitchen counter. A regiment of soldiers, ready for combat. Emma took her coffee and turned her back on them.

'Do you mind if I take this to my room?' Emma asked, surprised and saddened by how quickly she had adapted to a new life where she felt it necessary to ask permission to leave the room. 'I could do with a bit of a rest.'

Alone in her bedroom, she cleared a space on her bed and lay down fully clothed, leaving her coffee to go cold, untouched. She felt completely drained but as she let herself drift off to sleep she was already constructing the world she planned to build with the power that Mr Spelling said she held at her fingertips.

3

I hated flying. If there was an alternative form of transport, I would take it and if there wasn't, I had more often than not changed my destination. It made going on holiday complicated but my latest adventure was business, not pleasure and there really wasn't any other way of getting across the Atlantic Ocean, not if I wanted to make the nine o'clock meeting on Monday at Alsop and Clover's New York office.

I looked out of the tiny window and peered across the broad wing of the plane. It shone with the full force of a sun that was no longer obstructed by the dense cloud cover that had looked so dark and impenetrable from the ground. The only clouds I could see now floated gently below us, white and fluffy and, with any luck, bouncy if the plane should suddenly drop altitude.

My stomach was being twisted into tight knots and I tried to convince myself that it was with excitement and not fear. I had been thrilled that Kate Barton had made such efforts to track me down and offer me a job if not a little suspicious as to why she would be so eager to take me back. I had begun my working life as her apprentice, one of half a dozen graduates who were to be nurtured and groomed for corporate life, but only some would achieve the success that the company demanded. I had been one of them, for a time at least.

I had been twenty-two when I joined the company and within six months I was trusted with my own projects and in two years I wasn't just a team player, I was a team leader. I enjoyed working for Kate and I think she saw me more as a protégé than an apprentice. We had similar tastes, the same sense of humour and one day I hoped to have the same quiet fortitude that could speak louder than the most vociferous tirade in the board room. My career had been all mapped out but it wasn't long before my tumour began to cut off the avenues to my success.

The disease had been cruel and insipid. It hadn't arrived overnight and severed my options in one neat, clinical blow; it had crept slowly into my life. My symptoms had caused chaos and what I had assumed was irreparable damage to my career and reputation. The blurred vision affected my ability to research properly or produce reports on time. The headaches prevented me from getting out of bed, let alone getting into the office and worse still, I had bouts of memory loss. How was I supposed to convince a client that I had come up with an unforgettable tag line if I couldn't remember it myself?

Kate had been understanding at first and we both assumed that my lapses would be short-term, a mystery illness that would clear up of its own accord. But it didn't, it only got worse. I tried to build in contingencies to my projects wherever I could but when it became apparent that I was relying on the team more and more, when I became a liability rather than the asset Kate had groomed me to be, it was almost a relief when she severed the umbilical cord. Almost, but not quite. I was too busy dealing with the trauma of my diagnosis to feel anything close to relief.

And here I was, facing my past as I prepared for my future. I had to remember the person I had once been, the woman who had climbed the corporate ladder two steps at a time. That was who I was, not the victim of a brain tumour, not the bit player in someone else's success. But I was fooling myself if I thought it was excitement I was feeling. It was pure terror.

The plane suddenly dipped and the seatbelt warning lights flashed on as my stomach lurched and a wave of nausea washed over me. I gripped the armrests tightly where another hand gently covered mine and gave it a squeeze.

'You're going to be OK,' Alex told me. 'I'm here.'

When Emma awoke she thought she was at home, in the house she shared with Ally and Gina, tucked up safely in her own bed. It was only as she prised open her eyes and saw the jaundiced yellow of the walls, warming in the weak morning light, that her memory returned with a sickening stomach punch. The room hadn't changed since the last time she had been held captive within its walls and the paint had clung on in much the same way as her cancer cells. Emma stretched and untangled herself from the bed sheets. Despite the deep sleep that always seemed to arrive before dawn, she had spent most of the night tossing and turning thanks to her restless thoughts that were kept in perpetual train by the steroids.

With an unerring sense of timing that she had acquired in the last few days, Meg popped her head around the door. 'Are you awake?' she whispered. 'Would you like anything?'

Emma had to remind herself that she was a grown woman and not a schoolgirl as she pulled herself up to face her mum. 'No, I'll get up now,' she said as her eyes adjusted to the light. 'You look nice.'

Meg had looked tired and worn for weeks but at last she looked a little like her old self. 'I've taken your advice and made a bit of an effort. I might pop into work today if you think you can manage without me,' she said, stepping through the door to show off her transformation. She was wearing a light grey suit with a silk blouse. It had been easy to forget that she was a fully qualified and experienced solicitor but the shadow of a woman who had hovered at the side of her daughter's hospital bed had been given substance once more.

'I'm glad to hear it,' Emma said with a nod of approval. 'At least one of us is earning our keep.'

'We'll manage,' Meg told her. 'And I don't intend to stay out long. I'll do what needs to be done in the office and bring some of my case files back home with me. With any luck I'll be back by mid-afternoon.'

'I might take a string out of your bow and pop into the office too,' Emma said, trying to sound nonchalant.

To Emma's surprise, Meg smiled. 'If I didn't know better, I'd say you've already made plans to go in.'

'Who told you?' demanded Emma with a raised eyebrow.

'Gina,' they both said in unison.

'She mentioned it when she phoned last night,' Meg confessed. 'I'm surprised you're telling me now and not after the fact.'

'As if I'd do that,' Emma said. 'It's not as if you might try to put me off.'

Meg bit her tongue but clearly not hard enough. 'It is just a visit, isn't it? Please don't let Alex persuade you to get involved in one of his projects.'

'Is it my fault if I'm so indispensable?'

'I'd better go,' Meg said, sidestepping the argument. 'I've printed out the list of your meds, what you need to take and when, and your pill boxes are all filled for the day. Don't forget to take them with you when you go.'

'You didn't have to do that,' scolded Emma.

'One less thing for you to do.'

It was Emma's turn to bite her tongue. She wasn't looking for fewer things to do. An image of a tree being stripped of its leaves by autumn winds came to mind as she thought of her life being slowly deconstructed, leaf by leaf.

'Is anyone going to pick you up or do you need a lift?' Meg continued.

Emma wasn't allowed to drive and Alex had an early morning appointment so couldn't help although he had promised to meet her at the office later. Ally had offered to pick her up but Emma was intent on getting to Bannister's under her own steam. It had been four days since her seizure and she was hoping that her anti-seizure drugs would continue to thwart her tumour's best efforts to disrupt her life.

'I can manage, Mum. Now go!' Emma said, shooing her Mum out of the bedroom as she slipped out of bed and prepared to face the world. She glanced in the dressing-table mirror. As she traced a finger across her cheekbone, following the circle of grey beneath her eye, she realized that she would have to work hard on her own transformation and it was going to take an extra layer of concealer to prepare her mask for the day.

Her epic journey had involved a bus ride where she could feel the contents of her head being jostled about every time they went over a pot hole, followed by a ten-minute walk. By the time it was over, she felt completely drained and frustrated by the failings of her body and her arrival at the office did little to buoy her spirits.

Mr Bannister was away on business but she had expected that. They had had a lengthy telephone conversation, during which he had assured her that her job would be there waiting for her whenever she was ready to return. It was the reaction of her other colleagues that had surprised her. There had been plenty of 'hello's on her way to her office but her co-workers had looked distinctly uncomfortable and quickly made their apologies, insisting there were other places they should be. She could only assume that they thought her cancer was contagious. Alex was still out at a showroom with Jennifer so only Gina had been there to greet her and to give her the hug she desperately needed.

Emma sat down behind her desk and let her fingers slide along its surface. It was only chipped MDF but it felt like home and she was glad that only Gina was there to share this moment. Gina was nearer to Louise's age but that hadn't stopped them quickly forming a close friendship when Emma joined Bannister's and sharing a house with her and Ally had been the perfect arrangement.

Despite Emma's best efforts to make herself presentable that morning, she was pale in comparison to her friend's glowing health. Gina was the girlie-girl who never left home without being perfectly made up and, even today, with her long chestnut-brown hair captured in a messy ponytail, she looked sweet and fresh and full of life. She sat patiently watching Emma, only allowing the breath she had been holding to escape when she saw a smile creep across Emma's face.

'Did I tell you Mr Bannister said that my job would be waiting for me whenever I wanted?'

'And will you come back?' Gina often came across as quite blunt, mainly because she had a habit of speaking before thinking, but it was a question that everyone was wondering about, Emma included.

'I can't imagine why anyone would want to come back to this insane asylum,' remarked Ally, who had appeared at the door. For her sins, she worked in the office next door, which housed both the accounts and sale sections, a combination that made Ally's remark entirely appropriate.

Emma hesitated, not because she didn't know what to say but because she knew it would be painful for her friends to hear. 'Because when everything is being taken from you, you hang onto what you can,' she said.

'But you're not coming back now, not today,' Ally insisted. It wasn't a question.

Ally had always been the serious one. She was wearing dark clothes as usual to complement her deep brown, short-cropped hair. Her eyes were almost black and framed with dark-rimmed glasses. Emma and Gina had made numerous attempts to liven up her appearance but Ally's only concession so far had been to put multi-coloured streaks in her hair. At the moment, she had bright red streaks, which matched her red lipstick.

'You're beginning to sound like my mum,' Emma scolded. 'I'm here for a visit, that's all, just to say hello to people.' She looked at Gina and said, 'I can't believe Dan hasn't made an appearance yet.'

Ally recognized and took the bait. 'Oh, he's been in already this morning.'

'Only once?' Emma asked. 'If Mr Bannister hadn't been so quick to bring Jennifer into the office, it would have been Dan taking up residence at my desk, I bet. I suppose he's still in here every chance he gets, things can't have changed that much. It's a wonder he ever has time to fit kitchens.'

Neither Ally nor Emma was looking at Gina and ignored her vain attempts to interject. 'Maybe I need to look into this, see how many jobs Gina has been signing off for him instead of genuine customers,' Ally said.

'You might be onto something there.'

Ally shook her head sadly. 'As an accountant I have a duty to look into these things.'

Gina banged a stapler down onto her desk to get their attention. 'Firstly, Ally, you're not an accountant and, secondly, Dan had a genuine reason for visiting this morning. He has some good ideas about changing the rotas to make things run more efficiently. A proper accountant would see that as time well spent.'

'Firstly,' responded Ally curtly, 'I'm a trainee accountant, which is practically the same thing and, secondly, just admit it that you're encouraging him. You wouldn't be coming into work dressed up like a Barbie doll if you weren't.'

'Jealous?' challenged Gina.

'No,' snorted Ally. 'There are no men in my life because that's my choice.'

'Liar! You wish Emma was still in hospital so you could go and flirt with her nurse.'

Ally drew a sharp breath. 'I would give anything for Emma never to have been in there in the first place.'

Emma tried to keep her smile but it trembled. She had found respite in the inane chatter of her friends but her cancer had come crashing into the conversation. Two sets of tear-filled eyes looked at her for strength that she didn't have. 'I know,' she managed to say but she could already feel her throat constricting. She stood up and was about to go to her friends when a flash of colour swept into the room.

'You're back!' screeched Jennifer, rushing over to give Emma a hug and a kiss on each cheek.

Emma looked over her shoulder at Ally and Gina, who had been shocked out of their despair. Ally started sticking her finger down her throat and only just missed being caught out as Jennifer spun around.

'I told you to text me as soon as she arrived,' she chided. Jennifer stood with her hands on her hips as she looked from one fixed smile to another. She was wearing a brightly patterned winter coat, its pinks and blues clashing dramatically with her ginger hair, which was cut into a neat bob with a sharp fringe. Ally had jokingly referred to Gina as a Barbie doll, but Jennifer had a far better claim to the title.

'We wanted it to be a surprise,' replied Ally, her fixed grin still fixed.

Jennifer turned back towards Emma. 'I want you to know that I'm doing the best I can but I have been thrown in at the deep end.'

Emma wondered if she was actually expecting her to feel sorry for her. Jennifer had been cosseted and spoiled from an early age by her parents, and when her mum died, when she was a teenager, Mr Bannister had ensured that his daughter lacked for nothing to fill the gaping hole in her life. Working for a living was going to be quite a culture shock for her. 'Yes, it's not as easy as it looks,' Emma said.

'The girls are helping as much as they can and, of course, Alex is doing his best too. I just hope I don't mess it all up.'

'Speaking of the devil,' muttered Ally as Alex entered the office.

'Sorry I wasn't here for you,' he said, going over to give Emma a kiss on the cheek.

'Nothing new there,' Gina chipped in.

Emma gave both her friends a warning look. She had enough battles of her own without playing referee.

'I'll go make us all a cuppa,' Gina said.

'I'll help,' Ally added, and they both disappeared from view.

By the time they came back, Emma was busily tapping away at her keyboard, with Alex and Jennifer peering over her shoulder. Alex had already managed to clear her password, while she was in hospital, to access her computer, but he hadn't been able to find the files he wanted.

'It's all down to my training at Alsop and Clover,' Emma explained. 'You can't be too careful when it comes to security. All my important files are encrypted.'

'Here, write down the passwords,' Alex said, kissing the top of her head before pushing a notepad towards her.

Emma felt her chest tighten. The files he wanted held all of her ideas for future projects and campaigns, the ones that would help Jennifer fit a little more snugly into her shoes, not to mention help Alex do his job without even thinking. A voice in Emma's head was telling her she was being manipulated, violated even. The voice was insistent, strained with barely contained fury, telling her she was a fool. Alex had rushed to her side, eventually, but not to help her. He had wanted to strip the assets, gathering up her work to pass off as his own and to impress Jennifer. The voice told her to stand up for herself.

But that voice wasn't alone in her head; there was something else there too. She had promised Mr Bannister that she would help as much as she could. If there was a chance that she would never return to work, then all of her ideas would go to waste.

She picked up a pen and jotted down the passwords. Most of them, anyway. As Gina gently placed a mug of coffee in front of her, Emma glanced meaningfully at her watch.

'If you don't mind, I think I'll call it a day,' she said.

Ally and Gina looked purposefully at Alex, but he was too engrossed in the document he had just opened to notice them. Ally cleared her throat and he eventually looked up. 'Oh, sorry,' he said. 'Do you want a lift?'

'It's alright, you're busy. Besides, I could do with some fresh air.' Emma had missed Alex, had missed being in the office too, but now she needed to escape.

'Oh, OK then,' he said. 'Hey, how about we go out for dinner on Saturday?'

'That would be nice,' she said, but it was a lie that burned like acid at the back of her throat.

'I'll have had a chance to go through your files by then and I can pick your brain.'

'You and everyone else,' Emma replied under her breath.

There were plenty of hugs as she said, her goodbyes but it was Ally who insisted on seeing Emma out. 'I can give you a lift, if you want,' she offered.

'I think my life's in enough jeopardy already, don't you?'

They both made a good attempt at a laugh. 'My driving is getting better and I'll take good care of your car until you're ready to take it back.' Emma had seen no point in having her car parked outside her mum's apartment unused. Ally had borrowed it often enough so it seemed only logical to leave it at the house, and her friend had promised to be her chauffeur whenever she deigned to admit that she needed help.

'I may never be ready. You do know that, don't you?' Emma told her as gently as she could.

'We know. We just don't want to believe it. You deserve better,' she added.

Emma knew Ally was veering neatly towards another sensitive subject. 'I know, but for now I have to work with what I've got.'

'Really?' asked Ally, unconvinced.

'Really,' confirmed Emma. 'Although I may have to check the returns policy with my shopkeeper.' When Ally gave her a worried look, Emma laughed and it was genuine this time. She gave her one final hug. 'Don't worry. I've not lost the plot just yet.'

As Emma pulled her coat around her and headed into the early afternoon sunshine, she realized that she was going to have to give some serious thought to the image of the hero she had created in her mind. His shining armour was looking distinctly tarnished. As her mind whirred with ideas of how she could mete out justice and revenge in equal measure, the impotence she had felt sitting at her desk was slowly replaced by a sense of power that made her fingers tingle.

Emma's trip to the office had been far more physically exhausting than she had imagined. She could feel the pressure building up inside her head so she abandoned her plans to start writing and spent two days recovering. By Friday morning she was crawling the walls of the apartment but still she couldn't escape into her imaginary world. Her self-imposed break had given her time to doubt the direction her story should be taking and the claustrophobic atmosphere of the apartment was fuelling her writer's block. She knew she didn't have time to waste prevaricating; time wasn't on her side so she packed away her laptop, picked up the pill box her mum had prepared for the day and called a cab.

The Traveller's Rest was on a leafy avenue not far from Sefton Park on the boundary of Liverpool city centre. Her sister's restaurant had a bohemian feel to it with bare timber floors and mismatched tables and chairs. To the front, there were floor-to-ceiling windows with flowing crimson drapes and, to the rear, rows of intimate booths.

Weekday mornings were never a busy time for the restaurant but at first glance it appeared closed and, as Emma pushed open the door, she half expected it to be locked. The temperature in the bistro was only marginally warmer than outside where winter had started to bite. There were two tables occupied so if Louise had been relying on warm bodies to heat up the place she was going to have to recruit more staff. As it was, Steven, the only waiter on duty, was at a loss with what to do with himself. He was keeping one watchful eye on his customers, ready to pounce at the slightest suggestion that they needed something, and the other on the door. He looked briefly disappointed when he realized it hadn't been more custom walking through the door but that was quickly replaced by genuine excitement at seeing Emma.

'We weren't expecting you until the weekend,' he explained, taking her by the arm and leading her towards one of the booths at the far side of the restaurant. 'Not that I'm complaining, it's lovely to see you back again.' The look he gave Emma was enough to let her know that he was sorry to hear her cancer had returned, sorry that she may not beat it this time. As with most people, the look alone would have to be enough as he failed to voice his thoughts.

Emma gratefully accepted the look and then moved onto safer ground. 'I thought I'd check out business. See how Louise has been getting on without my interference.'

Steven winced as he made a point of looking around at the empty tables. 'She's out at the cash-and-carry at the moment but we're doing fine,' he lied. 'Here, let me take your coat.'

'No thanks,' replied Emma, pulling her jacket protectively around her. 'It's freezing in here.'

'Cost-cutting measures.'

Emma raised her eyes to the ceiling in disbelief. 'It's hardly providing a warm and welcoming atmosphere. I'm officially back on the case and here's my first suggestion: turn the thermostat up.'

'But . . .' began Steven. He had been working for Louise from the very beginning and was treated like one of the family, which meant that he had experienced the wrath of both sisters. He now faced a dilemma. Louise was the one supporting his personal development by allowing him to fit his shifts around a catering course and occasionally letting him loose in the kitchens. He could stay in her good books or he could do what Emma told him.

Emma made it easier for him to decide. 'I was being polite when I said it was a suggestion,' she said. 'I don't care what Louise says, she'll lose the few customers she has left unless she starts taking action. Please, Steven. Turn it up, if only for me.'

'You're the boss,' Steven relented with a playful smile. 'How about a nice hot cup of coffee?'

'This place is going up in my estimation all the time.'

The booth Emma was using had red leather benches along three sides, which would comfortably seat six and, under better circumstances, she would have felt guilty taking up so much space. The table was bare wood with a collection of condiments and menus lined up in a row along its centre. Emma pushed these out of the way so she had room to set up her laptop.

She took a deep breath and held it as she stared at the blank page that appeared in front of her and waited for inspiration to strike. A steaming cup of coffee, complete with swirls of creamy foam and a sprinkling of chocolate appeared in its stead.

Emma let out a sigh and her body visibly sagged as she looked up, expecting to see Steven. However, she discovered Ben watching her instead. Ben was in his early thirties, medium height with broad shoulders and dark short-cropped hair peaking through his catering hat. His eyes were the deepest brown with the longest lashes and he had the kind of expression that Emma missed. Someone was looking at her without pity in his eyes and the look lifted her spirit and her body along with it.

'Not got anything better to do than serve front of house?' Emma asked.

Ben looked around the restaurant in the same way that Steven had. 'No,' he said. 'But I'm not here to serve, I'm here to complain.'

'Complain about what?' Emma wondered if Steven had told him about her order to crank up the heating but would be surprised if Ben would disagree. He had been in the middle of many arguments between Louise and Emma before now and, more often than not, he had sided with Emma.

'I've been staring at the phone waiting for you to ring me with that order. I thought steroids were supposed to make you eat more.'

Emma laughed. 'Yes, they do, but if I give into temptation, you'd never get me out of this place.'

'I wouldn't complain and, besides, we could always roll you out when you're done.'

Emma's smile was so wide that her cheeks began to ache. There were muscles being used that hadn't been for quite some time. 'Never mind the steroids. You're good enough medicine, Mr Knowles.'

She had first met Ben when she and Louise had interviewed him for the job after Joe had left. Louise had still been in shock at the time. Her heart had been broken and her confidence shattered, but Emma had believed in Louise even when Louise hadn't believed in herself. Her sister had told her she wanted to prove that she could make it without Joe, and Emma had been determined to make that happen. So whilst Louise was assessing candidates purely on their cooking abilities, Emma was looking for something else. She wanted someone who would bring a calming influence, who would be an anchor to the occasional storms her sister could brew up and maybe, just maybe, be the person to mend her sister's heart.

Ben had stood out for both of them. He had learnt his trade in Liverpool and then travelled further afield to expand his culinary knowledge. Along the way he had transformed his trade into a passion, which translated not only onto the plate but came across in his whole demeanor and for once the sisters hadn't argued about their choice. Since then, Emma had watched and waited but the only sparks between Louise and Ben were confined to the kitchen.

'And you are an amazing woman,' he said, dropping down into the seat opposite her. He rubbed his cheeks, wiping away the gentle blush that threatened. 'I have to admit though, when I picked you up from hospital, I was scared.'

'Of me or my cancer?' Emma asked.

Ben took off his hat and scrunched it in his hands. He looked like he was about to lose the composure that had become his trademark, in and out of the kitchen.

'Of what the cancer might have already taken from you, I suppose. I thought you'd be a little less . . .' he began.

'A little less alive?'

Instinct told Emma that the usual commiserations weren't about to roll off his tongue and she was proven right. He rested his head on his hand as he scrutinized her face. His eyes fixed in concentration. 'Perhaps. But you don't look like someone who's ready to give up.'

Emma had always felt at ease in Ben's company and she had often surprised herself at how much she could open up to him. She respected his opinion and his judgement when it came to the bistro and as he sat in front of her, sharing his fears, she didn't think there was anything she couldn't trust him with.

'Not when there's still so much left to do,' Emma told him. 'I won't rest until I've knocked Louise into shape so she can run this place properly on her own, and then there are things happening at work that would have me turning in my grave, so I suppose you're right. Giving up isn't an option.' Emma took an excited breath. At last she had found someone she could talk to who wouldn't wince at the vaguest mention of death and she was tempted to take Ben hostage.

'So why were you frowning at your laptop?' Ben asked.

As if Ben had magically summoned its return, the frown reappeared on Emma's brow. 'That would be because of the book I'm trying to write.'

'And is this how great writers work? Direct thought transfer rather than actual typing?'

71

'Hmm, very funny. I was waiting for inspiration to strike.'

'So what's this story about?' Ben asked, little knowing that so far only Mr Spelling had been trusted with the premise of her opus.

There was something in Ben's eyes that made Emma pause only briefly before opening up her heart. 'OK, this is top secret. You tell no-one,' she said, as if he had spent hours trying to wear her down into a confession. 'It's a story about someone like me, who has battled illness but, in her case, she wins. She gets the one thing I never did, the all-clear.' Emma paused long enough for Ben's nod of agreement, which he dutifully provided. 'I need to write about what she would then do with her life. I know you're supposed to write about what you know but that's the whole point, I'm writing about what hasn't happened in my life.'

'Your life? So this someone that's like you, is you?'

Emma pursed her lips but it was too late to take it back. 'I still can't escape the fact that I haven't experienced enough to draw upon,' she said.

'Somehow I think you're doing yourself a disservice. I would have thought that someone who's gone through what you've been through has had more than their fair share of experiences.'

'Experiences of facing death, yes, but not of living. I haven't been anywhere, I haven't done anything,' Emma said, almost in a whisper that sizzled with emotion. Her head dropped, as she felt the little hope she clung to fizzle and die.

Ben leaned over and, hooking his finger under her chin, lifted her head so she had to look back at him. 'I thought we had just agreed that you hadn't given up on life yet. There's still time to make those experiences happen and write about them.'

Emma dropped her eyes and tried to lower her head but Ben's hand remained firmly in place. She turned her head to escape him. 'Time to write about them, perhaps, but not time to experience them too,' she said softly.

Ben took his hand away and Emma's gaze came back to meet his. 'Tell me what I have to do to stop you simply frowning at that computer all day and make something happen,' he demanded.

'I need to do some research, I suppose,' conceded Emma. 'Trying to decide on the plot is hard enough but I can't even describe the places I want to go to.'

'And where do you want to go?'

'Everywhere,' Emma said, as if it would be that easy. Her imagination was supposed to be limitless but her experiences weren't. 'I'm on my way to New York but I don't want to stop there. I want to see, I don't know, the Seven Wonders of the World and then some. But in reality I haven't been further than Spain.'

Ben grimaced. 'I don't want to burst your bubble, but I'm afraid the only one of the original Seven Wonders of the World still in existence is the Great Pyramid at Giza.'

'See! I don't even know where I *can* go.'

'May I?' he asked, turning Emma's computer towards him.

Emma watched as he tapped a few buttons. There was a look of concern on his face that didn't fill Emma with confidence.

'It doesn't have an Internet connection,' he complained.

'Because the bistro doesn't have WiFi,' Emma said, making a note to develop that thought later when she was a little less preoccupied.

It was Ben who was wearing the frown now as he returned his attention to Emma's laptop. Emma watched him work his own magic tapping away at her keyboard. He was too deep in concentration to notice that she was staring at him. 'Voila!' he said after a couple of minutes of concentrated effort. He turned the screen back towards Emma to show her that he had miraculously connected to the Internet.

'How did you do that, or shouldn't I ask?'

'I've got a wireless connection upstairs. Well, technically, Steven has, but he won't mind. I've logged you onto the network, so you're in!'

Emma felt a pang of guilt as she was reminded that Ben and Steven had become the new residents of the flat above the bistro whilst her sister was now technically homeless. She briefly toyed with the idea of trying to persuade Ben to squeeze in another lodger who also happened to be his landlady but she reined in her predilection for solving other people's problems and returned her attention to the problem at hand. 'Now what?' she asked.

'The Traveller's Rest is aptly named in my case. Here, let me take you on a journey of discovery.'

Ben had logged into a photo-gallery site to access his online photo albums. Emma braced herself to be bored to tears by a collection of holiday snaps of drunken friends with cheesy grins and bottles of beer, posing in front of an assortment of bars or sprawled across nondescript beaches.

'New York!' she gasped. Even with her limited experience she recognized the Manhattan skyline.

'Apparently, the design of the Statue of Liberty was based on the Colossus of Rhodes, which was another one of the Seven Wonders of the World.'

Emma was too engrossed in the photographs she was flicking through to be impressed with the wealth of Ben's knowledge, which he was determined to share. 'These are amazing.'

And they were. His collection of photographs marked a journey that had stretched to all four corners of the globe. They were a mixture of panoramic views and colourful close-ups, breathtaking scenery, wildlife in motion and wizened locals, all taken with the kind of precision that needed an artist's eye to choose the right lighting, the right focus and the right moment. They were photographs that wouldn't look out of place in *National Geographic* magazine.

'I was a bit of a photography geek for a while.'

'You should take it up professionally,' Emma told him.

Ben shrugged off the suggestion. 'It came in useful during my travels but it was only ever my second love. My first love is food.'

Emma was starting to warm up at last, so she shrugged off her coat and settled back in her seat as she turned her attention to Ben's life. 'But you could really make something of your life,' she insisted, all thoughts of not interfering long gone.

'I am making something of my life,' corrected Ben. He tried to look offended but the smile tugging at the corners of his mouth gave him away. 'I travelled the world to discover new cuisines. Now don't laugh, but goat's cheese and chutneys are my speciality. I'm experimenting for now but my long-term plan is to go into partnership with a farm and sell my own produce.'

'But . . .' began Emma.

'But we were sorting out your life, not mine,' he said.

Emma nodded obediently, having the good grace to let Ben keep his own dreams. 'You're right. I'll have a proper look at your photos. Seeing the world through your eyes is better than not seeing it at all and I suppose there's always Google Earth.'

'How about a trip to the museum? It's not exactly travelling the world but it has to be better than relying on a computer for all your inspiration. The World Museum has tons of exhibits that might give you more ideas. You can take a notebook and I'll take my camera.' The enthusiasm in Ben's voice was being exaggerated to make up for the lack of reaction from Emma.

'I'm not sure,' Emma replied, not quite knowing why she was unsure or at least not acknowledging that it was more than Ben's offer attracting her.

'OK, I won't push but if you're at a loose end on Sunday, give me a shout.'

'Thank you, Ben,' Emma said, and she felt her heart lighten a little.

'Any time,' he said with a wink.

'Any time except maybe now,' added Emma. Louise had appeared and was busily looking for her wayward chef. Dutifully, Ben disappeared back into the kitchen and as Louise made her way over to join her sister, Emma felt ready to face a world where she would choose her own wonders at which to marvel.

4

Kate Barton had made the transition from forties to fifties with effortless ease. Her blonde hair was clipped back in a tight French bun as always, her makeup immaculate and her dress understated but somehow still making a bold statement. I felt a familiar sense of awe. This was the woman who I had aspired to be and, once upon a time, I had felt I was getting close, but now the gulf seemed unassailable.

'More champagne?' she asked.

I looked down at my empty glass; nerves had clearly got the better of me. 'Maybe I should keep my head clear,' I told her. I wanted to pinch myself but, with the view I could see out of the window, there was no doubt about where I was. The night was anything but dark as the Manhattan skyline stretched out before me, a myriad lights sparkling in eclectic symmetry. A manmade universe where the stars could be commanded by the flick of a switch.

'Well, you won't mind if I indulge, will you?' she said, nodding to a waiter who immediately picked up a bottle and began to pour. 'Alex? Can I tempt you?'

'Like you wouldn't believe.' He grinned.

I grimaced.

It had seemed such a good idea to bring Alex along on my life-changing journey. We were a partnership and it had been a long time since I had taken on any kind of new project on my own. When Alex had arrived at Bannister's, I had wanted to resent him for getting the job I thought I deserved but he had been genuinely surprised when he realized how experienced I was and wanted to involve me as much as he could. I liked the idea that he recognized my abilities even if Mr Bannister had not and, when our unofficial union extended beyond the confines of the office, it became the perfect arrangement. I could continue with the day job as office manager and also be involved in marketing without the pressure or the responsibility. When things went well, and they usually did, I could revel in my boyfriend's successes as if they were my own.

That had been my starting position as I headed for New York but the flight over had given me some thinking time and the reception from Alsop and Clover had given me a much needed confidence boost. Unlike me, they remembered my successes not my failures and it was clear from the moment the limo picked us up from the airport that they believed in me far more than I believed in myself. As I started to see myself through their eyes,

I could look back at my time at Bannister's with a new perspective. I could stake my claim on Alex's successes; the best ideas had been mine, he had in many ways simply been the frontman. He had no marketing experience, not even a natural ability for the job. His only qualifications had been his family connections and his winning charm. But as I watched him try to work his magic on Kate, I could see through him as never before and so could Kate. Had it really been my idea to bring him along or had I simply been in his enthral, eager to please?

'So, Alex, you must be really proud of Emma,' Kate was saying as she watched him raise his champagne flute towards the waiter, awaiting a refill.

'I certainly am. It may have only been a small setup at Bannister's but Emma was a key part of our successes. I know she achieved so much when she worked for you and I just want you to know that she has continued to develop under my wing too,' he said and then had the temerity to drop his head a little in false modesty.

'I think I will have that drink,' I said, catching the waiter's eye.

'It must have been a big decision for you to follow Emma over here. I understand you've given up your job too.' Kate was relentless in her efforts to get something out of Alex.

Alex raised his glass to eye-level, taking a moment before answering. He appeared mesmerized as the bubbles rose to the surface and burst into oblivion. 'We're a partnership. Wherever she goes I go,' he said, taking another pause before delivering the killer blow. 'And vice versa.'

Kate looked at me, there was a glint in her eye. Only those who had seen her at work in the boardroom would know to take cover. 'How much do you love her?' she asked.

The question took Alex by surprise, as it did me, not least because I didn't know how he would answer. We had been together for less than a year and whenever we had discussed any long-term plans it had been separately, not as a couple who intended to spend the rest of their lives together. I'd had my own ideas of moving to London and we had both presumed that it would mark the end of our relationship, a move that would be sad but not heartbreakingly so for either of us. I didn't think for a moment that his determination to join me on my adventure to the bright lights of New York had anything to do with love.

Alex was let off the hook as Kate continued without pause and without taking her eyes off me. 'You see, I have great ambitions for Emma. I was sorry to lose her when I did and although her replacement was good, she wasn't good enough. We are both being given a second chance and she would be a fool to refuse this opportunity. But she knows me well. I expect complete focus and absolute commitment to the job. Emma will be required to travel the world, flitting from one assignment to the next and she can only do that if there is no-one standing

81

in her way. She knows that it takes sacrifice to succeed; she knows it because she is following in my footsteps.' Kate finally broke eye contact and looked back at Alex. 'So, if you came here expecting a similar job offer then you are going to be sorely disappointed. And if you think Emma is about to turn her back on her dream job for the second time and for a man who still hasn't had the strength of feeling to interrupt me and tell me how much he loves her, then you're the fool, not she.'

I had to stop myself from standing up and applauding her. When I looked at Alex, his jaw had dropped and his champagne flute was tipping sideways, threatening to spill. I suspected it was the look on my face that knocked him back to his senses. 'Emma?' he asked.

'I'm no fool,' I confirmed.

Emma's hands trembled over the keyboard but it wasn't only because of the emotion pumping through her body. She was also very, very cold. She was sitting out on the balcony and, even though she was wrapped up in layers of clothing and blankets, her fingers had to remain uncovered so that she could type and they were starting to go numb. She tried to ignore the cold as she read back what she had just written. It was as if she was reading her words for the first time and she was shocked to see her innermost thoughts revealed. They were laced with regrets, resentments and a long-forgotten recognition of her own abilities. There was something in the written word that Emma knew she should take to heart and not leave to fade on the printed page.

Shivering uncontrollably, Emma rubbed her hands together then tried to warm them on the sides of her mug, but the coffee was as cold as she was. December had whipped away not only the warmth but the colour from the world with its harsh winds. The steel balcony was painted black and frozen raindrops gave the handrails a pebble-dashed effect. Below her, the river looked murky, the buildings in the distance fading to shades of grey, the furthest blending seamlessly with the lifeless sky, which had already erased the hills and mountains that Emma was so often drawn to.

Reluctantly, Emma picked up her laptop and, dragging her blankets behind her, slipped back into the apartment, which was deathly silent. It was Saturday but her mum was still working hard to catch up on the time she had lost while she was at the hospital with Emma. Emma didn't object; in fact, she was happy to be left to her own devices.

Her writing was going well and it was helping to put her in the right frame of mind for her date with Alex. Their relationship had been put to the test in recent weeks and the results were far from promising. She had discovered a newfound confidence in herself and she hoped it wouldn't be eroded by the time evening came.

Emma retreated to her bedroom, where the yellow walls were only marginally better than the grey world outside. The only splash of colour in the room came from a series of framed photos, an eclectic mix of family snaps frozen in time. One was a four-year-old Emma holding a precious new sister in her arms, another was of the two girls with their arms wrapped around each other with matching cheesy grins. Although none held images of her father, there were one or two where Emma imagined him there, on the other side of the lens. She thought of him as little as she could but as her relationship with Alex stumbled on, she couldn't help but wonder if he was the root cause to her distinctly low expectations in men. Her parents' marriage had survived through her childhood but her father's presence even then had been debateable. Home had been a place he went to when there was nowhere better to be. He had walked out of the family home once Louise had reached sixteen and then completely out of their lives two years later without a backward glance, not even when his firstborn was fighting for her life.

Emma took a deep breath as she tried to dispel the ghosts of the past. She had a feeling her heart would remain frozen, which didn't bode well for Alex.

The Traveller's Rest had been an obvious choice for Emma's dinner date with Alex. She wanted some reasurance that business wasn't as dire as it had appeared the day before, but that wasn't the only reason. She wasn't sure how the evening would fare and she wanted to be close to family and friends if it ended badly. Surprisingly, however, she was going to have to make do with friends and not family. Louise had chosen to stay away and was spending the evening at the apartment where no doubt she and her mum would be putting Emma's world to rights.

The gentle chatter of customers, broken by the occasional clatter of plates or burst of laughter, gave the place a welcoming atmosphere, and the windows to the front of the restaurant reflected the warm light of the interior against the impenetrable blackness of the night beyond. Emma felt cocooned and safe as she sat with Alex in a discreet corner. Their table was draped in shadows that flickered in the candle-light, giving, Emma thought, Alex a demonic glow, but she pushed it to the back of her mind. She told herself that she needed to give their relationship a chance. There was a part of her that wasn't ready to go it alone, not now.

'How about some wine?' Alex said, reaching for the wine list.

Emma shook her head. 'Sparkling water for me, I think. I don't want alcohol reacting with my medication.'

'No, of course you don't,' agreed Alex. 'Then I won't either.'

Emma smiled at Alex's chivalry but the moment was short-lived.

'Well, maybe just a beer,' he added as the waiter appeared at their table, notepad at the ready. If he recognized Steven from previous visits, he didn't let on, even when Emma greeted him like the friend he was.

'Are you ever away from this place?' she asked with a raised eyebrow.

'No, not really,' Stephen said, lifting his gaze to the ceiling and the apartment above. 'I don't even think I've got a coat any more.'

They shared the joke but Alex was at a loss. He had never taken much interest in her sister or the bistro.

Emma placed the order for drinks and, when Steven confirmed that Ben was on kitchen duty, she left it to them to choose the food. Alex shrugged his agreement – he seemed less enthusiastic about leaving such a decision to the staff but clearly felt obliged to agree. The only interest he had ever shown in the bistro was the healthy discount Emma received on the bill. She swallowed back her disappointment as she realised that Alex would never appreciate how much affection and care went into the meals prepared on her account. He seemed incapable of understanding that level of sentiment so Emma didn't even try.

'Could we have some bread and olives while we're waiting?' he asked.

'Goes without saying,' Steven said, with a wink to Emma before he left.

Alex sat back in his chair and looked Emma up and down. 'I still can't believe it,' he began, shaking his head. 'You look amazing.'

'What?' asked Emma playfully in an attempt to divert the conversation from the state of her health, 'you can't believe how lucky you are to have such a gorgeous girlfriend?'

Alex wouldn't be distracted. 'I can't believe you're so ill.'

'Would it make you feel better if I looked like I was dying?' she replied, her words full of hurt. The truth was that when she had looked in the mirror before Alex picked her up from the apartment, she had seen a beautiful young woman staring back at her. She had dressed up in all her finery for the first time since leaving hospital. Her complexion had improved in the last week and her hair was in better condition and set in soft flowing curls that covered her head wound. The dark circles under her eyes had started to fade and she could almost convince herself that her eyes sparkled. She would even go as far as to say she felt alive.

'I'm sorry. I just mean it's hard for me too. I don't know what to expect.'

'I know it's hard and it's going to get harder,' began Emma, forcing herself to be kind. 'And the time will come when I will look ill, very ill, and I'm afraid that time will come sooner than anyone wants, especially me.' The words stung, not least because Emma wanted to be the one hearing words of comfort and support, not having to cajole others into staying the distance with her.

There was a long silence and when Steven appeared with their drinks and nibbles he picked up on the growing tension and disappeared as quickly as he'd arrived. Alex took a long swig of beer as Emma poured a glass of water for herself.

'Tell me what I'm missing at work,' she asked in desperation for something easier to talk about.

Alex launched into a lengthy diatribe about all the work he had to do, how Jennifer was doing her best but was mostly in awe of what was involved, having no experience of running any office, least of all her father's, and how it was quite tense at times. He was also at pains to tell her how Gina was being cool with them both to the point of being obstructive, and generally how he was running the place singlehandedly. It wasn't long before he revealed the plan he had been alluding to. He suggested that while Emma had relative health, she should make the most of it and spend more time, if not in the office, then at least working on some of the projects. It would give her something positive to focus on, he told her. It would be for her own good.

For her own good, Emma ignored his brazen attempts to manipulate her and zoned out. She stared down at her drink, on the table, watching the bubbles in her water sprint to the surface. She was concentrating as much on holding back the tears as she was on the glass and at first she didn't notice her heart pick up a beat, not until the warm glow of her surroundings began to make her feel clammy. The warning signs of an imminent seizure were all too familiar and she sensed the darkness that resided in the corner of her vision extend beyond the periphery. She looked around in panic, her eyes drawn to the large windows, which no longer reflected flickering candlelight but looked out onto a sheet of blackness that was pierced with a thousand lights, each one of which twinkled conspiratorially. New York stretched out as far as the eye could see.

Emma gasped as her heart thudded hard against her chest and, with a blink of her eye, the image had gone. She turned back to Alex but for a confused moment she was surprised to see only him. She looked around expectantly for a slender, sophisticated figure with blonde hair pulled back in a taught French bun.

'Emma? For God's sake, Emma, what's wrong?' There was genuine fear in Alex's voice. It trembled almost as much as Emma.

Emma's mouth was completely dry as she tried to lick her lips. She looked at the water in front of her but didn't feel composed enough to pick up the glass safely.

'What did you mean?' persisted Alex.

Emma frowned in concentration as she tried to control her breathing and slow her heart rate. Eventually, she picked up the water and took a tentative sip. Her drink had an unexpected and not immediately recognisable taste as the bubbles burst on her tongue. Even when she did recognize the flavour, it made no sense and so she took another sip. This time there was no trace of champagne tickling her taste buds. It wasn't one of the usual aftereffects of a seizure but she was certain she had just experienced one. 'Why, what did I say?' she asked. She couldn't remember, she could only remember feeling clammy.

'You said something about being a fool but you sounded weird. You looked weird.'

When Emma saw the expression on Alex's face she could read it as easily as she could read words on a page. He was horrified at the monster his girlfriend had become. She wanted to tell him that the real monster was hidden from view as it burrowed its way into her head and into her life but she didn't waste her breath.

'I don't remember but I'm guessing I actually said that I'm no fool,' Emma said. The sound of her written words spoken out loud brought such a relief that she could barely hold back an impulse to laugh. 'I don't have time for this. I'm sorry. You're on your own now, Alex.'

Alex stared at Emma, shaking his head in disbelief. 'But you need me,' he said.

'You are the last thing I need, Alex, and I want you to leave. Please. Right now.'

'Two very delicious Salmon Teriyaki,' announced Steven, making Alex jump.

'Alex isn't staying,' Emma told Steven. 'Take his meal back to the kitchen.' If there was a tremor in her voice it was only an aftershock from her seizure. Emma's composure was as cool as the atmosphere that had descended in their little corner of the bistro.

'Not a problem,' Steven said as he placed one plate in front of Emma, turned in one smooth move and headed back to the kitchen carrying the other.

By the time Ben arrived at the table, Alex had vanished.

'My compliments to the chef,' Emma said, licking her fingers. 'The salmon is delicious.'

Ben wasn't about to be fooled by false bravado. 'Are you alright?'

'I'm fine,' she said with a note of steely determination. 'Alex had to leave, that's all. I'm going to finish my dinner and then head off home.'

Emma wasn't ready to tell the world that Alex was no longer her leading man. She especially wasn't ready to tell her family, and Ben was an extended part of that. Her visit to the office and outpouring into her book had been the catalyst for a breakup that had been brewing for a long time but it wasn't over yet. Her emotions were still rattling around inside her head and she would tell no-one how she felt until she knew herself.

'I'm stuck in the kitchen but I'll get Steven to take you home. We can manage without him for an hour. Unless you want me to phone your mum?'

'If I didn't know better, I'd say that was almost a threat.'

'As if anyone could manipulate you, Emma Patterson,' Ben said, holding up his hands in all innocence.

Emma shrugged. 'Maybe once, but not any more.'

Ben was torn between staying and returning to the kitchen, which demanded his attention. Emma could read his mind.

'Go! I think I can smell burning,' Emma insisted with a smile that took all of her strength to maintain. 'And tell Steven I'm ready whenever he is.'

As Ben stood up, he took one more look at Emma. 'That offer still stands if you fancy going to the museum tomorrow.'

'I'll see how I feel,' Emma said, not knowing how she would feel, physically or emotionally.

'Well, if you ask me, you're looking pretty amazing tonight.'

Emma's smile came naturally but it was tinged with sadness. 'So I've been told,' she said as she remembered Alex's fumbled and backhanded compliment. From Ben, it sounded genuine. 'Now go before we need to call the fire brigade.'

Emma watched Ben disappear back into the kitchen, rubbing his face as he went as though his cheeks were burning as much as the meals he had abandoned.

Emma was silent throughout the journey home and thankfully Steven didn't try to make small talk. It was possible he had heard some of her conversation with Alex but then the atmosphere alone would have been enough for him to know that their relationship was floundering.

'Do you want me to walk you up to the apartment?' he asked when they pulled up in the car park.

Emma shook her head. 'No, you get back to the bistro. I've taken enough of your time.'

'You can have my time, any time,' Steven told her. 'Me and Ben are at your service, you know that.'

'Like the brothers I never had,' Emma said as she clambered out of the car.

Steven's response was muffled by the strong gust that tore at her flimsy dress. 'Goodnight, Steven,' she shouted above the wind that had whipped across the river and tasted of salt.

She waved Steven off but the car didn't move. He was determined to wait until she was safely inside the building so, with Steven's eyes upon her, she made her way across the tarmac. To her left, a path wound its way around the apartment block, towards the promenade and, if she hadn't been watched, she might have been tempted to forgo the confines of her luxurious prison and head to the river instead. The howl of the wind and the shriek of the seagulls would be background noise compared to the scream she held at the back of her throat. Instead, she turned to wave goodbye before stepping into the light and being swallowed up by the building.

The cold air off the river had cleared her mind enough to think so she took her time reaching the apartment on the sixth floor. She felt so alone. The tumour was in her body, nobody else's. Those closest to her were still on the outside looking in. They might be brave enough to stand by her but they could only hold her coat while she steeled herself for the fight. Perhaps it was too much to have expected Alex to take this journey with her but if she was going to die, she wanted it to be in the arms of a man who loved her. She had her mum to hold her and that was important but when the end came, she wanted to die as a woman, not a child.

The thought of dying had become so familiar to her

in the last few years and so intrinsic to her way of thinking that she often felt no emotional reaction to the idea, but her last thought burned into her mind as she was about to put the key into the lock of the front door of the flat. In reflex, she dropped her keys as if they were hot coals. She didn't want to die, she screamed to herself.

It took all of Emma's willpower to stop herself from slipping silently into her bedroom without announcing her return. She didn't want to face her mother's scrutiny and she didn't have the energy to even appear sociable. As she walked dutifully through to the living room, her body tensed as she prepared herself for the cross-examination.

Emma appeared in the room as silently as a spectre and Louise jumped with fright. She had been sitting at the dining table next to her mum, poring over a mess of papers that had been scattered across it, some printed, some handwritten. Lines of words and rows of numbers.

Meg's responses were a little more controlled as she swept up the pages without even looking at them. Her eyes were fixed on Emma. 'What are you doing home so soon? What happened? Where's Alex?' she demanded.

It didn't take much imagination for Emma to conclude that whatever plans they were concocting, she was at the centre of them. She didn't want to know but she asked anyway. 'What are you two up to? You look guilty.'

'I'm helping Louise tie up some loose ends with the

business,' Meg replied levelly. 'So why are you back so early?'

'The company was enthralling but I was tired so I thought it best to call it a night.' Emma knew the irony would be lost on them but it amused her.

'Did you have another seizure? Like the other one you didn't tell me about?'

Emma looked over towards her sister. 'Thanks, Lou.'

'So?' Meg had stood up and was now doing the one thing that mothers are expert at. She laid her hand on Emma's brow to diagnose the problem.

'A minor one,' Emma told her.

'We'll mention it at the clinic next week. I imagine your meds just need a little tweaking.'

'Yes, I imagine so,' agreed Emma, knowing that neither of them had a good enough imagination to believe that her health problems would ever be righted by *a little tweaking*. 'Now, do you mind if I go to bed?'

Meg had removed her hand from her daughter's brow only to plant it with a kiss. 'Of course not. I'll bring you in a warm drink in a little while.'

'Thanks,' Emma said, already wondering how long she would have to wait until she could safely switch on her computer and let her writing make sense of the emotions churning up her insides.

5

'Have I done the right thing?'

'Only you can answer that one,' Kate said. She had an inscrutable look on her face, similar to the look my favourite shopkeeper had given me, and my mind drifted to my last encounter with him.

He had been very understanding as he let me rant on. I had slammed down the box that contained my failed relationship on the counter in front of him. Its tattered gift wrapping had lost its sparkle and looked torn and crumpled. I told him I wanted my money back, no exchanges. I'd had enough disappointments in my life. They were going to stop now. In my fuming state, I even suggested that he might find a space on his shelf for me to see out the rest of my days.

'Let's get rid of this one first,' he said.

I watched open-mouthed as he flung the box over his shoulder. It missed the shelves completely and vanished from view with a rattle and a thump.

'I hope Alex's flight home isn't as bumpy,' I remarked.

'And I hope it is,' retorted the shopkeeper. 'Now, as for your other request, my firm view is the customer is always right.'

'Good,' I told him, slightly taken aback by his hasty agreement. I wasn't ready to give up, surely he could see that?

'Yes, I do see that,' he whispered. 'And I'm not the only one, am I?'

The image vanished before I could answer. He had left me to ponder my destiny. The customer was always right he had said but this customer still didn't know what she wanted.

'I feel so lonely,' I told Kate. 'I wanted someone to share in my adventures.'

'And was that ever going to be Alex?'

We both knew the answer to that but I didn't want to dwell on my humiliation or admit to the extent of my foolishness. I had been gullible and naive, words that I had never expected to associate myself with. 'Perhaps I had more confidence in Alex than he deserved,' I told her.

'Perhaps you didn't have enough confidence in yourself,' corrected Kate. 'You're on your own now, I can't tell you otherwise, but it's not necessarily a bad thing. True, you have no-one to share your life with, no-one else's expectations to live up to, but you also have no-one to let down. No-one except yourself.'

'And you,' I reminded her.

We were in a boardroom on the top floor of a building tall enough to not only scrape the sky but to pierce the atmosphere. The sun felt stronger and its rays streamed across the room, sending the shadows scuttling away into the deepest corners. The view took in the width of Central Park with its seamless layer of treetops, a tangle of paths and the glint of a lake in the distance. But I wasn't there for the view. My full attention was given to the series of files on the table. They may not have been glittering boxes lovingly prepared by the kindly shopkeeper, but they were still glorious in my eyes. A curve of brightly coloured folders, spread out like a rainbow before me, each one holding the promise of adventure. Kate stood beside me.

'Yes, and me,' she agreed. 'Which is why I'm giving you your choice of assignment. This is where the rest of your life begins, Emma. Choose well.'

The city centre was bustling with Christmas shoppers as Emma waited for Ben outside the museum. The decision to accept his invitation had been easy in the end. She needed to escape, not only the four walls of her bedroom but the fears that festered inside her head. Her future was uncertain and she didn't know who she could count on to be there to the bitter end. Alex had been the first casualty but there would be others who would distance themselves when the going got tough. That made the offers from those who wanted to step closer to her all the more precious but she didn't want more disappointments in her life, she reminded herself. She would have to tread carefully.

Emma stomped her feet to keep warm and looked up the steep stone steps that led to the original entrance to the museum. She could remember climbing those steps with her dad, gripping his hand tightly. Colossal columns stood guard on each side of the huge main doors, which had seemed tall enough for giants and she could remember as a little girl feeling very small and quite terrified. Nerves tickled her insides now and she wasn't sure why. Her emotions were in flux. She was still reeling from the news of her diagnosis, and the drugs she had to take only contributed to her constant mood swings. There was the emotional fallout from her breakup with Alex to deal with. And now there were her feelings for . . .

'Looking for me?'

She hadn't noticed him walking towards her; she realized she had been looking out for someone in chef's whites. Ben was as particular about his appearance as he was about his food in the kitchen. He may only have been wearing jeans and T-shirt beneath his winter jacket but it was a perfectly co-ordinated casual look that had taken time and effort.

As they walked towards the new entrance at the side of the building, Emma couldn't quite shake her nerves. It was still early morning and they practically had the place to themselves. She felt obliged to sneak into the building but the heels of her boots clicked harshly against the atrium's stone floor, loudly announcing their arrival. Emma tried to keep her weight on the balls of her feet and managed a few steps without making a sound but then Ben stopped her in her tracks.

He looked completely bemused. 'What are you doing?' he asked.

'It's alright for you, you're wearing trainers,' Emma whispered.

Ben laughed softly. 'We are allowed to be here. Look,' he said, pointing at the signs all around them, 'this is the World Museum. What's the point in seeing the world if you can't leave your impression on it? You can clomp around like a troll in a dwarf mine if you like.'

It was Emma's turn to laugh. 'Thanks! If I wasn't feeling self-conscious before, I am now.'

'Come on,' Ben insisted, pulling her towards the lift. 'The world awaits.'

They inspected the floor plan as they waited for the lift to arrive. 'Where shall we go first?' Emma asked.

'We could start at the top and work our way down,' suggested Ben.

'The planetarium? If you're suggesting that I include space travel in my story then I think you should start writing your own book and leave mine alone.'

'Me?' Ben laughed, shaking his head. 'In case you hadn't noticed, the sum total of my writing involves a Specials Board. You're the one with the degree in English.'

They had already stepped into the lift and, ignoring Ben's advice, Emma chose to begin her explorations in the ancient worlds on the third floor. 'Of course you can write,' she told him. 'Look how much you've helped me with my research already. That shows you have imagination. And you understand computers, know your way around the Internet . . .'

'Managing an Internet connection is easy and I can even come up with the odd idea or two,' Ben insisted as the lift swept them upwards ever closer to the destination of Emma's choice. 'It's getting those thoughts into a sensible order, finding the words to describe them. That's the problem.'

Emma wouldn't give up. Her moment of anxiety had passed and she was an adult again, ready to take on yet another project. 'I could teach you the basics of creative writing,' she offered as her imagination whirred into life. She could transfer her knowledge over to Ben so that her writing could live on, even if she couldn't. She pictured it like a scene in *My Fair Lady*, only she would be Professor Higgins. 'We could start with the mundane stuff like grammar and sentence structure, figures of speech.'

Ben laughed, still shaking his head as they stepped out of the lift. 'I never could get my head around that stuff at school. I was like a fish out of water.'

'See!' gasped Emma excitedly. 'That was a perfect use of a metaphor. Of course you're a writer, if only you would believe in yourself.'

Ben was grinning at her. He had laid the bait and she had snapped it up in her eagerness to take on a challenge. 'Let's just concentrate on the job at hand shall we? Point and click, that's the limit to the skills I can offer you,' he said, lifting up his camera, which had been hanging from his neck.

'I've seen your photos, remember. I think your skills are a little bit more advanced than pointing and clicking,' she scolded.

Before Ben could answer, Emma was striding ahead, clip clopping all the way to ancient Egypt. She breathed in the musty aroma of another world and time. The temperature of the room didn't have the heat of North Africa but the scattering of mummified remains rising out of the shadows allowed Emma to transport herself to the ancient tombs of a lost world. The touch of the stone relics felt cool but not cold and Emma closed her eyes and pushed her imagination to the limits.

'I want to walk through the Valley of the Kings,' she whispered.

'Good choice,' agreed Ben softly.

They barely spoke as Emma moved from one artefact to another, pausing to read the descriptions of the exhibits and information boards. As they paused in front of a large stone sarcophagus, Emma looked up to meet Ben's gaze. He was decidedly uncomfortable.

'I'm starting to think this wasn't such a great idea,' he confessed as he cast his eyes over the exhibits, which seemed focused on one common theme.

'Why?' Emma asked, her eyes narrowing and daring Ben to continue and not be like the rest, not run in fear of the word.

'I thought I'd be giving you inspiration to write about life but this,' he began, pointing towards a cabinet that housed the mummified remains of some poor, ancient soul, 'this is all about death. In fact, the whole museum is about the past. It might celebrate humanity and the living world but the exhibits here are far from alive.'

Emma didn't reply immediately, she wasn't sure how to, so she carried on moving through the exhibits, eventually stopping at one particular display board, which she read out loud: '*Knowing that death lays us low, knowing that life lifts us up, the house of death is for life.*' It was a quote from the teaching of Prince Hardjedef and there was something she found quite profound in his words.

'And what does that mean? To you?' asked Ben gently.

'It means I'm still alive and it means I want to make my own mark on the world, however brief my time here is. Those words were written nearly five thousand years ago and people are still reading them today. I don't expect my writing will survive such a test of time but I want it to matter and that way it will give me eternal life too.'

'You're unbelievable, did you know that?' Ben whispered as Emma gazed into another glass-fronted display cabinet, this one housing the tiny remains of a small boy.

'I'm as fragile as the next person,' she told him. Emma took a breath of warm and slightly stale air, the mustiness of the exhibits leaving a distinctive, ancient taste on her tongue. Then she set her shoulders straight. 'Come on, there's still plenty more to see.'

'Fragile but with a will of iron,' Ben added as they headed towards ancient Greece and Rome before moving on, with the simple press of an elevator button, to the rainforests, the jungles and the African plains. It was only when they took time out from their travels for a cup of coffee that Emma was ready to talk and make sense of the jumble of ideas that had flooded her mind.

'I need to plan my first big assignment,' she began. 'I want to storm the business world, flitting between London, Paris and New York, but I also want to see some of the greatest sights the world has to offer. I've got so many ideas spinning around in my head that I'm not sure where to begin.' She was sitting in the museum's cafeteria, her elbows on the table, and she was holding a large cup of coffee to her lips but she had yet to take a sip. For the moment, it was enough to smell the aroma and feel the warmth of the steam as it wafted across her face.

'You said you wanted to see the Valley of the Kings,' Ben reminded her.

Emma smiled. 'So I did. Yes, I think that might be a good place to start. We can learn a lot from the past.'

'Our own included,' Ben said.

Emma thought about that for a moment. 'If I'm relying on my past, then I'm going to end up with a rather miserable story,' she said, finally taking a sip of her coffee, which was now disappointingly tepid.

'All the more reason to make some good memories,' Ben said. 'And I'm sure your family and friends will help, and you have Alex.' His last words were more of a question than a statement.

Emma eyed him suspiciously. 'So what exactly did Steven tell you?'

Ben's face was a picture of innocence but Emma could see through him and he knew it. 'He only mentioned that the atmosphere looked a little frosty between you two.'

'And?'

Ben grimaced as Emma glared at him. 'And he sort of mentioned that you ordered him out of the restaurant.'

Emma sighed heavily. One of the reasons she had wanted to leave so early that morning was to avoid further questioning from her mum about her dinner date. 'So now everyone's going to find out that we've split up.'

Ben shook his head. 'No, Steven isn't a gossip and neither am I. We won't say a word.'

Emma's anger softened a fraction. 'I'd rather people didn't know, for now at least.'

'Does that mean you haven't even told your family?'

'I have so little privacy these days, I'd rather keep some things to myself, and besides, I'm not expecting them to be particularly sympathetic.'

'And do you need sympathy?'

Ben's question was probing. But by letting him into

her secret world of fiction, she had opened doors to other parts of her life and Emma didn't hesitate in baring her soul. 'I'm getting used to being on my own,' she said as she stirred her cold coffee with a spoon as if it would revive it. 'And I'm starting to realize it's better that way. It might add a bit of a challenge to my writing but every story needs a dilemma.'

Ben took the cup from her. 'Would you like me to get you another cup?' he asked. 'And then maybe I can convince you that you're not on your own.'

Emma shook her head, refusing the coffee. The air felt cool against her glowing cheeks. She had been so busy watching for signs of mutual interest between Ben and Louise, only now did she suspect his interest had lain elsewhere all along. 'How am I not on my own?' she asked, taking a tentative step outside her comfort zone.

'Because I'm your sidekick,' Ben said rather slowly, as if explaining something very complicated to a small child.

Emma's cheeks sizzled as she retreated back into the safety of her box, housed on a dusty shelf in the shop-keeper's store. 'You've been planning it all along . . . you want to be in my book!' she said.

Ben wasn't fazed by the accusation. Instead, he beamed a smile. 'It hadn't crossed my mind but now you've mentioned it . . .'

'Now I've mentioned it, wouldn't it be a good idea?' she said with a smile.

No matter how much he tried, Ben couldn't wipe the

smile from his face in time to convince Emma that he'd had no ulterior motives in offering her his assistance so readily. 'If you insist,' he said with false modesty.

Emma laughed. The physical act of laughing felt good. Why on earth had she even contemplated any romantic involvement, she asked herself, when all she needed right now was a friend to share her adventures with. 'Well, I might be able to find a part for you somewhere but be warned: you should be careful what you wish for.'

It was less than two weeks to Christmas but Emma and Meg were too preoccupied with hospital visits to even acknowledge the season. The appointments were unwelcome reminders that Emma was gravely ill and served to add to her misery. She had to be measured up for the mask that would keep her head still during the radiation therapy, which was still scheduled for January. Meg was adamant that the preparations were unnecessary as she was more confident than ever that she would find her daughter's miracle cure further afield. Amongst Emma's other visits, she had a clinic appointment where her medication was reviewed by a registrar who suggested tapering off her steroid dosage. Her anti-seizure drugs were increased slightly but Emma was relieved not to have to face Mr Spelling, who would have been able to extract a confession from Emma that the seizures she had experienced were far more disturbing than she was letting on. They were different from any she had experienced before and different was never a good thing. But while the doctors remained unaware, Emma could ignore it too and, after all, she was regaining her health in so many other ways. She was feeling stronger in body if not in mind and she was hoping that one would compensate for the other.

It was Thursday morning before she had her first taste of freedom when Meg at last returned to the office to catch up on work. Left to her own devices and in a repeat of the previous week, Emma opted for a trip to the bistro. This time she decided not to phone for a cab; she gathered up her things, laptop included, and stepped out into the grey and damp December morning.

When she reached the pale grey railings that stretched the length of the promenade, the damp air became an incessant drizzle as wintry gusts swept droplets of broken waves into the air. Turning eastward, she headed towards Otterspool, which was about two miles upriver, an expanse of parkland that rolled towards the water's edge but was currently hidden from sight by the curve of the river. The slapping of the waves against the sea walls gave the Mersey its heartbeat and Emma matched it beat for beat with her footfalls, steady and unstoppable as were her thoughts.

She hadn't heard from Alex since Saturday and as the days passed, she had waited for her broken heart to mend. It took less time than she would have thought possible but she was starting to realize that there was little point in mourning the loss of something she had never had. She had wanted someone to be there by her side, through the good times and the bad. That person had never been Alex, even in her wildest dreams. Her book was testament to that.

The news of their break-up was still restricted. Ben and Steven had been true to their word and she had also enlisted Ally and Gina's help to keep the news from reaching her mum's ears. She knew that the longer she left it, the harder it would be to break the news but she still felt like she needed the breathing space.

Seagulls screamed overhead but it was the flock of brightly coloured kites that caught Emma's attention as she neared the park. Her pace had slowed and, although the walk had been revitalizing, she knew when to call it a day. She searched out a cab and completed the remainder of her journey to the Traveller's Rest in less than ten minutes.

Emma was relieved when she reached the sanctuary that the Traveller's Rest offered, but as she pushed the door, she found it firmly locked. Confused, she peered inside, leaning her forehead against the cold glass. She glimpsed only dark shapes and shadows before her breath fogged up the window and obscured her view.

'I don't think it's open in the mornings any more,' said a cheery voice. 'But if you're looking for a cuppa, there's a café open just around the corner.'

Emma peeled her eyes away from the gloom and found herself staring at two elderly women, one very tall and thin, the other much shorter and wider but both wrapped up in brightly coloured padded coats, hand-knitted scarves and matching woollen hats in garish colours. The animal-print Wellington boots weren't an obvious choice to finish off their outfits but somehow it worked.

'It's my sister's place,' explained Emma.

The shorter woman shrugged. 'You need to tell her to lower her prices. Have you seen how much she charges for a cup of tea?'

'I'm surprised the place is still in business. No-one I know bothers with it,' added the tall lady.

'It was open as normal last week,' Emma said, more to herself than to the ladies. She wondered if this had been the cause of the guilty looks from Louise and her mum when she had walked in on them on Saturday night. She felt a stab of guilt as she recalled all the promises she had made to Louise about helping her get back on her feet when Joe first left. And she had done a lot to help Louise at the beginning . . . but circumstances had taken over. She had become involved with Alex and had been too busy taking on his work as well as her own to find time for much else. She had taken her eye off the ball and even the promises she had made to Louise after leaving hospital hadn't been followed through. She had been too focused on her own problems to give her sister the support she needed.

'Oh, don't listen to Iris. I'm sure it does well enough while we're tucked up in bed. Your sister must know what she's doing. She probably doesn't even want to attract old biddies like us.'

'Speak for yourself. I'm not an old biddy and if that

place was run properly it would be doing a roaring trade right now.'

The two women launched into an argument about whether their generation's custom would be of any value to the bistro. Emma coughed politely. 'Well, you've certainly given me plenty to think about.'

'I'm sorry,' said Iris. 'We didn't mean to worry you. Come on, Jean, let's leave the poor girl in peace.'

'But if your sister ever wants some more of our advice, we have very reasonable rates. A cup of tea and a slice of cake should do it,' offered Jean. Her plump cheeks wobbled as she laughed at her own joke.

Iris raised her eyes to the heavens. 'Ignore her,' she told Emma. 'But if you can convince your sister to have special rates for pensioners, you might find there's enough trade to make it worth opening in the mornings.'

'And nicer biscuits,' Jean called back as Iris pulled her away. 'Not those ones you could break your teeth on.'

'It was nice meeting you,' Emma called after them as they disappeared around the corner.

Turning her attention back to the bistro, Emma sighed. The ladies were right, the bistro should be doing a roaring trade. There were plenty of visitors in and around Sefton Park who would be eager for a warm drink on a cold, winter's morning. Iris and Jean may have been a little eccentric but they could be the demographic that Louise should be encouraging into the bistro during the quieter periods. It had to be better than shutting up shop.

Emma felt a thrill of excitement at the prospect of

launching into a campaign to save her sister's bistro and new ideas were already beginning to take shape in her mind. This was exactly the kind of purpose she had been searching for. Now all she needed was somewhere to work. She considered using the intercom at the side entrance that led to the apartment above but that would mean interrupting Steven or Ben. The thought was appealing but there were still some areas of her life where she was feeling far from assertive. The walk had left her wet and windswept and she dreaded to think what she must look like. She turned away from the bistro as she considered her options and that was when she noticed her mum's car parked on the other side of the road. Her taxi must have pulled up next to it but she had got out on the other side.

Meg had distinctly told her she was going into the office. There had been no suggestion of a detour. Emma turned and took another look inside the bistro, hands cupped around her eyes in an attempt to chase away the shadows that were intent on holding onto their secrets. It didn't take long for Emma to spot the tops of two familiar heads, partially hidden as they conspired within the walls of a booth at the rear of the restaurant.

'Need some help?' This second interruption was more familiar. The voice was deep and smooth, although at present, slightly breathless.

Ben was standing next to her, hot and sweaty and catching his breath after what must have been a jog around the park.

112

'Yes, you can let me in,' Emma told him. 'Why is it all closed up anyway?'

Ben looked guiltily at the closed door. 'It has been all week. Louise decided that it's not cost-effective, so we won't be opening until lunchtimes during the week now.'

Emma was about to launch into an argument about why it could and should be bringing in a profit but she closed her mouth tightly before the first words had a chance to escape. This wasn't Ben's argument. 'I think I'd better have words with my sister,' Emma told him, nodding towards the shadows.

'So have you made it to Egypt yet?' Ben was asking as they made their way into the bistro through the side entrance.

'No, still in New York,' Emma said, only half listening.

'If you need more inspiration, I was thinking that a trip up to the top of St John's Beacon might give you some ideas.'

They were in the hallway, which had stairs leading up to the flat above and a door that led through to the kitchens and restaurant. This was where they would part company. Emma stopped, trying to halt the thoughts racing through her mind so she could concentrate on Ben. 'What ideas?'

'It's not exactly the Empire State Building, but . . .' Ben was starting to lose the enthusiasm that had laced his initial suggestion.

'I don't know,' Emma started but she couldn't ignore the look of dejection in his face. Self-consciously, she tried to smooth a hand over her bedraggled hair. 'I'll think about it,' she said, summoning a brave smile that had slipped by the time Ben had turned to go upstairs. For the moment, there were other plans being laid on her behalf that she needed to find out about.

Emma stared at the back of her mum's head as she approached the booth and a sense of unease crept over her. She wasn't sure if she really wanted to know what they were up to but if she had any last-minute doubts, the chance to run away was lost as Meg turned around at the sound of her footsteps.

'Emma? What are you doing here?' she asked.

There was a now familiar collection of papers spread out across the table and Meg was already gathering them up as Emma answered. 'I could ask you the same thing.'

Meg took a breath as if she was going to answer but the lie forming on her tongue was swallowed back in one gulp. Instead, she looked over to Louise and Emma detected a slight nod of encouragement. 'I've found a clinic,' she said, already raising her hand to silence the questions that hadn't yet formed in her daughter's mind. Her hand trembled slightly. 'It's in Boston. They're running a clinical trial, which has been showing promising results, and we think you'll be eligible.'

'We? It wasn't mentioned at clinic yesterday. Does Mr Spelling even know?' Emma's fear of the unknown had swiftly been replaced by the fear, if not sheer terror, of the known.

'It's one of the programmes we were talking about when you were in hospital,' Meg said, carefully side-stepping the question.

'And exactly how far along in the process are you? How far have you taken this without consulting me or Mr Spelling?' Emma demanded, her voice trembling in sync with her mum's hand.

'You knew I was looking at alternatives; don't make this sound like I've been going behind your back,' countered Meg.

Emma bit her tongue and chose not to point out that the only reason she was being told now was that her mum had been doing exactly that. It was a trivial detail; there were more important issues to discuss. 'Is it going to be worth it?'

'Yes, it is,' insisted Meg. She rummaged through the briefcase lying by her side and plucked out a file. There was a flicker of excitement in her eyes as she passed it to Emma.

Emma remained standing, trying her best to ignore the wobble in her knees as nerves took over. She took her time leafing through the correspondence and the data sheets but her mum was there to talk her through the detail. It was evident that it wasn't only the day job that had kept her busy.

The trial involved chemotherapy and radiotherapy, the same treatment that Mr Spelling could offer, but it also offered surgery. The procedure was still experimental but, to use Emma's own joke, the doctor's in Boston had sharper knives. The doctors in Boston were asking for access to all of her medical records; they would liaise with Mr Spelling and then arrange for further tests to be undertaken, after which they would decide if Emma was eligible or not.

It was still possible that the offer could be withdrawn but Emma couldn't argue with the facts. The outcomes were extremely promising and Meg really had come as close as she could to finding that miracle cure. Emma knew she was supposed to feel relieved but she didn't. A voice in her head had to remind her that she was dying in an attempt to summon up the courage she needed to grab hold of this last hope. But she had buried that primal fear of death before and she did it now. There was a certain sense of security in remaining under Mr Spelling's care and accepting her fate.

'And who's paying for all this?'

It was the first question that Meg didn't have an immediate answer to and alarm bells began to ring as she watched her mum's fingers fidgeting nervously with the corner of a rogue piece of paper. 'We'll manage,' she replied.

'Who's paying for all of this?' Emma repeated, more slowly this time and she looked towards Louise for an answer.

'We should only need to cover some of the incidental costs, like accommodation for Mum while you're over there and loss of income because neither of you will be working. There are grants available but even with that, there will be a shortfall.'

'And?'

'And we'll manage,' Meg said.

Emma's heart thudded solemnly as she felt a very large penny drop into place. 'That's why you've been working so hard,' she said to her mum. 'That's why you're practically exhausting yourself.'

'We're all doing our bit,' explained Meg with a dismissive shrug. 'Louise is going to refinance the bistro so I can release some of my investment.'

'Really?' Emma asked. 'Who on earth is going to want to invest in a business that's grinding to a halt?'

'I'll find a way.'

The restaurant wasn't only filling with tension but with light too. Emma felt her heart thudding and her skin began to tingle with beads of sweat. 'But it could destroy your business, the business you've been working so hard for. Hell, we've all been working so hard for. I can't let you do this,' she said. Her hand was trembling as she slammed the file back down on the table.

Louise shook her head. 'It's not your choice.'

Emma turned away from them and, as she did so, bright sunlight radiated all around her, obliterating not only the shadows but the entire restaurant. She was standing in a vast boardroom, complete with highly polished walnut tables and leather upholstered chairs but it wasn't the furniture that drew her attention. In front of her, more light exploded through the window and a ghostly grey world was replaced by blue sky and, far below, a bright green canopy of trees flowing around a maze of paths and a sparkling lake. Emma knew there was a choice to be made as she prepared to turn around towards the files that would be spread out like a rainbow across the boardroom table. Before she had a chance to turn, the grey shadows slipped around her like tentacles and, with a gasp, returned Emma to the Traveller's Rest.

Emma put her hand to her mouth and felt her breath warm her fingers, which were as cold as ice. She slowed her breathing as silence crowded around her.

'Emma, please just say something,' her mum prompted, concern building in her voice.

Emma took a deep gulp of air. 'It's my choice,' she said, turning around to face her family. 'I'm still in control of my own destiny.'

'OK, having the treatment is your decision but the funding isn't,' insisted Louise. 'I can do what the hell I like with my business and if you decide to refuse the money then at least we can say we tried. That's my choice and Mum's too.'

Emma cast her eyes over the table, expecting to see a rainbow of folders but there was only one.

'But I can't see any bank or investor agreeing to a loan given the state that your accounts must be in at the moment.'

There was that silence again and Emma took a breath of heavy air in preparation for whatever was coming next.

'I'm going to contact Dad,' Louise said.

Emma had thought she had calmed her heart rate but

it hammered with a new ferocity, which transferred to her voice when she spoke. 'Are you serious?' she snarled.

'He can help and, besides, he needs to know.'

'What? Needs to know what?' stammered Emma. 'That I'm ill again? What do you really think he'll do? He didn't exactly rush to my aid last time, did he?' She was starting to pant, almost to the point of hyperventilating.

'Maybe he didn't understand how sick you were. We don't know.'

'That's the point, Louise. He didn't even try to find out. He was told I had a brain tumour and all he did was send a get well card. I was fighting for my life, for God's sake. He wouldn't have even known if I'd survived, not unless he was scouring the obituaries.'

Louise looked unconvinced, stubbornly clinging to the idea that their father could save the day. Emma turned to her mum. 'And you're alright with this?'

'If it helps with the finances,' she said with a shrug. 'And if you don't want to see your dad, that's fine. I don't exactly relish the thought of having John back in our lives either but Louise will contact him and if she can twist the knife and bleed him dry then she has my blessing.'

'No,' Emma said, and with one word she had dismissed the plan to go to Boston in its entirety. 'It's not worth it. I'll take my chances in this country. You don't need his money.'

Meg's fist thumped down on the table with such force

that it made both her daughters jump. 'I won't let you give up, Emma!' Meg cried. 'If you don't want John involved then fine, we'll find another way, but I swear I won't let you give up. I'm prepared to sell everything, lose everything, it's only money.' Meg stopped only long enough to swallow back a sob. 'I don't want to lose you, Emma, and I'll never forgive myself if I haven't tried everything I possibly can.'

Louise was silently crying, her hand covering her mouth even as she spoke. 'Mum's right. We'll find another way and if I lose the business, it's not the end of the world. Losing you is the end of the world.'

Emma felt all the fight leave her body as countless options ran through her mind, from running away and seeing out her last days on her own, to coming up with some amazing fundraising scheme to secure the funds without her father's help. But there really was no escape. She picked up the file, pulling it from beneath her mum's clenched fist. There really was only one choice.

6

My choice of assignment wasn't simply a question of choosing something that would take me to the most exotic locations, although that was still appealing. I had to choose something that would prove to the higher echelons at Clover and Alsop that Kate's faith in me was well placed. It wasn't only my neck on the line and I knew I was going to have to push myself to the limits.

It was no surprise, then, that I was too frightened to be excited as I boarded my flight. I wouldn't relax until the job was done and there was a lot of work to do. My new assignment was for the Museum of Fine Arts in Boston. A new exhibit was being planned and it was my job to deliver the publicity campaign that would draw in the crowds. The artefacts were going to be loaned from the Egyptian government and I had convinced my client that before they were sent from Cairo, it would be a good idea to produce some marketing material with the items in situ.

My nerves would not be calmed as the plane took off and I headed for the clouds once more. I had chosen the assignment because, as a child, my dad had dragged me around pretty much every museum in the UK. He and my mum had worked in the same solicitor's office although, for my dad, the office seemed to hold more appeal than his own home. When he did spend time with the family we always tried to make the most of it and would often think up little excursions. His hobby was antiques and he spent lots of his free time researching in museums and the remainder visiting flea markets and car-boot sales. He said it was his Scottish blood that gave him the thirst for a bargain.

Louise being four years younger would complain loudly every time we entered yet another musty and cramped junk shop but I shadowed my father's every step, desperately wanting to understand his obsession for the dusty relics of the past. I had feined interest at first because it was the easiest way to secure his attention. I didn't have Louise's cute blonde locks and rosy cheeks, which gave her the confidence to demand attention whenever she wanted. I was darker, a little too serious for my own good and I felt I had to work at it to be liked. But whatever my motives, my imagination and curiosity had eventually taken over and I began to share my father's passion where simply holding an ancient piece of pottery in my hands could give me a tantalising glimpse of the past. I had picked up the assignment from the pile Kate had offered me without hesitation. I really had no choice.

The plane lurched and my stomach with it and my thoughts of my dad turned towards another memory. I was no longer a child but a young woman on a flight home from a family holiday in Spain before setting off for university. Looking back, it had probably been a last-ditch attempt by my parents to save their marriage but it had failed miserably, the holiday that was, although the same could eventually be said of the marriage.

We had two weeks of sea, sand and snarls and the flight home was torture. I had been seated next to Louise and we were half the plane's length away from my parents. She would have been fourteen at the time and there was only so much of her hormone-fuelled surliness that I could take. Midflight, I had slipped into a vacant seat behind my parents. They hadn't realized I had joined them, so weren't aware that I could hear their whispered arguments, which led to a painful dissection of their marriage, stripping it bare until there was nothing left to resurrect. I had wanted to return to my seat next to Louise but the plane hit turbulence and I was trapped, forced to bear witness to what could later be marked as the beginning of the end of their marriage. I had hated flying ever since.

I tried to focus on the future although that wasn't easy when my assignment involved delving into the ancient world, but I did my best to put my own ghosts to rest and concentrate on the task in hand. The trip was all planned out although I'd already upset the production company who had the challenge of meeting my uncompromising demands. But I wouldn't let myself or anyone involved in the project ease up.

I could do this I told myself when we landed at Cairo. I was in control. Then I stepped out of the airport and was hit by a wall of heat. I tried to take a deep breath but it was as if I had just walked into an ancient tomb rather than open air and I almost choked on the taste of acrid dust. A car was waiting for me but rather than the plush taxicab I thought I had ordered, I was met by a dishevelled-looking man with a handwritten sign bearing my name, held between his nicotine-stained fingers. He was leaning against a dirty and dingy car that may once have been white. I looked around in hope that there was another sign for Miss Patterson but no such luck.

I tried to exchange pleasantries but it was clear that the driver knew only a few words of English and I knew absolutely no Egyptian. At least he recognized the name of my hotel, which, if the reviews were to be believed, should be more sanitary than the back seat of the cab. The upholstery was covered in equal measures of dust and grime, the only form of air conditioning was an open window and there was a distinctive smell of sweat and fear, the fear mostly mine. I opened up my laptop in an effort to keep my mind occupied and went through some of the storyboards for the photoshoots. It wasn't long before I felt motion sickness as the driver swerved from one lane to another, seeming not to notice or care if he was driving on the wrong side of the road.

It was inevitable that we would hit something as we sliced in between traffic and the occasional pedestrian and the inevitable arrived in the form of a young man in a brightly coloured shirt that was, to his good fortune, loud enough to draw the driver's attention in time for him to hit the brakes. The taxi managed to slow enough to allow the poor man to dive for cover in a flash of orange and blue and in the end it was only a traffic sign that took the brunt of the impact. I was probably more surprised that the brakes actually worked than I was about the accident itself.

Everything stopped. The traffic, the people on the street, my heart. The only thing that seemed to move was the sweat as it trickled down my back.

I tumbled out of the car but my legs had turned to jelly. I staggered towards the man who was rising tentatively to his feet and, as he turned slowly towards me, I could barely believe my eyes.

'Oh, my God, Ben!' I cried. 'What on earth are you doing here?'

'Mostly trying not to get killed by a maniac driver,' he said, laughing.

I took a long look at him. I had briefly considered hiring Ben as photographer for the Cairo shoot but he had once said that food was his first love and I had been loathe to draw him away from his chosen vocation. But it wasn't only his appearance in Egypt that had me bemused, it was how he looked too. He was dusty and his clothes were crumpled; his hair was longer than I was used to, and he had at least two days' stubble on his chin. 'Nice shirt,' I said with an approving nod at the Hawaiian fashion crime, before bursting into laughter and giving him a hug.

I had been doing well enough on my own but it was good to feel his arms around me. I needed a friend. Fortunately for me, we were within walking distance of my hotel and Ben offered to escort me there once we had escaped the clutches of the taxi driver, who was busily explaining himself to a local policeman.

'So what are you doing here?' I asked, wanting a proper answer this time.

'It was the weirdest thing,' he began. 'A package arrived on my doorstep. It had a camera in it and an aeroplane ticket. Not to mention an assignment that would pay me more in a month than I could earn in a year. It was like a dream come true.'

'Sounds like you have a benefactor,' I said with a smug smile. My kindly shopkeeper clearly shared my penchant for meddling in people's lives and could see that Ben deserved something better than slaving over a hot stove for the rest of his life.

'Yes, but I was once told that you should be careful what you wish for. The project manager is a real pain in the neck, by all accounts. She's had everyone running around in circles and she's not even in the country yet.'

'*I think you'll find she is,*' I replied.

Ben stopped in his tracks and looked at me, a cloud of dust swirling at his feet. He wiped his eyes again, still not sure if he could believe what he was seeing. 'Please, don't tell me you're working for Alsop and Clover?' he said.

'*I'm afraid so.*'

Emma was starting to enjoy her writing far more than she could ever have imagined. It was the realization of a long-held ambition to write a book but it was so much more than that. It was giving her a break from reality and the more she wrote, the more it drew her in. When she closed the lid of her laptop, the world around her was a darker place but at least she kept the smile that had accompanied her on her latest journey. She wondered what Ben would think of her latest entry. He certainly wouldn't like the shirt or the fact that she had more or less driven a car at him, but she was feeling mischievous, an emotion that didn't come easily to her these days.

Emma had an appointment for an MRI scan later that afternoon and she was dreading it. The image taken today would provide the benchmark for her future treatment and, more crucially, it would decide where that treatment would take place. Emma had arranged for Ally to take her but, rather than pick her up from home, she had insisted on calling into the office first. She wasn't about to make it easy for anyone to forget her. Her mischievous streak was still showing.

'Are you sure you don't want me to take you?' Meg asked when Emma emerged from her bedroom.

'No, I'm fine,' Emma said, picking up a piece of toast as she watched her mum set out an assortment of pills. 'If you can give me a lift to Bannister's, Ally can take me the rest of the way.'

Meg seemed completely absorbed as she counted out the pills but the act wasn't convincing. There was something on her mind.

'You could spend the rest of the day relaxing for once,' Emma added. She wanted to add that her mum looked tired, exhausted even, but she bit her tongue.

Meg shrugged. 'If you'd given me more notice I could have organized some appointments with clients.'

'That was the reason I didn't tell you,' Emma confessed. 'Take some time out, Mum. You deserve it.'

Meg's smile was so weak it trembled at the edges. 'One day,' she said, 'but not today. Once I've dropped you off, I'll pop into the office.' She was now pressing her finger down on one particular pill, building up to say whatever it was she needed to say. 'Are you sure you want to go into Bannister's?'

'I'm not going to throw myself into work, if that's what you're thinking.'

'I was thinking maybe you would want to avoid any upset.'

'About?' Emma asked, but she suspected she knew the answer. When Meg shrugged, it confirmed her suspicions. 'Who told you?'

'When Gina phoned last night and you were in the shower, we had a bit of a chat and she might have inadvertently mentioned it. You could have told me, Em. I know I wasn't particularly impressed with the way Alex treated you but I would have been sensitive. If you're upset I want to know. I want to help.'

Emma felt strangely relieved. 'I know I should have told you straight away. Sorry, Mum, but I couldn't face you telling me I'm better off without him or, worse still, telling me it would be best to break the ties now before we leave for Boston.'

'I wouldn't,' Meg began with a half-smile.

'And I'm sure you won't,' Emma added.

'So how do you feel about it?'

'Put it this way, I'm looking forward to going into the office. If anyone is going to feel uncomfortable about that, it isn't going to be me.'

'Hello, stranger,' Gina said, rushing over to give Emma a hug. She had been waiting at the entrance to welcome Emma personally.

'Hello, stranger still,' replied Emma.

When Gina released her, Emma was giving her an accusing look. Gina blushed. 'Oh, God, what have I done now?'

'Your conversation with my mum last night?'

Gina bit down on her lip. 'Did I drop you in it?' she asked, before launching into her explanations. 'I knew I wasn't supposed to say anything and I didn't but then

I said something and then I tried to back track and then she asked me what I meant and then I had to say I didn't know anything.' Finally, she took a breath.

'And Mum didn't believe that you didn't know anything? Normally, you're so convincing,' Emma said, laughing at Gina as they linked arms and made their way through to the office. 'So what do I need to prepare myself for?'

'I hope you're not going to be too disappointed but Alex has disappeared on a site visit. It's obvious he's trying to avoid you, the meeting wasn't in his diary yesterday.'

Emma shrugged. 'Well at least I can talk about him if he's not here.' She felt a tug of regret as she walked into the building. The prospect of ever returning to work at Bannister's seemed remote and even if she could return one day, Emma wasn't sure she would want to, not now she had set her sights higher.

Emma had a few hugs and hellos from colleagues along the way to her old office. There was still that sense of discomfort in their greetings, but, to Emma's surprise, Jennifer wasn't one of the ones who showed it.

'It's lovely to see you,' Jennifer told her.

'That plant needs watering,' Emma told her curtly. She was looking at the desk that had once been hers but that Jennifer had made her own. Emma's spider plant had withered and all but died, its leaves limp and tinged a deathly brown at the edges.

'I'll get some water,' Jennifer said with a blush of embarrassment to rival Gina's. She was on her feet before Emma could stop her.

'No, don't worry,' Emma said, giving into the guilt. Life was too short to hold grudges, she told herself, and it was hardly Jennifer's fault that she had been dragged in to cover her work.

Rather than sit back down, Jennifer gave Emma a hug. It was only then that Emma noticed how her clothes were less gaudy, almost verging on the professional. 'It really is good to see you,' Jennifer repeated. 'I've been looking after your files much better than I've been looking after your plant. I can't believe how organized you are and the ideas you were developing . . . they're filling in a lot of the gaps.'

'I'm sure Alex has found them invaluable.'

'My dad has, that's for sure. Are you able to hang around, he's out at the moment but I know he would be sorry to miss you. He's thinking of taking on consultants and wouldn't mind your input.'

'What kind of consultants?'

Jennifer took a furtive look around, only Gina was in earshot. 'Marketing,' she whispered.

Emma blinked. She looked at Gina and then back to Jennifer as if to confirm that she was hearing correctly. In Emma's case, she had every reason to doubt her own senses. Then she looked at her watch and her heart sank. She had timed her visit so that it would be brief. She had wanted to make her presence known but no more than that. 'I really wish I could but I'm already cutting it fine as it is. Where is Ally anyway?'

'I'm here,' she panted. 'Sorry, I was stuck in a meeting but I'm ready to go now.'

Before Emma was dragged away she gave Jennifer one last quizzical look. 'If you need any help, you know where I am. Gina can give you my mobile number.'

There was a flurry of goodbyes and then Emma and Ally were hitting fresh air. Emma checked her watch again as she settled into the passenger seat. Then she made the mistake of mentioning to Ally that they might only just make it.

Ally took no prisoners and if her life wasn't already in the balance, Emma would have been brought face to face with impending doom on at least two separate occasions as they drove through the Mersey Tunnel. They were lucky to escape the wrath of the tunnel police for changing lanes. Ally's driving skills were questionable at the best of times and Emma wondered if she had unconsciously been the inspiration for her Egyptian cab driver.

'So what were you talking about in the office? You looked as thick as thieves,' Ally asked, oblivious to the mayhem around her.

'Did you know Mr Bannister might be about to take on marketing consultants?' Emma knew Jennifer's news was meant to be a secret but Ally was most definitely in the circle of trust; besides, if she didn't mention it, there was no way Gina would keep tight-lipped.

Ally chanced a look at Emma but the frown on her

132

face suggested it was news to her. 'I suppose it was only a matter of time. Without you there, Alex can't pretend to know what he's doing.'

Emma cringed when she thought about how she had been blinded by Alex's charm, too eager to hear his glowing praises of her work to take time to judge his efforts. 'I wonder if that means they're about to sack him,' she mused. For a moment she could almost feel sorry for him but Ally was quick to put her straight.

'I don't think Mr Bannister can afford to upset Alex's dad. Do you know how much business they actually do together?' she asked.

'But he's a dentist. How many kitchens and bathrooms could he possibly need?' asked Emma.

Ally shrugged her shoulders and although it was in response to Emma, it could equally have been to the red light she had chosen to ignore. 'Maybe he has a sideline in property development.'

Emma's moment of concern for Alex's future was a distant memory; anger and a sense of injustice took its place. She shook her head in disbelief. 'I knew it was his family connections that got Alex through the door, but I didn't realize it was a business deal. Why didn't you tell me this before?'

'You were already involved with Alex when the account was set up, I didn't think you'd appreciate me tarnishing your shiny boyfriend's reputation.'

'I feel like such an idiot.' Emma sighed, closing her eyes and reliving her foolishness over the last year.

'You were,' Ally agreed.

Emma laughed but when Ally didn't share the joke she stopped. 'Ally?'

Ally took a deep breath. There was a speech on its way and if Emma didn't know better, she would say it was rehearsed. 'I kept quiet, Emma, but I wish I hadn't. I'm your oldest friend and I should have done something. Yes, you were an idiot but you're no fool, whereas Alex is a fool. The Emma I used to know, the one I went to school with, would have seen through him.'

'I don't know why I didn't see it myself. I just enjoyed working with him, or rather, I enjoyed doing the work itself, work he was meant to do. The fact that he didn't lift a finger only made our relationship work better. There was nothing to disagree on. I suppose he thought he was manipulating me but I was a willing victim.'

'The old Emma wouldn't have done that,' repeated Ally.

'I'm not the old Emma though, am I? I'm the Emma who has been fighting cancer for nearly five years. If that doesn't destroy a person's confidence, I don't know what would.'

'Just promise me you won't be an idiot again. Please.'

'I promise,' Emma told her. 'It's over now; I sent him packing. And if it puts your mind at rest, he was quickly despatched in the book I'm writing too.'

'Hold on, Alex is in your book?'

'It's a book about my life or at least a different version of my life,' Emma confessed. 'Alex has to be in it, one

134

way or another.' She was starting to feel ready to share her secrets. Her first reaction to the diagnosis had been to put up barriers, as if that would protect others from the battles she was facing. She was feeling stronger now but she was also feeling lonely and was ready to let people into her life again. She enjoyed telling Ally about her adventures so far, if only to prove to her friend that she wasn't a completely lost cause.

'So, am I in it?' Ally asked eagerly.

'Why does everyone ask me that?' Emma laughed. 'No, I'm afraid not. I've put Ben in the story but that was under duress and I'm going to make sure he regrets it.'

'Ben?' Ally asked. There was an accusation in her tone and Emma knew what it meant.

'No, Ally,' Emma said firmly. 'We have been seeing quite a bit of each other lately but it's all business. He's been helping me with some of the research for my story, that's all,' Emma explained.

'But you do seem to get on so well together and I don't think anyone would accuse him of being another Alex . . .'

Emma interrupted Ally mid flow, refusing to be cornered. 'No. It's not going to happen. It can't. OK, he's nothing like Alex but that doesn't mean anything. I'm not looking for more disappointment.' When Ally didn't look convinced, Emma knew she would have to say more than she would even have admitted to herself. 'Even if he could make me happy, Ally,' she began softly, 'it isn't going to end well. The treatment abroad is still a long shot. I don't want to add Ben to the list of potential casualties, if the treatment doesn't work out. It wouldn't be fair.'

Ally peered ahead of her with more concentration than she had given the road throughout the journey so far. Emma was afraid of saying any more; even the kindest words would have the tears spilling down her friend's cheeks. 'Here's the turn off,' she said, thankful that the hospital was now in sight.

'Shall I drop you off at the entrance?' Ally said as brightly as she could. 'I can take my time then finding a parking space and we can meet up in the cafeteria when you're finished.'

Emma checked the time and to her amazement they had arrived with a good five minutes to spare. 'That sounds like a plan,' she agreed, zipping up her coat and wrapping a scarf around her neck ready for a quick exit.

They were through the main gates and driving past myriad signs pointing this way and that when Ally started to get flustered. 'Should I go that way?' she asked, looking to the side instead of straight ahead, oblivious to yet another collision that was narrowly averted thanks to the quick action of a fellow driver who was angrily shaking a fist at her.

'Anywhere it's safe to stop,' panted Emma, her hand hovering over the seatbelt button, ready to release it and jump out as soon as the car stopped.

'Oh, my God, isn't that Peter?' asked Ally with panic rising in her voice. She leaned further over towards Emma for a better look.

'Watch where you're going!' cried Emma, but her words were barely audible over the sickening crunch of tangled metal. Ally had driven into an exit sign.

The engine shuddered and died. Despite the plummeting temperature outside, Emma could feel the temperature rising. As she took a breath, the air felt warm and acrid and there was a lingering taste of ancient dust in her mouth. She felt the sweat trickle down her back.

'Uh-oh,' murmured Ally as she watched Peter approaching them, but Emma didn't hear her.

The grey world had been transformed with the flash of an orange-and-blue Hawaiian shirt. Harsh yellow sunshine blazed all around her, obscuring her vision. She looked away, turning her attention to the interior of the car. There was a layer of dirt and dust covering every surface and she could smell stale sweat and something else, her own fear. She pushed open the car door and stepped out but her legs felt like jelly as she approached the front of the car. A road sign had been knocked over by the impact, that was all, but she knew there was something wrong; there was something or someone missing.

'Emma!' Peter called.

Emma turned towards him and the slap of the cold air as it replaced the cloying heat was enough to chase the sunshine back behind the leaden clouds. Ochre tones gave in to the grey.

'Emma, do you know where you are?' Peter asked in a serious voice as he reached her.

A flash of frustration zigzagged across Emma's confused mind. Of course she knew where she was but it was where she had been that evaded her. She wanted to tell Peter to stop testing her. She didn't need someone proving to her that her mind was malfunctioning. 'I'm fine,' she said firmly.

Ally gave an embarrassed cough to get their attention. She was also out of the car but hadn't ventured towards the point of collision. 'Is there much damage, do you think?' she asked weakly. She had remained trapped in the car by her own humiliation so hadn't noticed Emma's unusual behaviour.

'It's only a small dent,' Peter said, but he was still looking at Emma. 'I don't think you've done too much damage.'

At last, Ally approached the front of the car for a better look at the damage. The arrow on the exit sign was now pointing down to the pavement.

'Ground, eat me up,' Ally murmured.

'There's the way.' Emma laughed, pointing to the broken sign. The laugh was forced but she let it ease her back into reality. She took a deep breath of frost-laden air to clear her lungs of the heat and the dust. 'I'm sorry, Ally, but I really do have to get going.'

'Where do you have to go? Do you want me to take you?' offered Peter.

Emma shook her head. Ally, looking at Emma closely for the first time since the accident, was about to say something, but a glare from Emma assured her that she was her old self.

Emma returned her attention to Peter. 'If you want to make yourself useful, why don't you help Ally sort out her car.'

Not waiting for an answer, Emma turned away and to her relief, she found her jelly legs were strong enough to carry her, but only just.

Emma lay deathly still in the scanner as if she were in her coffin already. Her head was strapped firmly into place and she wore earplugs to muffle the noise as the machinery thumped, whirred and hammered around her. But it was the noise inside her head that preoccupied her. She could feel her pulse throbbing against her temples and she imagined it was the steady heartbeat of the monster lurking inside her head.

She tried to make sense of what was happening to her. The impact from the car crash was nothing compared to the impact of her latest seizure. She couldn't remember any of the seizures in detail but each time she was left with a feeling of déjà vu, ghostly remnants of where her mind had taken her, bewildering hints of colours, tastes and smells. The connections she was making with her story were unmistakable.

She didn't like the mind games her tumour was playing with her. As the MRI sliced through images of her brain, she wondered if there was a doctor alive who could save her. Emma closed her eyes. She fought against the growing fear creeping up her spine and retreated to the world where she was determined to retain control over her own fate no matter how much the monster tried to leach into reality.

7

I ignored the heat bearing down on me from the uncompromising midday sun. My latest schedule was proving to be just as gruelling and even more demanding than the assignment in Cairo. The Egyptian exhibit in Boston had been a runaway success and I was in demand. My only problem was trying to fit everything in that I wanted to achieve.

My current assignment had brought me to Tanzania. If I was going to produce a campaign for luxury safari holidays, I had to sample the goods first, but there would be no time to relax. I hadn't travelled across the world to take it easy, much to the dismay of the crew I had mustered together at first light to capture the rise of the sun over the snow-capped peaks of Kilimanjaro. Not for the first time.

'We've been working for ten days without a break,' Ben said. 'We already have good shots. We don't need to take and retake shots every day from dawn until dusk.

Much as I love your determination, Emma, I have to agree with the rest of the crew.'

'Agree what?'

'Agree that if you don't wrap it up now, then we're going to the village elder over there to see if we can swap you for a couple of goats.'

I had allowed two weeks on location and Ben was right, we had more than enough material for the campaign but when our guide had suggested a detour to a local village rather than head straight back to our hotel, I had jumped at the chance and I was glad I had. I was enthralled by the Maasai village and their way of life. It was the women I had been most drawn to, watching them at work with bright-eyed babies wrapped tight against their bodies in colourful swathes of cloth. When we arrived, some had been returning from their daily trek to fetch water with younger children trailing behind, their arms full of kindling. I eavesdropped on the exchanges between mother and child and though I couldn't understand a single word, the tones were familiar. Words of encouragement and love with the occasional scold to keep their children in check.

The scene took me back to my own childhood and a day out in Southport when I was about eight. We had spent a glorious day on the beach, which had seemed as vast as the Sahara desert and the sun just as hot. The tide was out and my dad had persuaded us to go in search of the sea, which had retreated out of view. I remembered holding his hand as we watched Louise running, and occasionally stumbling, ahead of us. When, after what seemed like forever, we failed to see even the faintest glimmer of silvery sea on the horizon and with Louise's squeals of delight turning to complaint, we had given up and turned back. Instead of paddling in the sea we settled for wading in sludgy mud pools and collecting shells, which we took home and with Mum's help glued them onto picture frames.

Along with the odd good memory, inevitably it was the bad memories of my father that rose quickest to the surface, ones like the day he left home. I had been in my final year at university, home for a quick break to provide moral support for my mum who had told me what was about to happen. My dad was about to give up all pretence of being a caring husband and father and as he walked out the front door and out of his marriage, he turned to me and said, 'Always remember I love you.' In hindsight, what he really should have said was, 'Remember I love you because I'm not going to be there for any more of your birthdays or Christmases, not to mention all of those important times in your life like the day you get told you have cancer.'

I released a deep sigh as Ben waited for my decision and there were another half a dozen expectant faces watching me. Taking my time, I stretched my spine, pulling my head back until I was staring into the raging sun. The scarf I wore to protect the back of my neck scratched against my sunburn. 'OK, but only on the condition that everyone remains on call. I'll make final selections today and run everything past Kate, but if there's a gap to be filled, then I expect the team to be in a fit enough state to resume work if we need to.'

'It might be a good time for you to take a break too,' Ben suggested. 'Maybe we could have dinner later?'

'I'm not sure,' I said, and I wasn't. It had been good for me having Ben around and I felt comfortable in his company. He was certainly a distraction, his presence in my life as bold as his shirts, but I wasn't sure if that was something I should encourage. We were friends, good friends, but there was an invisible but nonetheless important line between that kind of friendship and something closer.

'But I've been wanting to tell you about this small-holding that came onto the market just before I left for Tanzania. It would be perfect for my cheese-making venture and if I can put together a convincing business plan for the bank, I might be able to buy it.'

'Then how could I refuse?' I said with a lightness I didn't feel. Ben's dreams were the reason I kept that line firmly between us. His plan wasn't only about setting up business, it was about putting down roots. Our paths had crossed but our lives would not run in parallel and there was no point in dreaming that they ever would.

As Ben helped the others pack up camp, I turned my back on the village and the children's laughter. It was a sound that pulled at my heart and I envied the women's arduous but uncomplicated lives where their most precious possessions were the little ones chasing each *other around the village, kicking up dust and trying the patience of their mothers.*

'I won't rush off and abandon you, if that's what you're worried about,' Ben said as we loaded the last of our equipment into the jeep. 'However tough you like making it for me, I enjoy our adventures.'

'Good, because I've already got the next assignment all lined up,' I began as Ben stepped nearer, his shadow bringing a moment of relief from the harsh sun. I felt protected and I let him move closer still. He reached out and put his hand on my arm. My skin tingled as he moved closer. I looked into his beautiful brown eyes, slowly turning my attention to his lips. I imagined the invisible line underfoot. Instinctively, I took a step back, not forward and wondered why I couldn't summon up the confidence to go with my feelings.

Emma took a deep breath and held it in her lungs, letting it burn as she closed the file. When she released it, she expelled unwelcome desires as well as stale air and she let her mind retreat from the path her imagination had pulled her towards. To her surprise, there was a cup of coffee next to her, placed on the table whilst she had been engrossed in her work. It was early morning and the bistro was dimly lit, not yet open for business but Emma was working on that particular problem too.

By the time Louise took a seat next to her, Emma had finished her coffee and had a new file open and active. 'Right,' Emma said, twisting the screen towards Louise.

'You're going to have to act fast but I think I've found a good market for us to tap into.'

Louise didn't baulk at the idea of slashing the prices for their Christmas Day menu. There had only been a single booking and she had been on the verge of cancelling Christmas completely. What Emma was proposing might only mean breaking even but it would be better than a loss.

'And that's only the start of it. Once you've got them through the door, you need to convince them to come back, which is why there are all kinds of discounts and special offers that will target this specific demographic.'

'What kind of offers?'

'Free tea and coffee with breakfasts, special lunchtime offers and afternoon teas. By focusing the new strategy on the earlier part of the day, it doesn't affect your established clientele in the evenings, which works reasonably well already. We're simply building on your successes.'

'I didn't realize I had any,' replied Louise glumly.

'Give yourself some credit.'

Louise smiled at her sister and her eyes brightened. 'Maybe I could look at adapting the menu, include some traditional dishes.'

A figure cast a shadow over the computer screen as Louise and Emma pored over the spreadsheets. Emma could feel the glow from Ben's smile before she saw it. 'I take it your mission has been accomplished?' she asked.

'You're a hard task master but, yes, I have in my hand

the contact number for Iris and Jean and I've also secured their boundless enthusiasm.' Ben was holding up a folded piece of paper but when Emma reached for it, he snatched it to his chest. 'Not so fast,' he said. 'I want something in return.'

Emma narrowed her eyes at him. 'I would have thought keeping your job would be incentive enough.'

Ben wasn't about to crumble so easily. He held her gaze but said nothing.

There was a flutter of excitement in Emma's stomach, which she tried her best to ignore. 'OK, what is it?'

'Get your coat, we're going on another adventure.'

Once Louise had been tasked with inviting Iris and Jean over to the bistro to start putting their plans into action, there was no other reason for Emma to refuse.

St John's Beacon stood over four hundred and fifty feet tall and was a prominent feature of the Liverpool skyline. On a clear day it could offer amazing views that stretched all the way to Snowdonia and as far up the coast as Blackpool. Luck was on Ben's side because although the day was cold and the city was still thawing out from recent snow fall, the sky was bright and clear. The tower housed a local radio station but offered tours and Ben had bought the tickets before Emma had even agreed to go.

'Shall we?' he said, letting Emma step into the lift first as if suspecting she might make a bid to escape if his back was turned.

Emma squeezed in between an old couple and a woman with a small baby in a pram and a toddler in tow.

'Emma?'

The woman with the pram was looking at her and the frown on her brow eased when the spark of recognition lit up in Emma's eyes too. 'Claire? Wow, I haven't seen you since sixth form.'

In the few seconds it took to reach the viewing platform at the top of the tower, Emma had already decided not to share her complete life story with Claire. She found it liberating to pretend to be as normal as the next person and they had swept excitedly through the last ten years of each of their lives by the time they stepped out of the lift. Claire's little boy Jake was four years old and he didn't have an ounce of fear as he pulled his mum towards the floor-to-ceiling windows that leaned ominously outwards to give a unique view across the city.

Emma and Ben meandered off to find a window that looked towards Snowdonia. From the apartment, the silhouette of distant hills had been only an appetizer for the view in front of her. She could glimpse the snowy Welsh peaks glinting temptingly. 'Is it helping with your creative juices?' Ben asked. He was standing slightly behind her, his head peering over her shoulder to capture the view that she found so alluring. 'That could be the Hudson river in front of us.'

'I'm looking at Mount Kilimanjaro,' Emma corrected

him, a whimsical lilt in her voice as if she were in a trance, but this had no hint of seizure about it.

'You do like to travel.'

'I didn't, but I do now,' Emma said, turning to smile at him. He was standing close and she tried to tell herself it shouldn't feel so comfortable. 'I suppose you're going to tell me next that the stadium we can see over there is the home of the Yankees.'

Ben turned in the direction she was pointing but remained tantalizingly close. Emma could feel her skin tingling, anticipating his touch. If there had been a voice in her head about to tell her to step away, it was over-powered by the sound of a child bawling. Claire hurried over to them, steering her pram with one hand and pulling Jake with the other.

'I'm really sorry,' she said. 'I need to change the baby and Jake here is refusing to come with me into the Ladies'. 'Could you keep an eye on him for two minutes? Please?'

'Of course we can,' Ben answered, patting the dewy eyed little boy on the head.

Jake's face brightened and he ignored his mum's instructions to behave as he pulled at Ben's hand and led him towards the view he wanted to see. Emma was the last to move. She felt a tug in her heart at the sight of the little boy, the same feeling she had been trying to write about but for which so far she hadn't found the words. Upon meeting her old schoolfriend, her initial reaction had not been curiosity or delight, it had been envy. Four years ago, when Claire had been busily giving new life to the world, Emma had counted herself lucky to hold onto what life she had. Cancer had taken away her belief in the future and with it the hopes of becoming a mother herself. Having children had been one of her most treasured dreams from a very early age and unlike some of her other ambitions, it was the one that she had never doubted would happen. To lose that certainty had been devastating and even after her first battle with cancer had been won she dared not raise her hopes again. She had buried her desires to be a mother so deeply that it was a shock to feel them resurface.

'Emma?' Ben called when he noticed her reluctance to follow.

Jake stopped and turned towards her, copying Ben's every move. 'Emma?' he called. When Emma didn't respond, Jake rushed back towards her and grabbed her hand. 'Come on, lazybones.'

If cancer had frozen her maternal instincts then Jake was thawing them out as he squeezed her hand tightly and escorted her across the room. When they reached one of the windows, he lifted up his arms for Emma to pick him up. Ben didn't dare ask Emma if she could manage but he couldn't quite hide the look of concern. 'I'm fine,' she told him.

Jake giggled and writhed in her arms as Ben tickled him but she didn't mind, it gave her an excuse to hold onto him more. Ben started pointing out landmarks, convincing the little boy that they could spy magical lands full of trolls and giants.

'Oh, isn't he lovely,' cooed an old lady who had broken free from a party of pensioners. 'How old is he?'

'Four,' Emma said brightly.

'They're lovely at that age, aren't they? You'd better make the most of it though. Take it from me, he'll be all grown up before you know it.'

The lady was called away so didn't see the shadow of grief cross Emma's face. 'Here, you take him,' she said to Ben, feigning aching arms.

'Mummy!' squealed Jake, wriggling out of Ben's arms as soon as he'd taken him.

Claire returned but she was still flustered, explaining that she had used the last of her nappies so had better be heading home. A well-placed bribe of a visit to the toy shop was enough to persuade Jake to call it a day and with some fond farewells and promises from Emma that she would pass on Claire's regards to Ally, Emma's brief taste of motherhood was over.

'You're quiet,' Ben told her when they had concluded their viewing with a cup of coffee from the vending machine.

'Time to go home,' Emma said, taking an empty cup from Ben and dropping it in the bin.

'Did I do the right thing bringing you here?' he asked. There was an element of doubt in his voice.

'Of course,' she said, trying to shake her mood. 'You always do the right thing.'

'Good, because it means a lot to me, Emma. In fact, I'd like to do a lot more of this.'

151

Ben had taken her hand in his before she realized what he was doing. Her heart had been the first to notice and was beating furiously. Her mind flashed back to her conversation with the old lady, when Jake had been in her arms and Ben by her side. The image of a perfect family that could never be. She pulled her hand away. 'No, Ben.'

'Sorry, Emma. I thought . . .'

His dejection only compounded her misery. 'I like you, Ben. Too much to hurt you.'

Ben did the one thing that Emma didn't want to see. He smiled. 'Don't worry, I'm not Alex. I won't run away. I know I can't begin to imagine how tough it's going to get but I do know I want to be there for you. Don't think about me, Emma, think about what you want.'

'You think I'm being selfless in all of this?' she fumed, as Ben's smile faltered. 'Why do you think I put up with Alex? I *was* thinking of me. I don't want to be with someone worth loosing, Ben. I can already imagine what I'm missing out on.' Jake's face flashed across her vision again. 'And I don't want to get any nearer to it than I have to because it's going to hurt all the more when it gets ripped away from me. I know you won't let me down and that's the problem. You would be good for me but right now that's too painful to contemplate, so much so that I can't even bear to imagine it.'

Ben paused long enough to collect the thoughts that flickered like shadows across his face. 'I can't agree with you, Emma, but I don't want to upset you. Under other circumstances I could crawl away in embarrassment now and let you calm down. We could spend days if not weeks avoiding each other but you and I both know there isn't time for that. So I'm sticking around and I want you to know that I'm here for you under whatever terms you want. And who knows, maybe we can have this chat again when you've had enough of watching life from a safe distance and you're ready to try living it again, when that heart of yours thaws a little.' He paused and the smile that had fuelled Emma's anger returned with a vengeance. 'I think we'd better get you home before you hit me, though.'

Even Christmas couldn't thaw Emma's heart. She had always enjoyed this time of year, not least because it was the winter solstice, which marked the point in the year when the world halted its descent into darkness. The days would start to lengthen and no matter how harsh the winter, Emma could start looking forward to the arrival of spring. But this year, 21 December also marked her return to hospital to face Mr Spelling, and the tension was building long before she stepped into his office, her mum her constant shadow.

It was late afternoon and the sun had already surrendered the day, so it was the artificial lighting that bounced off the window behind Mr Spelling's desk and the only view to greet Emma was her own frightened reflection against a sea of darkness.

Mr Spelling greeted them with an enigmatic smile but

whatever secrets he was about to share, Emma knew the best she could hope for was a lack of bad news. The results of the MRI would have to wait, however, as Mr Spelling demanded that Emma perform her usual tricks, including walking a straight line and squeezing his hands. Then there were questions to be answered, questions about any changes to her motor skills, her memory, her speech. When Mr Spelling asked about seizures, Emma shrugged. It was her mum who filled in the gaps but Emma refused to elaborate. Whatever treatment she would have was already in train, it really didn't matter in the scheme of things. There were far more important things to discuss and as Mr Spelling shone a light into her eyes, he finally got the message and acknowledged her silent plea.

'Right then,' he said, turning to his computer, tapping a few keys and then swivelling the monitor towards Emma and Meg so they could peer at the screen, which revealed cross sections of Emma's brain, before and after shots. Emma sensed her tumour smiling smugly at her but it wasn't a smile she returned.

Mr Spelling gave a guided tour of the scans, explaining where the biopsy had been taken and, more importantly, how there had been some minor changes in the tumour but nothing to raise any alarm. The size of the problem was clear to see and now they needed to make that all-important decision: what to do about it.

'*My* approach,' he began, his inflection directed at Meg in particular, 'would be to start with six weeks of radiotherapy and low-dose chemo combined.'

'But that's only to start with?' asked Emma, recalling how tough it had been first time around and that had been without the radiotherapy.

'We would take an MRI about a month later to check for any initial indications of how effective the radiotherapy had been and to give a new baseline before we start you on six months of high-dose chemotherapy. I know it sounds intensive and it is,' he said, noting the look of trepidation on Emma's face. 'But then the treatment we're trying to secure for you in America will be even more rigorous.'

'And do you think they'll accept her, now you've seen the scans?' asked Meg.

Mr Spelling nodded. 'I think so, but that will be for the clinic in Boston to decide and, of course, it will ultimately be Emma's decision whether or not she wants to go ahead with the treatment.'

The blind spot in the corner of Emma's eye hid her mum from view but she could sense her bristling at the comment. 'We've come this far,' Meg told him curtly. 'I don't think it's helpful revisiting the options. That particular decision has already been made.'

Emma knew that Mr Spelling was testing her resolve one last time and she fought the urge to get up and run rather than confront what lay ahead. She didn't particularly savour the idea of the treatment awaiting her overseas and she certainly didn't want her family to face the inevitable financial strain but she also didn't want to rip out the final shred of hope from her mum's heart. There was something else that kept Emma pinned to her chair and nodding in agreement with her mum. Something far more obvious but still difficult to face. She didn't want to die. Not yet. 'When will we hear from Boston?' she asked.

'They've promised to get back to me by the first week in January at the latest. That way we can keep to the schedule here if for some reason Boston doesn't accept you.'

'When would we go to America, do you think?' Meg asked, ignoring the suggestion that there was still a chance she wouldn't get her own way.

'That would be in their hands but I would think you'd be over there before February.'

Emma could feel the clock counting down. She began to make a mental list of all the things she wanted to do in the time she had left before treatment so she tuned out of the verbal ping pong that continued between Mr Spelling and her mum. She needed to make sure her plan for the bistro was followed through and then there was the issue of her dad. She still didn't know if Louise had contacted him, she had refused to be involved, but she would need to know if he was willing to plug a gap in the funding for her treatment, otherwise all her plans for the bistro's future would go to waste.

And then there was still her friendship with Ben to smooth over. She hadn't seen him since their argument and although they had parted on good terms, she needed to know that she could still feel comfortable with him

156

again. She missed him. Thoughts of Ben led naturally to thoughts of her book. She wanted to continue to write more than ever and she started to consider where her imaginary life should lead her next but her musings were brought to an abrupt end when she realized there had been a lull in the conversation around her. Mr Spelling was looking at her with a raised eyebrow, aware that her mind had wandered.

'Wouldn't you agree, Emma?' he asked.

Emma matched his raised eyebrow and returned the wicked smile he was giving her. 'If by that you're asking if you're boring me yet then the answer is yes.'

Despite the sharp intake of breath from Meg, Mr Spelling laughed. 'Then we'll call it a day,' he said, 'and I'll see you in a few weeks. Until then, have a good Christmas.'

'But not necessarily a happy new year,' muttered Emma to herself.

8

I returned to earth with a bump when the plane landed at Kennedy, and as I walked out of the airport, I lifted my face to the sun in a feeble attempt to warm my spirits. It was April, cool and crisp, a refreshing change from the relentless heat but that hadn't been the only thing I had left behind in Tanzania. I was already missing Ben and that worried me.

At my insistence, he had returned to England to follow up on the smallholding he had talked about, while I continued with my own dreams. I had promised him I would be in touch to arrange our next expedition but now I wasn't so sure. Wasn't I delaying the inevitable? Our paths would separate one day so wouldn't it be better to end things now? I kept telling myself that Ben and I were never meant to be.

'But isn't that what I'm here for?' the shopkeeper asked me. 'To make it be?'

I played with the wrappings on the box he had placed

in front of me. I didn't need to read the label to know what the contents held. Ben would make a wonderful husband and father one day.

'We have different dreams,' I insisted.

'Really? You don't want to spend your life with a man who loves you? To raise a family together?'

'He wants to settle down on some Godforsaken farm and make cheese,' I said with a laugh that felt hollow and empty.

'But settling down was in your original plan, wasn't it?'

The shopkeeper's persistence was unnerving; it was as if he knew every twist and turn of the life I had mapped out for myself. I had been twenty-two when I had first joined Alsop and Clover and had been ready to give the company the best years of my life. My intended reward would be a senior associate position by the age of thirty, after which I would spend the next few years establishing myself in my chosen career before concentrating on the other aspects of my life, such as finding a soulmate. And that would lead nicely to the next phase. Unlike my mum, I intended to carve out my career first. Family would be the cherry on the cake rather than a pebble in my shoe.

'I've had a lot of catching up to do,' I reminded him. I was thirty-three already and my career wasn't quite back on track. There was no reason why I couldn't let my plans slip a little. 'I haven't landed my promotion yet or seen half the things I had in mind.'

'What is it you're afraid of, Emma?'

I put my hand firmly on the lid of the box and willed myself to push it back towards him but the box didn't move. 'What if it's as wonderful as I suspect it will be?' I asked. 'What if it's so precious that for the rest of my life, I spend every day paralysed by the fear of losing it?'

The shopkeeper hooked his fingers around his chin and stroked his beard. 'You wouldn't be the first but answer me this. What would be worse? To die knowing what a wonderful life you're leaving behind or to release yourself from a life barely worth losing?'

'The second option would be easier,' I answered a little too quickly.

'So what are you doing here in my shop of dreams?'

I wanted to tell him I didn't know but the image of the shopkeeper flickered and vanished, replaced by the April sun as it reflected off a river of yellow cabs flowing down Fifth Avenue. My phone buzzed in my pocket. Kate was calling to ask why I was late for our meeting. She was impatient to hear the details of my latest trip and to go through my next assignment. I had been excited by the prospect of exploring the Amazon but as I considered the possibility of making this trip without the man who was intent on leading my heart astray, the dream lost its lustre.

Emma knew it could be her last Christmas but as a family, they had all been there before. After the initial shock of her first diagnosis, there had been an inordinate amount of energy put in to making every day like Christmas Day, to be grabbed desperately by the throat and have the life throttled out of it.

But Emma had learnt that it was too exhausting to make every day special. She quickly became tired of being the constant centre of attention, of having nothing denied and of having every waking moment captured for posterity on film. At one point she had almost forgotten what her mum looked like because she spent so much time peaking at life through a camera lens. Everything that Meg did to make life special for her daughter only served to amplify their fears, so that there was no room left for life. So, in Emma's inimitable style, she had brought the frenzy to an end. Cameras were put away and normal life was embraced with a new sense of appreciation that needed no fanfare.

Some of those harsh lessons lived on and this Christmas was going to be as normal as it could be. It was a special day that would leave special memories but no more or less lavish than for any other family. There would be no extremes: it would be business as usual, and that included the bistro, and Emma and Meg planned to be there, hopefully to witness its success, and to help out if need be.

Louise was looking relaxed despite the chaos as she slipped between crammed tables to welcome her mum and sister into the noise and vibrancy of the bistro. It was midday and the Traveller's Rest was to remain open until four o'clock, at which point, the well-oiled customers would be sent on their merry way, leaving a select gathering of family and friends to make their own merriment.

The day was dazzlingly bright but icily cold and Emma was grateful for the warmth of the bistro. After a relaxing morning opening gifts and eating breakfast, she and her mum had gone for a brisk walk along the promenade and Emma still needed thawing out.

'Happy Christmas,' carolled Louise, hugging her mum and then Emma.

'Wow, it's so busy. You must be rushed off your feet,' Meg said, having to shout above the lively chatter.

'Yes, I know. Isn't it great?' replied Louise with a broad smile. 'Now, I'm sorry but there isn't a single table free at the moment but I have set aside some chairs at the bar. If you would like to come this way, ladies.' Louise turned to escort them to their seats.

Meg and Emma's feet remained rooted to the spot. 'We will not,' Meg told her firmly. 'We're here to help.'

'Yeah, I can help in the kitchen and Mum can serve out here,' suggested Emma.

'Don't even think about going into the kitchen. It's battle stations in there at the moment. Ben was adamant that he and Steven could manage the service but I'd be surprised if they're still talking to each other by the end of the day.'

'Steven's cooking Christmas dinner?' Meg asked, her jaw hitting the floor.

'He's been doing really well on his catering course, although it might be a case of sinking or swimming. From the way it's looking at the moment, I'd say it's more like sinking,' Louise explained with a half-smile. She clearly had more faith in the two of them than she was letting on.

'All the more reason for me to go in and help,' insisted Emma. She still hadn't seen Ben since their disagreement and the irresistible pull towards the kitchen was difficult to ignore. 'We don't want anything going wrong today of all days.'

Louise put her hands on her hips. It was a stance that Emma had often assumed with her sister but now the roles were reversed and Louise was enjoying the switch. 'No,' was all she said to put an end to Emma's temptations.

Emma bit down on her lip to stop herself from begging. 'OK then, we'll both help with the waitressing,' Emma said, knowing that there would be ample opportunity to break the ice with Ben once she started taking orders.

'How about you two look after the tables in the far section over there?' offered Louise.

Emma looked over to the section they had been assigned and spied two familiar faces who had been pivotal in filling the bistro to the rafters. Emma made a beeline for them.

Iris and Jean were chatting away merrily with a couple of friends when Emma arrived at their booth. The table was strewn with wrapping paper, precarious piles of gifts and a collection of drinks. They were wearing lopsided paper hats, matching grins and all had very rosy cheeks. Jean had a crumpled tissue in her hand and she was wiping away the tears from her eyes, which were clearly tears of laughter as her body was still heaving with repressed giggles.

'Hello, ladies, and a merry Christmas to you all. My name is Emma and I'll be serving you today.'

'Ooh,' chorused the women, 'very professional.'

'And this is my assistant, Meg,' Emma continued before leaning in towards Jean to whisper conspiratorially. 'It's my mum, so go easy on her.'

Meg coughed politely. 'I'll have you know I've been serving hot dinners since before you were born.'

'But I have a feeling this crowd are going to be difficult to please,' replied Emma.

Iris wafted a hand dismissively. 'I have no idea what you mean. We're going to be perfectly well behaved.'

'So how is my plan working so far?' Emma asked eagerly. 'The place is packed out and if you don't mind me saying so, they look like they might know you.'

'If by that you mean it's full of old biddies then, yes, you can thank us for that. Pretty much everyone here is a fellow escapee.'

Iris and Jean lived in a sheltered community and they had been flattered when Ben had tracked them down to ask their advice. His powers of persuasion had then secured their help and by the time Louise had contacted them they had already been plotting how to save the day.

164

Apparently, there was an annual dispute over who organized the communal Christmas dinner. A clique had formed from which Iris and Jean were consistently excluded, and so this year they had led a revolt to the Traveller's Rest.

'Our gratitude will be reflected in the bill,' Meg promised. 'It's wonderful to see the bistro so busy. I only hope it stays this way.'

'I think you'll be onto a winner if we get those special discounts,' Iris said.

'I'll make sure Louise keeps to her promises,' Emma assured them with mock severity.

'She's lucky to have you,' Jean told her.

'We all are,' Meg added, giving Emma a tight squeeze.

Iris and Jean nodded in agreement. In Emma's dealings with Iris and Jean she had been determined not to mention her illness but their inquisitiveness had worn her down and Emma had eventually confessed. She had hoped the death sentence that shadowed her wasn't quite so visible and had asked them if she looked so obviously ill. They had assured her that she didn't, that they were perhaps more in tune to recognize the signs at their time of life.

Before the mood was allowed to turn morose, Emma directed her mum to another table that demanded attention whilst she tried to take the order for Iris and Jean's table. The sooner she had her first order, the sooner she would be allowed into the kitchen. 'Now, ladies, what can I get you?'

'We had our order written down somewhere,' Jean said, riffling through discarded pieces of wrapping paper.

'You look like you've been having a great time so far,' Emma said as she took another look at the Christmas debris strewn across the table.

'Santa has been very generous this year. Look,' Jean told her, pulling an envelope from the bottom of her pile of gifts, which threatened to topple over. She handed Emma an envelope containing a voucher for an experience day.

'Hot-air ballooning?' stammered Emma, wondering how Jean would manage to clamber into the basket without breaking a hip. 'That's, that's unbelievable.'

'Hmm,' added Iris. 'I don't think Santa would have been so generous had he realized that some of us weren't going to be spoiled so much this year.' From her pile of gifts, Iris lifted up a gaudy printed headscarf and a pair of pink fluffy dice with a distinct lack of enthusiasm. 'I don't even have a car to hang these from, not unless Santa's got a new car parked outside.' She looked expectantly towards Jean.

Jean giggled. 'Now I don't think my pension would stretch quite that far, but . . .' she said, rummaging between the folds of her cardigan before pulling out a similar-looking envelope to the one Emma held in her hand. She proffered it towards Iris with a flourish.

Iris tore at the envelope and her growing excitement spread to the rest of the group. They all peered over to get a better look at the voucher she was staring at open-mouthed. 'A rally-driving experience?'

Emma looked on in disbelief but Iris was bubbling with excitement.

'Isn't that a bit . . .' began Emma, still stumbling over her words. 'Isn't that a bit too extreme?'

The four ladies gave their new waitress an imperious look. 'And why would that be?' Jean asked.

Emma suppressed a smile as she recovered from the shock and started to feel sheer admiration for the ladies. 'I thought maybe something like a spa day might have been a bit more, I don't know, relaxing, maybe?'

Jean tried to maintain her offence but couldn't contain her giggles for too long. 'It was tank driving last year,' she confessed. 'But she's seventy-five now, so I thought I'd calm it down a bit.'

'Have you ever thought of giving more practical gifts?' asked Emma with a wicked smile. 'Cookery books, bath salts, that kind of thing. Or hand-knitted scarves, even?'

As the table erupted into a counterattack, Emma tried to get back to the business at hand. 'Jean, have you got that order for me or would you prefer Christmas dinner served on Boxing Day?'

Jean obliged by handing over their order, which was scribbled on a scrap of wrapping paper, and from that moment on, Emma didn't stop. She barely had time to say more than a brief and chaste hello to Ben but the rest of the afternoon passed in a blur. It was no surprise that Iris, Jean and their friends were the last to go home and when they did leave, they left the staff, even the temporary ones, exhausted but smiling.

'Right, who's ready for a party?' Louise said.

*   *   *

As leftovers go, Christmas dinner was fit for a king. Ben and Steven weren't allowed, at Louise's insistence, to lift another finger. The day had been a resounding success and with so many of their customers promising to visit again in the very near future, there was finally something to look forward to.

After toasting their triumph, it took forever to get through the entire meal simply because there was so much chatter but no-one seemed to care. Emma, Louise and Meg were trying to outdo each other with family anecdotes, the more embarrassing the better.

'Just look at the way she's nibbling at the corners of that chocolate cake,' Louise said with a critical eye on Emma's plate. 'Now you may think it's all innocence but you mark my words, she'll make sure she's the last one with something on her plate so that she can taunt us with it.'

'She's welcome to my share. I'm stuffed,' Ben said, rubbing his belly, with a painful sigh.

'OK, maybe not taunt everyone, but taunt me.'

'Louise,' replied Emma, 'I can't believe you'd think I'd be that devious.' In truth, Emma's appetite had fallen away as a result of the reduction in her steroid dosage but she was happy to play along.

'You don't fool me. Every year without fail, you made sure you had at least one Easter egg left after I'd eaten all of mine.'

'I'm sorry, Emma, but she's right,' added Meg. 'You did. It used to drive me crazy the way you tormented her with that last egg.'

'But I always gave her some. Eventually.' Emma had been suppressing a grin but now she couldn't hold back the laughter and it felt good. She barely noticed how exhausted she felt.

'Yes,' cried Louise, waggling an accusing finger at her sister. 'After I was literally crawling on the floor, begging you.'

'Mmm, this cake is so delicious,' teased Emma, wafting a heaped spoonful of chocolate cake towards Louise's now empty plate.

As the laughter continued, Meg produced a gift bag from under the table. 'I think it's present time,' she suggested. They had already swapped gifts but this was a little family tradition. They were small tokens, mostly consisting of yet more luxury foodstuffs and novelty socks thrown in for good measure.

'Louise warned me you'd be sharing gifts, so we've come prepared,' offered Steven, pulling three brightly coloured packages from a gift bag he had brought with him from the kitchen. 'Although I hold my hands up and confess that my contribution was wrapping them up. Ben deserves all the credit.'

Emma looked at the gift that Steven had placed in front of her, identical in shape to the ones handed to her mum and her sister. As Emma explored its contours she felt a twinge of disappointment when she realized it was a picture frame. She would have preferred an envelope worthy of Iris or Jean but she was aware that Ben's eyes were on her, so she practised the look of delight in her mind as she tore at the wrapping.

When she turned the frame over her heart quickened as she came face to face with her own image in black and white. She had never liked looking at pictures of herself but this one took her breath away. In the photo, she was peering into a display cabinet at the museum, clearly unaware that she was being photographed. It had been taken at such an angle that the photo captured not only her face but its reflection on the glass-fronted cabinet.

'Do you like it?' asked Ben.

The picture provoked a surge of emotion that surprised Emma. It captured a moment where she had been deep in thought and there was a sense of hopelessness in her eyes. Incredibly, whether it was a distortion of the light or the skill of the photographer, the reflected face had an altogether different expression, with eyes that searched towards some unseen point in space and time. That face had a look of determination and anticipation. The photograph had captured not only her image but her soul too. 'It's beautiful,' she whispered as she met Ben's gaze. 'Thank you.'

Ben smiled. 'I'm just relieved you like it. From what Louise kept telling me about how you don't like having your photograph taken, I thought you'd take one look at it and throw it in the bin.'

'That was why we made sure to give Meg and Louise a photograph too,' added Steven who, unlike Ben, had been watching the others. They had each been given a different photo of Emma, all taken with equal skill but not quite matching the dramatic impact of the one Emma was holding.

Emma shook her head. 'You could have picked a better model,' she said modestly, 'but this is amazing.' The more she looked at it the more she felt moved by it.

'They all are,' Meg added. Tears were threatening so she painted on a smile and lifted up her own camera. 'You have an amazing talent, Ben, and one I can put to good use. Right everyone, photograph time.'

Emma didn't have a chance to reply as everyone jumped up and gathered around her, ready to pose for their photographs. She smiled at Ben as he pointed Meg's camera at her and in her mind she was making her own mental record of the moment when she had been reminded of what hope looked like.

Emma didn't want the night to end and there was a sense of panic deeply rooted within that desire, a belief that it really could be her last. Although she refused to allow that fear to sully the moment, she couldn't ignore how tired she was. It hadn't only been her appetite that had been affected by the tapering of her steroids; fatigue had replaced the restlessness and a headache that had begun as a dull ache that morning became searing pain by nine o'clock and forced Emma to accept that it was time to take a rest.

Ignoring Meg's insistence that they go home, Emma opted instead to take painkillers and lie down in one of the booths for a short nap. She made herself comfortable on one of the long upholstered seats as best she could and let the gentle sound of chatter lull her to sleep.

She had used a cardigan as a makeshift pillow and was dozing when she felt someone drape a blanket over her. When she opened her eyes, she could make out the silhouette of a man in the flickering candlelight.

'Sorry, did I wake you?' Ben whispered.

'No, it's alright. How long have I been asleep?' Emma croaked. She felt like she had only just closed her eyes but her seized-up joints were telling a different story. To her relief, the vice that she had felt tightening around her skull had relaxed its grip.

'About an hour. I fetched a blanket from the apartment in case you were cold,' Ben explained. 'Go back to sleep, I'll go.'

Emma pulled herself up to a sitting position but she moved too quickly and began to feel woozy. She started leaning to one side but Ben slipped next to her on the bench and let her rest her head on his shoulder. 'I'll be alright in a minute,' she said.

'There's a drink of juice there and your mum's put your next set of pills out ready.'

'Of course,' replied Emma solemnly, reaching out for the tiny little reminders of the cancer that refused to give her a day off, not even for Christmas. 'What's everyone else up to?'

'Playing poker,' Ben told her. 'It would seem I don't

have a poker face. I think I must wear my heart on my sleeve.'

Emma tentatively lifted her head and looked behind her. The others were gathered around a small table on the far side of the restaurant, absorbed in their game. She dropped her head back down on Ben's shoulder, less self-conscious now she knew they weren't being overlooked. Her aches had eased and a sense of homely comfort settled around her.

'How's the book going?' Ben asked innocently.

'Where shall I begin?' Emma asked, already wondering how she would skirt over the current dilemma in her story.

'How about everything you've done and everywhere you've been,' Ben asked, before adding more pointedly, 'so far.'

'Let me see. I jetted off to New York for my dream job and since then I've been handed one amazing assignment after another. Egypt was only the start of my adventures. I've seen sights you wouldn't believe.'

'And next?' urged Ben, his curiosity piqued.

'Next, I'm off to the Amazon.'

'Ah, I see. There seems to be a lot of work involved in your story so far.'

'But I am seeing the world.'

Ben went quiet for a moment so Emma lifted her head to look at him. There was a sadness in his eyes that she didn't like.

'So why do I get the feeling that you're looking at the world instead of stepping into it?' he asked.

'I have stepped into it,' replied Emma indignantly but the next look he gave her cut through her defences like a knife through butter. 'You were in my story for a while.'

'Only for a while?'

'I sent you away.' Emma put her head back on his shoulder and felt him rest his cheek on her forehead. 'You're probably setting up your cheese-making business as we speak.'

'So is there anyone else to share your life with in this book of yours?' he asked. Emma shrugged, which Ben took to mean no. 'I think I understand why you're scared of getting involved in real life but does that have to mean you carry those barriers through to your story too?'

'My two worlds are more difficult to separate than you would imagine. I know I have to take a leap of faith.'

'So take it,' Ben said, his voice deepening as if it was a command from on high.

'I'm nearly there,' she promised with a smile.

'And I'm still here to help. And if it doesn't offend your sensibilities, I wanted to invite you on a New Year's Day trek.'

'Really?' It was Emma's turn to have her curiosity piqued but she wouldn't look up at him again, she didn't want to break away from the touch of his skin on hers.

'I was planning a walk up Moel Famau with Steven but he'd rather spend time in the kitchen experimenting while the bistro's closed. I could go on my own, I suppose, but if you fancied doing something?'

'Really?' she said again.

'It wouldn't have to be Moel Famau. We could try something a little less challenging.'

'I'll have you know I've been building up my stamina,' Emma told him. 'I could manage a mountain.'

'Really?' Ben said in a poor impression of Emma.

'But if we go, it will be just as friends.'

'I'll be anything you want me to be, Emma.'

Emma drew herself upright, pulling herself away from his touch. Contact was broken and reality settled around her. She knew he wanted more. He had a determination that would see his heart broken; she only had to say the word. 'I'll think about it,' she lied.

The blind spot in Emma's vision meant that she didn't notice her mum until she had slipped into the seat opposite. 'Steven has managed to clean me out of all the winnings I took from Ben,' she said. 'So, what have you two been up to?'

'I was suggesting that Emma come with me on a New Year's Day walk,' Ben told her.

Emma pulled the blanket that had been draped over her knees and began to fold it, the manoeuvre carefully choreographed to create more space between her body and Ben's. 'We're going to walk up Moel Famau,' she told her mum, lighting the touch paper.

Meg's eyes widened in shock. 'What? Emma, you can't!'

And so it began. Emma played her part like a

professional and by the time Meg had finished her lecture, even Ben was agreeing that it had been a bad idea.

'Come on,' Emma said, punching through the depressing fog that had descended in front of her eyes. 'Christmas isn't over yet.'

9

I had no idea why Kate had insisted that we take a trip to the top of the Empire State Building. She had remained tight-lipped since my return from South America and there had been numerous furtive meetings to which I hadn't been invited. I was beginning to wonder if my luck had run out. Even though I had delivered this latest project to the company's exacting standards, it had been more of a struggle than previous assignments. I hadn't had Ben there as my driving force and in my eyes, my latest offerings didn't have the same kind of spark.

Knowing how ruthless Kate could be, I couldn't help wondering if I would be taking the elevator back down to the ground floor or a more direct route to the pavement.

Kate waited until we stepped out onto the viewing platform before she broke her silence. 'We did it!' she cried, stretching out both her arms as if the whole world was hers for the taking.

Her hair was pinned back tightly as always but a golden strand slipped free and rippled in the warm winds that swirled around us. I hadn't had the foresight to tie back my hair so my unruly curls slapped against my face, stinging my eyes. When I tried to speak, I almost choked on a mouthful of hair. There was still so much I had to learn from my mentor. 'Did what?' I asked.

'I've been invited onto the board of directors,' she told me. 'But credit where credit is due: I couldn't have done it without you and that's why you're being promoted too. Look around, Emma. The whole world is yours for the taking, the highest profile campaigns, the biggest budgets – and you'll deliver the best results. I have no doubt about it.'

I looked out at the soaring city where I had lived for four years, looking over the tops of the skyscrapers that usually towered above me to the crowded horizon and the glittering water. In the distance, the Statue of Liberty looked impossibly small. Directly below us, lines of miniature taxis crawled along the avenues like yellow caterpillars, slipping past an army of scurrying ants that tried to cross their path. 'It all looks so far away,' I said.

My new perspective only served to highlight how much I had distanced myself from real life. I had lost my way at some point, somewhere between Tanzania and the Amazon. Distracted, I wandered over to the north side of the viewing balcony, my eyes still searching for something to ground me, but even Central Park couldn't give me the inspiration I needed. I glimpsed the vast green *between the skyscrapers and the smog and I knew it held an intricate beauty brought to life by the flora and fauna that could be found there. I knew it was there but I had placed myself too far away to see it clearly or touch it. As my eyes desperately scanned the horizon, I became aware that I too was under intense scrutiny.*

'You made the right decision, Emma,' she told me. 'You can't get to these dizzying heights without keeping your focus on the big picture.'

'But I don't want to spend the rest of my life seeing the big picture without ever stepping into it.'

'Work gives me all the reward I need and I had hoped you would have the same kind of mindset, but if you want something more,' she began, carefully choosing her words. 'I'm not saying it isn't possible. There are a few women that have juggled their careers with a fruitful family life, but they all made sure they had secured their position in the business first. I have to warn you, Emma, you're not quite there yet.'

Her last words were a veiled threat that I would be foolish to ignore but as I looked out at the sights that failed to inspire, that left me feeling cold and alone, I knew I had reached a crossroads in my life. 'Life's all about taking risks,' I said.

Emma was sitting on her bed, cross-legged with her elbows on her knees and her palms propping up her chin. It was still early morning and the world outside was struggling to emerge from the darkness of the night.

Its progress was slow, as was Emma's. She had woken with a headache and the painkillers she had taken had fogged her mind. The only light in the room came from her laptop but so far she had been unable to continue with the chapter she had started shortly after Christmas. She felt frustrated, having psyched herself up to begin the next phase of her life and step into the world she had created, to give her heart the release that she denied herself in her real life.

It wasn't the start to the New Year she had been hoping for. She massaged her temples in a futile attempt to release the pressure. Unlike her friends, who had been partying since the first strand of tinsel had been pinned up in the office, Emma's poor health had nothing to do with overindulgence. She and her mum had opted for a quiet night at home on New Year's Eve. They had stayed up long enough to stand on the balcony and watch the fireworks split open the darkness, their reflections shimmering like ghosts across the river. They raised a small toast to the success of their endeavours, or more precisely Meg's endeavours, to secure Emma a place on the clinical trial: the news had arrived that day and Emma tried her best to share her mother's enthusiasm. At least now she had a firm date to work to. She would be travelling to Boston on 23 January.

Emma could hear her mum pottering about in the apartment. Meg had been torn between working all the hours she could to fund Emma's treatment and spending precious time with her daughter. For New Year's Day at least, she would ease her guilt by spending the day at home. She had suggested they go for a walk along the prom and then order a takeaway to eat while they watched some old movies. It was a plan that might appeal to another Emma, one half her age or, more likely, twice her age, but this Emma was looking at the clock and thinking about escape. It was eight thirty and she wondered if Ben would be having a well-deserved lie-in after a busy night at the bistro or if he was already preparing for his trek.

To occupy her mind, Emma checked out the latest photos that Ally and Gina had posted online. Her motives were disguised as mild interest but in reality it was a form of self-torture, a reminder of the life she had already lost. There were plenty of snaps of her friends at the office party posing drunkenly for the camera but Emma's focus was on those standing on the sidelines. There was something more appealing about seeing people in mid-flow. The way Dan was looking at Gina, a yearning in his eyes that would, by all accounts, be satiated by the end of that night. There were other silhouetted figures and one reminded her distinctly of Peter, but if there was a reason for her oncology nurse to be at the party that Emma had excluded herself from, then Ally hadn't made her aware of it. There was one photo that Emma would have preferred not to look at but it came as no surprise, a glimpse of Alex with his arm around Jennifer, whispering in her ear. Jennifer had her head turned away so it was difficult to tell if she found his tall tales as enthralling as Emma once had.

She was about to switch the computer off there and then but a message appeared at the bottom of her screen. An email had arrived and it sent a chill down her spine. As the sender's name faded and then disappeared like an unwelcome ghost, Emma continued to stare at the empty space until her eyesight blurred.

Rather than read the message, she shifted her gaze to the collection of picture frames on the dressing table. The latest addition was the one Ben had given her but it was a frame covered in seashells that drew her attention, an image of Emma and Louise building a sandcastle. Her dad had taken the photograph and she wondered what he had seen when he looked through the lens. What did his family mean to him? The answer was within touching distance and when she was ready, she opened up the email from her father.

With the words barely registering, she closed down the computer and dragged herself off the bed. She had pins and needles from sitting too long in one position and her left leg in particular took its time to wake up. She limped over to raise the blinds and then opened a window before taking a deep breath to clear her mind. The air was bitterly cold and had a salty tang reminiscent of the grey mist that lingered over the Mersey.

Emma struggled with her thoughts as she picked up the seashell frame from her dressing table, gripping it tightly as the anger built inside her. She didn't notice the tingling in her hand until it went into spasm and she didn't notice when it slipped from her grasp. She was already two thousand miles away.

The air she expelled from her lungs in one harsh gasp was as warm and acrid as the smog that enveloped her. The wind whipped her hair across her face as she tried to find her bearings. Emma pushed away her unruly locks, and glanced out towards the river, which seemed impossibly far below her, half obscured by tall angular buildings that reached up to scrape the sky but still failed to reach her. The distant hum of traffic drew her gaze further over the edge of the Empire State Building towards the yellow caterpillars that crawled along the streets.

The picture frame clattered to the floor as the bedroom walls were effortlessly reconstructed around her. She tried pulling the hair from her mouth, only to find that it was already neatly tied back. Carefully, she picked up the photoframe. It had lost a couple of shells but was otherwise undamaged.

Emma closed the window but kept her eyes on the horizon as she tried to focus her mind. Her seizures didn't frighten her but rather left her with a sense of comfort, leaving only remnants of the places she had been. One thought persisted and she spoke it out loud. 'Life's all about taking risks,' she said. The Welsh mountains were obscured by murky skies but they still managed to pull at her heart. She looked at the clock. It was nine o'clock.

*   *   *

'Do you mind if we take a rain check for today? I'm going out with Ben,' Emma said, sweeping into the living room.

'Going where with Ben?' Meg asked, looking up from the kitchen counter where she had been preparing a breakfast of fresh fruit and yoghurt for them both.

'Going for a drive to Wales,' Emma said lightly but her body was already tensing up for the fight. She was dressed and ready to go, kitted out in walking shoes and waterproofs. 'He's on his way over to pick me up now.'

'You're climbing Moel Famau?' her mum asked pointedly, not fooled in the least by Emma's use of the term 'drive'.

'Don't, Mum,' Emma warned. The anger that had sparked to life as she read her dad's email still simmered.

'No. Don't *you*, Emma. Don't make me be the one forcing you to face reality.' There was less anger in Meg's voice than Emma had expected but the pain in her voice was no less difficult to hear.

'Don't you think I face reality every day?'

'I don't know, Emma. Do you?' Meg said, the last words coming out as a guttural sob. 'I'm not sure you have faced up to what's about to happen. You were ready for the fight last time but now . . . now you're putting all your efforts into the bistro or that book thing of yours.'

'And why shouldn't I? What's wrong with escaping this prison once in a while, whether that involves going through the front door or into my imagination?'

'You can't run away from your cancer, Emma. If it was that easy, I'd have bought you the plane ticket years ago.'

The tears that had sprung to her mum's eyes had dampened Emma's anger enough for her to speak more calmly. 'I know, Mum,' she said. 'But it's so damned unfair, especially when other people are getting more than their fair share of life. Far more than they deserve.'

'Alex?'

'No,' Emma said, pausing to take a deep breath. 'Dad.'

'You've heard from him.' It wasn't a question. It had been inevitable. 'What did he have to say for himself?'

'He's living in Edinburgh and doing very well, by all accounts. He even has a nice little replica family, complete with two new daughters. It's as if he's been allowed to wipe the slate clean and start again.'

Meg looked down at the food she had been preparing. She breathed out an 'oh' and let her body sag.

'So,' Emma continued, 'I may not have that kind of luxury but what I do have is a small window of opportunity between now and 23 January. I want to enjoy the little freedom I have left. Please, Mum. Let me go.'

Meg was still looking down, cutting up an apple into chunks that were becoming so tiny they were practically dissolving into the cutting board. 'Promise me, you'll be careful,' she said.

'I will.'

'Don't take any chances.'

'I won't,' Emma said. 'We'll have a proper talk when

185

I get back. And you might want to warn Louise. I'd like to know why she gave him my email address.'

'Did he mention anything about finances?' Meg asked, her voice still strained.

'No, but maybe he'll contact Louise about that side of things. He certainly sounds like he's doing well, so we might be in luck.' Emma moved tentatively towards Meg until she was standing behind her. She gently rested her head on her mum's shoulder. 'Happy New Year, Mum,' she whispered.

Meg made a sound a little like a laugh and a lot like a sob. 'I hope so, Emma. Oh, God, I hope so.'

The day was cold and the skies above Liverpool were clearing by the time Emma and Ben set off for North Wales. Meg had helped load up the car with enough supplies to cover every eventuality, including an entire bag of medical supplies to counter her daughter's recklessness.

'She didn't seem that pleased with me,' Ben said once they were on their way. 'Are you sure you're well enough to go?'

'I know my limitations,' Emma told him, secretly thanking the cocktail of drugs she had taken, which had cleared the headache she had woken with. 'I wouldn't have phoned you if I didn't think I could do it. I climbed Moel Famau when I was at school so I know what I'm doing.'

'I never doubted it,' Ben said, knowing it was time to

change the subject. 'Great news about your treatment, by the way.'

'I wish I could share everyone's enthusiasm,' Emma said as they drove into the yawning mouth of the Mersey Tunnel. 'I'm being sent halfway across the world to go through treatment that won't only attack my cancer cells but pretty much every other cell in my body too.'

'But there must be a chance the treatment will work,' Ben said, and the irrefutable note of hope in his voice had a familiar ring to it.

'I want to believe it will but, realistically, this monster in my head will kill me eventually,' she said solemnly. 'I need you to understand that, Ben. This treatment might give me more time but it's not a proven cure.'

Their conversation was not the ideal start to the day but Emma had enough guilt to deal with, knowing what she was putting her family through. She had to warn him off, her conscience demanded it.

'Then that's all the more reason to make the most of today,' Ben said. There was a twinkle in his eyes as the daylight that appeared like a beacon at the end of the Mersey Tunnel lit up his features.

Moel Famau was still an hour's drive away and it wasn't long before Ben steered the conversation to Emma's book.

'So tell me, where are you up to now?' he asked. 'Are you back from the Amazon yet?'

'Yes.'

'And?'

'I'm still pondering my next move,' she said.

'Ah,' Ben replied. 'Could it be that you're taking on board my suggestions?'

'I've realized that I don't want to give my life to a corporate machine without demanding something in return. I've been seeing the sights the world has to offer but it's meant living like a nomad. Now might be the time to put down some roots.'

'I don't know where you get your ideas from,' Ben said with a self-satisfied smile. 'So have you finally given in? Am I going to be your leading man?'

Emma laughed as she shook her head. 'I thought we agreed to be just friends. Besides, how could I possibly have a humble cheese-maker as my hero?'

Ben gave a self-important sniff before he spoke. 'Who says I have to settle for one dream. I'm still young,' he said but then paused. 'I am still young, aren't I? I know what you writers are like with your poetic licence. You haven't turned me into a gnarled, old hack, have you?'

Emma pictured an unkempt Ben, complete with Hawaiian shirt. 'As if I would mess around with your immaculate image,' she said. 'You're not old, not yet at least.'

'Not yet? So you are planning on me being around for a while.'

'Let's see what the day brings.'

'You might want to make that tomorrow. Today, we have a mountain to climb,' he warned.

'I beg to differ,' Emma said firmly. 'I have my laptop in my backpack.'

Ben shook his head but he knew better than to argue. 'So, go on, tell me. Assuming you have the man of your dreams in your sights, what is this new phase of your life going to look like?'

Emma looked ahead but not at the road stretching out before her but to a distant point in time. 'I'm not sure I can see it yet. I suppose I'd want to return to England or, then again, maybe I'll settle in Wales,' she offered as they drove past a Welsh Dragon picked out in winter pansies along the road embankment.

'A stone cottage set into the hillside, looking down onto a green and lush valley with a river running through it like a silver ribbon glinting in the sunlight.'

Emma gasped in amazement. 'My literary prowess is obviously rubbing off on you,' she said.

'That and the inspiring view,' he said, tipping his head towards the hills and valleys looming on all sides. The patches of bright blue sky above them were few and far between but where the sun peaked through the clouds, it lit up the grey landscape with vibrant colour.

'Yes, I think I can see myself in a little cottage,' she agreed as she stared straight ahead and let her thoughts wander. She imagined herself in the picturesque setting that Ben had described, standing at the door of her cottage, first as a young woman but then gradually aging. There was a man standing behind her with his arms around her waist as they looked out at the rolling landscape. They were laughing as a young girl pushed past them, chasing her little brother who was toddling towards a swing hanging from an apple tree where the pink blossom showered them in soft petals. The man let go of her so he could follow the children and she looked on as he took out his camera and captured the idyllic scene. 'In fact, I can see myself there for a very long time.'

As they neared their destination, the murkiness that she had spied from her bedroom window still clung to the peaks above her. 'Do you think the weather will clear before we reach the top?' she asked. It had been a glorious summer's day the last time she had climbed Moel Famau and the view had been breathtaking.

'I think we'd better wrap up well in case it doesn't. You know, if it's still misty when we get to the top, we'll be lucky if we can see our hands in front of our faces. We could just climb until we reach the cloud cover and then turn back,' he suggested.

'Are you trying to bail out on me already?'

'Not a chance. I'm here for the long haul,' he said.

Emma fell silent as Ben pulled into the car park, which was nestled between steep mountain slopes covered in a seamless carpet of pine trees that disappeared into the mist. The anger that had fuelled her determination to escape the confines of the apartment had dissipated and thoughts of her dad were far from her mind. She couldn't escape her illness so easily and she felt a knot of anxiety growing inside her. She looked down at her trembling hands. She hoped it was only nerves as she slipped them into her pockets.

The air felt damp and, although it wasn't raining, the information board that displayed the various routes they could take, glistened with raindrops that trickled down paths of their own making.

'I say we follow the easiest route, don't you?' Ben asked. 'It takes a bit longer but it's safer.'

It was only as his voice echoed off the wall of trees that Emma noticed how deserted the place was. The car park was completely empty and there wasn't another soul in sight. Surprisingly, the sense of freedom she had craved for so long only added to Emma's nerves.

'You lead on,' she said. The walking stick she used to point the way had been forced on her by her mum but judging by how steep and muddy the slopes looked, she was glad she had taken it.

There were deciduous trees along the trail, denuded and overpowered by the evergreens that made the winter's day feel a little less lifeless. Despite regular walks, Emma wasn't prepared for how tough the climb was and she was struggling after the first twenty minutes. When they reached the top of one particularly steep incline, she had to stop to catch her breath.

'And this is the easy route?' she asked Ben in disbelief.

'I can see a fallen tree up ahead. We can use it as a seat and take a breather.'

*   *   *

191

Emma sat down with a thump and would have toppled backwards if Ben hadn't caught her. 'I told you that backpack was too heavy for you,' he scolded. 'At least let me put your laptop in my bag.'

'I will not,' countered Emma stubbornly.

'You won't have a chance to use it,' he insisted.

'We'll see. Who knows when inspiration will strike?'

Around her, the trees shivered in the cold arctic breeze, which transformed her breath into vaporous ghosts that danced in front of her face. Emma didn't shiver in sympathy, in fact she felt warm, too warm. Beneath her many layers of clothing she started to feel hot and clammy and that was when the panic set in.

'Actually, I think inspiration is about to strike right now,' she told Ben as she tried to breathe through her anxiety.

'You're the boss,' he said, doing his best to hide his disapproval as he helped her retrieve her laptop from her backpack.

'Why don't you go for a little wander, check out the weather conditions further up the slope?' suggested Emma.

'If I didn't know better, I'd say you were trying to get rid of me. Afraid I'll look over your shoulder?'

Emma faked a smile and watched him trudge up the path. She took off her gloves. Her hands were shaking badly as she fumbled in her pockets for the pills she had set aside in case of emergency. Try as she might to explain away her current state as overexertion, Emma recognized her symptoms. If she had wanted to outrun the monster in her head, it was nevertheless catching up fast and she needed to take cover in the realms of her imagination.

When I stepped into the cottage, I crunched shale underfoot. Daylight trickled down through the rafters whilst fat, lazy drops of rainwater from the recent downpour continued to drop heavily to earth with a chorus of thuds.

'Ben?' I called, my voice echoing off the stone walls. I could hear footfalls that weren't my own. 'Is that you?'

The sound of heavy breathing grew nearer. If I had been in a nightmare, a blood-crazed, axe-wielding maniac would be only moments away from meeting his next victim but I had no such fears. Even though I had failed to track down Ben so far, I held out hope that my heart had led me to the right place.

I'd had no forwarding address for Ben but I knew his plan was to go into partnership with a large farm, running his business from a small-holding connected to it and one which needed substantial renovation. All I had to go on was that the farm was in North Wales, but Ben's enthusiastic descriptions had made the task of finding him far easier than it might have been. His clarity of vision made my own view of the future seem hazy in comparison. When cancer had invaded my head and my life, I had learnt to forget the picture of the world I had once imagined, reluctant to invest emotionally in a life that had no long-term guarantees. Even now that I had escaped the clutches of my tumour, I wasn't sure that I could resurrect those dreams. I had advanced in my career but my journey up the ladder of success had been a lonely one. I was meant to move onto the next stage of my life now but it was a daunting step and I knew I couldn't do it on my own. That was why I had gone in search of Ben.

I was standing in what would have been the front hall of the cottage, and could only guess what might await. I could stay put or I could move towards it. As I did, I was almost knocked off my feet by a heavily breathing man coming from the opposite direction. On the upside, at least he dropped his axe.

It was Ben and he looked like he'd been hard at work demolishing the house rather than building his dream home. 'Emma?' He had caught hold of me before I had a chance to fall and he pulled me to him. 'What the hell are you doing here?'

'Looking for you,' I told him. 'You don't know how much trouble I've had finding you.'

'But I've been here all the time,' he said with a wry smile.

Emma rubbed her eyes as she looked up towards the sound of the clicking camera. 'Have you got nothing better to do?' she asked. She closed the lid of her computer and returned to the real world, which was as daunting as ever but at least the wave of panic that had threatened to overpower her had receded.

'I could always climb a mountain, that might be a

better thing to do,' Ben offered, holding out his hand to help Emma to her feet.

She looked up at him and did her best to absorb some of his enthusiasm. 'So, do I have blue skies and bright sunshine to look forward to up there?' she asked.

'I didn't go too far but all I'd say is, if there's anything you want keeping dry then wrap it up well,' he replied, looking at her laptop.

The rain started as a fine mist that swirled gently around them but as they climbed beyond the layer of trees and into open landscape, it grew more intense and sheets of rain slapped across Emma's face, encouraged by gale-force winds. The path to the very top of Moel Famau dipped before rising steeply and they had to clamber across shale to reach the top.

The remains of the Jubilee Tower awaited them at the summit and it was vaguely familiar from the school trip she remembered but there the similarities ended. That day had been dry and bright and the view mesmerizing whereas now, Emma could barely lift her head against the wind and the only view that met her was a complete whiteout.

'I'm not quite sure how this is supposed to inspire me,' she admitted with a resigned smile.

'Ben Knowles makes a complete mess of things yet again,' he shouted above the wind.

'It looks like you've brought me into the eye of the storm,' Emma agreed as the rain pelted against her face, obscuring her vision.

Ben grabbed her arm and pulled her towards the safety of the doorway of the tower where they found a corner to shelter from the wind. He made a brave effort to unwrap a silver-foil blanket for added protection. It flapped around them, trembling against the wind that had found its way into their hideout and was now trying to wrench the flimsy sheet from his grasp. Eventually, it took two pairs of hands to keep it over their heads.

'I wanted this to be special,' he confessed. 'You can't frighten me off, Emma. I know you're trying to protect me but I can't give up on us before we've even had a chance. I don't believe you want to give up either.' He paused, making sure he had her full attention. They locked eyes. 'I think I love you . . . no, I know I love you and I have for a very long time.'

'Me?' she asked, unsure if she had even heard right. The sound of the wind against their makeshift cover was deafening but not as loud as the sound of her heart thumping in her chest.

'Yes, you,' he said as softly as he could whilst still being heard. 'We've wasted so much time, please, let's not waste any more.'

His words hung in the air as the world transformed around Emma. The vicious wind was silenced and she could hear soft lazy drops of rain thudding against the floor of an abandoned cottage. 'You don't know how much trouble I've had finding you,' she said, taking Ben's hand. She led him back down the hallway to the front door. The sun had broken through the cloud and the warm air had already started to soak up the dampness left by the April shower. She felt Ben's arms encircle her waist. Children's laughter filled her ears and her heart leapt as two small figures swept past her. She gasped in delight, torn between pulling away from the comfort of Ben's arms and the desire to chase after her children and sweep them up in her arms. She turned to Ben and her breath was taken away as he kissed her. Emma closed her eyes and let her body melt and meld into his.

When she opened her eyes, the real world came crashing back into her consciousness. The security she had felt was as illusory as the world her mind was still trying to construct amidst the windswept ruins she and Ben had sought refuge in. The only warmth she felt now was from Ben's lips. He was kissing her but as her body became paralysed by shock, he pulled away, concern etched painfully on his face.

Emma could still sense the cottage walls around her, the dampness of the derelict building and then the warmth of the family home that had taken its place. Currents of confusion skittered across her brain and it took long painful seconds for her to make sense of it all. Her previous seizures had left only vague impressions of the world she had created but this time the images circled her like predatory ghosts. She took a breath. Her lungs felt ready to implode as fear gripped her heart.

'Emma, what's happened? Are you alright?'

'I don't know,' she said, shaking her head to force away the remnants of her alternate reality from her mind.

It wouldn't release her and she still couldn't trust her own senses; nothing she felt or saw could be relied upon. She wasn't even sure if Ben had really kissed her. Had he actually said he loved her?

Instinctively, she pulled away from him and barely noticed the foil sheet being snapped up by the storm raging all around. She started to run, heading back the way they had come as if her life depended on it. She slipped and slid down the first slopes on her bottom, her walking stick trailing behind her. She could hear Ben chasing after her, calling her name but she wouldn't stop even as he appeared next to her.

'Slow down, Emma, please,' he begged her. 'You're going to hurt yourself.'

Emma stopped as Ben caught hold of her arm. She was sitting in the mud but didn't turn towards him. 'I'm scared, Ben,' she told him with a pitiful sob. 'I'm so scared. My mind's playing tricks on me and what happened up there was like nothing I've experienced before.'

'What did happen? Was it me?'

Emma shook her head and immediately regretted it as stars appeared in front of her eyes. 'I had a seizure, Ben. A little reminder that the monster in my head is alive and kicking.'

'I'm sorry, Emma. I shouldn't have brought you here, it was a stupid, stupid idea. I wouldn't rest until I told you exactly how I felt.'

Emma turned to him, searching out for a friendly face

to anchor her. 'You did tell me that you loved me, didn't you?'

Ben nodded gently. Rain was trickling down his face in tiny rivers but at least there were no tears. Emma didn't want to make him cry, not ever. She tried to smile but she couldn't when the words she was about to speak were already breaking her heart. 'The Emma in my story would make you happy, but I can't. For every ounce of love I can give you, you'll receive a pound of pain.'

'Do you love me?' he asked.

Emma felt his arm slip around her waist and her mind began to pull her back to the cottage on the hill. 'I can't trust myself to know how to feel,' she said, aware that there was a perverse truth in her white lie – even their first kiss had been snagged between two worlds. 'It's as if what I'm writing is coming to life around me but it can't and it won't. I'm not the Emma in my story and I can't have what she has.'

'Why not?' Ben said. 'You're writing about all of those lost opportunities but not all of them have to be missed. The Emma you're writing about is still you.'

Emma closed her eyes as she tried to rein in the torrent of emotions building inside her. She wiped at her running nose and imagined what a sight she must look. Her nose and eyes would be red, her makeup running down her face. 'You couldn't be more wrong,' she sniffed. 'It's the Emma in my book that has more substance, I'm the shadow of the woman I was meant to be.'

'You feel real to me,' Ben said as he lifted his hand to her face but Emma knocked it away angrily.

'I don't want to hurt you,' she told him fiercely. 'I won't hurt you.'

Emma stumbled to her feet and continued her descent. Her head felt hazy, the left side of her body tingled but she refused to give in and stumbled down the steep slopes. Ben caught up to her again but rather than stop her this time, he helped her as much as he could without saying a word.

The rain started to ease as they reached the forest layer but the air was still thick with mist, partly obscuring her view. Emma reluctantly acknowledged that she was running out of energy and slowed her pace so she could catch her breath.

She chanced a look at Ben as they stomped along the spongy forest floor. His head was down and a frown furrowed his brow. When he caught her looking at him, his features softened. 'I think you need to take a rest. How about your usual table, madam,' he said with a weak smile, pointing to the log she had been sitting on earlier.

Emma sank gratefully onto the fallen log and Ben sat beside her, his head lowered. 'I'm sorry, Emma. If today is anything to go by, then you're better off without me.'

Emma turned to him. A sigh escaped and took with it some of the terror that had accompanied her flight down the slopes. She hadn't wanted to hurt him but she already had. Emma lifted her hand nervously to his face, turning his head so that he was looking directly at her. 'There are plenty of uncertainties in my life but if I'm certain of one thing, it's that I wouldn't be better off without you. I'm tired and I'm scared and I still can't quite trust my senses but whether I'm stumbling through this world or the one in my imagination, my feelings for you are the same. I think I love you, too.'

'Think?' Ben asked. His voice was hoarse.

'I love you,' she said, 'but I still don't want to hurt you. And if you insist on being a part of my life then I will hurt you.'

'I know, but let me worry about that.' His voice was no more than a whisper and his lips trembled.

Emma let her thumb sweep over his cheek, where she imagined the trace of tears yet to fall. Instinctively, he moved closer to her and slowly their lips touched. This time she was fully aware of what was happening and it was a sensation she wouldn't forget. His kisses were gentle, far more gentle than the electric current surging through her body.

'Let's get you home,' he whispered.

Emma agreed but Ben had to drag her to her feet. 'Are you sure you can make it?' he asked.

'I'll be fine once we get out of this damned mist.'

Ben looked at her and there was a note of anxiety in his voice when he replied, 'It's not misty now, Emma.'

'Oh,' she said, lifting her hand in front of her face. Emma's vision was cloudy and blurred. Her ears pounded with the sound of her heart beating wildly as she felt a new surge of panic. Her head throbbed malevolently as she realized that her brief moment of euphoria was being stamped on by the monster that had pursued and now finally caught up with her. 'I think you need to get me off this mountain,' she said, before adding more urgently, '*now*.'

Ben didn't need any further explanation but helped Emma climb slowly and carefully down the path towards the car park. Where the ground was level enough, he carried her and she looked up at his face, fixed and resolute.

'Will you stay with me?' she asked.

'I'll never leave you,' he promised.

She tried to say something but couldn't grasp the word. Panic was flooding her brain and Ben was almost at the car before she had managed to catch hold of the word that had wriggled like a slippery fish in her fingers. 'Tabernacle,' she said with a relieved smile.

When the look of worry on Ben's face only intensified, Emma hoped he would understand what she meant but there was no time to explain, there were other more important things to discuss. 'Tell me about our life together in our little cottage. I want to hear it. I need to hear it.'

10

Emma felt like she was floating and as she peered up into mist that had followed her down the mountain she could perceive nothing but flashes of light and dark, light and dark. Slowly, she became aware that she was lying on a trolley, being pushed along at frantic speed. Her brain was being knocked from side to side although she couldn't feel it, nor could she feel the pain that had exploded inside her head as soon as she had started to thaw out in Ben's car. She was high above it all now.

The blind spot in her peripheral vision was devouring more and more of the light that flashed above her but she wasn't frightened. She could feel a hand gripping hers tightly.

'Stay with me,' she whispered.

We stood in front of the cottage, the whitewashed walls reflecting the sun and warming our faces. The rambling roses were little more than fragile stems at the edge of the doorway but they would grow, in time. The wiry plants were busily putting down roots but would eventually extend their reach, climbing taller, getting to know the feel of the place, making it their own. In time, roses would bloom and we would smell sweet heady perfume as we stood at the door and we would know we were home.

'Is it as you imagined?' I asked.

'Yes.'

'Look,' I said, as if there was still more to prove. I stepped over the threshold and pointed up to the ceiling. There were no rafters in sight and no glimpses of sky beyond. We had a roof over our heads. We were safe and secure.

'It's perfect,' she agreed and then Emma began to laugh.

I looked at her beautiful face in amazement, knowing that finally she was mine. I could walk right up to her and kiss her without fear of a slap in the face. It hadn't always been so. When I first met Emma, I was surprised that she and Louise were sisters. They were so different. Louise was the precocious one who commanded attention whilst her sister seemed the dark and brooding type and my first impressions were, I confess, not great. She didn't have a presence back then, not like her sister and not like Emma's then boyfriend. She had stayed in the shadows and seemed happy there.

If I could pinpoint that magical moment when my world was turned upside down, when I stopped seeing a shadow and caught the hint of fire in Emma's eyes, it was when the local rag gave the bistro a poor review. Emma had been furious and forgot herself. Her family had been attacked and she would have had the poor reviewer tarred and feathered if I hadn't blocked her exit to stop her from storming over to the newspaper's office. When she had calmed down she retreated back towards the edges of life but I kept her in my sights. I watched and I fell in love.

There was fire in her eyes now as she rushed into the garden, raising her arms to the blue skies above and spinning around in a victory dance until she made herself dizzy.

I ran to her and took her in my arms to stop her from falling. I was laughing too. When we stopped we were facing downhill. 'That's the rest of the world down there. Do you think it's ready for us?'

'I think I might just stay here and hide,' she said, but I wasn't going to let the old Emma back.

'You have an amazing job waiting for you. You've taken a well-earned sabbatical but your talents are still in demand, Kate has made sure of that.'

'And you?' she asked. 'What about your ambitions?' She was leaning back against me and our bodies were swaying gently together as we considered our options.

'If you have to go away then I could come with you, if that was what you wanted. Or if you insist on going on your own then I'll be here waiting for you, building my dreams and waiting for you to step back into them. I am the ying to your yang.'

'Yes, I think you are.'

There was no doubt about it, we were feeling smug. But we deserved it. Emma deserved it.

I turned her gently to face me. 'Close your eyes, Emma,' I told her. She did. 'I want you to picture the life you planned for yourself all of those years ago. At thirty-four years old, you're meant to have your career and at this point, your leading man.' As I spoke, I took a small box from my pocket and flipped it open in front of her. It sparkled. 'You can open your eyes now.'

'I think you should go,' Meg said. Her voice quivered and the nasally tone suggested that she had been crying. But behind the pain there was a growing tension and Emma knew her mum was angry.

'I'd rather stay if you don't mind.' It was Ben's voice. It sounded just as pained and equally tense. He was going to give Meg a run for her money.

'I do mind,' she replied.

'Ben, I think it's for the best. Emma needs her family here, that's all.' Louise's voice was accompanied by footsteps as she drew nearer. Emma could hear her breathing and the swish of her long, blonde hair.

'You don't understand,' Ben insisted. 'Emma would want me here, I know it.'

There was a rustling of cotton as bodies moved and hands fidgeted. Meg was smoothing the creases in her clothes as she thought about what to say next. 'You barely know my daughter. You don't know what she

206

would want and you certainly don't know what's best for her. You're the one who put the idea in her head to go up that damned mountain in the first place.'

There was the sound of someone swallowing hard. 'I know,' Ben replied, the fight leaving his body in a long, painful sigh. 'I know it's my fault. I didn't realize she wasn't physically up to it until it was too late. I didn't know.'

'None of us knew,' Louise offered. There was the sound of chairs creaking and more cotton brushing against cotton. Louise had put her arms around her mum's shoulder.

A heavy silence filled the room and Emma could feel it weighing down on her, pulling her closer towards the world she had been floating above.

'I shouldn't have given in to her. I won't any more,' sniffed Meg defiantly. 'She can't take risks like that, not if we're going to get her to Boston. I know you thought you were helping Emma but you're not. I don't want her distracted, not by anything.'

'Doesn't Emma have a say in all of this? In case you hadn't noticed, she's a grown woman perfectly capable of making her own decisions.' Ben gulped as if he had tried too late to hold back the words that cut sharply through the tension.

'That's where you're wrong. She wasn't making her own decisions, not about her treatment. She left all of that to me,' replied Meg, her words followed by a stifled sob. 'I'm not setting out to destroy my daughter's life; I'm trying to save her.'

'I'm sorry,' Ben said, his voice barely a whisper. 'I don't want to add to your pain, really I don't.'

'Then go.'

Emma could feel the grip on her hand loosen so she held on to it even tighter. 'Emma?' Ben asked and his voice sounded closer. He was leaning over her, his face only inches above hers. She could feel his breath on her face. She could smell his damp clothes.

'Emma?' repeated Meg.

Shadows danced across Emma's closed eyelids as more faces loomed over her. 'He stays,' she whispered.

'How are you feeling, Emma?' Mr Spelling asked. He was shining a light into her eyes and although she could sense light and shade, her vision was nothing more than ghostly shapes that floated across a sea of blackness before slipping into the river of morphine pumping through her body.

'I don't think I'll be able to walk a straight line today,' she confessed drunkenly.

'We need to take some serious decisions,' he told her. 'Are you up for that?'

Emma felt someone give her hand a quick squeeze. It wasn't Ben. He had gone home but promised to be back within the hour and Emma had only let him go when she had firm promises from both her mum and Louise that they wouldn't bar his entry.

'I can handle all of this for you if you want,' Meg told her with another squeeze of her hand.

'No, I'm up for it, doc,' Emma said.

She was determined to make her own decisions but it was difficult for Emma to concentrate as disconnected images flashed across her mind. She saw herself standing in the kitchen. Apples being sliced. Her mum's voice telling her she wasn't facing reality.

'I'm facing it now,' Emma replied with a soft sigh.

There was a pause. 'How can you expect her to make decisions while she's pumped full of drugs?' Meg asked.

'Your daughter has never had any problems getting her point across, morphine or no morphine. Am I right, Emma?' Mr Spelling replied firmly.

'Hit me with it, doc,' Emma murmured and fought through the fog to concentrate on the life-or-death decision she was about to take.

Mr Spelling explained in careful detail what he thought was happening inside her head. He was absolutely certain that Emma would not be able to travel to Boston in her current state. She needed an emergency operation to relieve the pressure caused by the sudden growth of her tumour. But that was the only thing her consultant was certain about. Everything else would need to be taken a step at a time.

'But if you operate, then it may affect her eligibility for the clinical trial,' interrupted Meg before Emma had a chance to respond.

'Emma's current condition has already put that in doubt, I'm afraid. We'll know better after the operation.'

'No,' Meg continued, 'that's not good enough. I want a second opinion. I want to hear directly from Boston before we agree to anything.'

'I'm still here,' Emma said. 'And it's still my decision.'

As Emma lay back on her bed, she felt like Alice in Wonderland rising above the figures that surrounded her, growing taller and stronger as the magic potion in her veins transformed her from a small defenceless child into a giant.

'Emma, we need to operate. I need your permission.'

'Then you have it,' she told him. 'Discussion closed.'

Days passed and the first sign that the operation had been a success, for the short term at least, was the return of Emma's vision, and one of the first things she saw with any clarity was Ben's face as he slipped into her dimly lit hospital room. It was early morning and he was the first to arrive. She watched through half closed eyelids as he crept over to her bed and leaned over to kiss her forehead.

'Nice shirt,' she whispered.

Despite the lighting being restricted to ease Emma's eyes, the colours on his shirt were bright enough to sting. She peered at the swirling patterns of oranges and blues, which morphed into life, a flurry of exotic flowers and birds that would look at home in Hawaii. For a moment she wondered if it was her mind playing tricks on her. She had been warned that it would take days for the swelling to reduce after the operation and she could still expect some symptoms to persist during that time and, of course, the morphine didn't help. But somewhere at the back of her mind, a more rational explanation emerged. 'You've read my book,' she whispered.

'Tabernacle,' Ben told her. 'It took me a while to realize that you had given me the password to your computer. You didn't mind, did you?'

Emma's story had been her secret domain and although she had shared so much with Ben, she hadn't shared everything. In writing her future, Emma had looked to the past and bared her soul. There was a brief hesitation but then she remembered Ben carrying her in his arms and she knew she could trust him with her life. She smiled. 'No, of course I don't mind. It's our story now, isn't it?' When Ben didn't immediately respond, icy fingers of self-doubt wrapped around her heart. 'It wasn't all a hallucination, was it?' she asked weakly.

Ben gently stroked the side of her face, pushing back a dark and, no doubt, sweaty strand of hair. 'No, it wasn't. It was as real for you as it was for me,' he told her.

'But now you've had time to think and . . .'

'. . . and write,' Ben added quickly, 'in your book.'

Emma's reactions were sluggish, her emotions subdued and she had to dig deep to identify the correct response. The idea of someone not only reading her story but weaving their own fantasies into her imaginary world was at first an uncomfortable thought. But this wasn't anyone, Emma told herself, this was her leading man. 'And what exactly did you write?' she asked.

Ben had been looking guilty but he relaxed when Emma showed nothing but curiosity. 'I began with the dilapidated cottage you described and I built a home for us.'

'So we are together?' Emma asked bravely.

Ben didn't answer her with words. He leaned in closer and kissed her lips softly. Emma let her fingers trail slowly up his arms before wrapping her own arms around his neck. Gentle caresses were not enough and she pulled him closer and their kiss became deeper and far more sensual. It was Ben who had to draw breath first. 'And not only in the book. I want to be a part of your real life too, Emma.'

'That might not be a long-term commitment,' she warned.

'It could have been even shorter,' Ben said, guilt returning to his face. 'I nearly killed you.'

'No, you didn't. This thing in my head nearly killed me. Besides, I was the one who ignored all the signs that there was something wrong and still decided to go. My fault, not yours. Please don't blame yourself.'

'If you say so,' Ben said but he didn't sound convinced.

When he perched himself on the bed next to Emma, there was no hint of awkwardness between them. Ben knew her like no other.

'Yes, I do,' Emma said. 'So have you finished with your confessions or is there anything else I should know?'

Ben shook his head. 'No, only that I love you.'

'Good, because I love you too,' Emma replied and despite the morphine, her heart raced. Ben's eyes were glistening and Emma was determined not to let his tears fall. She kissed him again.

The door to her hospital room opened with an unnecessary bang and Emma didn't need to open her eyes to know who it was. When she did look up, Meg was standing at the door, silhouetted in the bright lights from the corridor beyond. She looked small and Emma wondered how such a tiny frame could have towered over her life for so long. Emma was torn between trying to escape her mother's control and wanting to rescue Meg from the pain that consumed her and smothered Emma. She released Ben but held on tightly to his hand. 'Stay,' she whispered to him.

'You're in early,' Meg said to Ben. She seemed reluctant to go closer to the couple, moving instead towards the window. 'Do you want to see if you can stand a little light in the room, sweetheart?'

'Just a little,' Emma replied. She felt bubbles of anxiety starting to build in the pit of her stomach but it wasn't the fear of bringing light into the room, Emma was preparing herself for what she would say next. 'When am I due to see Mr Spelling?'

Light crawled slowly from beneath the blind as it was inched upwards. Emma could make out vague streaks of fresh raindrops slithering down the windowpane; they glimmered dimly in the grey light of dawn.

'Tomorrow at eleven thirty, he said, but he has clinic first so don't expect him before midday,' Meg said in a singsong voice.

'I want to see him alone.'

Meg was still adjusting the blind, judging the amount of light being drawn into the room. 'Is that OK? Not too bright?'

'It's fine, Mum. Did you hear what I said?'

Meg turned and looked from Emma to Ben and then back to her daughter. 'We'll talk about it later.'

'No, we don't need to talk about it,' insisted Emma, her tone soft but firm. It was the exact same tone her mum had often used when Emma was a little girl.

Meg waved her hand dismissively and the bubbles in Emma's stomach started to fizz. 'You need me with you,' she said. 'You won't remember all the questions let alone the answers.'

'There's nothing wrong with my memory,' Emma reminded her. It was one of the few symptoms that Emma had avoided this time around, so far at least. 'I can manage. I insist.'

Her words were left hanging in the air and it was Ben's turn to shift uneasily. Emma gave him a small, apologetic smile as she let go of his hand, which he flexed painfully to encourage the blood flow.

'I haven't told Emma yet how everyone is helping out at the bistro,' he said in an attempt to smooth over the tension.

Meg smiled stiffly, taking her seat next to Emma's

214

bed. She was looking down at her lap, picking at an invisible piece of fluff on her skirt. 'Jean and Iris are in their element by all accounts,' she replied. There was no singsong tone to her voice any more and she sounded much further away than she ought to be.

Emma felt the first sting of tears but she knew that if she didn't hold her nerve, she may never be able to take control of her life. She swallowed hard and painted on a smile. 'They're helping at the bistro? How?'

'They're my latest apprentices, although if you saw them at work, you'd swear I was the new recruit,' Ben said with a nervous laugh. 'They're already planning to introduce some of their own dishes. Give them a few more weeks and I could be out of a job.'

'They told me to send you their love,' added Meg. 'Everyone does.'

Emma smiled at her mum. 'Tell them I'll be back before they know it. I don't want to stay here any longer than I have to.'

'We can ask Mr Spelling about that,' began Meg but then she faltered as did her smile. She looked down at her lap again, took a breath and when she looked up, Emma knew Meg was seeing her daughter with new eyes. 'You can ask him.'

'Thanks, Mum,' Emma said, reaching out her hand, which Meg took and squeezed fiercely.

'It's your life, your decisions. I know that.'

Emma felt her chest expand as she took a breath and let her confidence build. She knew it wasn't going to be easy, her options were becoming limited but the decisions she would take from now on would be her own. No-one else would share the burden and that was exactly how she wanted it.

Her meeting with Mr Spelling went as well as expected. He answered Emma's questions as honestly as he could, something she had insisted on. Together they were able to form a clear and realistic view of the future so that she could plan accordingly.

Mr Spelling had offered to stay around to give Emma some moral support when she shared the news but she had refused, knowing that her mum would only open up a debate with the doctor. She knew what needed to be said and who needed to hear it.

Three faces stared back expectantly at Emma as she sat in her bed but no-one was ready to ask the question that was on everyone's lips.

'They were able to remove some of the new growth but the tumour isn't going to go away,' Emma began, knowing that she was doing precisely what she had asked Mr Spelling not to do. She was sugar-coating the prognosis but then she knew in many ways it was a harder pill for them to swallow. They would be carrying their grief far longer than she would. 'In a few weeks I'm going to go ahead with the original treatment that was planned for me here. A combination of radiotherapy and chemotherapy that will slow the growth but won't stop it.'

'And the treatment in America?' Meg asked.

Emma hesitated before answering, knowing it was the last thread of hope her mum had been clinging onto. 'Mr Spelling has had confirmation from Boston that I wouldn't be able to start treatment in my current condition and once I've had radiotherapy here, then I would no longer be eligible for their programme.'

'But there must be a way . . .'

'Mum,' Emma said. There was a note of authority in her voice and it cut through that last thread of hope. 'I've agreed my treatment plan with Mr Spelling.'

Meg was trembling and Louise put an arm around her shoulder as tenderly as she could manage, afraid that her mum would shatter into tiny pieces. 'I won't stop fighting, Emma. I won't,' Meg insisted. 'I can find another clinic, another trial.'

'Please,' interrupted Emma. She had been planning exactly what she had to say and she hoped she had it word perfect. 'I know how hard you've been fighting for me but what I'm asking you to do next is going to take a lot more courage. I don't want you working all hours to pay for a treatment that isn't going to happen. I don't want a warrior woman who's trying to take on the world to save her daughter; I just want my mum back. If you can do that for me, then you'll have no regrets, not one.'

A deathly silence followed and the only thing that Emma could hear was the thudding of her own heart. There was a dull ache behind her nose and for once she

217

couldn't blame her tumour, it was pressure from the torrent of tears she was holding back.

Emma was exhausted and she bit down hard on her lip to rein in her emotions. She wasn't the only one struggling but she knew that neither her mum nor her sister would crack, not unless Emma cracked first and she wasn't prepared to do that. 'Why don't you go for a nice cuppa with Louise,' she told her mum softly, 'I wouldn't mind some time on my own with Ben.'

Meg left the room quietly under Louise's gentle guidance. Emma pretended not to hear the howls of anguish that echoed down the corridor just before the door closed behind them.

'Are you alright?' Emma asked Ben.

'You're asking me?' Ben whispered, rubbing his face. He had sat as still as a statue, not saying a single word as the tragedy that was Emma's life unfolded before him. She knew he was numb with shock and she felt renewed guilt for bringing him into her world.

'I'd like to say this is as bad as it gets, but it's going to get worse, Ben.'

Emma looked away from him and smoothed the blanket over her legs, extending her hands across the width of the bed to claim her territory. She didn't want Ben to join her on the bed; she could only say what needed to be said as long as she didn't have to feel him next to her. She had to try one more time.

'I need you to think very carefully about this,' she began. The thud of her heart was almost deafening now.

She had already played out this scene in her head, only in her mind's eye, she was about to board a plane.

The flight to Paris had been delayed. Perhaps if it hadn't, things might have been different.

We had spent days doing nothing except lying in each other's arms, talking to each other, loving each other. The time we had was precious and we savoured every moment. I was about to resume my jet-setting lifestyle, two weeks before my thirty-fifth birthday. Ben had been insistent that I shouldn't compromise my own dreams for his and we had both agreed that it would be better for him to remain at the cottage to start work on his business in earnest.

'I'm going to miss you,' he said, taking both my hands in his. We were standing beneath a flight-information board where the delay had just been announced. Tenderly, he began to kiss each of my fingers, stopping at the third finger of my left hand where a single diamond glinted. A self-satisfied smile appeared on his face.

'You'll be far too busy to notice I'm even gone,' I told him.

'I wish it was that simple. I'm going to be lost without you.'

'You'll find your way,' I assured him.

'I'll be bereft,' he insisted and it was his insistence that made me visualize what our future might look like, especially what Ben's future might look like. The scenes that played out in my mind's eye horrified me and I cursed my furtive imagination.

219

I pulled my hands away from his as if an electric shock had passed between us.

'Emma?' he had asked. 'What's wrong?'

'I need you to think very carefully before you answer this,' I began. 'Is this how you pictured it? Finding the love of your life and then watching her fly away?'

Ben seemed confused, uncertain about where I was leading and not sure he should follow. 'I don't understand, Emma. It's not about how long we spend together it's about making the most of the time we do have.'

He was shaking his head, as if to deny what was happening before his very eyes. I had taken off my engagement ring. 'I won't let you do it, Ben. I won't let you sacrifice your own happiness for mine.'

Emma was struggling to catch her breath as she brought the scene to an end. She looked down at her left hand, which was shaking. There was no engagement ring but there never had been. She wasn't standing in the middle of an airport, she was sitting in her hospital bed,

She chanced a look in Ben's direction and as soon as she met his eyes, she was captured by him. He reached over and took her hand, kissed her fingers, never taking his eyes off her. 'I'm not sacrificing my happiness, can't you see that? *You* are my happiness. Don't condemn me to a life of regret, wishing I had spent more time with you.'

'But you will spend the rest of your life wishing you'd had more time with me, that's the point.'

220

'All the more reason to spend as much time as I can with you now. It ends here, Emma,' he said sternly. 'If you really care about me then stop pushing me away.'

'I do care. I love you.'

'And I love you, with all my heart and soul. I'm here to stay, come what may.'

It took Emma an immense amount of concentration to stop herself from floating away on a wave of euphoria. If she had still been on high-dose morphine she would have been unable to resist but she had Ben's gaze to anchor her. 'You do realize this means were going to get married, don't you?'

There was no gasp of shock as she had expected, only a mischievous smile. 'Really?' Ben asked.

'Don't worry, I'll do my best to keep it in the realms of my imagination.'

'Don't feel you have to try too hard,' he said.

There were still so many thoughts and emotions that Emma had to wrestle with and even as her mind cleared of morphine, the constant interruption and invasion of her privacy left no place to withdraw to and no time to confront the consequences of the decisions she had made.

Emma couldn't wait to leave hospital but her recovery was slower this time and her return to fitness was not expected to be as complete. At least her sight was improving day by day. She cast her eyes over the collection of cards lined up on the window ledge, conveying good wishes and much love. Not one said get well soon.

Even her father had been sensitive enough to avoid that platitude although his card remained in its envelope, along with a contribution to the treatment that was already being cancelled as he posted the card. Emma hadn't had a chance to reply to his email and gave little thought of ever doing so; there were more important things to consider, if only her mind could focus for long enough.

Above the line of cards, the window blind had been opened fully to reveal a wet and windy winter's morning. Bare treetops exposed barren bird's nests swaying precariously in the breeze. She was starting to fear that she would never see another spring.

Before her mood was allowed to spiral into despair, there was a timely interruption as Peter appeared at her door.

'I was starting to think you were avoiding me,' she told him.

Emma knew she had hit a raw nerve by his sheepish smile and her bruised and battered mind connected pieces of a puzzle she had almost forgotten.

'It's only a quick visit,' he said. 'I just wanted to let you know that I'm up to speed with your treatment plan. If you have any questions now, or once you've been discharged, I can get you the answers.'

'As always,' Emma said with a half-concealed smile. 'Here's your first question then. Why would you be photographed at Bannister's office party?'

Peter's cheeks reddened. 'What photograph?'

'A photo of Ally.'

'Oh.'

'Care to elaborate?'

Peter put his hands in his pockets and started kicking at an invisible spot on the linoleum floor. 'Yes, I was there . . . with Ally.'

'So why the secrecy? Even Gina hasn't mentioned it. You have been avoiding me, haven't you?'

'Has anyone ever told you how pushy you are?' he said with a note of exasperation in his voice.

'All the time. So what is there to be embarrassed about? Ally wasn't just a notch on your bedpost was she? A one-night stand?' Emma asked, half joking but the punch line fell flat. 'It was a one-night stand?'

'No, it wasn't like that,' Peter replied defensively. 'I know I'm a terrible flirt but for the record, I don't do that kind of thing.'

'But for Ally, you made an exception?'

Peter twisted his foot into the floor as he squirmed under Emma's scrutiny. 'I like Ally and under other circumstances I would have wanted to see more of her and I think she felt the same.'

'But?'

Peter stopped moving and looked up. 'But you, Emma.'

'Me?' she asked. Her fractured mind briefly considered if Peter was about to confess his undying love but re-assuringly, she hadn't become that delusional.

'You're Ally's best friend and she's struggling. I wanted to comfort her but I've seen too much here. There's no way I would be able to say anything that could put her mind at ease, I'd only make her feel worse. So I didn't get back in touch with her and she didn't phone me. I think we both thought it was for the best.'

'Oh,' Emma said guiltily. 'I'm sorry, Peter.'

He shrugged. 'Don't worry about it. There are worse things in life.'

'Yes, there are but I'd like to think that if I can't be there for my friends, I can at least make sure they have a shoulder to cry on. Do you think there might be a chance between you two?'

'I would have liked things to have worked out differently but it really depends on Ally now.'

Emma gave Peter a conspiratorial wink. 'Leave it to me.'

'Like I said, pushy,' he said with a smile.

'Speaking of pushy, can you tell Sally Anne that I want to take a bath? She seems to think I'm not well enough.'

Emma's nurse took some persuading but Peter eventually convinced her that there was little point in arguing.

Although Emma was looking forward to her first bath, she dreaded the part where Sally Anne had to help her to get into the bath. She felt self-conscious about her body now more than ever. Her skin was dry and sore from some of the drugs she was taking and she had put on a little more weight than she would have liked in the last couple of months thanks to the steroids.

Sally Anne filled the bath with warm water and an emollient to moisturize her skin and Emma held back until the last minute before slipping off her robe and clambering into the steaming water.

'I'll leave you in peace but I'll only be next door writing up my notes. Just make sure you don't get your scalp wet or I'll be in trouble,' warned Sally Anne. 'The alarm button's there if you need me.'

'Thanks,' answered Emma as she sat scrunched up in the bath to hide her embarrassment.

It was only when the door closed that Emma began to relax. She slipped deeper into the water. The rain was beating against the frosted window and a storm was raging but Emma felt cocooned in the bathwater, which soothed and warmed her. Closing her eyes, she allowed herself a moment longer to savour the peace before forcing herself to think about the future.

She waved her hand through the water, feeling its resistance against her palm and listening to the ripples radiate outwards and hit the side of the bath. The residue of morphine in her system provided its own resistance as she tried to focus her mind. Drawing strength from within, Emma sat up again and dipped a cloth in the water before placing it over her face. She let the water trickle slowly downwards, tickling her cheeks before dripping off her chin and softly falling into the water where new ripples caused the surface of the water to tremble.

With her eyes open, she looked beyond the cloth in

front of her, towards a place she was frightened to go. There were still more decisions to take and she was starting to realize that she couldn't delude herself into thinking that any part of her life was going to be normal ever again. She had already stepped away from work, now she had to accept that she would never return. Cutting back on her involvement in the bistro would not be so easy but there would have to be some kind of withdrawal. Her mum had been right, her sister really did need to learn to stand on her own two feet. Emma wasn't going to be around forever.

Finally, her thoughts turned to Ben and those thoughts immediately led to the fictional life they were creating together. She still hadn't been able to use her laptop and was beginning to wonder if it was worth continuing with something that she may not be able to complete. But the story had continued in her head of its own accord and she would be compelled to write it down when she could. Even now, her story was drawing her in and she didn't fight it. The more space it occupied in her mind, the less room that would be available for her cancer and her fears, she told herself.

I was still holding back the tears as my stomach lurched. It was the moment where gravity released its grip and the plane took flight, tearing me away from the man I loved. Sunlight flared against my face as I watched the clouds fall below me. The bright blue sky stung my tear-less eyes.

The plane dipped, my stomach lurched again and then the sun disappeared. Immersed in shadow, I felt tentacles of darkness reaching towards my heart. I closed my eyes and came face to face with the shopkeeper.

'Take the box, Emma,' was all he said.

The plane levelled off and I was returned to the light. I gasped as I thought of what I was about to do. Ben was the man I was meant to spend the rest of my life with. What had I done? Suddenly, I couldn't breathe. It was only then that I realized that I had already started to cry. Tears were running down my face, my nose was blocked and I was getting strange looks from the poor man seated next to me. I made my excuses, apologized for dropping drenched tissues on his lap and headed for the toilet cubicle to freshen up. My eyes were swollen and red and through blurred vision I made my way to the back of the plane. In my haste to be out of sight from curious onlookers, I snagged my skirt on someone's seat.

'Sorry,' I blubbed to the man looking up towards me.

'So you should be,' he said sternly. 'Do you realize what kind of hell you've put me through?'

I slumped onto his knee and buried my head in his neck as the torrent of tears restarted, falling down my face and onto Ben's neck with renewed force. I couldn't get rid of him that easy.

Emma pulled herself back into the real world, peeling the damp cloth from her face. She knew she had been possessed with a grim determination to take control of her life and accept that she was dying. It had been an unstoppable adrenalin rush that had swept away the drug-induced fog and it had got her through the painful conversations she'd had with her family, with Ben and with Mr Spelling. She had shrugged on a suit of armour, ready for battle and she already had some small victories under her belt. She knew she should be pleased with herself.

But as the water cooled, the cocoon she had slipped into didn't feel quite so safe any more. She had set aside her suit of armour and she shivered in her nakedness. The water shivered in sympathy. There were two enemies she knew she couldn't defeat and she had already spent the last five years getting to know the first, the monster in her head. The second enemy wasn't exactly new but she had only just learnt the measure of it. That enemy was time.

Emma had learnt long ago that it was best not to ask questions if you didn't want to know the answer but whilst her family hadn't asked the burning question, she had. When she asked Mr Spelling how long she had left, he had given her an honest answer. His reply was that he didn't know but his best guess was that she would be lucky to count that time in months.

The water she had splashed on her face dripped off her chin, falling into the trembling water below. A rogue droplet slipped between her lips. It was salty but she didn't recognize it as a tear, not until the first sob echoed off the tiled walls. Emma drew up her knees and wrapped her arms around her legs as she tried to hold herself together.

'Why now? Why me?' Emma whispered, her words reverberating across the bathroom. Her questions went unanswered other than by the steady dripping and the slow release of another sob that sounded more like the howl of a trapped animal.

'I don't want to die!' she sobbed, the sudden release of emotion taking her by surprise. Her words were louder now and she could hear her voice clearly as it rebounded off the stark white walls.

She wanted to scream and when she realized she couldn't, that it would only send Sally Anne crashing through the door to destroy the little privacy she had managed to secure, she wanted to scream even more. 'I'm not ready!' Emma howled as loudly as she dared. 'I haven't finished living yet!'

She stifled the next sob and then the next as a frown cut deeply across her brow. She had caught the sound of her words echoing off the walls and it pulled her back from her desolation. 'I want to live,' she said, breathing through her pain so that she could concentrate on the sound of the voice being returned to her. Emma chanced a smile and gulped back her tears, breathing in deeply to quell her trembling body.

'I will live a full life,' she said as she realized that her voice wasn't the only way her words could be echoed. Her writing could do the same. Her story was her route to a fruitful and fulfilling life, her only route. Emma managed a smile as she steeled herself. She was ready to slip back into her suit of armour and carry on the fight.

11

I lifted the coffee to my lips and breathed in the warm, damp aroma rising from my cup. My senses came to life as if the drink was a sacred elixir and had transformed the world around me. The river glistened like liquid silver and the grass along the embankment was a luscious green carpet. The blossom trees were a spectacle to behold, each precious flower quivering as if it was a soft pink butterfly preparing for flight. I imagined I could hear the flapping of their delicate wings amidst the ripple of voices and the hum of the traffic.

It wasn't the coffee that intoxicated me; it wasn't even the joy of being in Paris in springtime. It was the joy that I felt in my heart. I had foolishly thought I had been in love before but I was only now learning the difference between lust and love, between adoration and mutual admiration and between total submission and the melding of souls.

I was sitting outside a café with a perfect view of the

Seine and a glimpse of the Eiffel Tower glinting in the morning sun as I waited for Ben. He had set off to buy some supplies for my birthday picnic. Meanwhile, I was supposed to be finishing off a piece of work so we could spend the afternoon together but I had become mesmerized by my surroundings, overcome by my swelling heart and I could concentrate on nothing else.

How had it taken me so long to discover true love? As with many things, I could trace it back to my childhood. I had spent so much energy trying to please my father, relinquishing my own dreams to pander to his in a vain attempt to secure his rationed attention. Then, when he had honoured his family with his presence, it had been such a thrill that it had spurred me on to engender more. Unwittingly, I had been trying to replicate that feeling, that thrill, in my adult life; it had become the blueprint for my future relationships with men.

I scanned the legion of faces in the crowded square, searching out the man who had allowed me to rip up that blueprint and start again. With Ben, I hadn't needed to beg for morsels of attention; if anything it had been the complete opposite. He had been the one watching me whilst I had remained unaware and distant and it was that space in between that had connected us before I even knew it. I was only now learning that we could both have our place in the limelight, neither pushed into the shadows. We were equals and we would find a way to build a life that would satisfy both our needs and desires.

My past was firmly behind me and I was looking forward to the rest of my life and for the first time, I didn't run away from the idea of starting a family. I wanted to marry Ben and I wanted to return to our cottage in the Welsh hills, to be a wife and mother. Ben was not a man made from the same mould as my father and family life with him was going to be a whole new experience.

As I drained my coffee, the last sip left a grainy bitterness in my mouth. I played with the textures it left on my tongue as I watched a figure walking across the cobbles. He had a large bouquet of bright red roses in front of him, obscuring his face. I wondered if it was Ben but I couldn't be sure as he weaved through the crowd. Such clichéd gestures of love had peppered my past. Alex in particular had been a frequent visitor to the florist but I had never had the courage to tell him that if anything, I preferred pink roses. I glimpsed the man's face as he veered off course. To my relief, it wasn't Ben.

'Is that how you work these days?' Ben had come from another direction and was standing beside me. 'Direct thought transfer to your computer?'

I looked guilty at the unopened laptop on the table as he kissed my head. When he sat down, I could see that his arms were full. Ben's bouquet consisted of a brown paper grocery bag bursting with goodies and a French loaf sticking out of the top. The aroma of warm bread with undertones of sweet marinades drifted *towards me. The heady scents spoke more of love and our future together than any bunch of gaudy flowers. 'I've been distracted by a new kind of life,' I told him.*

Emma was out of hospital and busy planning the next phase of her life. It was going to be different, it was going to be tough and it was most definitely not going to be normal. The plan was to begin radiotherapy at the beginning of February, which was only a couple of weeks away. Intent on tying up loose ends, Bannister's Kitchens and Bathrooms was first on her list.

'Emma, how lovely to see you,' Jennifer said, rushing over to give her a hug.

Emma did a double take. To all appearances, the woman in front of her was a consummate professional, her clothes demur and businesslike. She looked a lot less like the Jennifer of old and more like . . . well, more like Emma.

'I've only dropped by to say hello and to pick up the last of my things,' Emma replied. 'I've already spoken to your dad.'

'I know.'

'He was very kind,' Emma told her as she recalled how Mr Bannister had refused to accept her resignation. He didn't try to convince her that there might still be a chance of her return. She had told him there wasn't and he had seen enough of cancer to know what lay ahead for her but he had insisted that she would remain an employee of the company. No arguments.

'I've packed all your things up like you asked,' explained Gina, coming up to give her friend a hug. 'You should have said you were coming in today, we would have put the welcome banners up.'

'I didn't want you all making a fuss and I'm not staying long, Ben's waiting outside.' The words burned at the back of Emma's throat as she thought about the door she was about to close on a huge part of her life. Her career. 'Is Ally in?'

'I'm here,' Ally said from behind her, her voice as broken as her heart.

Both Ally and Gina had visited Emma in hospital and she had delivered the news to them personally. The experience had clearly left them traumatized but at least in an office setting, they were all doing their best to staunch their tears.

'I have a bone to pick with you,' Emma told her.

'What have I done now?' Ally said with a trembling smile.

Emma pulled Ally into the corridor for a quiet word. She stepped closer to her and in a motherly gesture, brushed a lock of hair away from Ally's eyes. 'You've upset my favourite nurse.'

'I'm sorry, Emma,' she said, biting down on her lip. 'I should have told you about Peter but it was only a couple of dates.'

'Do you like him?'

'Yes, but . . .'

'I know,' Emma told her. 'Me.'

Ally nodded. 'I spent most of the time interrogating him. I think it was a matter of me dumping him before he dumped me.'

Emma shook her head. 'I won't have this on my conscience. Set the ground rules if you have to, work out how much you should or shouldn't talk about what's happening to me, let him know how much you can deal with hearing, but give it another try. You need to have someone with you and I think Peter would be good for you.'

With the lecture over and promises made, Emma returned to the office. She asked Jennifer if she could use the computer and when she was logged in she quickly found the files she needed. They were a hidden collection of archived creative notes, strategy and design suggestions, messages and reports. This would remove all doubt about the extent of Emma's input. 'These are for your dad. I know he's still prevaricating over appointing consultants, so here's all the background thinking to the present campaign. He might find it helpful,' Emma explained, hoping that Jennifer had more sense than she herself had once shown and wouldn't hand the files directly to Alex allowing him to lay claim to her work one last time. From Ally and Gina's reports, she had so far spurned all the attention Alex had been showering on her.

'I'll show him,' Jennifer promised.

There was something in her voice that gave Emma hope that she would. But it was out of her hands. She had been party to Alex's deception but now at least the truth was out. 'I'd better go,' she said. Her body tensed at the thought of leaving the office for the very last time.

'Do you want to take this?' Jennifer asked, pointing to the sprightly looking spider plant on her desk.

'I think you're doing a pretty good job, you keep it.'

Emma almost made it to the door without a tear being shed but Ally looked like she needed a hug. 'We'll come see you soon,' Ally promised as her eyes began to glisten.

There was nothing Emma could do to stem the flow so she wrapped her arms around her friend instead and let her sob. 'I'm depending on it. I still have plans and you and Gina are part of them.'

Ally eventually lifted her head from Emma's shoulder and looked at her expectantly. Emma glanced down at the damp patch she had left on her shoulder along with a black smudge. 'Although next time wear waterproof mascara.'

'Sorry,' sniffed Ally, whose face was also smeared with makeup.

Emma was about to make a second attempt at leaving when pitiful howls rose from behind her. They both looked around to see Gina crying like a baby. Jennifer was doing her best to comfort her and when Gina lifted her head, there was a mark on Jennifer's shoulder that mirrored Emma's. The burning sensation at the back of Emma's throat had crept towards the back of her nose and she knew she couldn't hold back the tears for much longer.

'I'd better go,' she said, picking up the box that Gina had set aside for her, building herself up for the moment when she would remove the last remnants of her existence from the place she had once thought would collapse without her. 'But if you still need me, you know where I am.'

'I might just hold you to that,' Jennifer told her with a tentative smile. 'I know it looks like I'm filling your shoes, but I'm not. I've still got so much more to learn but I'm getting there. I won't let anyone undo all of your good work.'

Silently thanking Jennifer for allowing her to leave with her dignity intact, she turned to the door and felt Ally gently place a hand on her back; no more words were needed.

She took two steps and then her perfect exit was hijacked by a huge bouquet of red roses blocking the door. From behind the blooms, a pair of furtive eyes appeared, but Emma was less interested in Alex's face as she was in the sense of familiarity that suddenly overwhelmed her. She closed her eyes to push back the hallucination that threatened, telling herself it was little more than a real-life coincidence. But as she swallowed back the bitter taste of coffee grinds that coated her tongue and the smell of warm bread and herbs filled her nostrils she knew the monster in her head was still playing its games. Relief flooded her when she opened her eyes and rather than a view of the Seine, she found Alex still standing in front of her like an idiot, unsure what to do next.

'Hello, Emma,' he said at last.

She could almost follow his thought process as it played out in the expressions on his face. The flowers were undoubtedly intended for Jennifer but it was the unexpected visitor in front of him that he proffered them towards.

Emma sidestepped the rather pathetic gesture and was met by a far more rewarding view. 'I thought you might like some help,' Ben said, casting a curious glance towards Alex who was now trying to creep past Emma.

With the box in one hand and an arm around Emma's waist, Ben led her away and she didn't look back. She let the sense of familiarity that had set every nerve in her body on edge slowly slip away. She felt safe again and what was more, she was strangely comforted by the sense that she had, if only briefly, stepped closer towards the world of her imagination.

'I expect you're wondering why I called you here today,' Emma said as she gave Ally and Gina her most stern look. She was holding court in what was now her own personal booth at the bistro. It was the ideal location, close to Ben, close to the action and it provided a welcoming meeting place for the friends and family who would play a key role in her evolving plans. Today's lunch date was part of those plans and would pave the way for one of the highlights in Emma's life.

'I assumed it was because you were missing us but by the look on your face, I'd say we have something to worry about,' replied Ally.

'Please say it's nothing awful,' whimpered Gina. 'I don't think I could take any more bad news.'

Emma chose her next words carefully. She wasn't as blasé about her mortality as she had been, not now she knew it was true. 'I've already told you I'm not going to get better. How much worse could it possibly get?' she said as kindly as she could.

Gina twisted a serviette nervously in her fingers. 'I don't know,' she replied with a shrug. 'Maybe that you were going to . . . hrmph, grmph.' Her final words were muffled by the hand clamped over her mouth and only when Gina stopped trying to talk did Ally remove it.

'I don't think we wanted to hear that,' growled Ally. 'So, Emma, put us out of our misery before Gina has a chance to open her mouth again. Please.'

'I want you to help me plan my wedding.'

There were gasps of shocked delight and Gina clapped her hands excitedly.

'You're getting married? To Ben?' stammered Ally, who had already been struggling to keep up with Emma's whirlwind romance.

'Duh, what's the point in planning her wedding if she isn't getting married? And you call me thick,' mocked Gina.

'Actually,' interrupted Emma, 'it's not exactly going to be a real wedding.'

'Oh,' Gina said, deflating like a balloon. 'But I wanted to be your bridesmaid. I'd have a midnight-blue dress, simple and elegant. The flowers would be cream to match your ivory dress with lime greens and yellows, maybe a flash of burgundy too. Naturally, Louise would be your maid of honour and Ally could be another of the brides-maids but we would have to do something about her hair.'

'It's got something to do with the story you're writing, hasn't it?' Ally guessed once Gina had replaced her ramblings with a pout.

Emma nodded but it was the picture Gina had painted in her mind's eye that made her smile. 'It certainly has,' she said, stroking her fingers reverently across the lid of her laptop, which was never far from reach.

When Gina looked more confused than ever, it was clear that Emma would have to bring them up to speed quickly so that they could help her with the next chapter. She ran through a brief synopsis, skirting as much as possible over the role that Alex had once played in her imaginary world. 'And now I'm planning on marrying Ben in the bombed-out church on the first day of spring.'

Gina looked startled but then quite impressed. 'St Luke's? Now that would be an interesting venue but can you get married there?' she asked. St Luke's stood in a prime position in the centre of Liverpool and despite its perfectly preserved façade, the interior had been totally destroyed by a bomb during the Blitz. It was still being maintained but it was by no means a working church.

'I've no idea, probably not, but it doesn't matter. It's not a real wedding,' Emma reminded her.

'So it's an imaginary wedding, am I correct?' Gina asked, suddenly sounding very officious as she pulled back her shoulders.

'Correct,' confirmed Emma, thankful that her friend was finally joining the dots.

'Budget?' asked Ally.

'Unlimited of course,' answered Gina with an alarming glint of excitement in her eyes.

Emma grimaced as she imagined where Gina's thoughts had turned and a view of fairytale carriages and white doves came to mind. 'It needs to be realistic,' she warned before leaning over to retrieve a pink envelope that had been pushed to the far end of the table, perched between a saltcellar and a bottle of olive oil. 'But I do have this.'

She opened up the envelope and prised open the card without removing it to retrieve a single piece of paper. She held it between her thumb and index finger as if it were contaminated.

Ally pushed her glasses up as she took a closer look. 'It's a cheque,' she said knowledgably.

'You don't need to be an accountant to work that out. How much?' demanded Gina, nudging Ally out of the way so she could read it. 'Wow.'

'It was supposed to be his contribution for my trip to Boston.'

'It seems a lot of money to waste on an imaginary wedding. Couldn't I tempt you to go on a real shopping trip?' Gina said.

Emma shrugged as she returned the contents to the

envelope and tossed it to one side. 'I don't want his money. Now, back to this wedding. Let's imagine shall we that my wonderful father has stumped up the cash. How are we going to spend it, ladies?'

It was late afternoon and the lunchtime mayhem hadn't eased; in fact, it was getting busier. Steven was being extra attentive despite the demands on his time and arrived at Emma's booth with yet another cup of coffee.

'Don't worry, it's decaf this time.'

'Do you think you'll need this table soon?' Emma asked, almost hoping he would tell her to go home. She was starting to feel tired and her head throbbed, punishment for starting to use her computer again but she couldn't help herself, there was still so much more of her life to explore and she wanted to write as much as she could before her treatment began.

Steven tutted. 'It's your table for as long as you need it.'

Emma's guilt couldn't be eased as she took another look around the restaurant. Louise was leading a couple to the last vacant table. They were both elegantly dressed and the gentleman insisted on helping his lady friend with her coat before pulling out her chair.

'Is that Iris?' Emma asked, not trusting her own eyesight.

'It's a first date,' whispered Steven. 'That's why Jean's offered to work another shift so she can make sure the food's perfect.'

'And have a sneaky peak at what's going on while she's at it,' guessed Emma.

They watched as Louise settled her customers and then rushed over with an excited glint in her eye.

'Steven, could you take their drinks order for me?'

He winked at Emma. 'I'll be back with an update.'

'So what do you think?' Louise asked.

'I can't really tell from here,' replied Emma, straining to get a good look at Iris's beau.

'Not him,' she said. 'The bistro. It's full!'

With the exception of Christmas Day, it was the first time that Emma had seen the restaurant so busy for a very long time. 'You've done well,' Emma agreed.

'*We've* done well,' Louise corrected. 'I couldn't have done it without you.'

'I gave you a few ideas, that's all.'

'And I've had a few ideas of my own, things like putting in WiFi but I'd like you to take a look if you have time?' Louise said and without waiting for a reply, she sat down and took out her order pad. She had been making notes and from the different coloured inks, it was clear that she had been building up ideas for some time. 'Right,' she said.

Emma reached over and closed the notepad before Louise could continue. 'It's about time you had a little more faith in yourself. Follow your instincts,' she said. 'I organized Christmas Day but everything you've done since then has been your doing. The new menu; Iris and Jean's specials; the discounts. It's all working and I have to say the only new idea I had was about installing WiFi but you've already got that one covered. Louise, there really isn't anything I could add that you aren't already capable of, not now.'

Tears sprung in Louise's eyes, she had waited a long time to receive her sister's approval but she knew better than to say anything too sentimental. Emma would have shot her down in flames and she knew it. 'Was that Dad's card I saw you showing Gina and Ally?' Louise asked instead.

'Yes, but don't worry, I'm not going to bank the cheque. He can have his money back.'

'I've been in touch with him and he's suggested meeting up with us.'

'Not a chance,' Emma said as an old anger glowed into life.

'But you need to resolve this,' began Louise.

'No,' Emma insisted, her tone harsh enough to raise curious glances from neighbouring customers. 'It was bad enough seeing the email from him, and no, I still haven't replied. He can wait and I'm too busy.'

'I didn't give him your email address,' Louise said when she saw the unspoken accusation in Emma's eyes. 'I think he must have found it online. If he went to all of that trouble . . .' Louise said, determined to push the issue.

'That hardly counts as putting himself out and the answer is still no,' Emma insisted, bringing the argument to a swift close.

Louise pursed her lips and held her tongue but Emma felt the need to reinforce her position. 'No,' she said again, sending Louise scuttling off to look after her more affable customers.

No sooner had she left than Ben appeared out of the kitchen looking hot and almost as exhausted as Emma felt. He was the reason she had been prepared to sit in the booth all afternoon. Even though he was working, it had been enough to know that he was near and that she would be there waiting for him when he finished work.

'Do I get to keep you this time?' she asked hopefully as Ben sat down with a heavy sigh.

'You certainly do.' They both looked up as Steven magically appeared with another coffee, this one for Ben.

'I was hoping to have you all to myself?' Emma suggested as Steven made no sign of moving.

It was Steven's turn to sigh. 'I just thought that if you were about to show Ben what you've been writing, that I could take a look too. It would help if I knew a little bit more about your wedding plans,' he said hopefully.

'Really?' Emma said.

Steven was a new admission to her circle of trust and whilst Emma had been working with her friends on the details of the wedding, Ben had been tasked with writing the wedding speeches. It had been a burden he was more than willing to share. The best man should write his own speech he had argued.

'It would help me get into the zone if I could picture all of those beautiful bridesmaids,' Steven said.

Emma made a point of pushing her laptop a little further out of his reach. 'You're persistent, I'll give you that.'

'I get the message,' he said, moving off at last.

'So can *I* see?' Ben asked but as he reached out for the computer, Emma slapped his hand.

'Not a chance,' she said. 'It's bad luck to see the bride before the wedding and we need all the luck we can get.'

'No, we don't,' Ben told her and the confidence in his voice left little room for doubt. 'I'm going to make sure you get everything your heart desires.'

Emma was about to tell him that he couldn't, that her dreams would never come true but she looked into his eyes and knew as long as she had his love, it would be enough to create their dreams on paper. 'OK,' she said, pulling at one of the many threads of the story she had yet to weave. 'What about the honeymoon? Where do you think we should go?'

Ben didn't even pause for breath. 'Hawaii.'

Emma wrinkled her nose as if to dismiss the idea. 'More opportunities for you to wear that gaudy shirt?'

'You started the trend,' Ben reminded her. 'But it's not only the fashion that we'd have to look forward to. Think of the golden beaches and the palm trees where we can lounge in hammocks, sipping cocktails. And then when we get itchy feet, there are plenty of exotic islands to explore.'

'Tell me more,' Emma replied as she started to warm to his tropical paradise.

'It's not only a new place to visit, it represents our relationship.'

'It does?'

Ben reached out and took Emma's hands in his before raising them to his lips. He didn't kiss them but she felt the warmth of his breath on her fingers and it made her shudder with delight. 'I want to show you the smouldering volcanoes where our passion can start to rise.'

Emma couldn't help herself. She laughed. 'I'm starting to think I need to keep my computer under lock and key or you'll be adding even more chapters while my back's turned.'

Ben began to laugh too but then he caught a look in Emma's eyes. It was a sense of grief she had been doing her best to hide. 'I don't want to miss a moment with you, Emma,' he said. 'I love you.' His words blew gently across her fingers and reached out towards her heart.

'And I love you,' she answered, her smile erasing the sadness in her eyes. 'And I don't think I'll ever get tired of hearing it.'

She focused her mind on the happiness she felt and not the thoughts that haunted her. She concentrated on the here and now, knowing it would be far too fleeting and hoping she would be able to remember this moment in all its glorious detail. It was a moment worth preserving.

Emma had weaned herself off the more powerful painkillers to keep her thoughts clear but she was once again taking steroids and the inevitable restlessness had returned. Despite yet another long day at the bistro,

Emma found herself wide awake long past midnight but it wasn't only her medication keeping sleep at bay. Emma was wrestling with night terrors of her own making. She was plagued with dark thoughts that couldn't be ignored in the pitiless depths of a lonely night as easily as they could in the hustle and bustle of the Traveller's Rest.

She was lying on her back with her eyes wide open, fighting an irrepressible conviction that if she closed them now she may never wake up. Her eyes strained against the darkness, producing beads of light that sparkled like a host of stars above her and she felt herself being pulled towards them as if she had found a window to the heavens. She could feel the gentle rush of air being pushed in and out of her lungs. For a moment, she held her breath and allowed the stillness to wrap around her like a shroud. She imagined herself lying in the sarcophagus she had seen at the museum. As if to reinforce the image, in the distance she could hear the persistent tapping of a deathwatch beetle, counting down towards her impending doom. She exhaled and pushed the thought away but the tapping continued.

The sound gave Emma an excuse to clamber out of bed and search out its source and as she padded across her bedroom, it became not just louder but identifiable. Emma rested her head on the door in disappointment and frustration. One of the battles she thought she had laid to rest had been resurrected.

As Emma crept down the hall, she could see the living room immersed in an unmistakeable soft glow that could only come from a computer screen. Meg was typing away and didn't even notice that she had been caught out, not until Emma put her hand on her shoulder, making her mum jump with fright.

'Should I ask?' Emma asked solemnly.

'Em, I didn't hear you,' Meg said, turning towards her daughter. Her face glowed in an ominous green light that gave her a ghostly appearance. By the heart-wrenching look she gave her daughter, Emma's appearance was just as spectral. Meg turned back to the screen and closed the online form she had been completing.

'Too late, I saw it,' Emma told her flatly. 'Which whacky doctor have you been trying to track down now?'

Meg didn't reply straight away, choosing instead to trace her fingers across the keyboard as she searched for an answer. 'I've been in touch with the Boston clinic, just to check,' she began.

'And?' Emma asked as she tried to keep her anger in check. She was trying so hard to come to terms with her fate, to accept that she was dying. It may not be the path she had chosen for herself but at least she could plan the time she had left with a degree of certainty. She had thought her mum had accepted that too but it had been yet another false hope. Meg may have stopped working long hours and was spending more time with Emma, but, rather than help her on her final journey, she was planning to pull her away at the last minute towards another path, one that could only lead to another dead-end, literally.

'They've officially taken you off the programme,' Meg said, trying to control her own anger.

'I'm glad. And if that was another application for another clinical trial, then delete it. I'm not going. I'm staying here.'

Meg swivelled her chair around to face Emma. 'I still think we need to keep our options open. I haven't bothered you with this stuff because I know you're so wrapped up with Ben at the moment but it doesn't mean I have to stop looking.'

'It has nothing to do with me being wrapped up with Ben. I don't want to look because I know there isn't any point.'

'But I've just been reading . . .' began Meg.

'Stop! For God's sake, Mum, stop!' begged Emma, tears stinging her eyes. 'I'll do what's necessary, I'll undergo the radiotherapy and the chemo and any other treatments Mr Spelling is prepared to throw at me to give me more time but I'm staying here. I've accepted that I'm dying, why can't you?'

'Because I can't!' Meg yelled back in the faintest whisper. 'Don't make me give up, Emma. Please, I can't do it!'

Emma didn't know how to respond and even if she had found the words, she couldn't physically speak. The two women stared at each other, both breathing rapidly in a desperate attempt to keep their tempers in check.

Meg couldn't hold Emma's gaze so she turned her back on her daughter and began to purposefully close down her computer. The room was plunged into darkness and an eerie silence descended as the machinery was silenced. Neither Emma nor her mum moved.

'I'm sorry, Mum,' Emma said at last, reaching out blindly towards her.

Through the darkness, Meg found her daughter's proffered hand and gripped it desperately in both of hers, lifting it towards her face, which was now wet with tears. 'All I wanted from life was for both my daughters to be safe and happy. Nothing else. That's all I wanted, that's all I want.'

'You can't fix this, Mum. Please stop trying,' begged Emma.

When Meg didn't answer, Emma felt an urge to fill the silence and it was almost as if the darkness was trying to extract a confession. There were some secrets that Emma had kept from her mum for too long. 'The book I'm writing, it's about me,' she said. 'I know it's going to be hard for you to take any comfort from that now but I hope one day you will. Mum, I'm going to live a very long and very amazing life. I am going to live happily ever after.'

There was a pause and Emma wondered if her mum was giving her one of her dismissive looks. 'Is that enough? To write about it?'

'It has to be enough. There aren't any other options.'

Emma heard her mum stifle another sob. 'OK,' she

said, the magnitude of her reply summed up in two innocent letters.

'And it's not like there aren't good things in the real world too,' continued Emma. 'Ben loves me.'

'And you love him too, don't you?' Meg replied and Emma sensed her mum smiling.

Emma nodded even though her mum couldn't see her. 'Yes, I do,' she said. 'He makes me happy, he really does.'

Meg stood up, still holding her daughter's hand tightly. 'Then I suppose if I can't keep you safe, the least I can do is keep you happy. If you think he's right for you and he won't let you down then that's good enough for me. You have my blessing.'

'I'm glad you said that,' began Emma as she thought back to her conversation with Ben earlier. He had said that he didn't want to waste a moment with her and she was struggling through the nights on her own. There was an obvious solution. It was far too soon to think about Ben moving in, they hadn't even slept together but in another lifetime they had just been married. 'I want you two to get to know each other better and it's his day off tomorrow. How about we have a family dinner here, just the three of us?'

'That sounds lovely,' agreed Meg. There was a pause as emotions were forced back with a hard swallow. 'Anything you want, Emma. I'll do anything you want.'

'Then stop creeping around in the middle of the night trying to find a cure,' Emma said. Her next words were so painful to speak out loud that they choked the breath out of her. 'At some point you're going to have to let me go, Mum.'

The sound of her mum gulping for air was heart wrenching. 'My heart's breaking, Emma and I can't bear the thought of losing you,' Meg said in a barely audible whisper.

'I don't want to be responsible for destroying your life; I won't have that as my legacy. Promise me that you'll get through this when I'm gone. Promise me you'll be OK, Mum.'

The only indication that her mum agreed was the soft swish of her hair sweeping her shoulders as she nodded. 'Ben isn't the only one who loves you, Emma,' Meg said, pulling her daughter towards her through the darkness and holding onto her for dear life. 'I love you so much.'

'And I love you, Mum. I always will. Always.'

Emma could feel her mum trembling and as they clung onto each other she knew that Meg was doing what Emma had done earlier that day, savouring a precious moment, committing every minute detail to memory. She could only hope that it would bring her mum some comfort when Emma was no longer there to hold.

12

It was hot, almost unbearably so and the shade of the lush palms that whispered to us in the sea breeze offered little respite. Dappled light played across our bodies as we lay intertwined, rocking gently in a hammock. A tall cocktail glass rested on my chest and I could feel the condensation dripping onto my body, the fleeting chill bringing delightful relief to the heat. I could feel the gentle rise and fall of Ben's chest as his breathing slowed, a telltale sign that he was drifting off to sleep again. His body felt damp with sweet sweat.

'Can you believe how beautiful this place is? Just look at that scenery,' I said, peeking through the swaying palms at the cliffs that rose up steeply from the shoreline.

Ben snored softly in response. I nudged him and he opened an eye to look at me. 'Hmm, beautiful.'

'You were the one who insisted on Hawaii, the least you can do is climb a volcano and take some pretty pictures.'

He kissed my shoulder. 'Where did that drink come from?'

As I laughed, my glass jiggled and my grip tightened on it. 'The waiter brought it to me while you were asleep. He thought I looked hot.'

'You are hot,' Ben assured me, leaving his lips hovering over my skin, which tingled with excitement.

'You have to say that, I'm your wife,' I told him. How could I feel anything but insignificant when surrounded by such perfect beauty, from the clear blue of the ocean to the gleam of the golden sands? How could I compare to the delicate shells scattered across the beach, each one a tiny work of art, intricately carved by nature with a lining that captured shimmering rainbows?

'You're beautiful,' he insisted.

'I can't believe you just did that!' cried Emma.

Ben was laughing and didn't look in the least bit remorseful. They were lying on Emma's bed, relaxing after a surprisingly enjoyable dinner with her mum. Emma had her computer perched on her lap with Ben lying alongside her. It had been against Emma's better judgement to let him watch as she typed and she was now paying for her misguided trust. He had pulled the laptop away from her and written the last line before Emma could stop him.

'You are beautiful,' he said. 'I won't have you thinking anything else, not in that world and not in this.' His tone was surprisingly serious.

Emma unconsciously pulled at the edges of her headband, which was wide enough to hide the latest war wound on her scalp. 'OK, I won't delete it as long as you step away from the laptop,' she conceded.

Ben dutifully shifted position on the bed. He was wearing his Hawaiian shirt but that hadn't been his only contribution to the story Emma was writing. The whole day had been about bringing a little of their imaginary world to life. They had toyed with the idea of going to the beach but gale-force winds were never going to summon up images of a tropical island despite Ben's best intentions. Emma had been willing to give it a go but Ben was still a little nervous about pushing her too far, he didn't want the responsibility of another disastrous expedition. So as a compromise, he had bought a DVD of *South Pacific*, leis made from artificial flowers to wear around their necks and all the trappings for making cocktails. It had reminded Emma more of a cheesy hen night than a honeymoon but she couldn't be happier. Simply having Ben with her was enough and she intended to keep him all night.

'Is it safe to continue?' Emma asked, raising an eyebrow. Ben was now facing Emma but he had remained close. He hooked his arm below her crossed legs and began to stroke the side of her thigh.

'I'm ready.'

'You're beautiful too,' I told him. 'I don't know how I got so lucky.'

Ben didn't respond and I guessed he was falling back to sleep. We're married, I told myself and savoured the sense of satisfaction that thought gave me. I felt safe and, more importantly, complete. If I could bottle a moment it would be this one, it really couldn't get any better than this.

'I love you,' Ben whispered and my perfect moment began to sparkle with its own rainbows.

'And I love you,' I said, almost choking with emotion.

Ben leaned over me, kissing his way up my arm, across my chest, following the strap of my bikini before finally reaching the cocktail glass still perched on my chest, leaving me breathless. I groaned as he kissed my lips briefly before returning his attention to the glass. He gripped the straw between his teeth and then wrapped his lips around it as he started to drink, never taking his eyes off me.

I held his gaze for the longest time, distracted by his beautiful brown eyes, exactly as he intended. The glass was practically empty by the time I realized what he was doing.

'Hey, you drank it all,' I cried, pushing him away. The hammock twisted in midair and then started to tip. I let go of the glass but not the hammock, clinging on for dear life. Ben wasn't so quick. He was unceremoniously dumped onto the ground along with the remnants of my cocktail, landing on the sand with a thump. I heard the distinct crunch of shells. As I swayed back and forth in the hammock, his shocked face came in and out of view,

*his mouth open and a sprinkling of exotic fruit slices
sliding down his body.*

'Did I really deserve that?' Ben laughed as Emma finished
reading her latest instalment.

'Maybe you'll think twice before you try to take over
my writing again,' Emma warned as she shut down the
computer and pushed it to one side so that there were
no barriers left between them.

Ben took advantage of the empty space and slid over
Emma's lap, which was still warm from the heat of the
laptop, before moving ever upwards until they were nose
to nose. 'I think we need to make another one of those
perfect moments,' he said, waiting until he was sure he
had her complete attention. She held her breath. 'I love
you, Emma, more than I've ever loved anyone, more
than I thought I possibly could.'

The words made every nerve in her body tingle and
she had to suppress a groan. She was about to tell him
she loved him too but he cut off her words with a deep
and lingering kiss. The kiss became more intense and
they synchronized their movements until they were lying
down, wrapped in each other's arms. When the kiss
ended, they were both breathless.

'Are we going too fast?' Ben asked between ragged
breaths.

'Yes,' replied Emma with a half-laugh. 'But I'm living
my life at lightning speed so you'll just have to keep up.'

'But that doesn't mean we have to rush everything,'

Ben replied. He kissed her nose, let his lips hover briefly over her mouth before moving down towards her neck as Emma groaned out loud this time.

'Will you stay the night?' she whispered.

Ben continued to kiss her neck as he replied, 'Yes.'

'Will you stay every night?' Ben stopped what he was doing and when he looked up, Emma didn't know what to expect.

His expression wasn't the look of horror that she had feared, nor was there a hint of reluctance. He looked ready. 'You want us to move in together?'

'I'd have to talk it through with Mum and I know it's not exactly an idyllic cottage in Wales, but it's a way for us to spend more time together, if that's what you want?'

'It doesn't have to be a cottage in Wales, just like it doesn't have to be a Hawaiian beach. The best memories I could possibly make are when I close my eyes and kiss you,' he said. 'It doesn't matter whether the wind is howling outside or we can hear the sound of waves crashing against the shore. Once I can feel your lips on mine, I'm home.'

'Then close your eyes.'

Emma slid her body on top of his and they both closed their eyes. Silently, they started to undress each other and when Ben kissed her bare flesh, she dug her fingers into the quilt cover and found warm silken sand.

When Emma awoke she felt different and different for Emma usually meant something bad. She was still half asleep but she felt warm, too warm, and her body felt heavy. A rush of adrenalin coursed through her body and with a sudden gasp she was awake. She opened her eyes. The room was still in darkness and dawn a long way off but she glanced towards the lightless window anyway, willing the day to arrive and save her from this latest night terror. She drew her eyes away as the last remnants of sleep left her body. She tried to turn on her side but couldn't move. More of her senses came to life, bringing with them alien smells and sounds. A long hiss of air almost made her jump and a fraction of a second later, almost made her laugh out loud.

Ben continued to snore softly behind her as Emma began to relax.

She looked at the clock. It was still early but she needed to take her medication. Her mum usually left a tray containing pills and a glass of water on her bedside cabinet for the morning but Meg had made herself scarce and Emma hadn't seen her since she and Ben had disappeared into her bedroom after dinner the night before. She felt like a naughty teenager but at least her mum was treating her like an adult. And like an adult, Emma would have to take charge of her own medication.

Slipping her legs from beneath the duvet, Emma eased herself out of bed without disturbing Ben. She went to stand up but the night had taken more out of her than she first realized and she felt dizzy. She let herself slip to the floor in a partially controlled fall. She was gasping but as quietly as she could so as not to wake Ben. If he saw her struggling, he might blame himself. He might be too afraid to touch her again. She thought of the night they had just shared and panic rose in her chest at the thought of losing it.

She was sitting on the floor, her back against the bed and her eyes closed as her mind began to detach itself from her surroundings. She stretched out her hands to ground herself as the hallucination took over and her fingers wrapped around a tiny object lying in the shadows beneath her bed. She felt warm and the light beyond her closed eyelids grew in intensity. When she opened them, the aquamarine waters sparkled all the way to the horizon. She looked from the shoreline towards the impossibly steep hillside. Lush palms obscured the sleeping volcanoes but she knew they were there. She heard Ben behind her, still snoring. She turned towards him and the pre-dawn darkness returned with a blink of the eye.

Emma slowed her breathing and was left with only tantalizing hints of where her seizure had taken her. She tasted coconut in her mouth and felt the gritty sand between her toes. She lifted her hand and when she opened it, there was no doubt in her mind where she had been. The iridescent rainbows captured within the shell burst into life as light flooded the room.

'Emma? What are you doing down there?' Ben had switched on the bedside lamp and was leaning over the bed, concern on his face.

She lifted up the shell towards him. 'I found this,' she said. There was more awe in her voice than fear. It was only as she lifted it towards him that she noticed a rough yellow line running around the outer edge of the shell. It was the remnants of glue, yellowed with age. It was one of the shells that had fallen off the photo frame.

'A souvenir from our honeymoon?' Ben asked. He was rubbing sleep from his eyes and didn't notice the look of disappointment on Emma's face.

'I wish.' She tentatively rose to her feet and this time remained standing. Discarding the shell on the window sill, she headed for the door where there was a tray containing pills and water waiting for her on the other side. She picked it up and returned to the safety of her bed.

'Did you sleep well?' she asked as she took her medication.

'Yes, I could get used to this,' he said.

'Me too.'

'I'm not too sure how your mum's going to feel about it, though,' Ben added.

'She'll be fine.' Emma was sure that if the day before had been anything to go by, her mum would enjoy Ben's company almost as much as Emma.

'Of course, we could always consider moving into my place.'

Emma shook her head. 'Would you mind if we didn't?' She knew there would be dark days to come and although Ben would do his best to help her through her treatment, there were going to be times when Emma would want her mum and besides, with a bedroom available above the bistro, she was sure she could persuade Louise to move in as Steven's new lodger. She had it all planned and she didn't think Steven would object, he was putting his heart and soul into the bistro and Emma suspected that it wasn't the restaurant itself that held his affection. 'It might be a good bargaining tool but I really don't think Mum will need much persuading.'

'I might make myself scarce when you broach that particular subject.'

'Don't go too far,' Emma told him.

'Never,' he said. Ben lifted his hand and gently pushed back a lock of Emma's hair, briefly sweeping his fingers across the patch of shaven scalp, her headscarf long since discarded. She was amazed at how relaxed she felt, confident that he wouldn't recoil from her. Emma had bared her soul and Ben had seen her beauty, not her flaws.

'Good, because I'm planning on spending the rest of my life with you.'

Emma watched as thoughts of the future passed across Ben's face like a dark cloud. He was aware that his fears had been exposed so blinked them away. He moved his hand slowly down her body until his palm came to rest on her stomach. 'How about a honeymoon baby?' he suggested.

It was Emma's turn to blink away the fears. The thought of immersing herself into a world where she would become a mother terrified her, not because she didn't want to have children but because she so desperately did. Having a family hadn't simply been part of the life she had once planned for herself, it had been fundamental to it. It was what everything else was meant to build towards. Her cancer had destroyed the foundations for that dream five years earlier and whilst her career had been the first casualty, the thing she grieved most was the probability, and now certainty, that she wouldn't live long enough to have children and see them grow.

'What is it?' Ben was asking. He was about to move his hand away, sensing Emma's reluctance, but she placed her hand over his.

'It's going to be a challenge, but I'm ready,' she said, knowing that her choices in life were limited but her imaginary life was not, not unless she applied her own restrictions.

'You're sure?' Ben asked, Emma's uncertainty transferring to him.

'I'm sure. Now, what time do you have to be at the bistro?'

'Ten at the latest,' Ben told her. 'Do you want to come with me, spend another day at the office?'

'I would love to but I have a hospital appointment later,' Emma replied, pulling herself back into reality. She had one week left before her radiotherapy started and she had mixed emotions about the treatment that would not only take over her life but drain her of it too. She was more than ready for the fight but she was frightened too. If her tumour failed to respond, it would mark the beginning of the end and she wasn't sure she was ready for that yet. There was still too much of life to experience. 'And after that I might just have a lazy day,' Emma told him. 'I need to slow down a little.'

'If I'm pushing you too hard, you will tell me, won't you?'

Emma kissed his nose. 'I didn't mean you,' she scolded. 'You're the best medicine I could wish for. But it is going to take a while for me to build up to the next phase of our life together and I want to get it right.'

'You will,' Ben said. 'I've seen the way you look after people. You'll make an amazing mum.'

Ben didn't see the tears as Emma shut her eyes, hiding the grief she felt for her unborn children. She let him kiss her and she drew from him the strength to build a magical world around her that would give her the baby to fill her empty arms.

When Emma found herself on her own a little later, the world outside looked bright and far too tempting to ignore. She had told Ben she would take it easy but she was getting cabin fever. He had gone back to the bistro and Meg was making an early start at the office, promising to return after lunch for Emma's trip to the hospital. But that was hours away. The stamina she had started to build before Christmas had been completely depleted by the surgery but she convinced herself that a brisk walk would do her the world of good.

She wasn't fooled by the clear sky and dazzling sunshine. The gales from the day before hadn't completely eased and Emma was glad she had wrapped up well when the wind knocked the breath out of her the moment she stepped outside. She had her chin tucked into her chest and didn't notice Louise until she had practically walked into her.

'What are you doing here?' she demanded, her heart sinking at the thought of returning indoors to play hostess to her sister.

'Nice to see you too! I just thought I'd pay my big sister a visit.'

'I was about to go for a walk along the prom.' Emma looked longingly at the path that led towards the river.

'That's alright, I'll come with you.'

Louise was dressed casually in jeans and a padded gillet but her hair was loose and already whipping around her. The heels she was wearing weren't dangerously high but high enough. 'Are you sure?' Emma asked suspiciously.

'Yeah, I could do with some fresh air,' insisted Louise, marching ahead while Emma stood frozen in disbelief. 'Are you coming?'

The sea breeze was practically gale force as they reached the promenade and turned eastward towards Otterspool. She wondered if anyone would be brave enough to be kite flying in this weather but her curiosity would have to remain unsatisfied, she didn't have the strength for such a mammoth task. The walk to the river's edge alone had tired her but she pushed herself onwards, concentrating more on putting one foot in front of the other than she was on Louise's chatter.

The bitter wind seemed determined to take her breath

from her and she stopped next to a huge anchor, abandoned by its ship to become a lonely statue that would never touch the sea again. As she leant against it, she had run out of patience as well as energy.

'So, are you going to tell me what you're doing here?'

Louise was about to deny any ulterior motive but hesitated. She glanced behind her as if to check her escape route but when she looked back, there was a glint of defiance in her eyes that was so unfamiliar it took Emma by surprise.

'You need to get in touch with Dad.'

Emma's heart sank. 'I've already told you, he can wait. In fact, he can wait forever. We don't need him now.'

'But this could be your last chance to see him. You might regret it,' Louise insisted through gritted teeth. Her blonde hair had wrapped around her face and she was spitting hair out of her mouth as well as the words.

'No, Lou, he might regret it but not me! I won't be here, remember?' Emma was shouting her words above the howl of the wind but that wasn't the only reason as her anger began to grow. 'I don't care if he spends the rest of his life regretting it; in fact I hope he does. He really doesn't deserve my pity.'

'And what about me? Don't I deserve your pity?' Louise yelled back.

Emma didn't respond, she didn't know how to. She didn't see the connection.

'I'm losing you, Emma, and the world I'm going to have to face without you frightens me . . . no, it terrifies me!'

Emma shook her head. She wanted to tell Louise to stop. She felt guilty enough. She didn't need to hear the detail. 'You'll cope. You've got Mum. You don't need Dad.'

'Have I? You really think I've got Mum?' Louise spat out the words. 'Emma, you come first and I don't blame her for that, I'm sure I'd do the same. But when you're . . . afterwards . . . how will I ever be able to turn to Mum for support knowing that whatever my problems are, they're not going to be as big as yours or as bad as this. And even if they were, I'm always going to be compared to you and I'm always going to fall short. I know I wouldn't be able to face what you're going through, not the way you do.'

Louise was shaking and Emma softened, if only a little, and put an arm around her. 'Don't be so hard on yourself, or Mum. You'll cope, you both will.'

'See what I mean?' Louise cried as the anger sunk beneath the waves and anguish broke the surface to take its place. 'You're doing it now! You're being the strong one. How am I ever going to be that strong, Emma? I don't even know how I'll keep myself together, let alone help Mum too.'

'You'll manage,' Emma told her but her breaking heart gave no conviction to her words.

Louise shook her head and her falling tears were quickly whipped away by the howling wind. 'You both keep telling me I have to stand on my own two feet and I'm trying to do that, honestly I am but I don't know how long I can keep it up.'

Emma wasn't aware that she was crying but the tears slid down her cheeks nonetheless. 'You can do it, Lou. You always could and if I hadn't fussed around you so much, you'd believe that too. You're my baby sister and after everything we've been through, I wanted your life to be perfect. I needed one of our lives to be perfect and it wasn't going to be mine,' she said. The confession was burning the back of her throat. 'But it's not my life, it's yours and it's going to go on long after I've gone. You will survive this, you're stronger than you think.'

Louise had her hand clamped over her mouth and for a moment Emma thought she would crumble under the weight of the burden that had just been placed on her shoulders but her sister surprised her. When Louise found the courage to speak there was steel in her voice. 'I wasn't blind. I knew you were trying to live your life vicariously through mine. I knew it and I let you because I felt so guilty. You were the one who got sick and if interfering in my life gave you some purpose then who was I to refuse? I love you, Emma, and I'll do anything for you but please allow me this one thing,' she said. 'I'm going to need a shoulder to cry on and if that can't be Mum then I want to be able to turn to Dad. But if you don't resolve things with him now then he'll never be able to face me. I may not know him as well as I should but I think we both know that's what will happen.'

'Of course he'll face you,' Emma insisted. 'You were his favourite. Why wouldn't he?'

Louise almost laughed. 'Me? You were Daddy's girl.

You were the one that he took with him on his little adventures. I was the spoiled brat, remember? The demanding one that would get what she wanted just so he could escape from her.' When Emma shook her head in disagreement, Louise persisted. 'I was the one who contacted him but who did he respond to? He sent you the money that would keep me quiet but it was still you he replied to.'

Emma moved away from the anchor and away from Louise. She gripped the railings that prevented her from plunging into the angry waters below. She couldn't think straight, her thoughts were as heavy as the churning waves and they sank without trace beneath the weight of her despair.

Emma already knew that she would give in to her demanding sister, it was a family trait. She turned back to Louise. 'What if he's not up to the job? After all, he walked out on us long before I was ill. There's nothing to say he'll ever be there when you need him.'

'But we have to try, Emma, please. Meet him, if only once,' Louise said. The look of defiance had been washed away by tears but Louise wasn't giving up.

'What if he doesn't want to meet me? If he says no, will you give up on this?' Emma asked hopefully.

'We've already talked about it,' Louise said. 'He wants to meet you.'

'Hold on,' Emma interrupted. 'Talked? You've actually talked to him?' Her reaction to the news took her by surprise. They were, after all, referring to their father.

The man Emma had lived with her entire childhood. The man she had once called Daddy. The man she had loved with all her heart. Why should the idea of him speaking to one of his daughters seem so alien to her?

'I'm sorry, Emma. I should have talked to you before now but you haven't exactly made it easy for me.'

'So you actually talked to him?'

Louise nodded.

Emma looked back towards the river and back in time, trying to recall the sound of his voice. 'OK,' she said. Her heart thudded. 'Next time you speak to him, tell him that I will meet him. In fact, tell him that I want to meet him this Friday at two o'clock in the Palm House.'

If she was going to see him, it would have to be before her radiotherapy started, while she still had the strength to face him. She wasn't quite convinced it was the right decision but she was pleased with the challenge she had set her absent father. But her sense of triumph was short-lived.

'Am I invited?' Louise asked.

Emma bit her lip as she considered her reply. She didn't want to cause more damage to Louise's fragile state. 'We both want different things from him,' she started. 'You want a future with him but that's not an option for me and I'm not sure I'd take it even if it was. I certainly don't want some dream reunion, Louise. I want the opportunity to speak my piece and to hear whatever kind of explanation he has to offer for erasing us from his life. So I think it would be better if we met separately. I'll leave it to you to sort out your own arrangements.'

Louise nodded; at last they were in agreement. 'And what about Mum?' she asked. 'What do we tell her?'

Emma sensed that telling their mother was going to be even harder than meeting the man himself. 'We tell her that this doesn't affect our relationship with her, that we're not abandoning her. And you make it clear that you're going to be strong for her and that you'll be there when she needs you. But most of all, we tell her exactly what we're doing. No more secrets,' Emma spoke the last words slowly and clearly as if Louise was hard of hearing. 'But since I've only just asked her if Ben can move in with me, I think maybe we'll leave it until all the arrangements are made.'

'Ben's moving in?' Louise cried, with excitement this time.

'Yes, and if you're done interfering in my life, let me do some interfering in yours.'

Emma was completely exhausted both physically and emotionally. She slipped her arm through Louise's and they began their return journey.

'Like that's something new,' muttered Louise as she huddled close to her sister, who was about to explain their new living arrangements.

13

I was working in London and I managed my time as best I could, commuting weekly rather than daily. Given that I could have been sent anywhere in the world, it was an ideal arrangement, but I was under no illusions. Kate had made London my base because that was where I was needed and she would expect me to relocate without question if the need arose, so I wasn't expecting her to be thrilled with my latest news.

'I can't say I'm not disappointed,' she began.

We were sitting in a riverside café, sharing a plate of sushi and looking out over the Thames. The warm yellow sun and bright blue sky above the river gave the grey waters a hint of colour but it was the bare treetops on the embankment that more accurately reflected the season. It was a few weeks before Christmas and whilst the drop in temperature barely registered in the heart of London, it was another matter at the farm where Ben would have been up early to break up the thick ice that formed on the water troughs.

'But it can't come as that much of a surprise,' I said.

'You know what? Actually, it has. I thought better of you.'

I couldn't help it: I laughed. 'Why do I think you might have taken it better if I'd just confessed to defrauding the company? Kate, I'm pregnant. It's not a crime and surely you could have seen it was only a matter of time. I'm thirty-five, I'm newly married . . .'

'I thought you were following in my footsteps. I didn't think you'd be happy to give up a highflying career to spend the rest of your life milking goats and changing nappies.'

I wanted to tell her goats didn't wear nappies but I was still reeling from what else she was suggesting. 'Who said anything about giving up my career?'

It was Kate's turn to laugh. 'Do you really think you can have it all? Emma, you should know better than to believe everything you read in the glossy magazines; after all, we write half of it.'

I abandoned the tuna roll on my plate, suddenly remembering something about not eating sushi when pregnant. I laid a hand protectively on my stomach, which was still flat and taught. 'I have legal rights,' I reminded her.

Kate dipped a roll into a bowl of soy sauce as she spoke. 'Of course you do and Alsop and Clover is a responsible company but as your employer, we have certain expectations. I'm not saying we can't reorganize your workload so that you can be at home more.'

'So what are you saying?'

'I'm saying it's not going to be the same workload, the same kind of projects. I'm sorry, Emma but you've clipped your own wings. You're not going to be in a position to take on the more demanding, high-profile projects; at least, not for a long time, and that will inevitably affect your status in the company.'

Kate popped the sushi roll in her mouth and swallowed. Then she made a point of having to rush off for a meeting, leaving me to settle the bill. I watched her go, my hand still resting on my stomach. Kate may have been surprised by my news but I was not surprised by her reaction. I was in no rush to leave and pondered my future as I let the river outside carry my thoughts all the way back to my childhood.

It had been a hot and sticky summer's day and the tall ships were sailing into Liverpool. The docks were heaving with sightseers and I had felt so tall, sitting on my dad's shoulders. From my lofty perch I was one of the first to spy the bright sails on the horizon heading towards the safety of the harbour. The day was only one of a handful of happy memories with my father that I could actually recall. The rest, if they had ever existed, had long since plunged into the deep waters of disappointment and betrayal.

It was far easier to bring to mind the more painful memories; they were the ones that had denied him a place by my side as I walked down the aisle. I tried to picture the very last time I had seen him. I had come *home from London to wish Louise well as she headed off for university, my motives far nobler than those of my father who also showed up at the family home. My parents' divorce had been settled and the house was being sold. He was there to collect some pieces of furniture, antiques that we had bought together at auctions and flea markets. Soon afterwards, he returned to his roots in Scotland and contact was severed. A couple of years later when I became ill, my mum had sent a message to him via her ex in-laws, which had prompted the arrival of the greetings card, officially my last contact with him.*

These were not the best memories to focus on as I took my first tentative steps towards parenthood but they were important. It was my father's failures that had made me determined to do things differently. Perhaps Kate was right, I couldn't have it all. I had choices and I was choosing not to follow in her footsteps or those of my father.

It was a bright and blustery day and as the clouds skittered across the sun, shadows played across the park. Emma was sitting next to Ben in the car looking out over Sefton Park. Her eyes were drawn to the Field of Hope, which, in a matter of weeks, would spark into life as one by one bright yellow daffodil heads emerged from the green shoots that peeked bravely through the surface of what was still a frozen landscape. By March, the whole field would be transformed into a seamless sea of gold but for now, Emma could only imagine the scene. Hope, like spring seemed a little beyond her grasp.

'It's nearly two,' Ben said. 'Are you sure you're ready for this?'

There had been a great deal of discussion about the logistics for the meeting. Emma would have preferred to make her own way and give herself time to build up to the moment she would come face to face with her dad, but her health would not allow it. Ben was her companion of choice, but only as far as the outskirts to the park. She would be on her own after that.

Emma continued to look out of the window. 'No, I'm not ready at all,' she said honestly. 'How can a man get fatherhood so wrong?'

'I don't know, Em,' Ben said. 'I promise I'll do a better job.'

'You will if I have anything to do with it,' Emma said but then she winced and was glad that Ben couldn't see her face. Of course he was going to make an amazing father but Emma wouldn't be the one to give him children. She still wasn't sure she had the strength to describe the precious babies that she would never get to hold. Her writing was about to become more challenging and, she feared, more painful.

'Are you sure you don't want me to drop you any nearer?' Ben asked when Emma remained in her seat.

'Here's fine,' Emma replied. From her current vantage point she couldn't see the Palm House. She had asked Ben to drop her off on the opposite side of the park in case she accidentally caught sight of her dad before she was ready.

278

'If he isn't there then phone me and I'll come and pick you up.'

'Don't worry, I can get a taxi home,' Emma insisted as she opened the door, having to push against the wind to keep it open. 'I doubt I'll be that long anyway, whether he's there or not.'

Ben gave her a smile of encouragement and Emma kept the image of his face in her mind as she braved the elements. The park was a beautiful mix of naturalized fields and wooded areas, separated by curving footpaths that gave Emma countless choices for her route to the Palm House. Rather than a direct path, she was drawn into the heart of the park, towards the boating lake. A handful of ducks gave her a curious look before continuing to stalk an excited toddler with a bagful of bread. Their antics distracted her briefly but she pushed herself onwards.

She felt more nervous than she had ever felt in her entire life and for Emma that was saying something. She knew what she wanted to say to her dad and the questions she wanted to ask but she didn't know what the outcome would be or, more specifically, what she wanted from the meeting.

Her head was down so she didn't notice the white frame of the Palm House looming above her, its countless window panes flickering in the sunshine. This part of the park was practically deserted with just two little girls kicking around a bright pink ball to keep her company. When Emma looked over towards their mum, she felt a pang of jealousy. She was tempted to take a seat and watch the children play if only to remind herself of what her father had so cruelly discarded, of what she herself would never hold, to allow her resentment to build and fuel the fire already burning inside her. Fortunately for her dad, Emma was too cold to loiter. She wanted their meeting over and done with.

As she walked through the entrance doors, a wall of heat brought her to a standstill. It wasn't the same kind of heat she had imagined in the dusty streets of Cairo or the golden shores of Hawaii. This heat was heavily scented with a mixture of damp earth and lush foliage. She looked up towards the heavy fronds that were silhouetted against the bright light streaming through the great dome above, deliberately directing her gaze above head height. Her neck began to ache but she wasn't ready to come face to face with her father if indeed he was there.

'Emma?' The greeting came out as a question, which struck Emma as almost comical. Her dad could have easily said, 'Excuse me, are you the daughter I walked out on? The one I haven't seen for the last seven years even though she's been fighting for her life?'

As she dropped her gaze towards the voice, towards her first encounter with her dad, pain cut like a knife across her skull and down her neck, far worse than anything she'd imagined. She grimaced. Somehow it seemed fitting. She was disappointed to see that her dad looked older and greyer but otherwise unchanged. He hadn't even had the decency to grow horns on his head.

She was tempted to refer to him by his first name but instead posed her own question. 'Dad?' she asked

'There's a table over there, would you like to sit down?' He led the way towards a cast-iron bistro table and chairs. 'Would you like a mint?'

Emma politely refused as she sat down with a sense of anticlimax. She had prepared for this moment a thousand times in her head and had never once imagined that their first exchange would be whether or not she wanted a sweet.

John, her dad, popped a mint into his dry mouth and the sight of his nerves helped Emma quell her own. She bided her time and waited for him to open up the conversation.

'It's really lovely in here, isn't it?' he began. 'I remember when this place was derelict and you weren't even allowed to get close to the site let alone inside.'

Emma narrowed her eyes. 'As lovely as it is to share notes on the transformation of the city you left behind, I think we have other things to discuss. Don't you?'

Her words echoed loudly across the Palm House and if her dad had hoped for a private conversation then he was going to be disappointed. An elderly couple looked curiously in their direction and the smile on her dad's face faltered. He was an experienced solicitor and would be used to tough negotiations but he was going to struggle with his daughter's cross-examination.

'So what would you like to discuss, Emma? I'll answer your questions as honestly as I can.'

Emma wondered exactly how much he was capable of sharing honestly with her. She had planned to open with some easy questions, find out a little about the man so she could fill in the intervening years, but her first question was out of her mouth before she could hold it back. 'What kind of man finds out his child has cancer and the best he can do is send a get well card?'

There was a long drawn-out pause before her dad answered. He was looking down at his hands and Emma willed him to have the guts to look her in the face. When he did lift his head, his eyes looked pained. 'I deserve your contempt, I know that.'

Emma stared at him, her eyes stinging from the bright sunlight and she hoped he didn't think she was on the verge of tears. She was too angry for that.

'I knew how ill you were,' he confessed. 'And I knew how you were getting on because I kept in touch with some of my old colleagues, ones who still worked in the same office as your mum.'

Emma's chest heaved with anger and she felt her whole body tingling with the heat of her rage. 'And you think that was good enough?' she demanded.

'Not for any decent father, no,' John replied candidly. He broke eye contact and nervously picked at the flaking paint on the cast-iron table. 'I don't think I really understood what it was like to be a dad. I worked hard to provide for you all and I thought that was my job done.'

'Mum provided for us too,' defended Emma.

'Yes, yes, she did.' Her dad's voice softened as he was

drawn into the past. 'You weren't planned and your mum's pregnancy threw our career plans into disarray. Neither of us had completed our law degrees at that point so your mum took a break and I qualified first. I became the breadwinner and saw it as my job to support you all. I didn't see the point in Meg completing her qualifications, she didn't need to work.'

'She had just as much right to her career as you had to yours.'

John nodded. 'I know that now but back then, I had this idea that what I was doing was noble. I was prepared to do all the work and let your mum reap the rewards. With persistence, she managed to complete her qualifications but as soon as she did I persuaded her it was time for another baby and we had Louise.'

'And precisely how does all of this explain why you turned your back on me?'

Emma watched as her dad continued to pick at the flaking paint. 'What I'm trying to explain, and not very well, is that I thought that was all I had to do. I was the provider and Meg was the carer. To put it bluntly, I paid the bills and your mum looked after the fluffy stuff. Even when we split up, I did what I thought was the right thing. I waited until Louise was eighteen before taking my share of the assets. My children were officially adults and my job was done. I swear, I thought of it as if I was closing a business deal. I'm not proud of that but it's the only explanation I have. I never thought of it as abandoning you.'

'Why? Why did you feel like that?' demanded Emma, confused by the brutal explanation her father was giving her. She had expected some lame excuse, something that described circumstances beyond his control. What she hadn't expected was a character assassination, not by him at least.

'I could start blaming my own family background but I won't. I take full responsibility for my own behaviour.'

'So you didn't rush to my hospital bedside because you thought it wasn't your job? You're really that heartless?' Emma's eyes continued to sting and the heat was overpowering, almost as much as her urge to stand up and punch him.

John looked towards the main doors, peering out into the distance. 'When I found out about your illness, I'd already remarried and we had a two-month-old baby,' he said. 'Emma, I've thought long and hard about what I'd share with you today and this part is probably the hardest thing for me to say and for you to hear but I said I'd be honest with you.'

They locked eyes again and as Emma prepared for his explanation, she clenched her fist, ready to throw that punch.

'It was only when I held Olivia in my arms for the first time that I finally got it. I knew in that split second that I would move heaven and earth to protect her, that it wasn't only about providing for her. I understood what it was to be a father and I swear I cried like a baby myself,' he said, his voice choking with emotion. 'And before you hate me even more than you thought you possibly could, I need to explain that it wasn't just about making that connection with my new daughter, it was recognizing what I'd lost with you and Louise. In that moment, I knew that what I'd done was indefensible, so when I heard you were ill, I felt too ashamed. I had no right to be a part of your life.'

Emma sat back in her chair and her breath hissed between clenched teeth like a steam engine about to explode. She had secretly wanted a fight. She had wanted to scream accusations at her father and storm off, finally able to close that particular chapter of her life once and for all but there was no fun in attacking someone who was practically begging her to rip out his heart. 'And now?' she asked.

'And now I know I would move heaven and earth to protect you, Emma.'

'It's too late,' she replied flatly and her response wasn't meant to be hurtful, simply truthful.

He nodded. 'I know.'

'And now I suppose it's my turn to be honest with you,' she said. 'I don't know how or if we would be able to mend our bridges but the truth is I don't have time. What time I do have left needs to be spent with the people who matter. A part of me wishes you were one of them, Dad, but you're not. I missed having you in my life and I've spent far too long being angry with you. I would love things to be different because right now I need to feel protected and safe and that's what dads are for, aren't they?' Emma lifted up her hand to ward off her dad who was reaching out towards her. 'This is all I'm prepared to give you, this one meeting to resolve as much between us as we can. I have to put myself first and I'm thinking about Mum too. I don't want to taint her last memories of me with any animosity that might arise from you appearing back on the scene. She doesn't deserve that.'

'I can't argue with that,' John agreed. His eyes were glistening with tears that couldn't be explained by bright sunlight alone.

Emma felt herself let go of the last remnant of anger and a huge burden was lifted from her. She welcomed the calmness flooding her body as she reached into her bag for an envelope. She had imagined throwing the cheque back in his face and screaming, 'Keep your money!' Instead, she handed it to him almost reverently. 'I don't need this any more.'

'I still want you to have it,' he replied, not taking it.

'Really, Dad, I don't want it. Money serves no purpose in my life now and you can make better use of it. Maybe it can finance all those bridges you're going to have to build with Louise. You are going to, aren't you?'

'Yes, if she lets me.'

'Louise will be easy compared to me,' Emma said with a wry smile.

'I hope so,' he replied, finally taking the envelope.

'Do you fancy a little tour of the Palm House?' Emma

asked, a question that surprised them both. She wasn't ready to let him go yet. She needed to know exactly how he was going to put things right with Louise and, if she could, give him some pointers to make it easier for them both.

By the time Emma was ready to leave, she had achieved everything she felt she needed to. She had answers to the questions that had plagued her for years and although they hadn't repaired the damage that had been done, at least now they understood each other a little better. For good measure, Emma warned him that she would come back and haunt him if he ever let Louise down again.

'There is one thing I haven't been completely honest about,' her dad told her as they walked towards the exit. 'I didn't come alone. My wife Carolyn and the kids are here too.'

'Here in the park?' asked Emma. She felt shocked and confused, unsure how to react. Her dad's new family consisted of two young daughters, Olivia, aged five, and Amy, three. They were her half-sisters and in other circumstances, Emma might have had the desire to get to know them but, like so many things, there wasn't time.

'Would you like to meet them?'

'I have enough trouble dealing with one sister,' Emma joked. As they stepped over the threshold, the blast of cold that hit her was possibly a blessing as it softened the next shock. Emerging through the gated entrance Emma caught sight of two little girls wrapped up in woollen coats and hats, playing with a pink ball. They were the children she had been coveting earlier and they were her father's daughters. 'I hope you realize how lucky you are,' she said, still prevaricating over his invitation. She recalled a saying about the worst regrets being the things you didn't do in life. 'Yes, I think I would like to meet them.'

An awkward smile passed between Emma and Carolyn as she made her way towards the girls. Her dad joined his wife and left Emma to make her own introductions.

'Hello,' Emma said, crouching down so she was on the same level as Olivia, although she still towered over Amy. 'You two look like you're having fun.'

Olivia glanced over towards her parents, seeking re-assurance that it was alright to allow this stranger into their lives. 'We're playing football,' she replied and Emma smiled sadly at the Scottish lilt in her voice, which only served to exaggerate the distance and the differences between her father's two sets of daughters.

'What's your name?' asked Olivia.

'I'm Emma,' she said.

'She's your sister,' John called from behind them.

Olivia scrutinized Emma. 'You're very big for a sister,' she said.

'That's because I'm your big sister. But I'm afraid I can't stay long and I probably won't see you again.' The words were blunt but Emma saw a little of herself in Olivia's eyes and she knew she would want to be told the truth.

'Why? Where are you going?'

Emma's head dropped as she wondered the same thing herself. She noticed a fluffy white feather lying on the ground and picked it up, twirling it in her fingers. 'I'm going to be an angel,' she whispered as if it was a secret only to be shared with the two girls. 'And if ever you see a white feather like this, you'll know I'm watching over you.'

'Wow,' gasped Amy, taking it from Emma. 'Look what I got,' she was shouting as she toddled off towards her dad.

Olivia ignored Amy's squeals of delight and sneaked a look behind Emma's back. 'I can't see any wings.'

Emma smiled. 'I don't think I've earned them yet.'

'Will you be able to play with us when you're an angel?'

'No, but you have another· big sister who's called Louise. She'll play with you and I want you to promise me you'll give her a hard time. She needs little sisters to annoy her like she used to annoy me.'

Olivia nodded, pleased, her rosy cheeks glowing in the sunshine. Then she did something extraordinary, or at least it was to Emma. She took off her glove and reached out to touch Emma's cheek. Emma put her hand over Olivia's, feeling the warmth of her tiny fingers. She turned and kissed the little girl's hand, smelling the sweet, baby smell mixed with the faint odour of damp wool. Emma could feel something stirring deep inside her that she knew could never be satisfied. 'You're so very precious,' Emma told her, 'don't you ever forget that.'

Olivia gave her a serious look as she noticed the tears in Emma's eyes. 'I won't,' she promised.

'Go tell your dad how lucky he is to have you and then go get some hot chocolate to warm yourself up.'

'OK,' Olivia said, turning swiftly towards her parents. The little girl seemed blissfully unaware of the magnitude of the meeting that had taken place but something made Olivia stop halfway and turn around. She ran back to give Emma a hug with such force that it almost knocked her to the ground. 'Love you, angel,' she said.

Before Emma had a chance to respond, Amy had appeared and was pushing Olivia out of the way and copying her sister. 'Love you, angel,' she repeated.

Emma remained crouching as she watched them gather up their things. She was wary of standing up because the pain in her neck had travelled down the length of her spine and she knew rising too fast would be excruciating, but that wasn't the only reason. If she stayed where she was then she wouldn't be expected to say goodbye to her dad, not properly. There would be no awkward moment deciding what to say or whether they should hug. She stayed where she was as her dad gave her a friendly wave before turning away. She saw him wipe his face and watched his wife put her arm around him but it was only when they were safely out of sight that she was ready to head back to her own family.

Emma expected to be interrogated the moment she stepped foot inside the Traveller's Rest but her arrival went unnoticed. The place was in uproar. A young waitress, Isabel, was the only member of the team front of house and she visibly groaned when she heard the door open to what she expected to be yet another customer. The bistro was two thirds full and practically every table was trying to attract her attention.

'Where is everyone?' Emma asked.

'Emergency meeting in the kitchen,' Isabel said, tearing a completed order from her pad. 'Here, take this in for me and tell them to either start sending food out now or at least send someone out to explain why not.'

Emma headed for the kitchen and could hear a clamour of voices before she had even opened the door.

'Cottage pie? Who's going to be impressed with cottage pie?' yelped Louise, pulling at her hair. She was leaning over one of the counters, tapping her pen viciously against the stainless-steel surface. Ben, Steven, Iris and Jean were crowded around her, looking intently at the scraps of paper littering the counter.

'It kept my family fed for generations,' muttered Iris, clearly offended.

'But the whole point of a Specials Board is about making it special.' Louise picked up the scrap of paper they had all been looking at and turned it face down.

'Steven's been experimenting with some new dishes? Why don't we try one of those?'

'How about because Steven's not a chef?'

'Yet,' Ben added before Steven could register the hurt.

Steven didn't look hurt. 'May I remind you that you

291

might be my landlady but you're also my lodger now. You need to watch what you say,' he told Louise.

The group held their breath as they waited for the counterattack. They had yet to notice Emma's arrival and she felt odd, as if she was standing on the outside looking into a world in which she didn't belong any more.

'And may I remind you that down here, I'm the boss,' Louise was saying.

Emma watched Louise and Steven intently as they traded threats. There was a certain frisson between the two, which boded well for the future that she had envisioned for them, but there would be no more interference. She didn't need to; they would find their own path in their own time. The feeling that she was witnessing the life that would continue after she was gone persisted. 'Am I missing something?' she asked. The sound of her voice had a solid presence that brought her back into the room.

Five faces turned towards her but it was Louise who spoke first. 'According to insider knowledge,' she said, tipping her head towards Steven, 'Derek Watkinson is coming to review the bistro, here, tonight.' Emma thought she detected a subtle wince as her sister said the man's name out loud.

'*The* Derek Watkinson?' Emma asked, hardly believing her ears. 'The very same Derek Watkinson who published that awful review last year? Here's a suggestion, let me cook for him and I'll give him a meal he won't forget in a hurry.'

'How did the meeting go?' Ben asked. Of everyone, he was the only one who didn't appear to be panicking.

'Oh, my God, yes, sorry, Emma. How did it go? I need to know.' Louise crossed the kitchen, a cloud of discarded notes trailing in her wake.

'It went fine. Better than I expected but we can catch up later. I think I'd better head home in case I do something I regret with the darling Mr Watkinson's food.'

'No, Emma,' cried Louise. 'I need you.'

'Louise, you'll be fine, really you will.'

'I'll give you a lift,' Ben said, moving towards Emma, without waiting for a reply.

Emma heard a sharp intake of breath from Louise but she didn't give voice to her objection, Emma beat her to it. 'No,' Emma told Ben firmly. 'You're needed here. I'll get a taxi. No more argument.'

Ben kissed her cheek. 'I know you're right, you always are. But don't you need to talk things through?'

Emma was already stepping back towards the door. 'I need to gather my thoughts first and you lot need to agree the menu. And don't leave poor Isabel out there all on her own.' Emma handed the waitress's order to Ben then turned and left before anyone could object.

As she sat in the back of the taxi cab, she was struggling against an overwhelming desire not only to cry but to sob uncontrollably. She was convinced that if she let the first tear fall she would never be able to stop. She couldn't quite shake the sensation she'd had as she stood watching the others in the kitchen. It was as if she were a ghost already and her sense of isolation intensified. She was heading home to an empty apartment and for once she didn't want space, she wanted company. It would be a couple of hours before her mum arrived home and until then Emma needed to find a place she could feel secure and safe.

There was a sharp intake of breath as another contraction rippled across my abdomen but I was otherwise calm. I still couldn't quite believe that there was something amazing growing inside me, something that for once hadn't been a hostile invasion. I had nothing to fight against and everything to fight for. I would endure the pain that arced across my midriff, knowing that soon I would be able to hold our baby in my arms.

Resting my head on the back of the garden chair, I gently rocked back and forth, letting the last rays of a summer's day warm my face. I could hear the soothing chime of goat bells in the distance and the sweet smell of jasmine wrapped around me like a comfort blanket. My idyllic labour was blighted only by my husband who was frantically running around like a man possessed.

'Should it be taking this long?' he asked the midwife who had arrived two hours earlier and was as laid back as I was, much to Ben's frustration.

'It'll take as long as it takes,' she assured him. 'Now get back into the house and make us all a nice cup of tea to calm our nerves.'

'I don't really want a cuppa,' I told her once he'd disappeared.

'Me *neither*,' she said, patting me on the hand before leaving me in peace with my thoughts.

I wanted to cry with joy. I had denied myself this dream for so long, believing that my cancer had taken it away. I had buried my longing to be a mother so deeply it had taken nine months to reacquaint myself with something that came naturally to me. A desire to nurture.

I could remember the exact moment I decided I wanted to be a mother above all else. I was four years old at the time and had been resting my head on my mum's stomach, which had swelled to mammoth proportions as my baby sister (or brother) grew inside her. I held my ear against her taught abdomen and convinced myself I could hear the baby gurgling and laughing inside her. I had turned to face my mum to tell her, expecting her to laugh too, but there was no smile to greet me, only tears rolling down her cheeks. I had been so scared, not knowing what was making her so sad, frightened that she didn't want the baby. After Louise was born, that fear never left me and I watched over my sister like a mother hen.

I still wonder to this day what had made my mother cry. Had it been the sacrifices she had made for her children, the career that she was unable to secure for herself whilst her husband convinced her to remain barefoot and pregnant? In giving life to us, had she felt that she was *losing her own sense of self? I too had been forced to make choices. I resigned from my job because it was clear, even before Kate had spelled it out to me, that I couldn't have everything. I could juggle my time between my family and my job but I would do justice to neither. I had to choose, but in the end there was no sacrifice. My job at Alsop and Clover was not my life, my family was. But Kate had been wrong. I could have it all; I simply had to work out how I could have it all in one place.*

Emma turned off her computer and leaned back against her pillows. Daylight had silently receded as she concentrated on her writing and her room was shrouded in deep shadow. The excitement she had tried to conjure in her story was quickly overwhelmed by dark reality. She felt exhausted and not just physically.

For years, Emma had been preparing for a showdown with her dad and now that it had happened she didn't quite know how to feel. But before her mood could plummet any further, there was a distant jangle of keys. She tried to imagine that it was the tinkling of goat bells and not her mum arriving home but a moment later Meg popped her head around the door, dispelling the image that Emma was trying to hold onto.

'What are you doing sitting in the dark?' she asked. 'Are you OK? Do you need anything?' With each question, Meg's voice had increased in anxiety.

'Mum, I'm fine,' Emma assured her. 'I was too lazy to get up and close the blind, that's all.'

'Tired?'

'That's an understatement. And well done you by the way,' Emma added.

Meg smiled as she stepped across the threshold and turned on a lamp before going to the window to shut out the darkness. 'I don't know what you mean.'

'Yes, you do. Well done for containing your curiosity and not bombarding me with texts and phone calls all afternoon.' Whilst everyone at the bistro had been distracted, she knew at least her mum would be desperate to know the details. 'Have you got time for a chat?' Emma asked, patting the empty space next to her.

Meg practically leapt onto the bed. 'Of course I have. It's Friday night, what else would I rather do than spend time with my daughter? So, what would you like to talk about?' she asked, still the image of innocence, much to Emma's amusement.

'I don't know. What would you like to talk about?' She laughed.

'We could always talk about the latest crisis at the bistro.'

'Ah, you heard about that. So you haven't been totally incommunicado.'

'OK, I give in. Put me out of my misery. Did you get the answers you wanted?' Meg asked, her tone more serious as she took Emma's hand in hers and gave it a squeeze.

'They certainly weren't the answers I was expecting.

I think he was trying to tell me that he didn't know how to be a dad until it was too late.'

'And is it too late?' Meg asked diplomatically.

'For me, yes. I've told him I don't want to see him any more; I don't need to. He doesn't get the chance to make up for lost time.'

'And you're alright with that?'

'I don't have a choice. Time isn't on my side,' Emma answered. She felt her mum's grip on her hand tighten. 'If nothing else, I'm glad I got to meet Olivia and Amy.'

'His daughters?' asked Meg.

'My sisters,' corrected Emma, looking towards her mum to check how she was dealing with the idea that her ex-husband had a new family. Meg gave her a weak but otherwise brave smile.

'So what did they think of their new big sister?'

'I don't think it takes much to impress a three- and a five-year-old,' Emma replied with a wry smile as she pictured the two little girls looking at her as if she would sprout angel wings there and then. 'They were so sweet, Mum,' she continued, and her voice cracked with emotions that had crept up on her without warning.

Meg didn't speak but waited patiently for Emma to compose herself. It took some time. 'I know I've said it before but it really isn't fair. When I saw those gorgeous little girls, I couldn't help thinking, why does he deserve to be a parent and I don't?'

Emma was determined not to cry but as she laid her

head on her mum's shoulder she could feel her tears pooling in the corners of her eyes.

'Maybe one day . . .' Meg began but then stopped herself. 'You're right, sweetheart, life isn't fair.'

Emma felt her mum's body tensing and she knew she was trying to hold back her own tears. The threat of the conversation degenerating into communal hysteria was enough to jolt Emma out of her desolate mood. She took a deep breath and lifted her head as she tried to focus on the things she could achieve and not those that were forever out of reach. She picked up her laptop and switched it on. 'I think it's about time I told you a little bit more about my book,' she began.

'I was wondering when I'd get to see it. I've been watching you and Ben poring over your computer as thick as thieves and I was starting to feel left out.'

'I'm sorry, Mum. You are alright with Ben being here, aren't you?'

Meg smiled. It was more genuine this time. 'Of course I am. I can see how happy you are together and how much he's helping you. I have no complaints. Now, enough delaying tactics.' She was looking expectantly as the first pages of Emma's alternative life came into view.

'This is a way for me to experience some of the things that real life can never give me,' Emma explained. 'One of the reasons I haven't shared it with you is because I wasn't sure you were ready to accept that. I didn't want to tell you only for you to dismiss it and tell me, to use your words, "Maybe one day . . ."'

299

'If it makes you happy, then I won't dismiss it,' replied Meg, taking her position firmly on the fence. 'And I'll help any way I can.' She put her arm around Emma as she watched her tap away at her computer until her most recent entry appeared on screen.

Emma took a deep breath, knowing that what she was about to reveal might not be easy for her mum to read. 'It's not only about the things that I would want in my life, it's turned into a bit of a reflection about the past as well. I think you'd better read this part.'

Meg scanned through the pages, the silence occasionally broken by the sound of a sob being swallowed back. When her focus remained on one particular passage, Emma knew it was time to ask the question: 'Why were you crying, Mum?'

Meg was silent for a while longer and her lip trembled. 'It wasn't because I didn't want Louise.'

Emma waited but Meg clearly wasn't ready to share the answer without further prompting. 'Please, Mum. I need to know.'

Meg stood up and stepped over to the window. Despite the closed blinds, the view was so captivating that she didn't turn to face Emma as she spoke. 'I was crying for you, Emma. I was crying for the guilt I felt then and carry with me still.'

'What guilt?' Emma asked. She was beginning to regret pushing her mum, not ready to hear another parent's confessions.

'You know you weren't planned. Having children was

something that I intended to think about later in my life, much later. When I found out I was pregnant, I wasn't going to keep it. You, I wasn't going to keep you.'

'And why didn't you have an abortion?'

'Because, eventually, I realized that I wanted you more than I wanted the law degree.'

Emma's hand flew to her mouth but it wasn't with horror, it was with relief. When her mum chanced a look over towards her, Emma had dropped her hand to reveal a smile. 'Thank God for that.'

'What?'

'You haven't been the only one feeling guilty. I always thought it was my fault that you had to struggle so hard to fulfil your ambitions. I thought I had got in the way.'

'Don't ever think that, Emma. It wasn't a struggle, it was a pleasure.' Meg picked up the photo of Emma and Louise building sandcastles from the dressing table. 'You and Louise are the joys of my life.'

'Really? I thought we were a handful.'

'OK.' Her mum laughed. 'Maybe I'm looking back with rose-tinted glasses. See this photo? I remember it took an age getting you two to smile at the same time. Every time I picked up the camera, an argument would break out . . .'

'I thought Dad took the photo,' Emma said, wondering how her memory had become so flawed.

'He'd already disappeared to make some calls to the office. We didn't have mobiles back then.' Meg put the photo down and took Emma's outstretched hand. 'I promise you, Emma, the only regret I have is that I ever contemplated not having you. That was why I was crying.' Meg's tears threatened to surface again as the thoughts that had plagued her all of those years ago came back to haunt her now.

'I'm sorry, Mum. I didn't want to upset you but I'm glad I know. It helps.'

Meg nodded and a rogue tear rolled down her cheek in spite of herself.

'So, back to this story of mine,' Emma said, waiting for Meg to sit back down next to her. Her voice held a warning; they both had to keep a tight rein on their emotions. 'I'm starting to get a little out of my depth. I need you to tell me all there is to know about childbirth,' Emma said before adding tentatively, 'is it excruciatingly painful?'

'First time round I was terrified and yes, it hurts a lot. But it's worth every single contraction because suddenly you have this beautiful little baby in your arms and you forget the pain. I suppose you have to, otherwise no woman would ever go through it a second time.'

There was so much more that Meg was eager to share so she and Emma spent the rest of the evening talking more about Emma and Louise's early childhood, memories that Emma had been either too young to have herself or had simply forgotten. It was strange listening to somebody else describing her reaction to Louise's arrival, recalling it from a completely different perspective to Emma who had looked back to that time with her own pair of rose-tinted spectacles. She had indeed played her part as doting mother hen but apparently the novelty of a new baby had quickly worn thin. Her mum was in the middle of yet another embarrassing anecdote when there was the telltale jangling of keys at the front door. When Ben appeared, Meg made her excuses and left them to it.

'Am I forgiven?' he asked.

'And what exactly do I have to forgive you for?' Emma asked, although she had a suspicion she knew.

He slid onto the bed, crawling the length of Emma's body until his chin rested on her chest. 'I didn't give you the attention you deserved,' he confessed. 'I shouldn't have let you come home by yourself. I shouldn't have left you alone after seeing your dad.'

'You had more immediate problems to deal with. I said I needed time to work things through and I did. I've had a good chat with Mum and it's really helped. You have nothing to be forgiven for,' she told him. 'So how did it go? Did Derek Watkinson make his presence known?'

Ben lifted himself up and kissed Emma gently on the nose. 'I'm not here to talk about Derek blinking Watkinson. I'm here to ask you how it went.'

Emma felt a warm rush of emotion rising through her body like a wave, and in its wake came much, needed peace. 'I may have been short-changed with some things in life but you are not one of them. How did I get so lucky?'

'Because you deserve it,' Ben told her.

Emma snuggled down into the bed so that they were lying next to each other. 'And from the deserving to the far less deserving. Let me tell you how my meeting with my dad went,' she began.

14

I felt complete; there really was no other way to describe it. The roses around the door of our cottage were in full bloom and so was my family. Barely a day old, I cradled my sleeping daughter in my arms and in perfect synergy, Ben's arms wrapped around us both. It came as quite a surprise then to close my eyes and find myself in front of the shopkeeper once more.

'The lady who likes to shop,' he remarked.

'Not this time,' I told him, my eyes for once not drawn to the shelves. 'I have everything I need or could ever want.'

'I can't tempt you with an exciting new career? I'm sure there's something here that would give you a good balance between work and home life.'

'I may not have access to all the trimmings but I think I'm putting together a pretty good package for myself this time.'

I told him all about the farm and my plans to work

with Ben developing his business. I explained how I was already planning my first novel and when I said I could do it all and bring up a family too, he had little doubt that I could.

'So what is it you want from me?' he asked.

'I'm happy. For the first time in my life I am truly happy,' I explained as the nerves I had been trying to ignore turned my stomach in knots. 'What I want is for it to last.'

'You want me to stop time?' the shopkeeper asked. There was a note of sympathy in his voice, which told me what I already knew. Even my kindly shopkeeper had his limitations. 'You know I can't do that, Emma. Change will bring new challenges and you will adapt, you always do, but I'm afraid happiness is fleeting, as is life in the scheme of things. Enjoy it while you can.'

I opened my eyes and looked down at the sleeping baby in my arms, taking in every tiny detail from the curve of her cupid-bow lips to the smell of her hair, which was dark and downy. I felt Ben kiss my neck as he told me he loved me and it sent a shiver down my spine, but it didn't stop the tear that was sliding slowly down my cheek. It would never get any better than this, I told myself.

'Are you sure you're OK?' Ben asked as we drove through the gates and away from the hospital.

'I'm fine,' Emma assured him with an encouraging smile. 'At least that's one down, only another twenty-nine to go.' Emma had her schedule all laid out: radiotherapy five days a week for the next six weeks and she was already counting down.

'I was thinking, maybe at the weekend we could do a bit more research, if you're up to it?' Ben was trying to sound upbeat but it was forced.

Emma shook her head. Although the side effects from her treatment would take days if not weeks to build up, she was already feeling fragile, if only mentally. 'I'm not sure there's anything to research at the moment.'

'OK, maybe not immediately but once we've had the kids and they've grown up, we could resurrect your wanderlust,' Ben said with an almost desperate persistence.

'I'm in no rush,' Emma told him, trying to disguise the annoyance in her voice. She was in no mood to consider skipping through the precious years of her daughter's life. Slowly and reverently, she raised her hand to her cheek as she tried to recapture the moment that Olivia had touched it.

'Are you sure you're OK?'

Emma nodded. 'But things are going to change whether we want them to or not. You're going to wake up one morning and you won't see me, you'll see a cancer patient.'

Ben wasn't fast enough to hide the look of pain on his face. 'I will always look at you and see my Emma.'

'The chemo I'm on at the moment is only low dose so if I'm lucky I won't lose all my hair just yet, maybe only a bald patch here and there where the radiotherapy has zapped me,' Emma added quickly. She had led the conversation in a direction that she wished she hadn't. She was dragging Ben into the despair she herself had slipped into.

Ben was silent, staring intently at the road ahead. 'Is that what counts as lucky these days?' he asked.

Emma reached out and rubbed his back as he continued to keep his eyes front, gripping the steering wheel so tightly that his knuckles had turned white. 'I thought you were the one supposed to be keeping my spirits up?' she said lightly but her words tore at Ben's heart. He swerved into a lay-by and brought the car to an abrupt halt. He was still looking straight ahead.

'I'm sorry,' he said, his breath becoming ragged, painful gasps.

Fear turned Emma's blood cold and the nausea she thought she had evaded following her first dose of radio-therapy hit her so hard she put one hand on the door handle in case she needed to throw up. This was where her happiness ended; this was where Ben would turn his back on her just like her Dad. She raised her other hand towards her mouth and felt it tremble over her lips.

When Ben turned towards her, the pain in his eyes was replaced by a look of horror as he read her mind. 'No, no,' he said, taking her hand and holding it tightly. 'You think I'm about to dump you? Jesus, Emma, I'm sorry, that couldn't be further from my mind.'

'Then what?' Emma stumbled on. 'What made you

react like that? Are you sure you're ready for this, Ben, because it's going to get worse, so much worse.'

Ben was shaking his head. 'I'm just so damned angry,' he said. 'Angry that I can't help you through this, that I wasn't allowed in that room to hold your hand while they microwaved your brain. But most of all, I'm angry with myself because you go through all of that and you go through it on your own and you're the one comforting me. How can that be? I feel utterly useless.' His voice was growing in intensity but he reined in his anger and even managed a smile before he continued. 'And don't you dare say something nice to make me feel better, Emma. Don't you dare.'

'You're completely useless,' Emma agreed, with a fixed smile of her own.

Ben edged closer to her. 'Thank you.'

'You're welcome.'

'I love you.'

'I love you too.'

They leaned towards each other until they were nose to nose with their foreheads touching but they didn't kiss. They kept staring into each other's eyes and the connection between them felt unbreakable. If it hadn't been for the growing ache in Emma's back, she would have been happy to stay there for hours. 'If you want to make yourself useful, you could fulfil your duties as chauffeur and take me home.'

'At last, something I can do,' Ben said.

Emma watched as he pulled himself together and if the first-day nerves had not been completely dispelled then they had at least been brought under control for the moment. She felt ready to pick up her story again.

'There is something else you can help with,' she said. 'We need to decide on a name for our new baby.'

'You've had the baby?' he gasped. 'That's why you've been so quiet? You were busy giving birth at the weekend and you didn't tell me? What did we have?'

Emma looked out of the car window as they sped down the motorway, watching the world passing by in a blur, and she allowed herself to disconnect from it. 'We have a gorgeous baby girl, seven pounds, nine ounces,' she said. 'She has beautiful dark hair and brown eyes, just like her daddy.'

The discussion about their baby's name was animated and kept Emma distracted and both of them entertained for the rest of the journey but they were no nearer reaching agreement when they arrived home. She managed to convince Ben to go to work, claiming it would be good for her to have the peace and quiet. Reluctantly, Ben agreed.

Left on her own, Emma didn't have the strength to fight the emptiness that settled around her. She felt drained and didn't know if she would have the energy to write but she retreated to her bedroom anyway. When she picked up the pink rose that Ben had left on her pillow, she had already stopped trying to be brave.

My daughter was simply beautiful although her name had caused quite a bit of debate between Ben and me.

'I was thinking of something that represented spring,' I had told him.

Ben looked around us for inspiration. We were sitting in the garden. It was alive with colour, the summer flowers stretching their vibrant petals wide, ready to embrace the sunshine. Our baby slept soundly in my arms. 'Spring?'

'What about Blossom?' I ventured. 'Or Bluebell?' I lifted our sleeping daughter's hand with my finger and instinctively she grabbed it tightly. I leaned forward and kissed her tiny fingers, breathing in the baby smell as I did. I brought her hand to my cheek and my skin tingled from the touch.

Ben was oblivious to the moment I had just shared with my daughter, he was too busy laughing. 'She's not a cow,' he cried, tears rolling down his face.

But spring was my favourite time of the year, I had explained. It represented rebirth, new life, and I was determined to find a name that suited my purposes as well as one that suited my daughter.

Ben reached up and plucked a flower from the trellis that arched above us. It was only when he handed me the beautiful rosebud, its delicate pink petals as soft as our daughter's cheeks, that I gave in. I wrapped my arms a little tighter around our beautiful Rose.

Emma's fifth radiotherapy session was identical to the first and, at her insistence, life was carrying on as normal and she did her best to hide her growing sense of isolation, retreating as always to the sanctuary of her bedroom to absorb herself in another life. She had become protective of her story to the extent that she was being evasive whenever Ben tried to involve himself. She wanted to savour the time she had with her baby with no distractions. She wasn't ready to rush through her daughter's childhood only for her to fly the nest and leave Emma's arms empty once again.

Emma stroked her fingers across the shiny black surface of the keyboard, each key smooth but cold and inflexible. Something caught at the back of her throat, a mixture of anger and sadness. Her baby was not made of flesh and blood and its touch was unforgiving.

Emma gave up the pretence of writing and headed for the kitchen for a drink, dismissing the row of healthy juices for a warming and hopefully invigorating cup of coffee. She made it strong but before she could take her first sip, the intercom buzzed. Emma wasn't expecting anyone, both her mum and Ben were at work and, besides, they had their own keys. She considered whether it might be Ally or Gina, and indeed it was someone from the office who had taken time out to pay her a visit.

'Jennifer, this is a nice surprise,' Emma said, her smile forced.

'Don't lie. I know you'd be more than happy to see the back of Bannister's Kitchens and Bathrooms.'

'Given a choice, I'd be more than happy to still be there,' Emma reminded her.

'I know, it was a stupid comment,' Jennifer conceded.

'What I meant was, I think you were always intended for bigger and better things.'

The last comment hung in the air, neither woman expecting or needing to delve further into a postmortem of Emma's career. 'Make yourself at home,' Emma said, finally remembering her manners. 'Would you like a coffee? I've just made one.'

'Wow, that's strong,' Jennifer said as she took the first sip from the cup Emma handed her.

'Sorry, my sense of taste is failing by the day and I'm in the habit of making everything really strong.'

A look of sympathy passed over Jennifer's eyes, which was the last thing Emma wanted to see. 'Is that because of the chemo?'

'Yeah, probably,' Emma said with a shrug, not wanting to discuss the side effects of her treatment with Jennifer. In fact, she didn't want to talk about her cancer at all. 'So enough about me, what are you after?'

Jennifer didn't baulk at the accusation, she actually relaxed and smiled. 'I suppose I'm after your forgiveness. I'm here to apologize.'

'Apologize for what?'

'I knew from Dad how good you were at your job so when I started, I had this image of you in my mind as an ambitious career woman.'

'I am,' Emma told her proudly.

Jennifer laughed and bravely took another sip of coffee. 'I was later led to believe that you had a ruthless streak, that you had no qualms about undermining others to make yourself look good, staking a claim on other people's work, that kind of thing.'

'Alex,' guessed Emma, to which Jennifer simply nodded. 'So why do I get the feeling that you don't think that any more?'

'Because now I know for myself that he's a complete moron,' Jennifer replied. 'We could all see that Alex had plenty of good ideas, the ones he said you had written up for him, so it was hard to understand why he still couldn't put a campaign together. I had my suspicions but it was only when you gave me all of your other files that I had the ammunition to convince Dad that we really did need to bring in the consultants. And it seemed wrong that he thought Alex was the driving creative force when it was you.'

'I wasn't sure what you would do . . .' Emma started but stopped herself. She was remembering her last visit to the office and the bouquet of flowers.

'You thought we were going out together?' Jennifer smiled. 'How could I possibly respect someone who treated you the way he did?'

'Your dad is still employing him, though, he's still Marketing Director,' Emma said, shaking her head in frustration.

There was a pause as Jennifer shifted uneasily. 'I know you can keep a confidence so I'll tell you. You know Alex's father is an old friend of my dad's but what you won't know is that, with a little creative accounting, he's been covering his son's wages.'

'Ah, it all makes sense now. That would be the regular orders going through the books for nonexistent work.'

'I suppose on the face of it, my dad thought it was a win-win situation. He was getting free labour and his friend kept his wayward son in gainful employment. But he didn't factor in what a liability Alex could be.'

'You mean now he has to pay for a marketing consultant?' Emma asked, and Jennifer nodded.

Emma suddenly felt tired and full of regrets. To shake off the mood, she asked, 'So what happens now?'

'If I have my way, Alex will get his comeuppance. Leave it to me,' Jennifer said sagely.

'For all his faults, though, I have to admit that I almost regret passing on those files to you. I was hurt and I was angry but I'm not sure I want to be responsible for Alex losing his job.'

'You're not. Alex's incompetence will be responsible for him losing his job. Don't you dare feel guilty, Emma,' Jennifer told her.

Emma looked at Jennifer with new eyes. She wasn't the wild child she had first met, nor did she seem to be trying to be Emma's clone any more. She had her own sense of individuality, which actually made her more like Emma than either of them would ever admit. 'Then I accept your apology.'

There was no more to say on the matter but Jennifer was reluctant to leave and Emma doubted it had anything to do with the half-finished cup of coffee. 'Are you scared?' Jennifer asked without warning.

The swift change of subject left Emma with no time to prepare a smart or evasive answer. 'About dying? Yes,' she said softly. 'Yes, I'm terrified.'

Jennifer was looking straight at her. A gentle smile curved her lips but it wasn't in any way mocking nor did it feel inappropriate. 'I know this is where I'm supposed to say how brave you are and how inspirational you've been, to which you'll reply that you're not, that you're doing what anyone else would do under the same circumstances,' she said.

'So you don't think I'm brave then?' asked Emma, returning Jennifer's smile.

'Of course I do. But I know from experience that's how it usually goes. It's what happened with Mum. We said all the things we were supposed to say and she said what we wanted to hear. Emma, I'm not family and you and I both know we could hardly call ourselves friends. You don't have to walk on eggshells with my emotions. If you need to tell at least one person how it is without holding back, then now's your chance.'

Emma's heart skipped a beat as she considered baring her soul. Jennifer was by no means the first person to make such an offer, there were a whole host of nurses, counsellors and end-of-life specialists who would be there for her, if only she would call, which she had stubbornly refused to do. What Jennifer was offering, however, was something unique. She knew enough of Emma's life to know the depth of her pain. 'OK,' Emma said tentatively. 'You want to know how it feels?'

Jennifer didn't look convinced when she nodded but at least she didn't put her hands over her ears as Emma waded into the emotions she had kept in check for a very long time.

'I'm scared, yes, but I'm also angry. Very angry,' she began. 'I was actually angry with you for taking my place at work and with Alex of course but that's only the tip of the iceberg. I'm angry with everyone and everything, angry when I hear all the petty complaints and trivialities. If it isn't life or death then it doesn't matter. So your anti-wrinkle cream doesn't quite make you look ten years younger? Be grateful you're getting old, it's a privilege some of us don't get. So they didn't have your size shoe in the sale? Get over it!' Emma spat the words out and her chest was heaving.

'They were Jimmy Choo's,' remarked Jennifer, if only to make Emma laugh and take a deep breath, which Emma obliged.

'There's something else too,' Emma said at last. 'I feel so lonely, Jen. No-one can climb into my head with me. No-one can feel what it's like in that treatment room when you have this ray gun pointed at your head. No-one sees the world through my eyes; they don't see that blind spot in the corner of my vision where I imagine my tumour stalking me. They can't walk in my shoes, Jimmy Choo's or no Jimmy Choo's. No-one can give me a break from this ordeal, not for a day, not even for one miserable hour, even if they wanted to and I know they do. This thing in my head is there all of the time. It goes

317

where I go, listening to my thoughts, messing with mind, messing with me.'

Jennifer moved closer as Emma ranted on. By the time she fell silent, her tirade finally over, Jennifer was sitting next to her. 'I want so much to tell you you're not alone but I know that would just be stupid,' she said, putting her arm gently around Emma's shoulders, which were still heaving.

'And you're not stupid,' Emma said, her voice now a mere rasp. She managed a tremulous smile. 'Thank you for not being a friend, Jennifer.'

I ran out of the newsagent's at full speed, barely stopping to check for traffic as I crossed the road and scampered up the hill towards the church. I could see Ben lying prone on the grass, camera in his hand as he tried to follow Rose with his lens. She was toddling further uphill, towards the virgin rays of sunlight creeping over the horizon and I practically leapt over Ben to rush after her.

'Where's my little sunshine?' I called and she squealed in excitement as she tried to outrun me. I swept her up in my arms and twirled her in the air before letting us both fall to the ground in a fit of giggles.

'Is that the remnants of a magazine in your hand?' Ben asked.

I had to put my hand over my eyes to shield them from the rising sun. Ben was silhouetted against the pink-and-lavender sky. 'Yes,' I said with a childish giggle.

'The *magazine?*'

'Yes.' Another giggle.

Ben flung himself onto the ground next to me and tickled Rose's tummy before returning his attention to the magazine. As he opened it up, our daughter made a grab for the pages so Ben scrambled backwards to get out of her way. His body hit solid stone.

'Sorry,' he whispered to the tombstone he had bumped into.

I raised an eyebrow. 'I didn't know you could talk to the dead.'

'I'm talking to angels,' he corrected. 'And you are the most angelic of them all.'

I kept one eye on Rose who had resumed her trek up the hill and went to join Ben. I said nothing and let him read the article.

'I knew you could do it,' he said. 'And if this review is anything to go by, I'd say you've just published a bestseller.'

'A bestselling author, that's me, with an equally successful husband by her side.'

'I would struggle to call myself successful. How many famous goats' cheese empires do you know?'

'Just the one,' I said, pulling an envelope from my jeans pocket and handing it to him. 'Your invitation to make a pitch to a national chain, no less.'

'You got me in?' he cried, tearing open the envelope.

'And this is only the start of it. I'd say we need to

start thinking about adding more lines, something that will appeal to a global market.'

'Let's not count our chickens,' he said, only half listening as he read and then reread the letter.

Rose was giggling in the distance as she did an about turn and started to toddle back down the hill towards us. 'I don't think it's that difficult counting to two.'

Ben looked up from the letter and eyed me suspiciously. I was still watching Rose and concentrating on hiding the smile that threatened to have me grinning from ear to ear and my cheeks ached with the effort. He reached over and turned my head so I was facing him. 'Tell.'

Beneath the shadow of a headstone, my smile erupted and I didn't need to say a word. Ben knew and he kissed me.

Two weeks into treatment and Emma was still managing the physical effects of it far better than the emotional ones. She had a long list of drugs to take, which helped reduce if not completely eliminate some of the side effects she had been expecting but strong pain killers had also been added to the list to combat the neck and back pain that was exacerbated as she lay still during her radio-therapy sessions. Her immunity was low and fatigue had started to set in but these alone were not enough to prevent Emma taking an active role in the real world, if only she had wanted to.

Emma couldn't be sure if it was her cancer treatment isolating her or if she was isolating herself. She didn't really care and would have been content to spend all her time in her bedroom, in her own little world where even Ben, the real Ben who slept soundly next to her every night as she wrestled with sleep, could not follow.

Fortunately for Emma, her family would not allow her to become a recluse and with some prolonged and forceful persuasion, she found herself back at her booth in the bistro one Saturday morning to join in what would be a rather special vigil.

Derek Watkinson's latest offerings were about to be published in the local paper and so far Steven's insider knowledge had failed to reveal whether or not his review of the Traveller's Rest would be favourable. As punishment for his failure to put her out of her misery, Louise had sent him out to the newsagent's to await the paper delivery.

Emma had made the mistake of bringing her laptop along with her, although so far she hadn't been left in peace long enough to even think about writing. She was being shadowed by her mum and Louise while Ben was in the kitchens. He wasn't supposed to be on duty but had wanted to keep himself busy. Iris and Jean were hovering in the background too, having volunteered to manage the morning's service between them.

Emma began to tap her fingers on the table impatiently. She didn't want to be there, she wanted to be able to write so that she could be with Rose, so that she could feel the new baby growing inside her. Her fingertips tingled with anticipation. It was this sensation she concentrated on rather than the oppressive atmosphere that was making her feel hot.

'Try the site again,' Louise demanded.

Emma sighed as she repeated the exercise she had carried out only two minutes earlier. She checked the newspaper's Internet site to see if the review was available online yet. She tried to keep a blank expression as she read the review.

'It's there, isn't it?' Louise said when she noticed Emma's body freeze. 'Let me see.'

Emma didn't notice the laptop being pulled from her. She felt the warmth of the early morning sun as it rose above the tiny Welsh village of her dreams. She was running uphill, running after Rose and then picking her up and spinning her around. She could feel the comforting weight of her tiny body in her arms and as they fell to the ground the little girl was shaking with laughter. Rose found her feet, touched Emma's cheek with a chubby hand, but then turned to run away. The shadow of a headstone crossed her face and the sunshine that had interrupted Emma's world disappeared.

'"The Traveller's Rest offers something for everyone, from cutting-edge cuisine to home cooking your mum would be proud of,"' Louise was reading out loud. She almost collapsed with excitement but not before she let out an ear-piercing screech. 'I don't believe it,' she said, as Meg wrapped her arms tightly around her daughter, almost knocking the wind out of her.

'Is it good news?' Iris asked, rushing over at full speed

despite the tray she had in her hands. Soup was slopping everywhere.

'A four-star review,' gasped Louise.

'So my Cottage Pie was special, after all,' Iris said with satisfaction.

Louise looked duly admonished. 'Yes! Well done, Iris, I don't know what— '

A loud bang and a cold gust of wind interrupted her as Steven rushed through the door. He was panting heavily and waving the newspaper in the air but then he saw their faces and he was momentarily deflated. 'You've already read it,' he sighed, now grinning ruefully.

'Four stars,' Louise confirmed, her smile becoming smugger by the minute as the news settled in.

'What am I missing?' It was Ben's turn to squeeze through the crowd, with Jean in tow. 'Did I hear right? It's good news?' he asked, only to be met with a silent chorus of nodding heads.

Suddenly everyone was talking at once, devouring every word of the review and congratulating themselves. Everyone except Emma. Her seizure had been relatively minor, lasting only a matter of seconds, but wherever her mind had taken her, she had brought back with her the sensation of holding her child in her arms. She felt numb to the excitement around her.

'We'll have to celebrate,' Louise said. 'Shall we have a party?'

'Ooh, lovely,' agreed Jean and Iris.

'But when are we going to fit it in?' Steven asked.

'The bookings are about to go through the roof. We can't turn business away.'

As the conversation turned into a debate, Ben slipped closer to Emma and crouched down next to her. 'Want to tell me what's wrong?' he whispered.

Emma could feel his eyes scrutinizing her face but she was too afraid to look at him. 'I'm fine,' she mumbled but as she felt his hand touch her cheek and turn her head towards him, tears were burning her eyes.

'Come on,' he said, taking her hand and pulling her away from the table.

'Emma? Is anything wrong?' There was a note of alarm in her mum's voice.

'She's fine,' Ben said casually. 'We just have our own catching up to do.'

Ben led Emma through the kitchen and into the small corridor that led up to the apartment. They sat on the stairs.

'So,' he began, taking her hand and kissing it gently. 'You were saying?'

Emma couldn't look at him; instead, she stared at the hand that was holding hers so tightly but which couldn't quite contain her tremors. 'I'm sorry. I know I should be happy for Louise and I am,' she began but her words held a conviction she didn't quite believe. 'I've been so determined to put everything right while I still can, whether that was at work, here at the bistro or even my relationship with Dad,' she explained. 'OK, in fairness, I was pushed into that one, but I still did it.'

'Getting your house in order?'

Emma nodded slowly and then bit her lip. She knew that what she was about to say would hurt but she had to say it. 'I'm going to die, Ben. We both know that and it's going to be hard for you all. We know that too.' She waited a moment, making sure Ben was still willing to listen. 'I wanted to soften the blow.'

Ben cleared his throat and narrowed his eyes. If the tears were there, he hid them well. 'I don't think that's possible but I understand why you're doing it. What you haven't told me yet is what's wrong.'

'Me,' Emma said. Ben clearly didn't follow so he squeezed her hand and waited. She took a deep breath. 'I thought I could give me what I wanted, too: career, children. I thought it would be enough to write them into my life but it's not.'

'Look at me, Emma,' Ben said. 'Not everything is confined to the page.'

Ben cupped her face in his hand and gently wiped away the first tear with his thumb. Little did he know, but the sensation of his hand on her cheek was the trigger for an emotional dam burst. 'I know,' she said, recalling the sensation that had remained after her latest seizure, of the touch of a little girl's hand.

Ben wrapped her in his arms as she began to sob. 'I'm not sure you do know, Emma. I want you to let me back into your life, I'm feeling lost.'

Emma's emotions were sending shockwaves along every nerve in her body. She knew he was right. Her determination to shoulder the burden alone had fuelled her sense of isolation. Her writing had stopped being the joint effort it should be, she was keeping out the very person she wanted to share the rest of her life with.

Emma looked up into his face. She took his hand and placed it on her cheek, her hand overlapping his. She attempted to smile but it quivered pitifully. 'I sent you away,' she agreed. 'I shouldn't have done that. I need you, Ben. There are things I can still experience. You showed me that once before. I'm going to need your help to see it again.'

15

We weren't perfect by any means. We had our disagreements and we liked to challenge each other. To my shame, it took me a while to recognize that in one particular respect, I had been pushing Ben so far out of his comfort zone that I risked trampling over his dreams.

'You could have won that pitch,' I told him, throwing my words at him like an accusation. I scrunched up the rejection letter, which had followed my latest bid to take Ben's business global, and was tempted to launch that at him too. It didn't help that he was smiling at me. 'It would have needed some investment but we could have taken on extra staff, maybe even someone to manage the business. Give you more free time.'

Ben said nothing. He stepped closer to me, tentatively, the sunlight streaming through the window highlighting his features. He was as handsome as ever but now he had a sprinkling of grey at his temples. Middle age suited him and he deserved a business that equalled his distinction.

'Time to concentrate on other things like your photography. Maybe go professional again. I had it all planned,' I persisted.

Still not saying a word, he took my hand and I dutifully followed as he led me through the house and out to the garden. He waited until we were both looking towards the apple tree before he spoke.

'I could expand the business, take on more work to earn more money and spend all my time wondering how to stay one step ahead of the competition. I could even make enough to pay someone to run my dream for me. I could carve out a new career as a photographer, travel the world for that winning shot. I could fill my life with so much more,' he said, not once looking at me, never taking his eyes from our children who were playing on the swing that hung from the tree.

'Sorry,' I said when I saw our life through Ben's eyes. 'Perhaps I have been losing sight of what was right in front of me.'

We watched our children as they played, blissfully unaware of the love being showered upon them by their parents, parents who didn't put them before their own dreams because they were part of those dreams.

Looking back at my own childhood, it seemed wrong that the happy times that came to mind so readily were the times spent with my dad. Why should that be? I had to ask myself. After all, it was my mum who had stayed at home until Louise and I were both at school, and even when she returned to work, she seemed to manage her hours so that she was still there in the evenings and during school holidays. I couldn't help wondering what memories my own children would choose to capture and keep. Ben and I were fortunate in that we were both self-employed and if there was a fight over who would pick the kids up from school, it was because we both wanted to do it and often we both did. Together we were the constant in their lives.

'Come on,' Ben said, pulling me towards the fun. 'Let's not stay on the sidelines.'

Charlie spotted us first and rushed over to me and if I thought all disagreements had been settled for the day, I was about to be corrected.

'It's my turn to go on the swing,' he said with a pout. He was four years old and I could see a tantrum threatening as if it were an oncoming storm.

Rose and Charlie were like chalk and cheese, in much the same way as Louise and I were. Rose was the practical one who didn't like taking risks, whilst Charlie was the wild child. When they fought, I became referee, trying to find a compromise that would keep them both happy.

'You can play on the swing as soon as Rose has finished her turn,' I promised.

'But she's been on it all day,' he sulked.

'You've only been in the garden five minutes. Why don't we count how many times Rose swings? When we count to ten, then it can be your turn,' I said, looking towards Rose for agreement but she was pretending not to hear.

'One, two, seven, ten,' counted Charlie as quick as a flash. 'My turn!'

When I couldn't hold him back any longer, Rose gave up trying to ignore us. She may have complained constantly about her brother but she took as much pleasure from Charlie's enjoyment as she did her own. She surrendered the swing without complaint.

We watched as Charlie swung higher than Rose had ever dared and the blossom from the apple tree started to fall to the ground in a shower of petals.

'I wish this could last forever,' I said to Ben and I meant it. It was the high point of my entire life, everything I could ever want was there within my grasp.

Beyond the perfection of the scene around me, I could hear the creaking of the branch as Charlie pushed himself back and forth. A doubt crept into my mind. A sense of fear shared by mothers the world over. I could barely comprehend what my own mum had gone through when I was ill and I imagined she never stopped listening out for that creaking branch.

'Are you sure you don't want to go global?' Emma asked.

'I'm sure,' he said, still reading from the computer screen. When Ben had realized the new direction Emma was leading him towards in their story, he had told her in no uncertain terms that his ambitions would always lie closer to home, and she had been forced to rethink her plans.

'I have the power,' she persisted, wiggling her fingers for effect.

'And I have a pushy wife,' he told her, taking her hand and kissing each finger.

They were at the hospital, waiting for Emma's name to be called for what would be her fourteenth session of radiotherapy. She had to concede that the side effects were finally starting to get to her. The anti-nausea drugs were doing their best to stop the constant feeling of sickness escalating to full-blown vomiting but it was the pain in her back and neck that she feared most. It was most excruciating when she had to lie on the treatment table, but each session lasted only five minutes and if she took enough painkillers beforehand then the drugs made it almost bearable. It was the fatigue that came with no miracle cure and it was becoming the one thing she found hardest to accept. The physical effort of writing was becoming far more of a chore than she would like. Even when she wasn't fighting sleep, her mind was sluggish and words were beginning to slip out of her grasp. If it hadn't been for Ben's subtle editing when it was clear she had given up on a particular sentence, not to mention his encouragement and unstoppable enthusiasm, she doubted she would have written a word in the last few days.

'I still think you could do something with your photography.'

'Maybe when the kids have left home,' he said, not dismissing the idea.

'I wasn't talking about in the story,' Emma said, closing down the computer and handing it to Ben for safekeeping.

'You do like to meddle, Mrs Knowles.'

Emma smiled at the sound of her fictional name. It suited her. 'I'm sorry; of course I was talking about the story and I promise I won't do anything without discussing it with you first.'

Ben laughed. 'You don't have to start walking on eggshells. It's your story. I want to be involved but I don't mind the odd surprise. Sometimes it can be good for the soul to face the unexpected.'

'Emma Patterson,' the nurse called.

'Back to reality,' Emma said as she stood up, unaware that it was Ben who was now being drawn back into their imaginary world as he watched her disappear from view.

'I don't think I've seen you here before,' the shopkeeper said. He stood with his hands spread wide across the counter as if protecting his wares from unwelcome eyes.

'Actually, I'm here on behalf of a mutual friend of ours,' I told him, doing my best to hide my nerves. I wasn't sure if I was doing the right thing and I was hoping the shopkeeper would see that my intentions were honourable. I needed his help.

'And who would that be?' he answered, not giving an inch.

'Her name is Emma. I believe she's a regular customer of yours.'

The shopkeeper eyed me carefully if not a little suspiciously. 'There is such a thing as customer confidentiality.'

'OK, I understand that and if I'm being completely honest, she doesn't know I'm here,' I confessed. 'But I know she needs help and I think that she trusts me enough to know I want what's best for her.'

'So why the secrecy? Why not bring Emma along with you?' he asked, unconvinced by my argument thus far.

'Because I think a surprise is well overdue, a nice one that is.'

Rather than reply immediately, the shopkeeper took a closer look at me. 'You must be Ben,' he said at last and then a broad grin settled across his face. 'How may I assist you?'

'I'm planning a little expedition and I need your help convincing Emma to accompany me, no questions asked,' I said, my eyes darting towards the shelves that the shopkeeper was still protecting. 'The problem isn't the gift itself, it's getting Emma to accept it.'

'I think between the two of us we can manage to persuade her,' he said.

Emma crawled out of bed where yet again she had failed to surrender to the restful sleep she had needed. Ben was already up and busily preparing for the day ahead. It was Saturday morning and by all accounts it was going to be a very special day. Emma had yet to discover what Ben had planned for her but as a whispered conversation came to an abrupt end as Emma entered the living room, she suspected that her mum did.

'Three bags,' Meg explained. 'This one has all the

medical supplies you could possibly need, this one has the food and this one's got blankets and extra layers in case she gets cold.'

'This is only a day trip, isn't it?' Emma asked.

Meg shrugged. 'I've no idea,' she replied.

'Liar,' Emma muttered.

'Now you will let me know when you get there,' Meg told Ben. 'And take things easy. Don't believe this one when she says she's feeling fine.'

'No more climbing up mountains,' Ben agreed dutifully.

The sight before Emma was worthy of one of her hallucinations as Meg lifted a motherly hand to Ben's face. He leaned over and kissed her cheek. 'You're a good boy,' she said.

'Are we ready?' Emma asked as the first bubbles of excitement burst into life deep inside her.

'For the time of our lives,' he assured her.

The drive was long. Very long. They were heading north but, despite Emma's frequent asking, Ben continued to refuse to tell her where he was taking her. She dozed through much of the journey and each time she opened her eyes, they were still following the same grey ribbon of road even though the landscape around them had changed. The manmade motorway embankments were eventually replaced by more natural peaks and valleys but it was only as the peaks became snow-capped mountains that Emma started to put the clues together.

She groaned as she shifted position and sat up straight in her seat. 'Scotland?' she asked.

'Might be.'

The look Emma gave Ben was lost on him, he was too intent on the road ahead. 'Given that we've already crossed the border and there's pretty much nowhere else for this road to go, I don't think you can quite justify a *maybe*,' she answered curtly.

'OK, it's Scotland.'

Emma went through all the possibilities in her head, trying to match them to the dream destinations she and Ben had talked about. She stared out of the window and followed the shadows of the clouds as they slipped across the mountains, white snow glinting brightly before falling to grey. 'Does this have anything to do with your suggestion about taking the kids to Lapland?' she asked.

When Ben didn't answer, Emma decided not to delve any further. It would be nice, she told herself, to wait for the surprise. But her stomach churned as their route led them away from barren landscape towards civilization once more, nausea caused by pure excitement and nerves rather than anything else. She didn't want to even dare to hope but as they pulled up outside a large Victorian terraced house and a little face appeared at the tall picture window, Emma wanted to cry with joy.

'We're here,' Ben said softly, turning off the engine and looking over to Emma for her reaction, which was exactly as he had hoped. 'It's all arranged and don't worry, this isn't some kind of forced reunion with your dad. He and Carolyn are going to make themselves scarce and we get to spend time with Olivia and Amy. We're going to be parents for the day, Em.'

Emma intended to say, 'OK,' but it came out as a muffled sob.

'I didn't have anything spectacular in mind,' he warned. 'I thought maybe a trip to the park, but otherwise, I think it's going to be a matter of keeping the girls occupied at home.'

'Not spectacular?' Emma asked. 'How is this not spectacular?'

The house was warm and so welcoming that it practically shone. True to the promise made to Ben, John and Carolyn spent only as long as necessary to go through some of the more practical issues. It was midday and lunch had already been prepared for Emma and Ben to share with the girls whilst their parents planned to spend the afternoon dining out and shopping. Emma had to rely on Ben to take notice of all the various instructions, she was too busy fielding the questions her sisters bombarded her with.

'Would you like to see my bedroom?' Olivia asked.

'Mine too,' interrupted Amy.

'Will you play house with me? You can play with my dollies,' offered Olivia.

'Mine too,' Amy said, jumping up and down with excitement and oblivious to Olivia who was manoeuvring herself between Emma and her younger sibling.

Emma looked at Ben, tears already glistening in her eyes. 'You go,' he said, 'I'll be up in a minute.'

When Ben arrived in Olivia's bedroom, all three of his girls were sitting on the floor surrounded by a mountain of toys. They all looked up expectantly at him. 'Now, ladies,' he began. 'I think it's time we all had something to eat.'

'Play first,' pouted Amy.

'We can eat later,' agreed Olivia.

Ben looked towards Emma for support but she was torn between siding with her girls or with her husband. 'I tell you what,' she said, applying the art of compromise. 'Why don't we have a picnic?'

'Can we?' screamed the girls, jumping up and dancing around the room.

Ben looked out of the window. The weather was clear but the temperature barely above freezing.

'We can have a picnic in the house,' Emma explained, to counter his puzzled look.

'Yes,' the girls screamed again.

'And then we can all walk off our lunch with a trip to the park,' offered Ben and, this time, he had the presence of mind to cover his ears before the screams of excitement could pierce his eardrums.

There had been moments that Emma wanted to preserve and then there were whole days and this was most definitely turning into one of them. When John and Carolyn arrived back home in the early evening, Emma and Ben were on the last leg of their journey through parenthood and had crashed out on the sofa, each with a sleeping child sprawled over them and a pile of storybooks lying close by. The children weren't the only ones sleeping.

John nudged Emma's shoulder to wake her as gently as he could. 'Have you had a good day?' he asked.

'The best,' she said, groggily trying to loosen her joints without disturbing Olivia who had her head nestled into Emma's neck.

Ben's groans matched Emma's as he tried to shuffle off the sofa with Amy in his arms. 'I'll take her up,' he said as Carolyn helped him to his feet. As they disappeared upstairs, John made a move to take Olivia from Emma's arms. Emma instinctively tightened her grip on the sleeping child.

She was unwilling to let go of the dream. She was holding Rose in her arms and didn't want to give her back. Her fingers weren't stroking the keys of an unforgiving keyboard; they were touching real flesh and blood.

John didn't insist, choosing instead to sit down next to his daughters. 'You and Ben make a perfect couple,' he said. 'And you would have made such wonderful parents.'

Emma noted his use of the past tense, it was something that most people struggled with and she was grateful for his honesty. 'Yes, I think you're right,' she said, relaxing her grip on Olivia. 'Considering how new it was to us, we coped pretty well, and I wouldn't have missed it for the world. I suppose Ben's told you about the book I'm writing?'

John nodded.

'The real thing is so much better,' she said. 'How did it take you so long to realize that?'

'Ah, indeed,' John said, trying to sound light-hearted. 'I ask myself that often.'

Emma rested her head on Olivia's and her damp hair tickled her cheek. She could feel the little girl's steady breath warming the skin on her neck and it sent a shiver down her spine. She felt an overwhelming desire to protect her above anything else. 'Don't you think it's strange that my most vivid childhood memories are of you? Why on earth would I covet the memories of the one parent who let me down so badly?'

'I get the feeling you know the answer. Tell me,' her dad said, surprising Emma with his obviously genuine need to know.

'It was such a rare event to have your attention,' Emma explained. 'Those times were so precious, from a child's perspective at least, but now I see things differently. While I was busy worshipping you, I barely noticed Mum, and she was the one person who was there every single day of my life, willing to give everything of herself for her daughters and never expecting anything in return, not even recognition for what she was doing.'

'I'm sure she knows how much you appreciate her,' John assured her.

Emma shook her head. 'No, how could she? Even I

339

didn't know how much I should appreciate her until now. Only now do I know that you don't have to take a starring role to be the best parent; in fact, you should be the opposite.' Emma looked towards her dad. She needed some sign from him that he understood what she was trying to say, because she didn't think she could hand Olivia over to him without it. The silent tears trailing down his face confirmed that he did. 'So, if you want some advice and if you want to be the best father you possibly can to this beautiful little girl, then be invisible, Dad. Be there for her, be a constant in her life and not a rare event.'

'I will,' he said. 'You have my promise.'

Emma and Ben drove through the Scottish wilderness in stunned silence. The world outside transformed into an impenetrable darkness as they put more distance between themselves and the city. All Emma could see was her own reflection in the passenger window, and for the first time in a long time, the reflection didn't scare her. She could see what she already felt, a sense of fulfilment that she had once thought unobtainable.

'Did I do well?' Ben asked when he noticed that she still hadn't succumbed to sleep.

'Yes,' Emma told him. She wanted to say more but words failed her. Thankfully, Ben didn't need further proof. He had been as intent on watching her as he had been watching Olivia and Amy. He already knew he had done exceptionally well.

'I thought you would have dropped off to sleep as soon as we left Edinburgh.'

Emma was undeniably tired and she knew she needed to sleep but her mind was busily trying to retain every single detail of the day she'd had. 'I'll try,' she said, slouching down a little further in her seat.

There was an indistinct line between her conscious mind adding new layers to her alternate life and the unconscious creation of dreams over which she had no control. On this occasion it seemed not to matter as both conjured up idyllic scenes of family life, but inevitably the dream had to end and she woke with a start. The car had come to a stop and when she turned towards Ben, he wasn't there. There was no time to panic as he appeared at the passenger window, a camera around his neck. He opened her door and crouched down next to her.

Still confused, Emma glanced over his shoulder to be met by the same inky blackness that had surrounded them earlier. 'Where are we?' she asked, rubbing away the sleep from her eyes and the remnants of her dreams along with it.

'I need you to get out of the car,' Ben told her. His voice sounded almost reverent. She released her seatbelt and he took her hand as she struggled out of her seat.

She could vaguely make out the silhouettes of mountains ahead of her, a ghostly impression of the snowy caps that seemed to float in midair. As her eyes became accustomed to the darkness, she felt unsettled. There was a quality to the night sky that didn't feel right. 'Is something wrong?' Emma asked, the chill in the air giving her the final shock to the system to make her fully alert.

'No, not at all,' Ben said, but his words were charged with emotion, which did little to dispel Emma's growing anxiety. He put his hands firmly on her shoulders. 'I need you to close your eyes.'

Emma gave a laugh, a nervous reaction to the building tension, but she did as she was bid. She allowed Ben to manoeuvre her towards the front of the car and then turn her around so that she was facing the opposite direction. 'Keep them closed,' Ben reminded her as he let her go.

She heard the crunch of stones underfoot as he stepped away and then his coat sleeves rustling. She suspected he had lifted up his camera but for the life of her she still couldn't think why.

'Wait,' he said again.

Emma kept her eyes tightly closed but then something magical happened. There was a flutter of light over her closed eyelids and she was already opening her eyes instinctively when Ben told her she could look. Her attention was drawn not to Ben but to the skies. There was a click of the camera to commit the moment to eternity.

It took perhaps two seconds for the sob to escape and for the tears to blur Emma's vision but she wiped them away furiously, intent on keeping the view perfectly in her sights. 'The Northern Lights,' she gasped. 'How the hell did you do that?'

Ben stepped closer and then stood behind her, his arms wrapped around her waist so they could watch together. Swathes of colour rippled across the sky, undulating ribbons of light on a cosmic scale that slipped from view behind the rugged landscape. 'I wish I could take credit for this but it wasn't part of the plan.'

They stood in silence and watched the sky continue with its incredible lightshow. 'It was on the list,' Emma said, almost to herself, 'but I could never have imagined it would be like this. I couldn't have described this without seeing it for myself, Ben. This is living it. The whole day has been living it.'

'In that case, do you think you could stand a little more real-life experience?'

'There's more?'

When Ben refused to reply, she reluctantly tore her eyes away from the lights that were still sweeping the sky and turned to face him.

'I love you, Emma, with all my heart and soul and if I could create a million days for you like this one, I would,' he said, taking her hand. 'I know I can't make all your dreams come true but there is one thing I can make happen.'

'And what would that be?' Emma asked, daring not to hope.

As Ben knelt down before her, she could feel the darkness around her falling away. The light grew as if the

Northern Lights had been on a dimmer switch and had suddenly been set to full power.

'Emma, will you marry me?' Ben asked, looking up towards her, icy determination in his eyes.

'Yes,' Emma replied, almost choking on that single word as Ben stood up and kissed her.

The children were growing up so fast and as much as I wanted time to stand still, I also wanted to see them grow. I wanted to know what they would make of the world once my little fledglings flew the nest. But there was still time to enjoy one particular joy of childhood. Rose was nine and Charlie seven and I guessed it would be the last year that at least one of my children believed in Father Christmas.

'I want a white Christmas,' I told Ben. 'Nothing else will do.'

'We might get snow on higher ground but I don't think we'll see any here.'

'Then you're going to have to climb a mountain and bring it back so we can make snowmen.'

'OK, I give in.'

'Give in to what?' I asked, my face a picture of innocence.

'We can close up shop and go to Lapland.'

'Thank you, I never thought you'd give in!' I said, opening a draw where I'd hidden the travel details for the trip I had already booked.

Ben opened his mouth to speak but words failed him.

* * *

'We're here!' squealed Rose, pulling at her dad's hand as we stood in thick snow outside Santa's Lapland home. There were twinkling lights all around us, reflecting off the white landscape that gave the lodge an ethereal glow. Above us, the jet-black sky only served to enhance the sparkle of a thousand stars.

'How about taking Charlie in to see Santa, Rose?' I asked, looking down at my daughter who had wrapped her arms tightly around my waist. Her whole body trembled and I wondered if she had resurrected her belief in Father Christmas or more likely, she was simply terrified at the thought of going into a hut to meet a man who made a living from dressing up in a silly red suit and persuading children to sit on his knee.

Though I was encouraging her, part of me didn't want to let her go and my heart wrenched when she pulled away. I could only hope that Santa would live up to my expectations.

I watched them disappear inside the lodge with my heart torn.

Ben pulled me towards him and wrapped me in his arms. 'They know where we are if they need us,' he reassured me.

Before I could answer, his body froze and I looked up into his face to see a shimmer of light reflected across his eyes. It was as if he could see heaven's gates in the skies behind me. 'You're not going to believe this,' he said.

*   *   *

Emma's neck and back pain showed no signs of letting up, but even when she left the treatment room crying in pain after one particular radiotherapy session during her fourth week, she insisted that she could continue to brave it through. It was Meg who wasn't prepared to let her suffering continue unchecked. Emma's next scan wasn't scheduled to take place until a month after treatment – it would only be then that the effectiveness of the radio-therapy could be properly measured – but with a little persistent persuasion, Mr Spelling arranged a CT scan for the following week.

Fortunately, Emma's deteriorating health was coun-terbalanced by a rise in her spirits. Whilst it was hard to silence her body, which was telling her to spend the weekend cocooned in her bedroom, she was determined to celebrate her engagement and to toast the recent successes of the bistro. Her compromise with herself was to organize a special but otherwise sedate Sunday lunch surrounded by family and friends.

When Emma walked into the bistro with Ben, everyone else had already arrived, holding court at one of the long tables in the centre of the restaurant. Even her mum was there before her, conspicuous by her absence all morning and now deep in conversation with Ally and Gina, who looked like they had demolished a bottle of wine already.

Jean and Iris were there, sitting either side of Steven and clearly enjoying the attention of a young man. They were all honoured guests for the day and Louise was making a concerted effort to show her appreciation by closing the bistro for a few hours and taking charge of cooking dinner.

The conversation came to an abrupt end as Emma took her seat. She looked from one guilty expression to another. 'So what have I missed?'

'Ally was just telling us about the dirty weekend she's planning,' Gina announced.

Ally glared at Gina, her face turning as red as the wine in her glass. 'No, I wasn't,' she growled.

Emma's tired body flared with excitement. 'Tell,' she insisted.

Ally groaned. 'You don't want to hear about my love life. We're here to celebrate yours.'

'Peter?' Emma asked, ignoring her attempt to sidestep the question.

'She's in lurve.' Gina giggled, ignoring Ally's second glare.

'Don't blow it this time,' warned Emma.

'Yes, for God's sake, Ally, don't be yourself,' Gina added, laughing at her own joke.

'Your first weekend away. How romantic,' Emma said but when Ally's blush deepened, it made her check her words. 'It's not the first one, is it?'

'We went away last weekend.'

'When I was in Scotland. Is there no end to the secrets you lot have been keeping from me?' Emma demanded and then was met with a wall of silence for the second time that day. 'OK, that's it. Tell me what's going on.'

'We were wondering what kind of plans you had for

your wedding,' Jean replied eagerly when everyone else simply shifted uneasily in their chairs.

Emma shrugged her shoulders shyly as the image she had described in her book came to mind. She was ready to accept that the real-life occasion couldn't be so magical but it was enough to know that she was going to marry Ben; it didn't really matter how or where. 'We'll probably opt for something low key, a registry office followed by a quick bite to eat,' she suggested.

'You will not,' Gina said huffily. 'I didn't go through all of those plans with you for nothing.'

'That was only my dream wedding,' Emma told her firmly.

'And I'm not wasting my very amusing speech over *a quick bite to eat*,' warned Steven.

'But when we had our imaginary wedding, we were spending imaginary money,' replied Emma, who wasn't in the mood for false hopes.

'But Meg and your dad have already stumped up the cash,' Gina said primly.

'What?' Emma asked, directing the question towards her mum. 'You've been making deals with Dad?'

'I'll do whatever's required to give you the wedding you deserve. You're going to be married on the first day of spring in St Luke's,' Meg said firmly.

'Sorry,' offered Jean. 'I was only being polite when I asked you what kind of wedding you wanted. I'm afraid it's out of your hands now.'

'We're the newly formed Wedding Planners,' Iris

declared, banging her hand on the table. 'And I hereby bring this meeting to order.'

'The Wedding Planners?' Emma asked but was duly ignored now that official business was underway.

'When is the first day of spring, anyway?' Gina asked.

'The beginning of March, isn't it?' Jean said. 'Oh, dear, that's tomorrow.'

Emma was shaking her head. 'Not necessarily. There are differing views and the one I prefer to go with is the vernal equinox.' Jean looked blankly at her. 'Twenty-first of March,' Emma added quickly.

There was a collective sigh of relief. 'Then that's plenty of time,' Jean said.

'Let's hope the weather improves by then,' added Ally, who was looking towards the window. It was a cold, murky day outside, growing darker and murkier by the minute, and the few souls who had braved the elements had their heads down and were holding onto their umbrellas for dear life.

'I'll second that,' Gina said. 'Only you could choose to get married in a church that doesn't even have a roof.'

'There is another problem,' Louise added. She had appeared from the kitchen, looking for volunteers to help serve up dinner but the conversation had distracted her from the task in hand. 'You can't have a legal ceremony there.'

'We can go to a registry office to get the piece of paper,' Ben said. 'That part doesn't really matter. Our wedding will take place on the twenty-first of March in

349

the bombed-out church. We're going to make it happen.'

Emma's gaze met Ben's and a delicious shudder crawled down her spine. She needed no more convincing. She really was going to have the wedding of her dreams. Any ideas of a low-key wedding were abandoned. Emma would be putting her faith in the Wedding Planners to perform their miracles although she would be insisting that the costs were tightly controlled. Any spare cash her mum and dad were willing to throw around would be invested in the bistro, Emma would see to it.

Emma's appetite for her lunch may have been wanting but the company was not. She was carried away by the collective enthusiasm for her wedding plans, but as the afternoon went on, so her energy levels receded. She felt much older than her years. The hot and sticky atmosphere was trying to overwhelm her but she was determined not to let it; her intent was to stay at least until the bistro opened for the evening custom.

'It's lovely to see you and Ben so happy together,' Iris told her when everyone else was busy clearing away dishes.

'Love is most definitely in the air. Wouldn't you agree?'

Iris smiled coyly. 'Yes, I confess, I'm all loved up too.'

'So how's it going?' asked Emma in a low whisper so no-one else could hear them.

'Oh, it's early days,' she said, 'but I can't afford to take things slowly.'

'You and me both,' Emma said with a laugh but Iris

350

looked mortified. 'Live for the moment. No-one knows what's around the corner,' she continued, holding her smile until Iris returned it.

'I know that better than most. Ted and I were planning our retirement when he died. I thought my life was over and I would have been happy to crawl into the grave with him. Never mind he was a grumpy old sod and such a miser, I was lost without him. That's the price of love, I suppose.'

The goosebumps that appeared without warning made Emma shiver. She thought of Ben and her guilt weighed down on her chest as did the air around her. 'At least you had Jean,' she offered.

'Actually, I didn't even know Jean then. We met when I moved into sheltered housing and quickly discovered how much we had in common. We had both lived very staid lives with husbands who kept a tight hold of the purse strings and now we're making up for lost time. Jean bought me one of those experience days as a joke for my birthday, but we caught the bug. We had a taste for life again and you've seen what we're like now.'

'Like a couple of schoolgirls, mostly,' observed Emma.

Emma wafted her hand in front of her face in a vain attempt to freshen the air around her. 'I hope your new man knows what he's letting himself in for,' she said.

'Are you feeling alright? You look a little flushed.'

Emma tried to convince Iris that she was fine but she was starting to feel distinctly clammy. 'I think I'll just step outside for some fresh air.'

As she stood up, Ben was there to take her arm. He seemed to have developed a sixth sense to be there exactly when she needed him. 'We'll catch up later,' she promised Iris. 'You still haven't told me about your new beau.'

'I can't wait for you to meet him,' Iris replied with a meaningful wink that was lost on Emma.

The air outside the bistro was blissfully cool. The wind had chased away the rain and now it had finally lost its breath, leaving the world quietly exhausted. 'I can't wait until the blossom starts to appear,' she told Ben wistfully, nodding towards the trees that lined the avenue. They were showing tantalizing signs of budding but wouldn't be ready to reveal their hidden beauty for a month or two.

A gust of wind appeared from nowhere and Emma heard nearby branches creaking in response. A sense of déjà vu crept over her and she squeezed her eyes closed as she felt her mind pulling her towards another world.

'It won't be long,' Ben told her, wrapping an arm around her waist.

It wasn't only the branches creaking that Emma could hear now. She could hear her children's laughter and in a leap of faith, Emma opened her eyes, blinking away the bright sunlight to reveal white clouds of apple blossom and a shower of petals raining down on Charlie, who was gently kicking his feet to propel himself back and forth on the swing. 'Not long at all,' Emma agreed as her vision settled back into reality.

16

My fingers danced over the keyboard more slowly than once they had but then life was slower too. To accompany my rhythmic tapping, I could hear the rain falling in heavy, lazy drops, thudding against the window sill. The usual morning birdsong had been reduced to the gentle cooing of a single wood pigeon. Beyond those sounds, silence.

I was aware of the sonorous springtime ballad being played around me as I worked and despite the pressures of a challenging deadline for my latest novel, I was relaxed. I was contented. I stopped typing and let the sound of my breathing join in the music. The air felt fresh and slightly metallic as I pulled it into my lungs.

I stood up from my chair, gently stretched my aching back, yawned. The house felt empty. My birds had flown the nest but I didn't feel the sense of loss I had feared. I stepped out of the study and as I glanced up the stairs, my mind's eye glimpsed a child running down towards me. Rose as a little girl with a sparkle in her eyes and a teddy in her arms, Charlie next, in a Superman costume. My arms reached out instinctively to catch him as he tried to fly. Then Rose, a little older, in her school uniform, the back of Charlie's head as he stormed up the stairs in his football kit, trailing mud behind him but refusing a bath. Charlie in his cap and gown, Rose in her doctor's whites, then her wedding dress. The memories flooded my heart and the rush of love and pride pumped through my veins.

Behind me, I heard the door opening and closing, followed by the scrape of boots against the mat, the flapping of a coat being shrugged off and the dripping of water as the rain fell from wet clothes. I didn't turn around but my body tensed. Playing to form, Ben crept up behind me, wrapped me in his arms and buried his cold, wet face into my warm neck.

'You're freezing!' I scolded but I didn't pull away.

'So what were you staring at? Waiting for the kids to come down the stairs?'

'I know they've gone,' I said, twisting around towards him. Raindrops that had pooled in the creases of his brow were dripping through the softer wrinkles around his eyes and when I kissed his wet cheek, the spring rain tasted sweet. 'But they'll always be my babies. They'll always be a part of me, no matter what.'

'You're beginning to sound like your mum.'

I smiled. 'I'll take that as a compliment. She wasn't as fortunate as I am. She didn't have someone like you by *her side but she still managed to create a secure and stable family. Louise and I never lacked for love and attention. She thought her heart would break when I left but she stayed strong. The bond between mother and child is unbreakable. She knew that and now so do I.'*

Ben kissed my nose and I rested my head on his chest. 'So, are you ready to face the next chapter of your life?'

I couldn't look at him. The contentment I felt for the life I had led so far didn't mean I was any less reluctant to face the future. I was about to turn sixty and was starting to feel my age but there was life in the old dog yet. I took a deep breath. 'I'm ready,' I told him.

Mr Spelling's office was deep in shadow, matching the dark brooding day outside. Emma was sitting in the chair next to his desk, watching the doctor as he stared at the screen in front of him, rubbing his chin. She lifted her head slightly as if to catch the warm rays of sun that weren't streaming through the window. Her eyes stung against the nonexistent light that nevertheless reflected off the pale butter-cream walls.

Emma had been summoned to receive the results of her recent scan but her mind was pulling her somewhere else. The sense of familiarity was at first difficult to place but once Emma recognized it, her heart quickened. This was where it had all begun. This was the moment that Mr Spelling would turn and tell her in his own inimitable way that it was over, that she had the all-clear. For a split second, she almost wished that she had asked Ben and her mum to come into the office with her rather than relegating them to the waiting area outside, but then reality pulled her back. She pushed away the feeling of déjà vu and planted her feet firmly into the carpet to stop her legs from trembling.

'I'm afraid it's bad news, Emma,' Mr Spelling said.

By the time Emma was ready to leave his office, the initial shock had been replaced by two very different emotions. Fear and relief. The relief for Emma was that she no longer had to face the torturous prospect of any more radiotherapy, or any kind of therapy for that matter. When Mr Spelling had explained that new tumours had developed on her brain stem, that these were causing the back pain, Emma had taken a deep breath and prepared herself to accept whatever treatment her doctor could offer. But it hadn't taken Mr Spelling long to convince her that there would be little to no benefit in continuing with treatment; it would not justify the unpleasant side effects. It was over and that was exactly how Mr Spelling had phrased it in a cruel perversion of the scene she had described at the very beginning of her book. The fight was over.

The fear she felt meanwhile had nothing to do with being told that she didn't have long to live, that particular prospect was strangely another part of her relief. There would be no more fear of the unknown and no doubts about what the future held. That certainty was reassuring, liberating even. The monster in her head had won but she would be a good loser.

The source of Emma's fear lay on the other side of the door. The two expectant faces that turned towards her as she left Mr Spelling's office would not share her relief.

Ben and Meg rose to their feet as she approached. Ben met her with a bright, innocent smile and no inkling of the news she was about to impart. It was her mum who had seen the warning signs, and the way Emma wasn't making eye contact as she approached was only the final confirmation she needed. Meg had been aware of the almost imperceptible deterioration in Emma's condition over the last few weeks, which couldn't be explained by radiotherapy alone. Clues that Emma had managed to hide from everyone except her.

Emma had played out a few scenarios in her mind on the long journey from the doctor's office to the waiting area. She considered beginning with the good news that she wasn't going to have any more treatment but that would be too cruel. There really was no way to soften the blow. 'I have three more tumours,' she began, 'and they've appeared really quickly. The only treatment now is palliative care.'

There was a deathly silence as Meg's face completely drained of colour and she almost stumbled. 'No,' she said in a painful mewl. She reached out and grabbed Emma's proffered hand with such force that it took the last remnants of Emma's self-control not to cry out.

Time seemed to stop as they all stood in stunned

silence, broken only by the sound of Meg's gulps for air. 'I'm going to be sick,' she gasped before staggering off towards the washroom at the end of the corridor.

As Emma watched her mum running away, the finality of her situation hit home far more than when Mr Spelling had given his grim prognosis. If there had been even the tiniest spark of hope in Emma's heart, it was brutally extinguished by the sight of her cavalry making a hasty retreat.

Ben's eyes were wide with shock and he seemed torn between staying with Emma and going to help Meg. He stayed but perhaps only because he couldn't trust his legs to carry him. 'Palliative?' he asked, still trying to digest the information.

'End-of-life care, Ben,' Emma said, reaching for his hand. His grip was tentative, as if he were holding a delicate flower he was terrified of crushing. 'Some drugs, specialist nurses, hospices, that kind of thing.'

'And that's it?' he asked, his voice trembling. He glanced back in the direction that Meg had gone.

'She knows,' Emma told him. 'A few months ago, I would have needed to call security to keep her from storming into Mr Spelling's office and demanding he cure me, but not now. I'm so sorry, Ben, it's time to start thinking of letting go.'

'But how can I let you go when you're not even mine yet?' he asked but it was a question that Emma couldn't even begin to answer.

* * *

There was no discussion about where they should go when they left the hospital. There was only one place to go.

'If I wanted to know what my wake would be like, you're all doing a very good impression,' Emma warned when the hushed tones around her usual table at the Traveller's Rest were too much to bear. 'Can't we at least put some music on to liven the place up?'

'I need to get back to work,' Ben said, making a move to leave. He hadn't left Emma's side since the news had broken but he had adopted the role of silent partner. He had been as brave as Emma had expected he would be, taking care of her and her mum, but after his initial questions, he could find nothing else to say.

'Oh, no, you don't,' Louise told him. 'I've already arranged cover. You're family now and we need you here with us.' When Ben tried to refuse, Louise interrupted him again. 'Besides, the state you're in, you'll probably burn the place down.'

'In that case, I'll go sort out the music,' Ben insisted.

When Louise looked like she was going to object again, Emma raised her hand. 'Let him go,' she told her, and when he left, her heart went with him. 'Let him do what he has to.'

It was Meg's reaction that surprised Emma the most. She may not have argued with the prognosis but she wasn't about to stop being her daughter's advocate and Emma knew it was going to test her strength to the limits. Her mum was prepared to discuss the practicalities of arranging palliative care and didn't even dismiss the suggestion of finding a hospice. Not that they had discussed it in detail, the news was still sinking in for all of them.

'You still want to go ahead with the wedding, don't you?' Meg asked.

Emma was about to reply that of course she did – preparations were underway and they had already posted their marriage notice at the register office – but then she stopped herself. She looked towards the kitchen door and noticed the continued absence of music. 'I need to speak to Ben first,' she said and with a knot of fear twisting at her insides, she went in search of him.

Ben wasn't in the kitchen, so Emma moved on, past the inanimate music system and headed towards the small corridor that led upstairs. Ben was sitting on the stairs, his shoulders hunched and his hands over his head, covering his ears as if the music he hadn't switched on was deafening. He was visibly shaking.

For a moment, Emma stood still, not sure if she should run up and wrap him in her arms or back slowly away without him ever knowing that she had been there to bear witness to his private torment. She did neither. She sat down gently beside him and waited for him to decide if he wanted her to see him.

Ben didn't look up as he reached for her hand and when she gave it to him, he wrapped his fingers around hers and reverently brought her hand to his chest. His tears fell like raindrops onto her hand and she imagined the tears following the creases of his skin, following wrinkles that were yet to reveal themselves. She felt a shiver of familiarity course through her body but her heart was beating too fast to let the image of an older, rain-drenched Ben to take form.

Ben took a deep breath and held it, trying to compose himself before he spoke. 'What if your mum was right all along?' he began, his voice sounding hoarse as if the scream he had been holding back for the last few hours had already torn his vocal chords to shreds. 'What if there is a better doctor out there who can help you?'

'I already have the best doctor, one who told me the truth and didn't pull any punches.'

'But I haven't had long enough with you yet, not nearly enough,' he said, giving her hand a gentle squeeze.

'I can't make myself better, Ben, and neither can you,' Emma said softly. 'It will have to be enough to know that I wrote myself better.'

Ben snapped his head towards her. His eyes were as red and pained as she had feared but they were also angry. 'I don't care about the book,' he said. 'It's not real. I don't care about anything but you.'

Emma raised an eyebrow and when she felt the spark of anger she went with it, it was an emotion she preferred, far better than the abject despair she had been facing. 'Don't care?' she repeated. 'Well, you damn well better care.' She let her words sink in before she continued. 'If you don't care about the book then there's no point in trying to bring any more of it to life. We might as well call off the wedding.'

'We will not,' Ben replied, his own anger filling his deflated body and forcing him to raise his shoulders.

'And I might as well throw the book in the bin,' Emma goaded.

'You can't. You put your heart and soul into that book. I won't let you destroy it.'

Emma stared at Ben's face and the trail of tears that slashed like scars across his cheeks. She wiped them away. 'No more tears,' she told him. 'Not while I'm still here. When I'm gone, you can howl at the moon, rip the stars out of the sky and stamp on them if you want to, but while I'm alive, no more tears.' Her words quaked over trembling lips, a mere fraction of the tremors that were coursing through her body but she would not let her own tears fall.

Ben tried to smile. It didn't quite reach his eyes but it was a brave attempt. 'I'll try,' he said.

'Trying isn't good enough,' Emma pointed out. 'We're getting married and then we're going to live happily ever after. Then, when I can't be with you and when your tears are finally spent, there will be happy times to remember and there will be our story to remind you how I lived my dreams.'

Ben stared at Emma, his eyes narrowing as he tried to unravel her inscrutable expression. 'Your Mr Spelling would be proud of you. You don't pull any punches either.'

Emma felt herself relax as he smiled, more easily this time. She wrinkled her nose and smiled back and the weight of the world on their shoulders lessened by a fraction. 'That's why you love me,' she said.

'That's one of the reasons,' he corrected before leaning in and kissing her.

'Egypt?' the young woman offered tentatively.

'Been there too.' I sighed, leafing through yet another brochure.

The poor girl did her best to maintain a semblance of enthusiasm. We had been in the travel agents for an hour and it hadn't taken our advisor long to realize that we had been to more places than even she had heard of. We were semi-retired and had taken what was meant to be only a year out to travel the world but every time we thought we'd had our last adventure we managed to find one last amazing place we simply had to visit. Now, after three years, we really had done it all and I didn't like the idea that this might be it.

'How about we go home?' Ben said. His voice was raspy, too much laughter and fine dining over the years. He stood up and I suspected he wasn't going to take no for an answer.

I lifted my hand towards him in submission and he pulled me to my feet.

'But . . .' I said and then stalled. Could there really be no more buts?

'Life isn't about seeing the world, it's about experiencing it,' he said, ushering me to the door. 'We have grandchildren now and maybe it's time we thought about spending more time with them.'

We had almost made it to the door when I stopped in my tracks. 'Yes, you're right. There are plenty of experiences we haven't tried yet,' I told him. 'Riding camels across the Sahara or deep-sea diving in Fiji, skydiving in the Himalayas . . .'

'Emma . . .' Ben warned.

'OK, maybe not skydiving. That might be pushing it at our age, but how about hot-air ballooning across the Serengeti?'

Ben laughed as if I had gone mad but the travel agent had pricked her ears and was busily gathering some new brochures for me. He stopped laughing when he saw that I was serious. I wasn't giving up, not yet. I was going to squeeze every last drop out of my life. I hugged him. 'If it makes you feel better, then we can always take the grandkids to Florida. I'd like to see you face the Tower of Terror.'

'There really is no stopping you, is there?'

'That's why you love me,' I replied, returning to my seat in front of the salivating travel agent who was about to work even harder for her commission.

'That's one of the reasons,' he said, taking the seat next to me and showing the first signs of enthusiasm as we started to trawl through our options. That was one of the reasons I loved him.

Emma had to agree that St Luke's wasn't an obvious venue for a wedding. By rights it shouldn't have survived the bomb that fell on it during the Blitz or the ensuing fire that swept through the entire church from the altar at one end to the tower at the other. But whilst the roof and everything inside the church had been destroyed completely, the yellow stone edifice had survived unscathed. The tall square bell tower was missing its bell, the ornate windows were bereft of their stained glass, but somehow each and every one of the Gothic pinnacles that adorned the edges of the absent roof stood proud and impossibly intact. It was a survivor and that was what had appealed to Emma.

The church was no longer a place of worship but it was still being used regularly for a variety of creative arts events and there had been some intense negotiating by the Wedding Planners to secure the venue. Emma had to be at the church at nine but her six o'clock alarm call was nothing compared to the early call some of the volunteers had. They'd been working around the clock to get everything ready.

'Someone must be looking down on you,' Meg told Emma as she watched benign, fluffy clouds ambling across a sky that had been molten red at sunrise. They were standing on the balcony of the apartment and everything around them glistened with spent raindrops. The air was fresh and the first day of spring looked like it was going to be a bright one.

Emma had been made up to within an inch of her life. Her hair had thinned and there were two significant bald patches where the radiotherapy had done its worst, but thanks to the creative use of a tiara and accessories, she was given a hairstyle befitting any bride. Her grey pallor and the dark shadows under her eyes had been hidden beneath carefully applied makeup that looked fresh and natural. Gina had succeeded where her doctors had failed.

'Enough fresh air,' Gina said, pulling Emma back into the apartment. 'It's time for the dress.'

'I feel sick,' Emma moaned as they re-entered the apartment, which felt very warm, as did she.

'You can't throw up now,' Gina cried, her eyes wide with alarm. 'Meg, do something.'

'Let's get you back outside,' Meg said, leading Emma carefully back through the patio door. She tipped up a chair with a large puddle in the middle of it and was wiping the seat with a tissue as she spoke. 'Ally, get her some water. Louise, get her anti-sickness tablets. Emma, sit down here.' Her instructions came out as fast as bullets and Emma, like everyone else, followed her orders without question, sitting down heavily on the damp chair.

'It's probably just nerves,' Emma told her mum.

Meg took a deep breath and calmed herself so her next words would be free from the anxiety building around her. 'Of course it is. We'll just have to take things a little more slowly. It's traditional for the bride to be late.'

When they arrived at the church, Emma was no less nervous but the drugs had banished the nausea. She hadn't been sick and her makeup had remained intact. As she stepped out of the car, she felt like she was stepping into another reality, leaving behind the Emma who felt tired and frail, the Emma who was dying. The young woman who stepped out of the car was radiant and as Gina and Ally adjusted the fall of her ivory silk dress and carefully arranged the veil over her face, Meg and Louise looked on with tears in their eyes.

It didn't register with Emma that the car was only a taxi cab. The driver, a bistro regular, had dressed his car with silk ribbons and flowers for the occasion and Emma couldn't have been happier if she had stepped out of the classiest limousine. Nor did she care that her dress had been acquired from a charity shop. It had been pulled apart and completely transformed by Gina to the extent that it was, in Emma's eyes, fit for a princess. The bridal bouquet was a spray of spring flowers and roses, provided by Iris and Jean, no questions asked. As far as Emma was concerned, the illusion was complete.

Meg looked anxiously at the steps that led up to the entrance to the church but before she could ask, Emma had her answer. 'I'll be fine, Mum,' she said. 'Let's not keep them waiting.'

Emma could hear the swish of silk as she glided up the stone steps and when she reached the top, the sound of church bells filled the air, coming not from St Luke's but the nearby cathedral, which was lending its voice to the occasion. As Emma reached the entrance, a figure stepped out of the shadows. Through her veil, Emma didn't recognize him at first, or perhaps didn't trust her own eyes.

'I know you're not exactly mine to give away,' he began, 'but I had to be here. Tell me to go if you want.'

Emma didn't answer her father but turned towards her mum who was following close behind. 'It's alright, I knew John would be here,' Meg said, although she avoided looking at her ex-husband. 'It's your day, Emma. It's your decision.'

John Patterson had played no part in the wedding day of her imaginings. This isn't a dream, she told herself. This is really happening.

Emma didn't say yes or no, instead she reached out her hand for her dad to take and the look of relief on his face was clear to see. 'Thanks, Emma. I don't know how I would have broken it to these two if we had to leave before the big event.'

Emma looked on as a tiny, cherub-like face appeared from behind him, closely followed by another. Olivia and Amy had little rosebuds in their hair to match Emma's bouquet and pretty satin dresses in the exact same shade of navy blue as her other bridesmaids.

'Rose!' cried Emma.

'No, I'm Olivia,' corrected the little girl with a giggle.

'Yes, silly me,' she agreed, ignoring the looks of concern from everyone around her.

'We've got flowers,' explained Olivia, holding up a small basket full of petals, 'and we're going to throw them on the floor.'

'And then you can squish them,' added Amy in excitement.

'Oh, they're too beautiful to squish. I'm going to have to tiptoe through them.'

Olivia thought about it for a while. 'You could always use your angel wings and fly over them.'

'Maybe not today,' Emma said. 'I haven't quite worked out how to fly yet.'

Before the girls could interrogate her further, Meg and John started to usher everyone into the church, managing to synchronize their actions without speaking to each other or even acknowledging what the other was doing.

Before Meg disappeared into the church she glanced back, a smile trembling on her lips. Soon after, the bells stopped ringing and beautiful music filled the air. The flower girls began the procession into the church and Emma prepared for her own entrance.

'Shall we?' John asked, giving Emma's arm a quick squeeze.

When Emma entered the inner ruins of the church, she was grateful for her father's arm. They stepped into a world of enchantment where the ethereal sound of violins echoed off the high walls with their Gothic peaks. Swathes of cream voile had been draped from high, falling in front of the windows and billowing softly in the breeze. The bare stonework, the charred timbers and the weeds growing from lofty crevices bore witness to the church's resilience and added to its charm. The makeshift aisle that led to the altar was dappled with sunlight that fought through the bubbling clouds high above them. The altar itself, with its curved walls and intricate windows, appeared to have kept the majority of the sunbeams for itself. Flickers of light glinted from tiny shards of stained glass that had remained attached to the windows with colourful determination.

The intimate gathering of family and friends stood to attention as Emma made her way down the aisle. With no pews to sit on, they would have to remain standing throughout the ceremony. Emma didn't look at their faces or note the tears being shed; she was looking at one person and one person only.

She hadn't seen Ben since they had stolen themselves away to the register office the day before to make their union official in the eyes of the law. That particular ceremony had been perfunctory with only Iris and Jean in attendance as witnesses. Emma hadn't wanted her family there. This was her real wedding, this was where the magic and the memories would be made and as Ben turned to look at her and smile, Emma's heart beat a little faster. It was the first time she had seen him in a suit. He looked impossibly handsome as he pulled back his shoulders and stared directly at her, strong and resolute. She fought an overwhelming desire to rush straight into his arms.

Ben stepped forward to claim his bride and gave her dad a wink. He lifted the veil from Emma's face. 'You're so beautiful,' he whispered.

Having reached the safety of Ben's side, Emma took in more of her surroundings. Delicate sprays of flowers decorated the altar and the sweet scent of the blooms drifted towards her. Candles flickered in a breeze strong enough to snuff them out but the candles simply burned brighter in defiance. To one side of the altar, a quartet of musicians stood to attention, their music having reached a heart-stopping climax as Ben took her hand. She glanced past his shoulder and Steven gave her an encouraging smile.

Without the music, Emma could hear the distant hum of traffic outside and the frantic cry of seagulls above, reminding her that they hadn't been magically transported to a dreamscape. There was the occasional sniffle from the congregation and she didn't need to look around to know that the person who had just blown her nose was Jean, not when she had also heard Iris telling her to shush. The distinguished-looking gentleman standing in front of her drew her attention back to the altar. There was something familiar about him but the dog-collar had distracted her. She had seen him at the bistro where he had worn less formal garb. She was staring into the benevolent face of Iris's new beau.

Ben and Emma had written their own vows and their words focused on the here and now, about their love for each other and their completeness. There was no talk of 'till death us do part', only of a love that was undying and of the memories they were now sharing, which would bring them eternal joy.

Emma's voice was clear and strong as it echoed around the church. It was Ben's voice that shook and his hand trembled as he placed the wedding band on her finger.

Her eyes were drawn in awe to the ring that symbolised their union and if there was ever a moment in her life when she felt truly complete, it was when the chaplain pronounced them husband and wife. A shiver of excitement coursed through her body and was electrified as her husband kissed her.

The unconventional venue meant that the wedding breakfast could be held there and then. The party could continue afterwards at the bistro but this was the place where all the formalities would take place, including the speeches and, thankfully, the weather didn't encroach on their plans. Champagne bottles were popping before Emma and Ben had time to draw breath and as they turned around, glasses were being lifted into the air.

'To the bride and groom,' everyone chorused, as the music started up and Ben led his new bride towards the well-wishers.

Emma didn't know who to greet first, there were so many familiar faces. Gina was linking arms with Dan, Ally stood a little more discretely with Peter's arm around her waist. Mr Bannister was there, as was Jennifer, but Emma had someone else in her sights, the person who deserved the first hug. She ushered Ben in the direction of his father-in-law whilst she walked over and let her mum wrap her arms around her.

'Thank you, Mum,' Emma said.

'What for? This is your day, your creation,' Meg told her, reaching up a hand to tuck away a rogue curl from Emma's face.

'Thank you for everything. For making me strong enough to be happy.'

'And are you happy?' Meg asked.

'Blissfully,' Emma assured her. Only now did she notice the eminent figure standing next to her mum. He looked quite different without his white coat and stethoscope. 'As long as you two don't come to blows in the middle of my big day.'

'I'll have you know, your mother and I never fought each other. We were always fighting for you, in our own, sometimes opposing ways,' Mr Spelling corrected.

'Hmm,' Emma replied, 'I'm going to have to trust you on that one while I go and say hello to some of my other guests.'

Emma gave into her curiosity and walked over to Jennifer and her old boss. She was keen to hear the latest news on Alex who, according to Ally and Gina, hadn't been seen for over a week.

'How lovely to see you both,' Emma said as the old man leaned forward to kiss her cheek. Mr Bannister was only in his sixties but years of drinking and smoking had aged him beyond his years. At least beneath his weathered skin, his spirit was still as indomitable and boundless as ever.

'We wouldn't have missed it for the world,' Jennifer told her, reaching over to touch Emma's arm gently; there wasn't a hint of the gushing insincerity that would once have greeted her.

'Why don't you get this girl a drink,' Mr Bannister

said, raising a meaningful eyebrow to his daughter. Jennifer dutifully disappeared out of earshot.

'I'm glad I've caught you on your own,' he began with a wicked smile.

'Yes, how did that happen?'

'I hope you'll indulge an old man and let me clear my conscience,' he said, waiting long enough for Emma to nod her consent. 'I made a mistake not putting you in charge of marketing, I know that. Alex wasn't up to the task.'

'I take it by your use of the past tense that he's no longer in your employ?' Emma asked and when Mr Bannister told her that he had been sacked the week before, she felt a sense of relief mixed with a little pity, which she knew Alex didn't deserve. 'Jennifer made you see sense, then?'

'You've influenced her more than you could even begin to imagine and I will be eternally grateful for that. I'm only sorry I didn't appreciate you when I had the chance.'

'Don't worry about me. Today isn't about regrets. To hell with the past, or the future for that matter.'

Mr Bannister didn't have a chance to respond even if he had been able to think of anything to say. The music had stopped and there was an insistent tapping on a glass as Steven drew everyone's attention. Emma was summoned to Ben's side and they stood in the centre of the church, next to a small pond that had been added after the church's demise. It gave life to an assortment of tall, willowy plants and there were white ribbons tied to every branch and twig, each one conveying a single-word blessing written by their guests, but there was no time to read them. The best man was about to give his speech and Emma wanted to concentrate on every word, even though she already knew it by heart.

If your soul had wings,
If it could fly away
Then hope is the anchor
That will help it stay

If your heart could sing,
If it had its own tune
Then the notes it would choose
Would never end too soon

If time was an ocean
If it touched no shore
Then your love is a raft
And through storms will endure

If your dreams could come true
If you could bring them to life
Then Emma and Ben have theirs
As husband and wife

17

It had been many years since I had thought of the kindly shopkeeper, decades in fact, but I thought of him now, standing in his mysterious shop full of life's hidden gifts that had been mine for the taking. He stood patiently watching as I scanned the shelves, searching out something I might have missed.

'By rights they should be bare by now,' he told me.

'Have I been too greedy?'

He laughed softly and his belly wobbled. 'Not greedy,' he said, 'just thirsty for life and that's how it should be. It would have been such a shame to leave the boxes unopened, wasted opportunities.'

'I'm glad you said that because I'm still very, very thirsty,' I confessed, but then self-doubt set in. 'Although I'm fairly certain that I've already had everything I could possibly think of.'

The shopkeeper narrowed his eyes. 'Now might be a good time for reflection.'

He was right of course. I needed to take stock of my life and although I had achieved so much, I hadn't done it all on my own. I owed a debt of gratitude to those around me, to the ones who had helped and supported me and most of all, loved me. Inspiration struck. 'Do you have a gift department?'

Reaching up towards the ceiling, which looked surprisingly like open blue sky, the shopkeeper pulled down a new set of shelves to reveal row upon row of brightly wrapped gift boxes. Each gift had its own handwritten label, a single word in beautiful script that succinctly described the blessing contained within. My eyes darted from one to the other.

'I can't see the one that says "happiness",' I told him, a mixture of disappointment and surprise in my voice.

'We don't carry that particular product, I'm afraid,' he said, but he didn't sound the least bit apologetic.

'But isn't that the one that everyone wants?'

'Happiness means different things to different people and at different times in their lives. What we have here,' he explained, 'are the basic ingredients. It's for everyone to make up their own recipes.'

I glanced back at the boxes and reread each and every label before I was ready to make my choices. I followed my intuition and settled on four: courage, love, hope, and peace. A buzz of excitement grew inside me as I imagined what each of the people I loved would make of their essential ingredients. The shopkeeper was right, each person would create their own recipe for happiness;

all that I could do was pass on my blessings for lives that I hoped would be as wonderful as mine had been.

'Do you deliver?'

'Consider it done,' he said, 'but before you go, I have a gift for you.' The shopkeeper took something from his pocket. It was a tiny box, as beautifully and meticulously wrapped as any of those on the shelves, but this was unlabelled and when he passed it to me, it fitted in the palm of my hand. 'This is something special from that man of yours.'

'From Ben?' I asked, looking at the box again. The brightly coloured wrapping paper reflected the light, a flaming mixture of oranges, reds and golds. I gently tugged at the bow that tied it all together and it crackled with the sound of dry, autumn leaves. 'Can I open it?'

'No, not yet. Ben will need to think about what he wants to put inside it first and speaking of the devil, I think he's trying to wake you up.'

'What?' I mumbled as I felt myself floating somewhere between sleep and consciousness.

Ben was nudging me, slowly rousing me from my slumber.

'Emma,' he coaxed. 'It's a bit early for a catnap, isn't it?'

A magazine slipped off my lap as I tried to sit up in my armchair. For a moment, it sounded like the flap of an angel's wings and as I opened my eyes, I felt disorientated. The room was in darkness whereas it had been a bright spring afternoon when I had closed my eyes.

378

Still groggy, I watched my husband as he switched on a lamp. He was still the man I had fallen in love with all those years ago. I didn't see the receding hairline or the gentle stoop of his shoulders or the groans as he climbed out of bed each morning and I hoped he could say the same about me. I was starting to feel old and I certainly couldn't do the things I used to, not without a lot more effort. But I didn't feel old. In my mind, I was still planning the next adventure.

We had pushed ourselves to the limit in recent years. It hadn't been enough for us to simply see the world, we had devoured it too. My greatest fear was that one day I would be forced to stop even though my thirst for adventure was barely satiated. Time and my body were my enemy.

'Another brochure?' Ben asked as he picked up the magazine that had slipped from my lap. 'We only got rid of the grandkids two days ago, don't you want to take a little breather first?' When he saw me look furtively back at the brochure, he sighed in resignation. 'Where now?'

'Deep-sea diving?' I said, as if I was asking him something simple like suggesting a cheese sandwich for lunch.

Ben gave a deep, throaty laugh. 'I need an oxygen tank walking up the stairs these days, isn't that bad enough?'

I couldn't help but laugh too, only my laughter turned into a coughing fit and left me gasping for breath. Ben's joke applied far more to me than him and he knew it.

I had to bang my chest the way that old people do, to remind my lungs that they were supposed to let me breathe and laugh at the same time.

Ben crouched down next to me and put his arm around my shoulder. 'You're still the apple of my eye but you can't go chasing halfway around the world in search of your lost youth. Maybe it's time we hung up our walking shoes.'

I looked at him and wondered where the conversation was leading. Was he getting too old for this or worse still, thinking that I was already past it? I knew I was struggling, the cough I'd had for months wasn't shifting, but I was still living and I certainly wasn't ready to be wrapped up in cotton wool. 'Really?' I asked.

Ben giggled like a schoolboy. 'Nah, of course not,' he said with a familiar twinkle in his eyes. 'The magic will never die.'

'Are you sure you're warm enough?' Ben asked. They were sitting on a park bench and, having fed the ducks with enough bread to sink them, had retired to a higher vantage point away from the lake. Emma had chosen a seat where they could bathe in the glory of the Field of Hope with its golden sea of daffodils, which had bubbled to the surface since her last visit to Sefton Park.

March was about to be overtaken by April and the weather continued to improve but despite the mild temperatures, Emma was wrapped in woollen layers complete with hat, scarf and gloves. 'Yes, Ben. The wool may not be cotton wool but I'm perfectly wrapped up,' she said, knowing he would recognize the reference to her latest entry in her book.

'I get the message,' he conceded.

Emma was working on her story every chance she had, desperate to cling onto the time she had left, but each time she placed her hands on the keyboard she sensed time slipping through her fingers. She was putting a lot of strain on her body to finish it and that building pressure was most evident inside her head. She tried not to rely too heavily on painkillers, which eased the back pain and headaches but which also numbed her mind. She had been forced to change the settings on her computer so the type was larger but it eased rather than cured her bouts of blurred vision. At times, she had resorted to touch-typing with her eyes closed but even that was becoming difficult. There was a distinct weakness in her left side and occasionally her fingers felt numb or completely forgot what they were supposed to do. There were also occasional periods of confusion, frustrating minutes that ticked away as she tried to find the right words.

All in all, her body could not keep pace with the story that Emma was still creating in her mind and that was where Ben came in. He wasn't only her fellow traveller and sounding board, he was the assistant who noted down new ideas as they developed and he was the copy-editor who corrected occasional lapses in Emma's literary prowess. Ben was now spending almost all of his time with her, rarely going to the bistro other than to delegate work to the many willing volunteers or working up new menus that he wouldn't have time to eat, let alone cook.

'So, are you ready to tell me what's supposed to be in the box?' he asked.

Emma stared out over the daffodils. There were hundreds if not thousands of fluted yellow heads, all swaying carefree in the breeze. Some daffodils had yet to bloom whilst others were looking a little frayed around the edges but the carpet of gold was seamless. In contrast, the sky above was dark and brooding and she had to wait patiently for the sun to pierce the cloud cover and make the field shine in all its glory. When it did, it stung her eyes.

She bathed in a sense of achievement. She had made it through the birth of spring and with a little more perseverance, she would be around to see what she considered to be the most spectacular prelude to the summer. 'It's like I said in the story, that's for you to decide.'

'And will my wife give me any hints as to what kind of gift she would like to be in the box or do I have to read her mind?'

Emma tore her eyes away from the daffodils and looked at Ben. 'This is my last spring,' she said, her heartbreaking statement a means of conveying how precious the scene in front of her was. 'It's such a remarkable time of year. How can anyone look at that field and not be amazed at the transformation? I only hope

I get to see the blossom trees in all their glory too. Only then will I be able to face the season that frightens me the most.'

Ben didn't answer at first but let his eyes take in every detail of Emma's face, only then would he turn to face the landscape that she held so dear. He didn't need to be told that for his wife there could be no natural order to the seasons, summer would not follow spring. 'You want me to give you your autumn,' he concluded.

'You read my mind and that's going to come in very useful,' Emma said, her words choking on the tears that she would not allow to fall. The tears weren't for herself but for Ben and what she was about to ask of him. She took his hand and squeezed it fiercely. 'You need to write the end of our story, Ben. I'm not going to be in a position to do that for myself.'

'I almost wish I didn't know you so well,' he said.

'No you don't,' corrected Emma.

'No, I don't,' he agreed with a sigh that barely hinted at the burden that had just been placed on his shoulders. 'I know what you're doing, by the way. All of those gifts from the shopkeeper.'

'I am what I am,' Emma told him. 'If there's a problem to solve, I want to fix it. The thing you will want most when you're facing your grief is me. I can't be there but my blessings can.'

'Courage, love and hope?' Ben said, trying to remember the labels on the boxes.

'And peace,' Emma told him.

'It's a lot to ask,' Ben said. His eyes shone with golden reflections but there were no tears to blur his vision. He was keeping his promise.

'I know.' Emma pulled off a glove and reached over to slip her hand beneath Ben's jacket. She had her hand over his heart, which was pounding fiercely, but it was his breast pocket that she sought with her fingers and it wasn't long before she felt the silken smoothness of the photograph he always kept close. 'This will help.'

It was the picture Ben had taken of the moment when Emma had come face to face with the Northern Lights. There was a sharp intake of breath and Emma pretended not to hear the suppressed sob that had escaped before he bit down hard on his lip.

'Courage, love, hope and peace,' Emma repeated. 'There to see in my face, just in case you forget what they look like.'

As she held out the photo, a large raindrop splashed onto its surface and Ben hurriedly returned it to the safety of his pocket. Emma meanwhile slipped off her other glove and then her hat to reveal a thin covering of hair and the slithers of silvery red skin that marked her battle wounds but even with her frailties exposed, she felt invulnerable. She lifted her head to the skies, her hands reaching upwards as she embraced the life she still clung to. Heavy raindrops hit the palms of her hand and for a moment they reminded her of tears falling, but as the rain hit her smiling face it washed away all painful thoughts. She was ready to enjoy the moment despite Ben's protestations that they should run for the car. The sun hadn't completely given up the fight and Emma was hoping for a rainbow.

'I don't know why we haven't done this before,' I said, slipping off my sandals and letting my feet sink into the warm golden sands. 'I always thought cruises were for old people.'

'We are old people,' Ben said, correcting my delusion. 'But this isn't exactly your average cruise. Not many people get to hitch a ride on one of those.' He was looking back towards the ocean where our very own yacht lay at anchor. It reminded me vaguely of the boats I used to watch fighting the choppy waters of the Mersey as they gathered like flocks during the Tall Ships parade, but in the aqua blue of the Caribbean Sea, this singular behemoth looked far grander if not slightly smug.

'True,' I granted with a satisfied smile.

Technically, it wasn't our yacht. It had been temporarily loaned to us from a very grateful and extremely rich client of Charlie's. My son was now a renowned photographer with a very select clientele. Whilst Ben had, to use the shopkeeper's description, left his box unopened and an opportunity missed, Charlie had shared his amazing gift with the world and thanks to a very grateful customer, Ben and I were reaping the rewards. Apparently, Charlie's flattering portrait had taken decades off the old gent's wizened features. We all had our own ways of trying to recapture our youth, I supposed.

'Now put your sandals back on if you want to explore the jungle,' he said, turning his attention to the tropical island we had washed up on.

'We could try living dangerously,' I suggested.

'We already are,' Ben countered. 'Do you realize this place has no toilet facilities?'

Beginning our trek through the lush tropical forest, our chatter and laughter echoed off giant tree trunks, but it wasn't long before we started to flag. Our lungs weren't good at multitasking and we soon fell silent, concentrating solely on fuelling our bodies with enough oxygen to keep going.

I heard the waterfall long before we saw it and as we broke through the tree cover we stepped into a fresh, cooling mist. I craned my neck to take in the full height of the crashing waters, powered by gravity.

'Can I take my sandals off now?'

'And anything else you want,' Ben suggested.

I may have been the wrong side of seventy but I blushed and Ben noticed my reticence. 'We share everything, remember? Wrinkles and all,' he said with a laugh as he started to pull off his T-shirt.

We stepped into the shockingly cool emerald lagoon, and as I approached the thunderous waterfall, its power reverberated against my bare skin. Fortunately, the choppy motion of the pool banished the chill and I lifted my head up as the falling water rained down on me, *washing away the years. I felt young and invigorated by the passion for life reflected in Ben's face as he took me in his arms and kissed me.*

When we emerged from the cold, churning waters, the air felt heavy and warm. I stared up at the wall of dark trees that marked the boundaries of our little oasis, creating a barrier between one world and the next. A beautiful rainbow arched resplendently between the two.

Emma reached her hand across the bed. 'Ben?' she whispered, clutching nothing except cold, empty sheets. Her groping knocked a pile of paper off the side of the bed and the printed pages of her book fluttered to the floor with the sound of angel wings.

Emma felt a hot and clammy sensation rising up through her body. She couldn't quite place herself as her mind stole her away towards a world of her imaginings and a future that was beyond her grasp. She thought she might be sitting in an armchair having an afternoon nap and so she waited in desperate hope for an aged and careworn Ben to switch on a lamp but the illusion refused to bring light into her life. She could feel a vice slowly beginning to tighten around her head and though her eyes were wide open, the impenetrable blackness remained.

With a sense of rising panic, Emma's breathing became more and more rapid and her heart started to race. 'Ben!' she cried. 'Mum!'

The door to her bedroom was flung open and a yellow

light pierced the darkness but for Emma, it only revealed her worst nightmare. A shadow passed in front of her face. 'Emma, what's wrong?' panted Meg as she touched her daughter's face, pushing away stray strands of sodden hair from her sweaty brow.

'I can't see,' Emma said. Simply saying the words out loud compounded her terror. 'Mum, I'm scared.'

'Shush,' soothed Meg, 'it'll be alright. I'll phone for an ambulance.'

'No, not yet. Please, Mum, I'm not ready. Just give me some time, I'll be OK. Where's Ben? I want Ben,' Emma gasped, desperately trying to calm herself as she clung to her mum for dear life.

'He's slipped out to the shop, I'll phone him. And I'll phone for the nurse too. I'll be two minutes,' Meg promised as she pulled herself away and Emma had no choice but to let her go.

She lay completely still, focusing on her breathing, slowing it down. She felt like she was being pulled into a dark abyss so she concentrated on the vague suggestion of light, a dull yellow blur but light all the same.

By the time her mum returned, Emma was much calmer. 'I've got you some water,' Meg said and helped Emma take a sip. 'Help's on the way.'

'And Ben?'

'He's on his way too,' Meg answered as she slipped onto the bed so Emma could rest her head on her lap. Meg began to stroke her hair gently as if Emma was so fragile that the merest touch might break her.

'Do you think I'll need another operation?' Emma asked when she felt composed enough.

'Is that what you want?'

The question sounded simple enough but it had taken Meg an immense amount of courage to ask it. This wasn't about whether Emma was ready for another operation to relieve whatever pressure was building up in her head. Meg was asking her if she was ready to die.

Emma had been determined to finish her book, almost at the expense of anything else. She had given Ben permission to continue the story but she really wasn't sure she was ready to hand it over yet.

'I want you to know how much I love you, Mum,' Emma began. It wasn't a direct answer to the question but it was an answer.

'And I love you too, Emma. So, so much,' replied Meg, choking back the emotion with a painful sob.

'I worry about you,' Emma said and her fear for her health lessened as she concentrated on the fear for those she loved.

'Please don't, not now,' Meg whispered.

'But I know you. You'll blame yourself.'

'Of course I'll blame myself, I already do. I made you, sweetheart. I gave life to you, I gave you the body that's letting you down. I wish I could have done better for you.'

'Don't ever question what you did or didn't do.' Emma had planned this speech for a very long time and it seemed strange to be finally speaking the words out loud

389

even if it was only in the barest of whispers. It was a surreal moment where she could almost step out of the moment to listen to herself talk, watching from a safe distance. 'You did everything you could and you couldn't have done more. You fought for me long after I'd already given up the fight. I know I gave you a hard time about it but it gave me hope even when I didn't recognize it, or appreciate it at the time. You're the best mum I could have wished for.'

Meg gulped for air before she was able to speak. 'And you're the best daughter.'

'But don't forget Louise. She needs you too and I've taken up too much of your attention for too long.'

'No, you haven't,' argued Meg. 'I'd give you all the time I had, if I could.'

'But it's been at Louise's expense. You have to be strong for her now, strong for each other. Promise me, Mum.'

Reminded of her obligation to stay strong for her children, Meg pulled back her shoulders. 'I promise,' she agreed.

'And you'll look after Ben too, won't you?'

'He'll be like the son I never had. He already is.'

'Then make sure he doesn't waste the life he has grieving for me. And encourage him to do something with his photography, he has talent,' Emma said.

'I will.'

'But only if it's what he wants. I wouldn't want to be pushy.'

'You? Never. Now stop panicking, Emma.' Meg's voice had taken on a familiar firmness. 'There'll be time to talk all of this through.'

Emma relaxed a little, knowing that she had said everything that needed to be said for the moment at least but she knew her mum was wrong. They didn't have time, not any more.

18

Emma's room was crowded and although she couldn't see a single person, she knew their faces would be etched with anxiety. She sensed each of them holding their breath, trying desperately not to breach the silence. As she fought through the fog, she felt two hands holding onto hers, guiding her towards consciousness. She knew that one hand belonged to Ben, the other to her mum and she tried to work out which was which but her thoughts kept slipping from her grasp. She squeezed her right hand.

'Emma?' It was Ben's voice and the sound made her smile drunkenly.

A wave of whispers lapped against her ears and she fought an impulse to giggle. 'Where am I?' she asked, her words slurred, making the effort to talk harder still.

'You're in the hospice,' replied Meg. Although sensations on her left side were not as distinct, Emma felt her other hand being squeezed.

'Is Louise here?'

'Yes,' she replied softly from the side of the room. 'Gina and Ally are here as well.' There was a stifled sob, then another.

'Jean and Iris were here earlier,' said Meg in a hushed tone. 'Steven's been in too. They said to give you their love.'

'Can you please stop whispering,' Emma told her. 'I'm not dead yet.'

'Still can't help bossing us around,' Ben replied, raising her hand to his lips. His remark hadn't quite disguised the muffled sob from her mum.

'Sorry, Mum,' Emma said as she tried to pull herself out of the haze, but it was as if she was wading through a syrupy sludge. 'Did someone bring my computer?'

'What? You can't want it now, can you?' replied Meg, the panic in her voice telling Emma that she hadn't. 'I never thought . . .'

'It's here,' Ben said. Emma heard shuffling and imagined him taking her beloved laptop out of his rucksack. She tried to look at him but saw only a vague image, a mixture of light and dark, mostly dark. Her blind spot had extended its territory once more.

'Give it to Louise,' Emma said and waited for the wave of mutterings to ebb away before she spoke again. 'It's up to you to organize everyone.'

'For what?' asked Louise.

'I want you all to read to me,' Emma explained.

There was a squeal of delight from Gina and she

clapped her hands. 'At last, I've been dy—' There was a sharp gasp of pain. 'I've been desperate to read your book.' Then in a whisper, 'Ally! That really hurt.'

'I've been dying to read it too,' smiled Emma woozily. She felt herself slipping back into unconsciousness but she didn't want to float into an abyss that had no sense of beginning or end. She wanted to stay with the people she loved and if she couldn't find the strength to keep the fog from consuming her thoughts, then she wanted to be led towards dreams of her own making, where night followed day and where autumn knew its place. 'I want you all to take turns reading to me and it doesn't matter if I'm asleep or awake, I'll hear it.'

'Then I'll go first,' Louise told her. 'Shall I start now?'

Emma smiled as she began her journey anew. She was back in Mr Spelling's office and the sun was shining through the window.

Emma's words took on a life of their own as they danced across her mind, which added colour and depth to the world she knew so well. She lost all sense of time and wasn't sure if her journey through the chapters of her life was being told over a matter of hours or days. To her, it lasted a lifetime. And when her words came to an end and silence fell, Emma found herself outside her beloved cottage, enjoying the spring sunshine. She was busily tending her garden as her grandchildren played around her. In a repeat of history, her children's children were now fighting over the swing.

'I'll tell you what, why don't you two push me on the swing for a change?' Emma suggested.

'What did you say?' asked Ben.

Emma frowned as she tried to distinguish one world from another but she wasn't ready to leave her garden. 'I could do with a sit down, just don't push too high.' There was a pause. 'How did I get this old, Ben?'

'You're not . . .' Ben said before stopping himself, not ready to extract Emma from the safety of her world either. 'You're still as beautiful as the first day I saw you.'

'Thank goodness that taxi had good brakes.'

Emma groaned as she tried to straighten up her arthritic joints. Thanks to the morphine, the pain was as imaginary as the butterflies that chased each other from flower to flower. Their white wings fluttered across her mind, whipping up confusion but slowly sweeping away the fog.

'Is the blossom out yet?' she asked Ben, holding desperately onto a brief moment of clarity.

'I can see apple trees from the window,' he assured her. 'The sun's shining and there's white blossom everywhere. It's beautiful.'

'You will think of me, won't you? When you see the blossom trees.'

'I'll think of you all the time, blossom or not.'

The room felt very quiet. 'Are you on your own?' she asked.

'No, I'm here,' Meg said. 'Steven's bringing Louise

back later and your dad's been in touch. He said he would come if you wanted him to.'

'We've said our goodbyes,' Emma said and she felt certain that the time for all her goodbyes was close. She had been told that she would more than likely slip into a coma and each time she drifted back to sleep, there was less and less chance that she would wake up again. 'I'd like to go outside. I want to sit under the blossom trees.'

'Emma, you're too weak,' Ben said.

Thankfully, Emma didn't need to argue, her mum was going to do it for her. 'If it's what you want, we'll get you outside.'

Emma heard the door open and footfalls receding into the distance.

'Thank you for making my dreams come true,' she told Ben. 'I'm sorry if all I've given you in return are nightmares.'

Ben didn't answer immediately but she sensed a shadow over her face, smelled his sweet breath on her cheek and then the touch of his soft lips on hers. 'I'm not ready for this, Em,' he whispered.

'Me neither,' Emma agreed, 'but I'm almost there. I need you to be strong for me. I need you to help me get to the end of our story in a blaze of glory.'

'Only if you promise me you'll never leave me, not completely. I couldn't bear that,' he said, panic rising in his voice.

'I promise,' she began. 'I'll be there in your dreams.

You'll see my smile in every rainbow and you'll hear my voice in every love song. If there's a way to connect to you, I'll find a way back.'

In the distance, Emma could hear a heated discussion between her mum and a man who Emma assumed was in charge of her care. 'I don't care about policy!' shouted Meg. 'Either you help us do it or we'll do it ourselves.'

Emma smiled to herself. Her mum was still fighting her battles for her.

Emma could feel herself floating. She was dimly aware of light and shadow but not the regular flashes of strip lights. She wasn't being hurried down a hospital corridor, not this time. She was basking in dappled sunlight and she could hear the branches swaying above her, laden with blossom and trembling in the breeze. She was lying in Ben's arms and her mum was close by, stroking her hair.

Emma's fingers tingled as they instinctively searched out the smooth resistance of a keyboard but she knew she wouldn't be the one to continue her story to its natural conclusion. Fear overtook her as she imagined the power she had held at her fingertips disappearing into the ether. She struggled to move, desperate to look at her hands. Out of the darkness, a flash of orange and gold caught her eye and the small gift-wrapped box that the shopkeeper had given her came into view. The fiery wrapping paper sparkled in the palm of her hand.

'It's time to open the box,' she whispered to Ben.

*   *   *

I had been truly blessed when I met Emma, humbled that she would return my love, astounded by her strength of spirit and immensely privileged to share my life with her. However, it wasn't only her spirit that was strong, so were her opinions. In short, my wife was pushy.

There was one thing we had never been able to agree upon and I was finally getting the chance to make my case. I would never forgive myself if I failed. Emma had argued that springtime, that vibrant eruption of life bursting out of the darkness to chase away the last remnants of winter, was the season to be celebrated. I couldn't disagree with that but what I wouldn't accept was that autumn was the season to be mourned. To prove my point, I was about to take her on a voyage of discovery. We had returned to Paris one last time, only this time there was no blossom fluttering in the breeze like wedding confetti. We were no longer looking forward to married bliss but marvelling at the life we had shared together.

'I'm out of breath already,' Emma complained.

Although I knew she was finding our walk through the streets of Paris a struggle, I suspected her reluctance had more to do with a stubborn refusal to accept my opposing view of the seasons but I wasn't about to give up on the challenge. I knew Emma wouldn't want me to.

'Come on, I'll race you to the park,' I said, daring her into action.

We set off at a sprint or at least what counted as a sprint by the standards of two octogenarians. When we eventually arrived at the gates to the park, we were both unarguably out of breath but somehow uplifted.

'What are you smiling at?' I asked as Emma tried to slow her breathing. She was leaning against one of the large wrought-iron gates, her grey hair having fought its way free from her woollen hat and falling across her beautiful hazel eyes, which were surrounded by a feathering of well-earned wrinkles.

'It's so beautiful,' she said, staring in awe at the russet-red trail of fallen leaves that led into the park. The path was lined with maples, burnishing leaves of golden yellows, oranges and reds, the exact same tones as the wrapping on the gift box the shopkeeper had given her. The occasional pine tree peaked out from the shadows and their inferiority was telling. They may remain forever green but they looked a tad worn and dull.

'Let's find somewhere to sit down,' I said, leading Emma by the hand and taking her through our enchanted forest.

As we walked, our feet swished through a sea of crisp leaves that crackled like fire underfoot. When we found a suitable resting place, there was still that look of awe on Emma's face.

'I wanted you to see this through my eyes,' I told her.

'It's as if the turning leaves are putting every last ounce of strength they have into making a burning impression on the world.'

'So *that they'll never be forgotten,*' I added, knowing *that at last she was seeing autumn in a way she never thought possible. This was not the sight of nature in the midst of its death throes. The trees weren't seeking her pity, far from it. Their glorious autumnal tones were a celebration of a life well lived in beautiful Technicolor. 'Emma, I know we haven't got long left together so I need you to understand something. This is nothing compared to your autumn. Your life has burned an impression on my heart that's never going to fade.'*

'*We've had a good life together, haven't we?*' she said *and the smile on her face warmed my heart.*

Emma was smiling as she tried to open her eyes but her vision was all but gone. She couldn't see the branches above her or even make out Ben's features. She lifted a hand towards his face. His cheeks felt wet.

'A good life,' she whispered. Her mouth was dry and her lips cracked and old.

'Yes, a pretty damned amazing life,' he assured her, his voice breaking almost as much as his heart.

She looked at him, suddenly focusing perfectly on his dark brown eyes and beautifully long lashes but not on the deep-set wrinkles that reached like spiderwebs towards his greying temples. 'You're still as handsome as the first day I met you,' she said with a sigh. 'And I couldn't love you more than I do now.'

'And I love you, Emma,' Ben said as he held her tightly in his arms. 'I'll always love you.'

'I don't know how we fitted it all in,' she continued, her smile broadening with self-satisfaction. She pictured the tiny gift box still clasped in her hand, its contents having been revealed.

The branches overhead began to sway again in the breeze and she could hear the crisp red and gold leaves sparking off each other. With her hand still touching Ben's cheek, she looked in awe at her fingers, which had held the power of life. And even when her hand slipped from his face, the impression remained. Her fingers had shone.

I could hear soft words that wrapped around me like loving arms. My family were telling me how much they loved me and I tried to hold on fiercely to the sound of their voices. As I struggled, I heard one voice, stronger than any other. She was telling me that it was alright to let go, that I had fought long enough, and her words calmed me.

I had reached my autumn years and with soaring relief, I gloried in all that I had achieved. The dazzling colour and light that danced across my closed eyelids was almost blinding, images of blustery days at the edge of the river, looking out towards the horizon; rippling views of barren desert with the pyramids rising up from the sands; piercing blue skies that remained out of reach no matter how tall the skyscraper; the smell of a newborn baby and apple blossom twirling like snowflakes through the air as a rickety swing swept back and forth. As so many breathtaking memories came flooding back, I felt compelled to visit the kindly shopkeeper one last time. It was time to close my account.

Yesterday's Sun

Newly-weds Holly and Tom have just moved into an old manor house in the picturesque English countryside. When Holly discovers a moondial in the overgrown garden and its strange crystal mechanism, little does she suspect that it will change her life forever. For the moondial has a curse.

Each full moon, Holly can see into the future – a future which holds Tom cradling their baby daughter, Libby, and mourning Holly's death in childbirth…

Holly realises the moondial is offering her a desperate choice: give Tom the baby he has always wanted and sacrifice her own life; or save herself and erase the life of the daughter she has fallen in love with.

'A haunting and heartbreaking story that stayed with me long after I'd finished'
Fern Britton

'Magical and unputdownable'
Katie Fforde

Coming in 2014, Amanda Brooke's next book

WHERE I FOUND YOU

will tug at your heart strings . . .

Maggie Carter knows Victoria Park like the back of her hand. She knows which routes around the park are easiest to navigate; she knows what time of year the most beautiful flowers bloom; and she knows which bench by the pond allows you to hear the joyful chatter of children throwing bread to the ducks. But she's never seen any of these things. Maggie is blind and has never felt held back by her unseeing eyes. And yet, newly married and expecting her first baby, Maggie is suddenly doubting her ability to cope.

Elsie is also expecting her first child, but unmarried, alone and without the support of her family, she's terrified her baby will be taken away. When Maggie meets Elsie one day in the park she tries to comfort her – but all is not as it seems. Because Elsie lost her baby sixty years earlier, and now, suffering from the first stages of Alzheimer's, she can't stop re-living the most traumatic event in her life.

Determined to bring Elsie back to the present, Maggie sets out to discover what happened all those years ago and bring peace to Elsie memories . . . before it's too late.